HEATHER GRAHAM

ghost MOON

MIRA®

MIRA®

Recycling programs for this product may not exist in your area.

ISBN-13: 978-0-7783-2796-7

GHOST MOON

For questions and comments about the quality of this book please contact us at Customer_eCare@Harlequin.ca.

www.MIRABooks.com

Printed in U.S.A.

For Sprout and Scout
and the Peace River Ghost Trackers
and a great time at the Spanish Military Hospital
in St. Augustine,
and Daena Smoller and Dr. Larry Montz
with the ISPR, New Orleans, Louisiana,
and the several great groups
who do ghost tours in Key West, Florida.

Key West History Timeline

1513—Ponce de Leon is thought to be the first European to discover Florida, which he claimed for Spain. His sailors, watching as they pass the southern islands (the Keys), decide that the mangrove roots look like tortured souls and call them Los Martires, or "the Martyrs."

Circa 1600—Key West begins to appear on European maps and charts. The first explorers came upon the bones of deceased native tribes, and thus the island was called "the Island of Bones," or Cayo Hueso.

The Golden Age of Piracy begins as New World ships carry vast treasures through dangerous waters.

1763—The Treaty of Paris gives Florida and Key West to the British and Cuba to the Spanish. The Spanish and Native Americans are forced to leave the Keys and move to Havana. The Spanish, however, claim that the Keys are not part of mainland Florida and were really North Havana. The English say no, the Keys are a part of Florida. In reality, this dispute is merely a war of words. Hardy souls of many nationalities fish, cut timber, hunt turtles—and avoid pirates—with little restraint from any government.

1783—The Treaty of Paris ends the American Revolution and returns Florida to Spain.

1815–Spain deeds the island of Key West to a loyal Spaniard, Juan Pablo Salas of St. Augustine, Florida.

1819–1822—Florida is ceded to the United States. Salas sells the island to John Simonton for $2,000. Simonton divides the island into four parts, three going to businessmen John Whitehead, John Fleming and Pardon Greene. Cayo Hueso becomes more generally known as Key West.

1822—Simonton convinces the U.S. Navy to come to Key West—the deep-water harbor, which had kept pirates, wreckers and others busy while the land was scarcely developed, would be an incredible asset to the U.S. Lieutenant Matthew C. Perry arrives to assess the situation. Perry reports favorably on the strategic military importance but warns the government that the area is filled with unsavory characters—such as pirates.

1823—Captain David Porter is appointed commodore of the West Indies Anti-Pirate Squadron, known as the "Mosquito Fleet." He takes over ruthlessly, basically putting Key West under martial law. People do not like him. However, starting in 1823, he does begin to put a halt to piracy in the area.

The United States of America is in full control of Key West, which is part of the U.S. territory of Florida, and colonizing begins in earnest by Americans, though, as always, those Americans come from many places.

Circa 1828—Wrecking becomes a big business in Key West, and much of the island becomes involved in the activity. It's such big business that over the next twenty years, the island becomes one of the richest areas per capita in the United States. In the minds of some, a new kind of piracy has replaced the old. Although wrecking and salvage were licensed and legal, many a ship was lured to its doom by less than scrupulous businessmen.

1845—Florida becomes a state. Construction begins on a fort to protect Key West.

1846—Construction of Fort Jefferson is begun in the Dry Tortugas.

1850—The fort on the island of Key West is named after President Zachary Taylor.

New lighthouses bring about the end of the Golden Age of Wrecking.

1861—Florida secedes from the Union on January 10. Fort Zachary Taylor is staunchly held in Union hands and helps defeat the Confederate Navy and control the movement of blockade runners during the war. Key West remains a divided city throughout the great conflict. Construction is begun on the East and West Martello towers, which will serve as supply depots. The salt ponds of Key West supply both sides.

1865—The War of Northern Aggression comes to an end with the surrender of Lee at Appomattox Courthouse. Salvage of blockade runners comes to an end.

Dr. Samuel Mudd, deemed guilty of conspiracy after setting John Wilkes Booth's broken leg after Lincoln's assassination, is incarcerated at Fort Jefferson, the Dry Tortugas.

As salt and salvage industries come to an end, cigar making becomes a major business. The Keys are filled with Cuban cigar makers following Cuba's war of independence, but the cigar makers eventually move to Ybor City. Sponging is also big business for a period, but the sponge divers head for waters near Tampa as disease riddles Key West's beds and the remote location makes industry difficult.

1890—The building that will become known as "the little White House" is built for use as an officer's quarters at the naval station. President Truman will spend at least 175 days here, and it will be visited by Eisenhower, Kennedy and many other dignitaries.

1898—The USS *Maine* explodes in Havana Harbor, precipitating the Spanish-American War. Her loss is heavily felt in Key West, as she had been sent from Key West to Havana.

Circa 1900—Robert Eugene Otto is born. At the age of four, he receives the doll he will call "Robert," and a legend is born as well.

1912—Henry Flagler brings the Overseas Railroad to Key West, connecting the islands to the mainland for the first time.

1917—On April 6, the United States enters World War I. Key West maintains a military presence.

1919—Treaty of Versailles ends World War I.

1920s—Prohibition gives Key West a new industry—bootlegging.

1927—Pan American World Airways is founded in Key West to fly visitors back and forth to Havana.

Carl Tanzler, "Count von Cosel," arrives in Key West and takes a job at the U.S. Marine Hospital as a radiologist.

1928—Ernest Hemingway comes to Key West. It's rumored that while waiting for a roadster from the factory he writes *A Farewell to Arms*.

1931—Hemingway and his wife, Pauline, are gifted with the house on Whitehead Street. Polydactyl cats descend from his pet, Snowball.

Death of Maria Elena Milagro de Hoyos.

1933—Count von Cosel removes Elena's body from the cemetery.

1935—The Labor Day Hurricane wipes out the Overseas Railroad and kills hundreds of people. The railroad will not be rebuilt. The Great Depression comes to Key West, as well, and the island, once the richest in the country, struggles with severe unemployment.

1938—An overseas highway is completed, U.S. 1, connecting Key West and the Keys to the mainland.

1940—Hemingway and Pauline divorce; Key West loses its great writer, except as a visitor.

Tanzler is found living with Elena's corpse. Her second viewing at the Dean-Lopez Funeral Home draws thousands of visitors.

1941—December 7, "a date that will live in infamy," occurs, and the U.S. enters World War II.

Tennessee Williams first comes to Key West.

1945—World War II ends with the armistice of August 14 (Europe) and the surrender of Japan, September 2.
Key West struggles to regain a livable economy.

1947—It is believed that Tennessee Williams wrote his first draft of *A Streetcar Named Desire* while staying at La Concha Hotel on Duval Street.

1962—The Cuban Missile Crisis occurs. President John F. Kennedy warns the United States that Cuba is only ninety miles away.

1979—The first Fantasy Fest is celebrated.

1980—The Mariel boatlift brings tens of thousands of Cuban refugees to Key West.

1982—The Conch Republic is born. In an effort to control illegal immigration and drugs, the U.S. sets up a blockade in Florida City, at the northern end of U.S. 1. Traffic is at a stop for seventeen miles, and the mayor of Key West retaliates on April 23, seceding from the U.S. Key West Mayor Dennis Wardlow declares war, surrenders and demands foreign aid. As the U.S. has never responded, under International law, the Conch Republic still exists. Its foreign policy is stated as, "The Mitigation of World Tension through the Exercise of Humor." Even though the U.S. never officially recognizes the action, it has the desired effect: the paralyzing blockade is lifted.

1985—Jimmy Buffet opens his first Margaritaville restaurant in Key West.

Fort Zachary Taylor becomes a Florida State Park (and a wonderful place for reenactments, picnics and beach bumming).

Treasure hunter Mel Fisher at long last finds the *Atocha*.

1999—First Pirates in Paradise is celebrated.

2000–Present—Key West remains a unique paradise, garish, loud, charming, filled with history, water sports, family activities, and down and dirty bars. "The Gibraltar of the East," she offers diving, shipwrecks and the spirit of adventure that makes her a fabulous destination, for a day, or forever.

Prologue

The sun was setting, casting a bloodred hue upon the land and the Merlin house.

The house was quite odd, sitting on a spit of peninsula that stretched in a small curlicue from the Old Town mainland of Key West. One of a kind, it was Victorian and elegant—and in a state of neglect and decay that made it appear as if it were haunted, almost a living, breathing entity. Shadowed windows might have been eyes, watching all activity that surrounded the place. The fading gray paint created a trick of light in the coming darkness, making it seem as if there was a pulse in the façade of the place. It sat, quiet, dormant, and yet alive... waiting.

Liam Beckett parked his car in the overgrown gravel drive of the old house, dreading what he would find within, and thinking back many years.

This had been Kelsey's home for so long. Until her mother had died, and her father had taken her away. Cutter Merlin had stayed behind, either mourning his only daughter or left behind by his son-in-law. Liam didn't know. He remembered Kelsey, though. She'd been his enemy—the little girl who tortured him with spitballs while he'd slipped behind her to tie knots in her hair—and then, somewhere along the way, they'd become friends. And then she had become the first real crush of his life, a dark-haired tomboy who had become a lithe and elegant young woman. He hadn't been able to say goodbye.

And now…

He walked to the front door and knocked. The house was nearly seven thousand square feet, and Cutter lived in it alone, so—with or without his sense of dread—there was no reason to fear because his initial knock wasn't answered. He pressed the buzzer for the doorbell, but he was certain that it hadn't worked in years.

He heard nothing within the house.

He banged on the door again, but there was still no response.

He stepped back on the porch. As Jason Fried had reported, the mail was piling up.

Maybe Cutter Merlin had gone somewhere. Out to see his granddaughter in California, perhaps.

But that wasn't the case, and Liam knew it.

Cutter Merlin hadn't left the island in a decade.

He walked around back. The house itself sat on a solid coral-and-limestone shelf that gave way to sand, sea grapes and mangroves. Bony pines and low scruff foliage surrounded the house, most of it appearing to be dead and unkempt, adding to the barren, forgotten and forlorn appearance of the property. Liam knew how to break in: when Kelsey had forgotten her keys, they had crept through the brush—once tended—to the rear of the house and the laundry room. There was a loose screen over the washer and dryer, and it was a piece of cake to move it.

Liam did so.

He slipped the screen out and crawled in, then leapt down from the dryer to the floor.

The odor assailed him immediately, and he knew.

He just had to find the body.

He flicked the switch, but the lights in the laundry room were out. He doubted it had been used in a long time. The connecting door between the kitchen and the laundry room was unlocked, though, giving to his touch. In the kitchen, he flicked another light switch.

A dim bulb came to life.

Cutter Merlin had been fixing himself something to eat. Flies buzzed around a bowl of tomato soup and the sandwich on the plate beside it. Liam touched the bread; it was hard as a rock. An odor different from the intense smell of death but nearly as bad rose from the sandwich.

He walked through to the massive dining room. A bay window seat to the north usually gave a beautiful view of the Gulf, a magnificent site to watch the sunset. But he couldn't see the dying sun except for a sliver of light; the drapes had been drawn.

There was a patina of dust over the house. Cobwebs covered the chandelier over the dining table.

"Cutter?" Liam called the man's name, and then felt like an ass, talking to himself. He knew that Cutter was dead. No living man could have remained in that house with the odor, a miasma that was palpable.

One tile step led to the grand living room. The

light from the kitchen wasn't enough to filter in, but, trying another switch, Liam discovered that it, too, was dead.

The room was cast in the eerie bloodred that was darkened by the shadows of the coming night.

It had once been beautiful, with Italian marble floors, elegant throw rugs and crimson Duncan Fife furnishings. Over the years, it had become cluttered, and not with the usual accumulation of silly souvenirs, magazines or papers. There were boxes everywhere. A suit of armor—real—stood in a corner, near a Victorian coffin with a window at the head and a painting beneath the window to display how the dead might have been shown. A mummy case lay to one side of the fireplace, and an authentic voodoo altar lay to the right. A glass dome covered a shrunken head he knew to be from New Guinea, and a stuffed raven took precedence on the mantel. Everywhere you looked, there was an artifact from somewhere, some in pristine condition, others worn and falling apart. Animal heads adorned the walls along with African masks and feathered spears.

There was so much in the room to attract the eye in the strange mixture of shadow and light that Liam didn't even see the dead man at first.

And then he did.

Like one of his relics, Cutter Merlin was covered in a thin patina of dust. A spider had spun her web from the edge of Cutter's reading glasses to the armrest of the rocking chair on which he sat.

Liam felt his heart sink. He'd known, of course. He found himself suddenly wishing that he—or someone—had kept up with the old recluse. Cutter Merlin had always been kind to children. He'd been filled with wonderful tales about distant lands: Asia, Far East, Middle East, the jungles of South America and the sands of the Sahara desert. But his daughter had died, his son-in-law and granddaughter had moved away and he had closed himself in with his treasures. Then there had been the strange rumors about the old hermit and his collections. He practiced black magic. He made deals with the devil.

He sat now, just sat, a book in his hands, dust motes dancing in the crimson air around him. Old and frail, his hair long and white, his cheeks covered in a stubble of white beard, he looked as if he might speak. But, of course, he would never speak again.

"Ah, Mr. Merlin!" Liam said softly, walking toward the old man. He noted then that the corpse's mouth was slightly open, while its eyes were wide-open as well behind steel-framed reading glasses. It was as if Cutter Merlin had died staring toward the foyer and the grand front entry, terrified of whatever he saw there. The expression on his face was so filled with horror that Liam found himself turning to look.

But there was nothing there. He turned and came down on one knee by the corpse. He realized that he would be saturated with the smell of death when he left, but it didn't matter; he had known the man. He was a sad old fellow who had given a great deal, and he had died alone, in fear.

He sighed softly, shaking his head sadly. He took out

his cell and called in the death; the medical examiner would arrive soon.

There wasn't a terrible rush; Cutter Merlin was dead. The spider that had spun the web about him emerged from the old man's mouth, causing Liam to start and shudder—and be glad that no one had been there to see his horrified reaction.

Liam frowned, noting the book on the old man's lap. It was large, with gold trim on the pages, and Liam judged it to be a hundred or more years old. He carefully lifted the cover, but the bloodred twilight was turning to darker and darker shadow, so he took his flashlight from his pocket, carefully lifting the book with the tip of the light.

In Defense from Dark Magick.

There was something in the old man's hand, as well. Liam knew not to touch him until the M.E. came, but he was curious, and it hardly appeared that this could be a case of murder. An old man had scared himself, and died from a heart attack.

His gloves were in the car, so he used the tip of the small laser light to shift the hand and see what was clutched in the fingers. The old man had long since gone in and out of rigor, so he wasn't stiff, and Liam was easily able to see what he clutched.

It was a casket, a little gold casket, like a jewelry box with its lid open for a special piece. Liam hadn't been an altar boy, but he had been brought to church every Sunday when he'd been growing up. It seemed to him that the box was some kind of reliquary. It appeared to contain a small gold ball, filigreed, with the ball designed to fit into the casket, and the casket designed just to fit the ball.

Beneath the book on his lap, Cutter held an old sawed-off shotgun.

"What were you doing, old man?" Liam asked softly aloud. He shook his head and stood, looking around the room again. Boxes and crates and pieces—some priceless, some surely pure junk—seemed piled en masse. Now, the shadows stretched out like bone-fingered tentacles. Liam walked across the room to the main entrance, and, once again with his flashlight, studied the door. Odd. Cutter Merlin had prepared his dinner, simple soup and a sandwich. But he had never eaten it. He had taken a book and an old relic and gone to sit in his rocking chair by the fire, staring at the front door.

Staring as if he were waiting for someone, but with a book and gold casket as his weapons, along with a sawed-off shotgun. He hadn't pulled out the shotgun to aim at anyone; it remained on his lap, beneath the book.

Cutter Merlin had been called eccentric as long as Liam could remember.

In the last years, he had been referred to as a crazy hermit. To keep their children from playing near the shoreline where the boats came and the water could suddenly become deep, local parents had warned that the man was loony, that he might have been the devil.

The front door was locked. In fact, there were three bolts on the door now, and they were all secured.

It was as if Cutter Merlin had become quite frightened of some visitor in his dotage. Who?

He'd probably begun to suffer dementia. Alzheimer's. And none of them had really known. Or cared. Liam felt horrible again; how had they all forgotten this man?

He walked back to the corpse. Cutter still stared at the door in fear—and determination. He had been clutching the little casket as if his life had depended upon it.

"Poor old fellow," Liam said. "You were always good to me. I'm sorry that I forgot you."

Hearing the approach of the M.E.'s car, he returned to the door. He was about to unlatch the locks when he decided that he just might want to investigate the death further. He headed into the kitchen for a towel and covered his fingers to unlatch the bolts.

The M.E. was Franklin Valaski, a veteran of many a death, natural and unnatural. He was nearly Cutter Merlin's own age, or at least he looked nearly as old. Maybe his years observing death had made him old early and given him that look of an old bulldog. He was short, stout, wrinkled and excellent at his job. He was followed by an assistant, one of the dieners at the morgue, who bore a stretcher.

"So, old Merlin finally bit the dust, eh?" Valaski said, shaking his head. "Tell you the truth, I had all but forgotten the old bastard was out here."

"Sad, huh?" Liam murmured. "Looks like a heart attack."

"Lead the way," Valaski said.

Liam pointed to the rocking chair, and Valaski went on over to the corpse. The young diener nodded an appropriately grim greeting to Liam, which Liam returned, and then stared around the house.

The diener was gaping at what he saw.

You didn't know Merlin! Liam thought.

Then, naturally, he found himself thinking about Kelsey. Her mother had died here. He didn't know much about it—he had been fifteen at the time. It had been a tragic accident, he knew, and Kelsey's father hadn't wanted to do anything except escape Key West—and the place where his beloved wife had perished.

He had been brokenhearted to see Kelsey go. But then, half his class had been in love with or in awe of Kelsey—all of them budding into adolescence, a bit slowly, being boys. She had been a whirlwind of smiles and energy. In grade school, she had been a freckled little thing with thick pigtails. But in middle school she had shot up, and she had acquired an amazing shape. Unruly dark hair had become a beautiful and sleek deep brown, so shiny it seemed black, like a raven's wing. Her freckles had faded, and her eyes had become the deepest shade of blue that he had ever seen. She had been friendly to everyone, kind to the kids other kids picked on, and she had eschewed as sophomoric the idea of being a cheerleader or belonging to any club.

Sometimes, when people had teased her about her grandfather, she had let her eyes grow big and assured them that he was the devil. Then she'd laughed and told them that he was an adventurer, and, until he had turned sixty, he had traveled the globe, battling primitive tribes on the islands of the Pacific and riding camels in the Sahara. She had defended him as the most magnificent explorer in the world. He'd even been to the North Pole!

Liam realized he hadn't thought about Kelsey in years, either. He'd heard about her father's death; he had succumbed to a virulent flu a few years ago.

He'd sent her an e-mail knowing that he had learned about it long after the funeral. No flowers to send—even if he had known where to send them.

Now, of course, he'd have to find Kelsey, wherever she was. Probably still in California—she had become a cartoonist, he'd heard. Naturally—she'd always been a good artist. He'd find a phone number; it was one thing to send sympathy in a note after the fact; it was quite a different matter to tell her about a death that way. He didn't know what she would feel; Liam was pretty sure that she hadn't seen Cutter Merlin since she'd left Key West.

"Odd," Valaski announced.

"What's odd?" Liam asked, walking toward the M.E.

"Looks like a coronary, but…"

"Yeah?"

"It looks as if he were…scared to death," Valaski said.

"He was an old man, and he probably wasn't under any medical care," Liam said. "He might have been suffering from delusions."

"Hmm," Valaski said, agreeing. "Odd, though—a man who lived with a mummy, shrunken skulls, coffins and voodoo offerings. Stuffed animals. Bones. Petrified flesh. You wouldn't think he'd scare easy."

"He was old," Liam said softly. *Old and forgotten.*

"Yes, of course. But what's really odd…"

His voice trailed off, as if he were deep in thought. Or memory.

"Valaski?" Liam prompted.

Valaski looked up at him. He seemed to give himself a shake, physically and mentally.

"Nothing. Nothing, really. It's just that… Well, he seems to be wearing the same expression I saw on his daughter's face. You remember her. Chelsea Merlin Donovan. I'll never forget. She was such a beautiful woman. She fell down the stairs—down that beautiful curving stairway right there. She died of a broken neck, and yet… Well, she had this exact same expression on her face. I remember it as if it were yesterday. Her husband was holding her, tears streaming down his face. She had fallen…and yet her eyes were open, her lips just ajar…and she seemed to be staring at the most terrifying thing in the universe. Just like Cutter here. Good God, I wonder what it was that they saw?"

1

Kelsey Donovan was at home, working beneath the bright light above her drafting desk, when her phone rang. She answered it distractedly.

"Yes?"

"Kelsey? Is this Kelsey Donovan?"

It was odd, Kelsey thought later, that she didn't recognize Liam Beckett's voice the minute he called, but, then again, it had been a long, long time since she had heard it, and they'd both been basically children at the time.

His voice was low, deep, confident and well-cultured, with the tiniest hint of the South. Naturally—they were from the southernmost city in the United States, even if that city had never been completely typically Southern or typically anything at all. Key West was an olio of countries, times, and people, and accents came from across the globe.

And still...

"It's Liam."

"Liam Beckett?"

"Yes, Kelsey. Hello. I'm sorry to be calling you. Well,

I'm not sorry to be calling you, I'm just sorry because of…the news I have to give you."

Her heart seemed to sink several inches down into her stomach.

"It's Cutter, isn't it?" she asked.

"I'm afraid so, Kelsey." He was quiet a minute. "I'm afraid he died a couple of days ago. We just found him."

A heart couldn't sink lower than into the stomach, could it? It seemed that the depths of her body burned with sorrow and regret. It was human, she tried to tell herself, to put off until tomorrow what should have been done today. She hadn't gone back.

Why in hell had she never gone back? She had meant to, she had promised Cutter Merlin, her only living relative, that she would do so. And yet…

Even after her father had passed away, there had been that dark, empty place that had made her afraid to do so.

"Kelsey? Are you there?"

"Yes, I'm here. I'm… Thank you. Thank you for calling me."

"Of course." He was silent, and then he cleared his throat awkwardly. "Well, there are matters, of course, that must be dealt with. The property is yours—and the decision on the final arrangements for his interment are yours as well, of course."

"Um…" She couldn't think. She didn't want to think. She didn't want to sit here and think of herself as being such a low and callous human being for not having gone back. Whatever had happened when she had been a teenager, she didn't think that it had been her grandfather's fault, no matter what her father had believed. And her father hadn't actually called Cutter evil, he had told her he was a good man. He hadn't even said that the house was *evil*. But there had been something. She had known that her father believed that her mother's death hadn't been an *accident,* and that he had taken Kelsey away from the house because he had wanted her away from Cutter Merlin.

But the man had been her grandfather, her flesh and blood! She had spoken with him on the phone after her father's death, and she had said that she would come out. But there had been the awful grief of losing her father, and then the flurry of work to learn to live with the fact that he was gone. And then…and then…

She had meant to go down to see him. She hadn't. And that's the way it was, and now he was gone, too, and she was a horrible human being. Liam had said that they had just found him, but…

He had been dead some time. He had died alone, and his body had just sat there alone in death, because he had been so alone in life.

"Kelsey?"

"I'm here."

"His attorney was Joe Richter. I'll text you the phone number and address. I suppose you can come here yourself, or make whatever arrangements you'd like with Joe."

"Sure. Thank you." She still felt numb—and filled with regret. She didn't like herself very much at the moment. She roused herself, though, curious as to why it was Liam who had called her.

"Um—how is it that you're calling?" she asked.

"I'm a cop these days," he told her. "And we've had a few shake-ups in the department lately, so… Anyway, old times, I suppose. When his mail carrier reported that he wasn't collecting his mail, I went to the house. I found him."

A cop. Of course, Liam was a cop. He'd wanted to solve every riddle, put together the pieces of any puzzle. Once, when a school lab rat had disappeared, he had discovered that Sam Henley had stolen the creature to take home; he'd pretended to find Sam's fingerprint on the rat cage, and Sam had quickly squealed—like a rat.

She closed her eyes. She was thinking about Liam. And Cutter was dead.

"Was it a heart attack?" she asked.

There seemed to be a little beat in time before he answered.

"Apparently. But his body is still with the M.E. Just procedure," he said.

But there had been something odd in his voice!

"Please go ahead and call Joe, Kelsey. Let him know what you'd like. Are you still drawing?"

The new question took a moment to comprehend. She was surprised that he remembered how she had loved drawing.

"I'm a cartoonist. I have a column, and we do a little animated thing on the web," she said. "I have an animator partner, and we're doing fairly well. Thanks for asking."

"That sounds great. Well…"

His voice trailed off. He was a cop. He was busy.

"Thank you again, Liam. I'm glad the news came from you."

"I'm sorry, Kelsey. Though I guess it's been a while since you'd seen Cutter."

"We had talked," she told him. Ah, yes, there were defensive tones to her words!

"Take care," he told her.

"Of course, thank you—you, too."

The phone went dead in her hands. She still didn't move for several minutes.

The room darkened around her. Only the bright light above her drafting table gave illumination to her apartment.

She liked where she lived. People often thought of the L.A. area as rather a hellhole of plastic people and traffic.

But Hollywood had neighborhoods. She didn't have to travel most of the time; she worked from home. She had great theater around her, and wonderful music venues. A decent, busy life in a place where there were actually local bars and coffee shops, where she knew the owners of the small restaurants near her and where, day by day, things were pleasant, good.

She didn't need to go back. She could call Joe Richter, and he could make any arrangements that might be necessary.

No, she couldn't. She owed Cutter the decency of arranging a funeral herself.

A beep notified her that Liam Beckett had sent her the text with Joe's information.

She would call him in the morning. She swiveled in her chair from the drafting board to her computer. And she keyed up the airlines, and made a reservation to reach Key West.

She was going home.

Once the reservation was made, she found herself thinking about her father. He'd been a good man. He'd loved her mother so much, and her, too. And he'd even loved Cutter Merlin, she thought. But when they had moved away, she had asked him why, and he had told her, "Because it isn't safe, kitten. Because it just isn't safe to be around Cutter, or that house, or…all that he has done. That man will never be safe, in life…or in death."

The call came when Liam was off duty, when he was down at O'Hara's having dinner—the special for the night, fish and chips.

His cousin David was frequently there, since David was about to marry Katie, Jamie O'Hara's niece, and the karaoke hostess at her uncle's bar. They'd all grown up together. Liam had stayed, while David had gone, until he'd returned recently. Sean, Katie's brother, had also spent many of his adult years working around the world. Like David, he'd gone into photography and then film.

There were others, friends of various ages, sexes, colors, shapes and sizes, who were local, and the locals came to O'Hara's with a standard frequency, though the place also catered to tourists—in Key West, tourism was just about the only industry.

The fish was fresh—caught that afternoon—and delicious, but he'd barely begun his meal, sympathizing with David about the problems inherent in planning a wedding when Jack Nissan called him from the station.

"I just got a call—something is going on over at the Merlin house. I know you cared about the old fellow and contacted his granddaughter. I thought that maybe you wanted to be the one to check it out," Jack told him. "If not, I'm sorry to have called."

"Who called, and what is the something going on?" Liam asked.

"Mrs. Shriver. She could see the place across the water from the wharf area. She said she saw lights, and knew that we'd found the old fellow dead. Should I just send someone on patrol to check it out?"

"No, Jack, thanks. I'll go on over," Liam told him.

"What is it?" David asked.

"A report of lights over at the Merlin house," Liam said.

"Want me to come with you?" David asked.

"No, it's all right. I'll be back. I'll see you later."

When he headed out to his car, Liam knew that he was being followed. He paused, turning around.

Bartholomew.

Not everyone saw Bartholomew, and frankly, he'd been among the last in their group to really *see* the pirate.

Bartholomew had died in the eighteen hundreds. First, Bartholomew had attached himself to Katie O'Hara.

Then, somehow, he had become Sean O'Hara's ghost, and now, with the world quiet—and, Liam assumed, because the others were all living basically normal lives and were romantically involved—Bartholomew had decided to haunt him.

It was quite sad, really. He'd listened to his cousin and the others talk about Bartholomew, but he might have actually believed that it was all part of a strange mass hallucination because of the danger they had been in.

But then, Bartholomew had decided that he needed to attach himself to Liam. It had been after the affair out on Haunt Island, when, his cousin David had assured him, the ghost had been instrumental in saving a number of lives.

At first, seeing a ghost was definitely disturbing. And as far as that went, he'd assumed you'd see some wisp of mist in the air—hear the rattle of chains—or the like. But seeing Bartholomew was like seeing any would-be contemporary costumed pirate in Key West.

The pirate—or privateer—had been a good man. He could be a fine conversationalist, and had certainly helped them all in times of great distress.

It was still unnerving to be followed about by a ghost few others could see, a man in an elegant brocade frock coat, ruffled shirt and waistcoat, and tricornered hat. Since it was Key West, with Fantasy Fest and Pirates in Paradise—not to mention Hemingway Days—it shouldn't have felt that odd to be followed about by anyone in any attire—or lack thereof. Though it was illegal to travel the streets nude, there were those who did try it during Fantasy Fest, when body paint was the rage.

Katie O'Hara, was the one who had been born with the sixth sense, gift, curse or whatever one wanted to call it that allowed people to *see* what others did not. Liam didn't think that the rest of them had anything that remotely resembled Katie's gifts. But they had all survived events in which what wasn't at all *ordinary* had played a major part.

And they all knew there were forces in the world that weren't visible to the naked eye.

And he should have been accustomed to Bartholomew by now.

In life, Bartholomew had surely been a dashing and charming individual. Even in death, he was quite a character: intelligent and with a keen sense of justice.

"What?" Liam said, spinning around.

Bartholomew stopped short. "What do you mean, *what?* Cutter Merlin was found dead in a most unusual way, and, God knows, the place had its reputation. You just may need me."

"It's going to turn out to be kids, I'm willing to bet," Liam said. "Teenagers who know the man died and want to break into a haunted house."

Bartholomew shrugged. "I'm just along for the ride," he said. "I haven't seen it yet. The place sounds extremely unusual, and I'm fascinated."

Liam groaned. "All right, let's go."

Liam supposed it was natural that people—young and old—would find the Merlin house fascinating, and that it did make a great haunted house. Once, of course, it had been a beautiful grand dame, but time had done its work, and with Cutter Merlin being old and alone, it had taken on that aura of decay long before the gentleman had passed. Then, of course, there was the truth—he had been a collector of oddities, including human remains such as mummies and shrunken heads.

It was a little more than a mile down Duval and around Front Street and then down around the little peninsula to reach the Merlin house. Liam parked in the overgrown yard. He exited the car and stared at the place, but not even the porch light he had left on after Merlin's body had been removed was still shining. A burned-out bulb? Or was a prankster inside?

"That's one eerie residence," Bartholomew commented.

Liam shrugged and walked up the path to the porch. He tried the front door and found it unlocked. He knew that it had been locked and they had sealed up the entrance over the washer and dryer. Merlin's attorney, Joe Richter, had the only other set of keys.

He stepped in. Somehow, the house still seemed to have an aura of death about it.

He tried the light switch by the front door, but nothing happened. He turned on his flashlight, and the parlor was illuminated.

An odd whisper emanated through the house. In his mind's eye, Liam thought about the layout of the house. The front door faced south and Old Town, Key West. Cutter's library or office was to the left, and behind it was a workroom. The living room stretched the rest of the way in the front, with a doorway leading into the dining room. The kitchen stretched across the back of the house and could be entered through the dining room or the living room. In the center of the living room there was a grand stairway.

The staircase where Kelsey's mother had died.

He hadn't been there when it had happened; he had seen Kelsey after, at the funeral. Throughout the service, attended by most of the city, Kelsey had stood, pale and stoic, trying to be a rock for her father, and for Cutter.

Later, when the formal services had ended, they had come here.

Friends and neighbors had helped; food had been set on the buffets, and on the dining-room table, and people had talked. And one by one, their other friends had gone, and finally he had been alone with Kelsey, and they hadn't said much; he had just held her while she sobbed, until she was so tired that she needed to be brought up to bed.

He had carried her. With her father's permission. Cutter had suggested that they just wake her; he had been loath to do so. "She's not heavy, sir," he had assured Cutter. But when he had brought her up the stairs and laid her down, she had clung to him, and he had stayed beside her in the darkness and the shadows until the exhaustion of her grief had brought sleep mercifully to her once again, and only then had he tiptoed away.

It had been the last time he had seen her.

He couldn't think about Kelsey or the past now. He wasn't the same; he was sure Kelsey wasn't the same. And the house certainly wasn't the same. It seemed like a shell, the bones of a family and happiness that had once existed.

He owed it to Kelsey, though, to keep the miscreants and thieves away until she decided what she wanted.

Two archways sat on either side of the stairway, one leading to the dining room, the other leading to an area that was a family room—in Victorian days, the family had seldom used the proper living room or parlor. The fireplace was dual; a mantel sat on the other side in Cutter's office. Though it was seldom that the temperature went below forty even in the dead of winter, it could be cold in the dampness of the semitropics. He had found Cutter in the rocker by the fireplace.

He cast the light over the parlor. It sat in still and brooding silence, boxes everywhere, the heads of long-dead animals staring down at him, spiderwebs reigning supreme along with the dust.

"Oh, God! Oh, God!"

The sound was coming from the kitchen. Frowning, Liam walked through the parlor and quietly continued, skirting boxes and crates and statues, until he reached the kitchen.

He cast the flare of his flashlight toward the far wall even as a bloodcurdling scream ripped through the air.

It startled and unnerved him; even Bartholomew gasped.

"What the hell…?"

"Oh, my God! You're alive, you're real!"

The light illuminated three people—three young people.

Teenagers, as he had suspected.

They looked like little Key deer caught in the head-lights, staring back at him with white faces and terri-fied stares.

"Yes, I'm alive," Liam said irritably. "Who are you, and what are you doing here? You're trespassing."

There were two boys and one girl. It was the girl who worked her jaw and gasped out, "There are things in here! Things! Horrible things, shadow ghosts, they touch you…they try to kill you!"

She had been hunched in terror against the wall. She had a frying pan clutched in her hands. She was dressed in capri pants and a tank top that left her stomach, and her cute little belly-button ring, visible. She was as skinny as a twig, maybe fourteen.

The boys seemed to gain courage from her. They both stood as well, and were each about an inch shorter than she was. One of them held a copper dough roller. The other was clutching a deep dish pan. Strange weapons—gained from the racks that stretched out over the brick island in the center of the room. Liam was surprised that none of them had grabbed the fire poker.

"Sir! There's something awful in here!" one of the boys said.

"Awful!" the other repeated.

"How did you get in here?" Liam asked.

"The door was open," the girl said. She was shaking. "Please…please get us out of here. We'll never come back, never!"

"You can take us to jail—it will be okay!" the boy with the roller clutched in his hands told him, his eyes still huge and panicked.

"Look, just stay here, and I'll check out the place and—"

"No!" The wail came out of the three of them in a chorus.

Liam sighed. "Look, if the door was open, someone was in here ahead of you. I've got to find whoever it is and—"

"No, oh, God, oh, no! You can't leave us here! Please?" the girl begged.

Liam pulled out his phone and called the station. Jack, on the desk, answered the phone.

"Get a car out to the Merlin place for me, will you, Jack? I've got some teenagers."

"Sure. Are you arresting them?" Jack asked.

"No, I just want them taken home. But I think there's still someone in the house. The lights are down. I need some backup."

The three teens were still huddled in front of him. He hung up and asked their names. The girl was Jane Tracy, the boy with the roller was Hank Carlin and the last was Joshua Bell. They had just come in as a prank.

"You know, it's like…it's like a haunted house. Like at Disney World," Hank said. "We just wanted to have some fun. We weren't going to steal anything. Please, can we get out? It can kill you, too, Officer, you don't know…it's terrible!"

"The Addams family…the Munsters…," Jane said. "We just wanted to see. They said he had all kinds of treasures…. Can we just get out?" she begged again.

He didn't blame them. There was something creepy about the house. The hanging utensils cast strange shadows in the glare of his flashlight, while a rocker by the fire seemed to move. Dust motes seemed like misted forms in the artificial light, as well.

"All right, come on."

He turned, and the three came running up behind him like metal drawn to a magnet; he thought he'd trip, they were so tight against him.

Scared. They had scared themselves in the place. They'd wanted a spooky challenge; they had found one in the Merlin house.

They went out to the porch. Liam hoped the patrol car would hurry. If the door had been unlocked, someone else had gotten in. That someone might have provided the shadows and touches that had scared them so badly.

He wanted to find the trespasser before it was too late.

The three remained stuck to him like glue while they stood on the porch. "Hey!" he said. "You'll be home in a few minutes. Look, there's someone still in there. That person was trying to scare you out. But it's a good lesson. No trespassing. It can be dangerous."

"They weren't just trying to scare us, and it wasn't any person," Jane said. "They wanted to kill us—they would have killed us. They were ghosts, evil spirits!"

"Jane, it's just a house," Liam said.

"Then the house wanted to kill us."

"What makes you say that?" he asked.

"Because we heard it!" she whispered. "We all heard it! It was horrible, a horrible whisper in the darkness saying, 'You're going to die. I'm going to kill you.'"

"And he was there," Joshua said gravely. "I saw him. I saw old man Merlin. His eyes were burning in the darkness. I felt him, felt him put his hands around my throat."

"He shoved me," Jane said.

Just then the patrol car arrived and Art Saunders and Ricky Long emerged. "Art, get these three home," Liam instructed. "Ricky, come with me. Lights are out, and I want to search the place."

"Yessir," Art called. "You three, get your little juvenile-delinquent butts into the car," he said to the kids.

Ricky Long had been with the department about three years. He was a good cop. He'd seen some bad things in his brief stint.

He looked sick as he walked toward the house.

"You want me to search it with you, sir?" he asked.

"Ricky, it's a house. If there's something in it, it's flesh and blood. Yes, we're supposed to guard lives and personal property. I'll take the upstairs, you take the downstairs."

Ricky nodded slowly.

Liam left him to search through the ground floor. Upstairs, he went methodically from room to room, aware that Bartholomew was at his back.

"I don't like this place," Bartholomew whispered.

Liam stopped. "Bartholomew, you are a ghost."

"I still don't like this place. There is something here. Remnants of evil and pain. Maybe it's in all this creepy stuff. Mummies, coffins, shrunken skulls. Evil spirits, the memories of pain and sacrifice and human suffering. Miasma on the air. Let's get this done and get out."

"Bartholomew, someone human was in here. Doors don't unlock themselves."

"What if evil spirits unlock them to lure in the innocent?" Bartholomew asked. "I may be a ghost, but we both know that evil isn't something that dies easily."

Liam wondered if Kelsey Donovan was going to have Joe Richter sell the place for her, or if she'd come to Key West herself. He'd have to ask Richter. If Kelsey was going to come down and move back into the house, he had to stop whatever the hell was going on.

"Cutter Merlin wasn't an evil man," he said.

Bartholomew sniffed, sidestepping a huge stone gargoyle probably procured from a medieval church somewhere in Europe.

The gargoyle's huge shoulders hunched and the eyes seemed to stare at them with malice.

"They say he practiced black magic!" Bartholomew told him.

"People make up whatever they wish regarding an old hermit," Liam said sadly.

"He was some kind of a wizard. Or a witch, maybe. Men can be witches, right? Yeah, that's right. They hanged men as witches in Salem, Massachusetts. And in Europe, too," Bartholomew said.

"They hanged a bunch of innocent people caught up in hysteria or a land grab," Liam said firmly.

As he did so, he heard a scream again. Male this time, hoarse and curt…and somehow just as bloodcurdling as the first he had heard that evening.

The sound came again, a scream of abject terror.

Then, it was broken off. Midstream, as if the screamer had...

As if the screamer's throat had been slit.

Ricky. Ricky Long, screaming from the ground floor....

And then—not.

Liam forgot Bartholomew and the idiotic imaginations of the masses and went tearing down the stairs.

2

Liam's call had opened the door to the past.

Odd—that was actually what she had done in her mind, she realized. Closed a door. And as if that door had been real and tangible, she had set her hand on the knob and turned it.

Cutter Merlin, her mother's father, had been so many things. He had doctorates in history and archaeology, and he had been the best storyteller she had ever known. His beautiful old house in Key West had been like a treasure trove, filled with *things,* and each thing had offered a story. She had loved growing up with the exotic. While her friends could be easily scared, she loved the idea that she lived with a real Egyptian mummy. At campfires she had told great tales herself, describing how she had awakened once to find the mummy standing over her… reaching out for her.

It had been great. The others had squealed with fear and delight.

Except for Liam, of course. She could remember the way he would scoff at her stories. He was two years older than she was, but in their small community they often wound up at the same extracurricular events, and even when they were in grade school, they had battled.

"Yeah, sure!" Liam said, mocking her story. "Like the mummy really got up. The mummy is old and dead and rotten, and if you let me in the house, I'll prove it!" he would say.

"Ask my grandfather!" she'd dared him.

"I'll be happy to," he'd assured her. But he never did. He didn't want to prove his words, because her stories made her popular.

And they were good stories, of course.

He'd been so elusive; that little bit older, somehow, even for a boy, more mature.

And sometimes, when they were grouped together out on the beach at Fort Zachary Taylor, she told stories that were true about the aboriginal tribes her grandfather had known, getting a little bit dramatic by adding the fact that Cutter had barely escaped with his life—and his own head.

Liam listened, rolling his eyes at her embellishments.

She had been tall, since girls did tend to grow faster than boys. But Liam had grown quickly, too, and by the time they had reached their early teens, he had stood at least an inch over her, and when she would talk, he would lean against a doorframe, arms crossed over his chest, that amused and disbelieving look on his face.

But when her mother had died, he had been like the Rock of Gibraltar, telling her to go ahead and break down when she had tried so hard not to cry in public, and he had held her while she had sobbed for an hour.

He had been her strength that night, smoothing her hair back, just being there, never saying that it was all right that her mother was dead, just saying that it was all right to cry.

And then…

Then she hadn't seen him again. Her father took her away from Key West, hurriedly, one night. She had left most of her belongings, taking only one suitcase, because her father had been in such a rush.

She'd told no one goodbye.

And no matter how real her life in Key West had been, everything about it had faded away. She had enrolled in a California school. She had acquired new friends. She had played volleyball in the sand, and she had finally learned to surf in cold water. Everything in their apartment was brand-new, and her father never even watched old movies.

There had only been one time when she had asked him about Cutter. She had never called him grandfather, grandpa, or even gramps—he had always been Cutter to everyone. And so she had asked her father, "Do you hate Cutter, Dad? Do you think that he hurt Mom somehow?"

He had hesitated, but then shook his head strenuously. "No, no. Cutter is a good man. Don't let anyone tell you anything different, ever."

"Then why did we run away from him?" she'd asked.

"Because bad things can follow a good man, and that's that, and please, I don't want to talk about it anymore."

And that had been it.

Key West had faded away, like a scene out of a movie, one she had seen long ago. Until her father was dying, and he had talked about Cutter again.

Cutter wasn't *safe*.

She'd loved him. She thought about it now, and she knew that she had really loved him. He'd had such a wonderful sense of adventure. His eyes had been brilliant while he'd described the pyramids in Egypt and the temples in ancient Greece. He talked about places like the Vatican, St. Paul's Cathedral, Westminster Abbey and Notre Dame with great awe. He'd talked about the catacombs in Paris, and about marvelous, creepy grottos in Sicily.

His talent as a storyteller had been amazing. And, of course, he'd turned her into one, she thought. No one had ever really known when Cutter was telling the truth— and when he was spinning a very tall tale.

She called Joe Richter, the attorney, to let him know that she would come in person, and then she called Avery Slater, her creative partner, to let him know that she was leaving and why. And naturally, Avery appeared at her door within twenty minutes.

He was seriously one of the most beautiful people she had ever seen, and she used his image for one of her characters, Talon, an angel who had come to live among men. Avery was tall, and he spent his free time at the gym, so he was lean and muscled, as well. He had luxurious, thick, almost black hair, his eyes were chestnut and his features might have adorned a Greek statue. He was a skilled animator, her partner and one of her best friends. She knew that people often thought they were a romantic pair, but Avery was gay, not in the closet in the least, but someone who was very private as well, unless he was among close friends.

He burst into her home with the ease of a best friend, heading straight into the kitchen, opening the refrigerator and finding the chardonnay. He poured himself a glass, didn't offer her one and swallowed it down as if it were water, staring at her all the while.

"You can't just up and go to Key West," he told her, setting his glass down firmly on the counter.

"I'm not moving to Key West, I'm just going down for a few weeks. My grandfather died," she said.

"Yes, yes, you told me that. But you weren't close—you hadn't seen him in years," Avery reminded her.

"I owe him a decent burial," she said.

"Send money," he said. He frowned. "Oh, wait—will you inherit money? A lot of it?"

She laughed. "I don't know. Maybe. He had a number of artifacts, but I knew, even as a kid, that he'd willed a lot of his things to various museums."

Thoughtfully, Avery nodded. "Yes, yes, a will. Of course. There you go. There's no need for you to go to Key West."

"Yes, there is."

"An attorney can arrange for a funeral."

"Avery, he was my grandfather."

"But we have work to do!" he said.

"Avery, I will bring my computer. And my scanner. And I will send you the strips, and you will set them up for animation. It will all be fine. Seriously. We're ahead."

"You can never be ahead in this business. We have to keep the Web stuff going daily—that's the only way to really acquire an audience. The bigger we get on the Web, the more the advertisers will pay," he reminded her.

"I have to go."

He frowned. "I don't think you should go."

"Why?"

"I'm seeing a guy who reads tarot cards," he told her.

"Okay…?"

"He warned me that a friend would want to go on a dangerous journey," Avery said, his expression somber and grave. "It's dangerous."

"The danger is in getting a serious sunburn," she said. "Avery, I lived there, remember?"

"And your mother died there, remember?"

She felt a chill, and it was almost as if she knew the words would haunt her later.

"You can take me to the airport, if you want," she told him.

He sighed deeply. "You're going to go no matter what I say, aren't you?"

"Yes."

He came over to her and drew her into his arms, hugging her tightly. She was touched by the gesture; she had thought that he didn't want her going because he was so ambitious, and he liked to work together, with her at his beck and call whenever he had an idea.

But he seemed genuinely concerned.

She drew away from him. He was so gorgeous.

"It's okay. I'll see to the house and his things. I owe Cutter that much. And I want to have a funeral for him. Then I'll be back. It will all be fine. Really," she assured him.

"No. That's not what will happen. You'll go home, you'll see old friends. You won't want to come back here."

"I left as a teenager. My life is here," she said. "I'll be back."

He wagged a finger at her. "If you're not back immediately, I'll be down there to get you. I'll take care of you. And if there's anything bad, well…I'm psychic, you know."

She laughed. "No, I didn't know. But by all means. Key West is beautiful. Come on down."

He sniffed.

At last he left, still offering dire warnings to her.

She needed to pack, but she wandered out to the porch and gazed at the pool she shared with the others who lived in the group of old bungalows. She stared at the water.

Cold water. Even heated, it was still cold, in her mind.

Key West had warm water. Beautiful, warm water.

A sudden scream startled her and brought her back inside. She had a habit of keeping the television on for company. One of the movie channels was running an all-day marathon of classic horror movies.

Someone was running from a werewolf.

She smiled and sat, and then stretched out on her sofa, watching the television. As she did so, her eyes grew heavy. A nap would be great; she had tossed and turned through the night.

As she felt herself nodding off, she thought about fighting sleep.

She knew that she would dream.

It seemed that a scene from a movie was unfolding. The house was distant at first, sitting on its little spit of land. The water around it was aqua and beautiful, as it could only be around Florida and the Caribbean.

But then dark clouds covered the soft blue of the sky, and the ocean became black, as if it were a vast pit of tar.

The camera lens within her dreaming eye came closer and closer, and the old Victorian with its gingerbread façade came clearer to her view. She heard a creaking sound and saw the door was open, that the wind was playing havoc with the hinges.

She was in the house again, and she heard the screams and the wailing, and she saw her father, as she had seen him that day, holding her mother, the sound of his grief terrible. She ran toward him, screaming herself, calling for her mother.

Then Cutter himself came running down the stairs, crying out in horror. He sank down and she felt herself freeze, just standing there as she had on that day.

Then her mother and father and Cutter all faded to mist, and she stood in the empty house, alone. There were boxes and objects, spiderwebs and dust, and there was something else in the house as well, something that seemed like a small black shadow, and then seemed to grow…dark, stygian, filling the house with some kind of evil.

The mummy rose from its sarcophagus and stared at her with rotted and empty eyes. It pointed at the black shadow, and its voice was as dry and brittle as death as it warned, "The house must have you. It's up to you. Now you—you must come, and you must stop it from growing, from escaping. It's loose, you see, the evil is on the loose, and it's growing."

The mummy wasn't real. The mummy was dead. Liam had said so.

Terror filled her. She heard her name called. She turned. Liam was there, a tall, lanky teenager, reaching out to her. "Come here, come to me, it isn't real, the mummy is dead, it's in your imagination, in all the stories. Don't believe in it, Kelsey—take my hand."

There seemed to be a terrible roar. She turned, and the mummy was a swirling pile of darkness, a shadow, and the darkness was threatening to consume her.

Kelsey awoke with a start. She was in her charming living room, in her charming bungalow apartment, and she had fallen asleep with the television on.

And the movie channel she watched was showing Boris Karloff in *The Mummy*.

She laughed aloud at herself, turned off the TV, and decided that she was going to get things done, batten down the house, pack so she could leave in the morning, and then get a good night's sleep. She wasn't a coward; she had spent her childhood with Cutter, and really, she had to have some kind of sense of adventure.

I owe you, Cutter! I'm so sorry. I should have

come to see you. I never should have let you die alone like that.

Please forgive me.

She wasn't afraid.

The house was just a house.

And Cutter's mummy was just preserved flesh that could now find a good home in a museum. Everything in perspective.

Cutter himself needed to rest at last, in peace.

She would see to it.

Liam shouted the officer's name. "Ricky!"

There was no answer. As he reached the bottom of the stairs, however, he saw him on the floor, caught in the glow of light from his own fallen flashlight.

"Ricky!"

He rushed over to the man. Hunching down, he called for backup and an ambulance. He instantly checked for Ricky's pulse, and was relieved to find that it was beating steadily.

Ricky groaned, and moved.

"Lie still. Where are you hurt? What happened?"

There was no sign of blood anywhere near Ricky.

As Liam spoke, Ricky opened his eyes, staring at Liam for a moment and then jerking around in panic. He stared across the room in the darkness. Liam aimed his flashlight beam in the area that seemed to be causing Ricky so much fear.

His light fell upon a suit of armor.

Ricky let out a scream, trying to choke it back.

"Ricky," Liam said evenly, "it's a suit of armor. Probably real, historic and worth a mint."

"It moved!" Ricky declared.

Liam walked toward the armor. It was just that. Metal. It was buckled together by leather straps that had been made to replace the originals. They were probably period, but not historic.

The metal display stand was not on rollers. It hadn't moved.

Liam turned to look at Ricky. He was rubbing the back of his head. It appeared that the man had seen the armor and backed himself into the edge of one of the display cases on the other side of the room.

"I swear to you, it moved!" Ricky told him.

He'd called for an ambulance. Even as Ricky stood, rubbing his head, and Liam checked all around the suit of armor, they heard the sound of a siren. Help was on its way.

Ricky winced, looking sheepish. "It moved. I'm telling you, it moved."

"It's dark down here, and you've heard all kinds of rumors about this place," Liam said. He sighed, shaking his head. "Or maybe it did move, Ricky. Maybe a trespasser was in here, hiding behind the suit of armor, and when you knocked yourself out, he got away."

Ricky's mouth fell open. He was young, twenty-five years old. He was a good officer. Strong, usually sane and courteous. He could break up a barroom brawl like no other.

He protested weakly. "No…no, I would have seen a person." He cleared his throat. "Oh, Lord, Lieutenant

Beckett, please…maybe we could not mention this?" he asked hopefully.

Liam was irritated; he might have just lost his chance of finding whoever had broken in. But he said, "I'm not going to say anything—hell, I don't want half the idiots in this city starting all kinds of rumors about haunted houses and animated suits of armor. Let the paramedics check you out. Just say you crashed into the display shelf, and that's what I'll say, too. It's the truth."

He walked out. The paramedics were exiting their ambulance with their cases in their hands.

"It's a knock on the head, self-inflicted," Liam said. "I think he's fine, but check him out, please."

The paramedics nodded and headed for the house. A patrol car came sliding up to park beside the rescue vehicle. He sent the two officers inside, telling them to secure the residence before they left.

He stepped down to the lawn and looked back at the house. He felt the presence behind him and didn't turn.

"Did you see anything?" he asked softly.

"No, I was with you," Bartholomew said.

"Well, what do you think?"

"I don't like the place, if that's what you mean."

"Is there anything in it? Anyone?"

"I sense—something," Bartholomew said.

"I'm telling you, this has to do with something human," Liam said flatly.

"Maybe. I'm *human*," Bartholomew protested.

"You're a ghost."

"But I was human. Evil isn't…it isn't necessarily human."

Liam groaned softly. "We both know that human beings are the ones who carry out physical cruelty and injury to one another."

"Well, we don't actually *know* everything," Bartholomew said.

"If I were going to be hounded by a ghost," Liam said, "you'd think it would be one who knew a little more about eternity."

"There's no one in the house now," Bartholomew told him indignantly. "No one who isn't supposed to be there. No one *human*."

"Someone else was in that house tonight," Liam said with certainty.

"I think so, too," Bartholomew said.

"And now?"

"Whatever is in there isn't human," Bartholomew said quietly. "So, what now?"

There was nothing else to be done for the night.

"Now? Hell, I'm heading back for a new batch of fish and chips," Liam said. But as he walked toward his car, he hesitated. It was dark now on the little peninsula. But there were three acres surrounding the house. There was a strip of beach on the property, and near that there were mangrove swamps and bits of pine and brush on higher ground. The house itself was built up on a large slab of coral and limestone, but surrounding it were dozens of places where someone could conceivably hide, or places where one might stash a small vessel like a canoe, or…

Hell. A decent swimmer could make it across to the mainland easily.

In the darkness, someone could hide with little chance of actually being discovered. He would need a helicopter and megalights to find someone in the night.

He made a mental note to get an electrician out there in the morning.

When he reached O'Hara's, he found Katie, David and Jamie at a table, all dining on fish and chips themselves.

"Well?" David asked curiously.

"Teenagers," he said.

"They mess anything up?" David asked.

"They were huddled together in the kitchen, terrified," Liam said. "They thought the shadows were coming after them."

Katie laughed. "I can well imagine that place at night. They must have been scared out of their wits."

"Hey, that place is frightening to an adult," Jamie O'Hara said.

Liam was surprised that Jamie might have ever found anything frightening. He was a solid man with gray hair, bright eyes, and the calm confidence that made him a good man in any situation and—in Key West—a good barkeep. He could stare down any man about to get in a brawl, and if a punch was thrown, he had the brawn to walk an unruly guest right out to the street.

He'd been both a friend—and something of a parental figure to all of them.

"Cutter Merlin was born and bred right here, and he was popular with folks when he was a young man. He was our version of Indiana Jones, I suppose," Jamie said. "When he got older, that's when folks started talking about him. They said that he got himself into too many places that maybe he shouldn't have gone. It wasn't until his daughter died, though, that folks started saying that he might have been a Satanist, or a witch. Trying to explain that wiccans, or witches, practiced an ancient form of religion that had to do with nature and that Satanism meant worship of the Devil didn't seem to go over. After his daughter died, people said everything in the world about him. He'd signed the Devil's book. He held Black Masses. You name it, people said it."

"He was a nice old man, and a great storyteller," Katie said. "I was out there a few times. Kelsey is a few years older than me, but we were in a sailing class together, and we all went to her place for a picnic after the final day. Cutter was great. He dressed up in a suit of armor, then showed us how heavy it was and why a knight needed a squire. He was wonderful."

Jamie shrugged. "Well, you know how people gossip, and you know how rumors start. People said that his daughter died because he'd signed a pact with the Devil—and that was why Kelsey's father got her the hell out the minute he could after his wife passed away."

"I wonder if it occurred to people that he might have been in tremendous pain—and that he wanted to raise his daughter without her having to remember how her mother had died on the stairs. A tragic accident," David said.

Liam hesitated, thinking about the things the M.E., Franklin Valaski, had said the day before when he had studied Cutter Merlin's mortal remains and mentioned the man's dying expression, comparing it to that of his daughter.

She had fallen, but her eyes were open, her lips ajar....

And Cutter had been found with a relic in his hands and the book in his lap.

In Defense from Dark Magick.

Just what the hell had the old bastard been up to?

"I wonder if Kelsey will come back?" Katie mused. "Actually, I wonder what she's like now. Do you think she became a Valley girl?"

"I don't know," Liam said. He was curious. He wanted to see her. It had been a long time. Other women had come into his life, and other women had gone. She was the only one who had ever teased his memory in absence. "I don't know," he repeated with a shrug.

And he suddenly prayed that she had become a Valley girl, that she would stay away and that whatever cursed the Merlin house, human or *other,* would never touch Kelsey.

The next night, it was a dinner of shepherd's pie that he had to leave. It had just arrived, and the call came from the station.

It was Jack again.

"Lieutenant, I know you found kids last night, and I can't believe they're back, but we've just gotten another call. This time it was a tourist who is staying at a bed-and-breakfast across the way. He saw lights on at the Merlin house, and he's certain he heard a scream."

Liam set his fork down. "There are lights on because I had an electrician out. The lightbulbs are all new. I left a light on inside the living room, and one on the front porch."

"Sir, the lights are coming from an upstairs bedroom. The lights didn't bother Mr.—" Liam could hear papers rustling as Jack checked his notes "—Mr. Tom Lewis, from New York City. What bothered him is that he could swear he heard a scream."

"All right. I'm going out," he said.

He slid off his bar stool. He'd been alone thus far that night, though Katie was working her Katie-oke, and he knew that David would be in soon. Clarinda had taken his order and delivered his food. She came by as he stood. "I take it you'll be wanting this reheated when you get back?"

He smiled at her. "Yep, thanks."

"The Merlin house again?"

"Yep. What made you say that?"

She grinned at him. "You don't usually leave your dinner for drunks on Front Street."

He nodded, thanked her and assured her that he'd be back.

On the street, he looked for Bartholomew, but he didn't see the ghost, who usually hovered near or around him. It disturbed him to realize that he wished that Bartholomew was around.

He wondered if he should call for backup, but decided that he would be able to see in the house that night, and he wanted to move in quietly himself.

So thinking, he parked out on the road and walked onto the property.

When he reached the house, he moved quietly up to the porch. When he touched the front doorknob, he carefully twisted it and once again found it open. He pressed it inward carefully, remaining as silent as he could.

To his surprise, he heard conversation coming from the kitchen. "Look, none of this stuff is worth stealing. I thought we could find some small thing that would bring in a few bucks, something that no one would notice, and maybe sleep a few nights in a place that wasn't a hellhole," someone said. "But there's nothing. We're going to take a shrunken skull? There aren't even any amulets or anything on that ragtag excuse for a mummy. And guess what? I don't like this place! It's creepy and scary. That damned door opened as if the house was sucking us in!"

"Don't be ridiculous. This is a house—that's all there is to it. Things are things. The dead are dead, and I don't know about you, but I'm certain there's got to be something that doesn't weigh a hundred pounds and can be sold easily," said a second speaker. "He's supposed to have all kinds of jewels, diamonds and so on."

"You know what? You're wrong. This is bad. I don't feel good about taking anything out of this place. It may be cursed, you know?" said the first voice.

There seemed to be a slight hesitation between the two; Liam almost moved forward, but then the second speaker said, "All right, so the house is…weird. Creepy. We look fast, we get out—fast. Hey, I was always kind of close to old Merlin. Ran errands and stuff. He owes me, honestly. So, nothing creepy will happen if we're just careful about taking what we need, and not robbing the place blind."

It was enough. Aware of his gun in its holster beneath his light cotton jacket, Liam stepped forward, walking casually into the kitchen.

The first man, with scraggly blond hair and a scruffy face, let out a startled yelp.

The second one spun around as if he were ready to pounce on the threatened danger; he saw Liam and backed down.

Liam knew them both.

The scruffy blond was Gary White, a guitar player who wasn't bad, with a voice that, likewise, wasn't bad. He could get work. Thing was, while he wasn't bad, he just wasn't *good*. That meant he didn't work all that often, but he was still convinced that he'd get rich one day, that he'd be discovered in Key West. His last name fit him—his hair was so bleached out by the sun, it was platinum, nearly white.

The second man was Chris Vargas. He was dark haired, about a decade older than Gary, an inch taller, and he couldn't play guitar at all. He had a beat-up old rickshaw, and made money running tourists up and down Duval Street. He had a home in a tiny apartment above the garage of a house on the south side of Old Town.

"What the hell are you two doing?" Liam asked tiredly.

Gary looked at Chris in alarm. His mouth began to work. "Uh—uh."

That was all that he could come up with.

Vargas said, "Oh, hey! We saw lights in here. We knew that old man Merlin just died. We thought we'd better check it out."

"Vargas, you ass, I just heard you talking," Liam said.

Chris Vargas reddened. He was a lean, lithe man in decent shape from running up and down all the time with a fair amount of weight behind him. He could probably be dangerous, under certain circumstances, Liam decided. His features were sharp, like a little rat's. He'd been scraping for a living too long, drinking to drown his unhappiness a few too many nights.

"All right," the man said softly. "We—we weren't after much, Lieutenant Beckett. Honest to God. Just some little thing."

"And you were in here last night, too, trying to scare those kids to death, huh?" Liam asked.

"No, we were not in here last night!" Gary White said, indignant. He stood straight, and seemed really hurt at the accusation.

Liam looked at Chris Vargas. Vargas stared back at him, shaking his head emphatically.

"Oh, God, we're under arrest, right?" Gary asked miserably.

"How did you get in?" Liam asked.

Gary looked puzzled. He wasn't the sharpest knife in the drawer. "Um—the door?"

"You walked in the front door. How? You picked the lock?" Liam asked.

"No, it wasn't locked," Gary assured him.

Liam believed him. Gary White was just a bit too dense to be a good liar.

"Look," Vargas said, "we just walked in because—"

"You were robbing the estate," Liam interrupted.

"Not really robbing," White protested. "Just… Ah, come on, Lieutenant. If you heard us, you know that we're just… All right, so we were going to take something really little. And, hell, we're not bad. The kids in here the other night—those little bastards have broken into other places. They don't steal, but they smoke pot, yeah, they smoke pot up in the rooms and play with all the stuff the snowbirds leave behind."

"If you weren't in here," Liam asked wearily, "how do you know about the kids?"

"Because everybody knows about the kids," Vargas said. "Ah, Lieutenant! You know this is a small town, really. Everybody knows everything. And it's true. I heard they got the bejesus scared out of them here. I hope it's true. It will keep the little rug rats from causing real trouble."

"That's right," White agreed solemnly, nodding at Vargas as if the two of them were the most solid citizens in the world.

Gary White must have seen something in Liam's face. He choked slightly, cleared his throat and asked, "Are you going to arrest us?"

This whole thing was beyond absurd. Two nights in a row. First, kids. Second? Two of the denizens of the place who weren't known for violence, who just eked out a living. If he arrested them, an attorney would have them out on bail. And what would they get for trespassing? They hadn't stolen anything; he had arrived too soon, and, from what he could tell, they couldn't find anything they actually wanted to steal anyway.

He thought about the paperwork.

And, to his knowledge, Gary White had never done anything to break the law that was more serious than jaywalking.

"Get the hell out of here," he said.

They both stared at him.

"Now," he said.

They bolted like lightning. He turned and watched them from the kitchen doorway. They had trouble opening the front door, the one crashing into the other, crashing into the door, then each other again.

Finally, they made it out.

He walked to the door himself. There was nothing wrong with it that he could see. The lock hadn't been picked.

Someone else out there had a key.

Tomorrow he'd have to have the lock changed.

Going from the West Coast of the States to the east coast made it difficult to arrive with much of anything left of daylight, especially once daylight savings time was gone. But Kelsey had found an early-morning flight that got her into Miami around three in the afternoon. She could have taken a puddle jumper down to Key West from Miami International Airport, but she wanted to drive. Baggage claim at MIA was insane, but eventually she was ready to head out for the rental-car agency, and by four-thirty she was driving south.

The turnpike took her to Florida City, and she headed down U.S. 1, past the gas stations, one real restaurant and fast-food eateries to the eighteen-mile stretch of noth-ingness that led to Key Largo and from there south and then west to Key West.

They'd improved the road, though she still saw signs and crosses where those in a hurry had tried to pass, only to pay the ultimate price. She managed to get behind a truck towing a huge boat trailer, but she didn't mind waiting for the passing zone.

It had been a long time.

The day was beautiful. The turquoise water glistened, the waves were gentle and calm. In a few areas, construc-tion workers were still claiming land to widen the road and the stench of stagnant water overpowered the view, but the sight of a cormorant soaring above the water seemed to lift the stench beyond her windows, and then she was past it.

A new overpass made getting into Key Largo a bit easier and faster, and it was still daylight when she ar-rived. Key Largo was built up. She assumed she'd see that all the way down the Keys.

By six-thirty she had lost the daylight, and she had come to the middle Keys where there were still vast tracts that didn't seem to have been built up much. Mara-thon had acquired another shopping center, but the lower Keys were still tiny and starkly populated. She slowed at the signs warning that her speed needed to be minimal in honor of the little Key deer that roamed the area, and at last, in darkness, she reached Stock Island and then drove on to Key West. Following North Roosevelt Boulevard around, she sought out the shopping plaza on the newer part of the island where the attorney had assured her he would leave the key to the Merlin house in a lockbox—a brand-new key because the police lieutenant had suggested new locks. She found the shopping center easily enough, decided she'd just stop quickly for a sandwich at a small Cuban restaurant and went to procure the key. As she punched in the number Joe Richter had given her, the door to his office in the plaza opened.

"Kelsey. Kelsey Donovan! Young lady, you have grown up!"

Joe Richter was probably about fifty. She remembered him the minute she saw him because he hadn't changed at all. His hair was snow-white, and he had a full head of it. He was lean, a gaunt man who managed to maintain a presence and a tremendous sense of dignity.

"Joe, I remember you, of course," she said. When she had called about Cutter's death, he hadn't reminded her that she knew him. But she had been distracted when she called—still wallowing in guilt.

"I was just about to leave—you just caught me. I wanted to let you know we can do a formal reading of the will anytime you like. You're the only heir, so… Then," he added, clearing his throat, "we do need to make arrangements for Cutter's burial. He's still at the morgue, awaiting your plans."

"Thank you, Joe, for handling everything so far," Kelsey said.

"He was my client for years, though even I had barely seen him lately," Joe said.

"When did you see him last?"

"About six months ago."

"That long? Was there any special reason you saw him then?"

Joe shook his head. "No. His will has remained the same since your mother died. I happened to be shopping down on Front Street, so I took a ride out. I told him he needed a maid—he said that he'd tried hiring someone once, but she'd left in the middle of the job, screaming. I guess the house isn't for everyone."

"No," Kelsey agreed, smiling.

"Well, young lady, I'm going to suggest you get some help to clean the place out. It's going to need a lot of work." He hesitated. "Can I do anything for you now? Would you rather stay somewhere else? I can get you a reservation.... Of course, you could have gotten your own reservation, if you had wanted," he added gently.

"No, I think I need to get out to the house. Everything is actually working, right? Electric, plumbing…that kind of thing?"

"Oh, yeah, the police saw to it. All I had to do was hire the locksmith—safety's sake, you know?"

"Sure, thank you. I'll talk to you tomorrow," she told him.

He nodded and watched her head out to her car. She revved the engine and found herself looking around the plaza. She might have been almost anywhere in America, in this parking lot. This portion of the island was fairly new, created by dredging salt ponds, digging some places, dumping others. Once she headed down Roosevelt toward Old Town, things changed. Hospitals, restaurants, tourist shops and bars were interspersed among old Victorian buildings, and grand dames from the past sat side by side with neon lights. The Hard Rock Cafe was located in one of the old Curry mansions—in fact, it was "haunted," of course. Robert Curry, unable to sustain the family fortune due to ill health and a lack of business smarts, had killed himself there. Also on Duval was St. Paul's Episcopal Church, rebuilt and rebuilt again—and still the haunt of a sea captain and a group of children tragically killed in a fire. Key West jealously guarded her ghosts, just as she did her bizarre history and all her citizens who had come and gone.

Kelsey didn't drive as far as Duval, though, turning to take Simonton down to the wharf and then turning onto the private road that led out to Cutter Merlin's house.

Her house.

She hesitated a minute at the overgrown gravel drive that led out to the house. Funny—as a child, she had never thought of the house as remote.

That night, in the darkness, the road looked like something out of a slasher film, and the house seemed to sit in a lonely jungle far from the mainland.

It wasn't far, she reminded herself. She and her friends had swum the distance from the house's spit of land over to the mainland many a time. Of course, they were good swimmers. They knew the currents that could sweep by, but the eddy would keep them closer to the road, and they had learned as kids never to strike out alone. Her mother had been an amazing swimmer and diver, and she had taught Kelsey that the biggest mistake those who knew what they were doing made was that they didn't take common-sense precautions.

Still, the house seemed so austere, so alone out here tonight.

All right. So much for the swimming. She had *walked* in and out of town as a kid. There was nothing far or remote about the place.

It was hers, and she had to take care of the place.

She could wait until morning.

That would be ridiculous. She didn't need a hotel room. She owned a house. Even if she planned on selling it, she owned the house.

She pulled the rental car around the side of the house, where they had always parked the family car. There were no cars there; she wondered if Cutter had stopped driving as the years had gone by. There was a lot she had forgotten to ask Joe. But she had just arrived; she'd spend time with him learning about the entire situation tomorrow.

If Cutter had employed a maid who had run away, he had stopped hiring a gardener as well, that was certain.

She exited the car, and was startled to feel an uneasy sense of being *watched* the second she did so. She looked around. She could see the lights across the tiny inlet, and the lights in the house itself. A porch light was on, and light glowed from the living room.

Parlor, she corrected herself. Cutter had always called it the parlor. Now it would be called a living room.

Maybe she was having a ridiculous argument with

herself about *semantics* because she just wasn't sure she wanted to go in.

She had always loved the house. Her mother's death had been an accident. She had tripped and fallen down the stairs. She might have just broken a leg, or an arm. She might have tumbled down and been fine, just bruised and shaken. But the way she had fallen...

She had broken her neck.

Kelsey dug in her over-the-shoulder bag for the new keys. On the porch, she discovered that there were two bolts, thus the chain of keys. She turned both, opened the door and walked on in.

She thought that memories would come flooding back, that she might feel weepy and nostalgic, but the house was actually different. Not the house per se but the appearance of the house. When she and her parents had lived here with her grandfather, the clutter had been at a minimum. There had still been strange objects everywhere: a hundred-year-old stuffed leopard on a dais, mounted heads on the wall—none of them killed by her family, and none less than a century old—native American art, dream catchers, Indian statues of Kali and other gods and goddesses, Roman busts, wiccan wands and so on. The items had been displayed on the wall, or in etageres, or freestanding on mounts. Now...items were everywhere, boxes were everywhere, and the objects on the walls were strewn with dust and spiderwebs. Cutter's glass-encased six-foot bookstand—which had held priceless first editions of many works—was open, and it seemed that the spiders and other crawling creatures had done their damage in there, as well. Sawdust and packing material was strewn haphazardly here and there, almost as if Cutter—or someone else—had been feverishly looking for something special among the endless supply of *things* in the house.

Standing there, looking around, she felt a sinking sensation. The work this place was going to require would be enormous. And yet…they had been her grandfather's treasures. Joe Richter had his will and his detailed papers on where things should go. Only Cutter would have known what had value, what belonged in a museum, and what had been sentimental to him.

A prickly sensation teased her spine, and she looked around quickly, having the eerie feeling once again of being *watched*. She didn't know how that was possible, except that….

Well, actually, anyone could be hiding just about anywhere.

She walked forward and turned on more lights. She frowned as she surveyed all the boxes and crates. She had nearly reached the kitchen when she heard someone on the porch.

They would knock—if they were legitimate.

They didn't knock. She heard a scratching sound, and something like metal against metal.

With her heart in her throat, she went flying across the room. She reached for the poker in the stand by the fireplace and grabbed the ash sweep instead. No matter; there was no time. She flew for the light switch, turned it off and dived behind one of the boxes.

A second later, she heard the knob twist; the door was unlocked.

Had she locked it again after she came in? She couldn't remember.

The door creaked open. She heard footsteps, and then nothing. Whoever was there was just standing, listening.

Seconds ticked by with nothing, nothing except the pounding of her heart.

Then, as if the intruder could hear that pounding, he zoned in on her exact location. The footsteps came closer and closer....

And he was right in front of her. In a second, she would be pinned in place, trapped where she crouched in fear....

She shot up, swinging the metal ash sweep. She heard a hoarse cry as the rod connected with flesh, but then it was pulled out of her hand and a body tackled her length, sending her, and him, crashing down between the boxes.

"Bastard!" she raged, struggling desperately.

Her attacker went still.

"Kelsey?"

She knew the voice. Years dissipated. She knew the voice well.

The boy had changed. The long, lean, muscled body bearing down on hers had definitely changed.

"Liam?" she breathed.

"Good God, Kelsey!" he said.

For another split second, he was on top of her, vital, tense, a mass of flesh and sinew like a brick prison wall that lived and breathed...and then he was up, reaching for her hand, hauling her to her feet.

"Kelsey!" he said again, rubbing his arm, staring at her in the shadows.

"Liam," she said.

Then he turned away from her and walked toward the light switch, and the eeriness of the night was filled with a glow of rationality once again.

3

It was good—and strange—to see Kelsey after so many years. The promise of great beauty that she'd always shown had come to full fruition, and the awkward, embarrassed smile she was giving Liam was nothing short of pure charm.

Kelsey had grown up. She was in a pair of rolled-up capri jeans, a soft cotton V-necked T-shirt and sneakers—she seemed as elegant as a swan. A little tremor ripped through him. Time could wash away so easily. Once, she had been the love of his young life, the seductress of an adolescent's libido and the object of many a dream.

And she was home.

"Liam!" she said again, and laughed. "Oh, Lord, I am so sorry."

"Hey, it's okay. I'm sorry—I tackled you," he told her. "I heard you were coming. I just never expected you to arrive so quickly."

"So, what were you doing here?" she asked him.

He shrugged. "Folks have been breaking in," he said.

"Oh, yes, I heard—Joe Richter, told me. He said the

police suggested that the locks be changed and—oh!" She stared at him, her brows arching. "Liam—okay, I guess that you *are* the police officer who told him to get the locks changed?"

He nodded. "Guilty as charged. I'm with the criminal investigation unit. Seems a lot of crime down here has to do with brawls on Duval and drugs but we've also had our share of serious crime lately."

Kelsey nodded in agreement. "I read about your cousin being cleared in Tanya Barnard's death and the awful things that happened." She grimaced sheepishly. "I was happy—David is a great guy. Just because I haven't been here doesn't mean that I don't read. And I read a really bizarre story about murders that took place near here—out on the islands. Sean O'Hara was involved, right?"

"Sean and David were filming a documentary. They meant to go through our history of oddities and wound up following the minds of the mad. But it's over. They finished up the filming a few weeks ago and are thinking about their next project. David has moved back—he's living at our grandfather's place. He and Katie O'Hara are planning their wedding now."

"Oh, that's wonderful! Katie—so, what is Katie doing these days? Cutter told me that she went up north to college, but came home."

"She's home. She runs Katie-oke at O'Hara's."

"I can't wait to see her," Kelsey said. "Katie was younger, of course, but we took a sailing class together, and I knew Sean fairly well. She was such a cute little ragamuffin, running around with him all the time!"

"Actually," Liam said, glancing at his watch, "you can see her right now, if you'd like. Have you eaten? I can take you to O'Hara's for some dinner and old-home night."

She hesitated. Liam wondered if her current life involved a boyfriend, a lover or even a husband. She wasn't wearing a ring but still he wondered if there had been a husband who was gone now. Maybe he was pushing too far too fast. It just seemed so normal and right that she was here.

"Sorry, no pressure," he told her.

She shook her head. "No, no...I was just looking around—before I panicked when I heard you at the door. This house is going to take...wow. A lot!"

"Were you really going to do much tonight?" he asked.

"Probably not. Um, why not? I had a sandwich, but I'd love to see O'Hara's." She smiled again. There were the dimples he remembered.

"Hey, by the way, how did you get here?" he asked her.

"I have a rental car. I drove down from Miami," she said. "The car is around on the side—that's where we always parked. I guess Cutter hasn't had a car for a while?"

"Not in years. He never left the house."

"How odd—he traveled the globe; and then he became a hermit," she said.

"He was a fascinating old fellow," Liam said. "Brilliant. A real-life Indiana Jones."

"Hmm. I think most of my friends thought of him

more as Uncle Fester, I'm afraid. Or Dr. Frankenstein, creating monsters out of his collections of strange things," Kelsey said.

"Well, you have friends here who cared about him. Shall we go?"

She hesitated, frowning. "Liam—you said you were in the criminal investigation unit. Why was Cutter's death investigated as a crime?"

"It wasn't. I chose to come out—old times," he said with a shrug.

"I see. Thanks."

When they left the house, she turned one key in its lock. "I think you ought to be locking both locks," he said. "In fact, I don't think you should actually be staying here."

She looked at him with amusement. "I grew up in the house. I'm not afraid of the mummy or the coffin—or even the shrunken head."

"Kelsey, I came out here tonight because the house was broken into twice. The first time, a pack of kids came in. The second time, two local lowlifes were looking for something to steal. That's why I told Joe Richter to get a locksmith out here and change the locks. The lowlifes said that the door was open when they got here, but I knew that it had been locked the night before. I'm not sure I feel good about this place," Liam said carefully.

She offered him her dimpled smile once again. "Well, obviously, there had been a key out there somewhere. The locks are brand-new. Honestly, most thieves wouldn't break into this place. It's supposed to house evil spirits, or something of the like. There's so much to be done here. It's ridiculous to own a house and go rent a room. Trust me, I'll be fine. The house likes me, honest!" she said teasingly. "Actually, though, it was a long trip. I'd love a good Guinness—and my dad always said that O'Hara's kept the cleanest taps in the state."

She was a grown woman, and maybe, Liam thought, his unease was unfounded. "Okay, then. Let's go. I'll drive."

He saw that Bartholomew was standing at the edge of the porch and seemed thoughtful. He prayed the ghost wouldn't start talking to him, distract him and make him appear crazy.

No such luck.

As he walked to his car, slightly behind Kelsey, Bartholomew fell into step beside him.

"I don't like it," he said.

You don't like what?

The words were on the tip of Liam's tongue. Somehow, he refrained from saying them aloud.

Bartholomew followed them to the car. He'd known the ghost for some time now; it still unnerved Liam when he simply misted through doors. The physiology was intriguing. Maybe it was the fact that he didn't want to believe in ghosts. Bartholomew could *sit* on a chair, but he misted, blended, faded—whatever!—right through doors. He loved boats, hated the water. He'd been around nearly two hundred years, and he knew the answers to many questions, but he *didn't* know a great deal that Liam felt a ghost should know. It was a different existence, Bartholomew believed. He didn't know every ghost—just as Liam didn't know every living, breathing human. Ghosts were still the essence of people. They were good, bad, clever, dedicated, lost…greedy, generous, loyal, traitorous. That's the way it was. But most of the time, they stayed behind because of a passion or a need. A passion for revenge, or justice—to save the life of a loved one or to right a terrible wrong.

Liam liked Bartholomew. But he wasn't sure he wanted him around right now.

As he pulled the car around the circular drive, he caught a glimpse of the ghost in the rearview mirror.

Bartholomew was staring solemnly at the house, his gaze intent. He was searching for something.

Liam paused and stared up at the house himself.

He thought of the other night. The house seemed to have a life of its own. Beneath the moonlight, constantly shadowed by clouds, it seemed to breathe, and to watch, and to wait.

"What is it?" Kelsey asked him.

"Nothing." He paused, his foot on the brake. "You're sure you want to come back here, stay here alone?" he asked.

"It's my house now," she said quietly, staring at it. "With all that it holds!" she added, and smiled.

O'Hara's was charming, and it hadn't changed a bit—at least, not in Kelsey's memory.

They entered a large open area with high-top tables scattered toward the rear; the space allowed for dancing and was right in front of a stage area that could be set for karaoke or live music. Tonight, rock music was playing, but Kelsey saw a sign that advertised "Katie-oke" four nights a week. If "Katie-oke" was going on that night, it either hadn't started or Katie was taking a break.

"There," Liam said.

"I see."

She had wondered if she would recognize anyone; in the time she had been gone, many people must have come through Key West—and possibly moved on. It could be a city that was warm, like a true neighborhood, yet it was also a city of transients. And most of her friends had been young when she had seen them last, and surely they had changed.

It was easy to see that David Beckett was there, seated at a far booth on the restaurant side, to the left of the dance area. He resembled Liam, or Liam resembled him. He was a tall man with a face made of rugged angles, striking eyes. Katie had grown up beautifully, her red hair having darkened to a gorgeous hue. Sean was easy to recognize, as well—he was a far more masculine version of Katie, and though Katie was definitely feminine, with fine features, they both resembled their uncle, Jamie O'Hara. Kelsey didn't recognize the young woman with Sean, but they were obviously together. She thought she recognized the woman with a tray standing by the table, and even the others who were there: another young couple who looked like flower children. His hair was as curly and long as hers was, and they both wore wire-rimmed glasses.

As they neared the table, unseen, Kelsey heard the last man at the table talking. He was very long and lean, but had a rich voice.

One that she thought she knew.

"They should really just bulldoze that house—let a major-league hotelier come in and put up one of the mega hotels—well, you know, a within-limits mega hotel," he said, slipping an arm around the waitress who hovered by the table. "No more than two stories, of course—you can't ruin the horizon."

"Jonas," Katie O'Hara argued, "don't be silly. That's an historic house. Why would anyone want to destroy it?"

"Well, please. Who would want to keep it?" Jonas asked.

Liam, his hand at the small of Kelsey's back, cleared his throat.

"Actually, Kelsey hasn't decided what she's doing with it yet."

It was almost funny, the way the eight people at or near the table swung around to stare at them.

It was Katie who gasped, then leaped off her bar stool with pleasure. "Kelsey! Oh, my God. You came home. How wonderful to see you!"

Her eyes were sparkling, and her words were sincere. She came forward, offering a hug, and Kelsey was glad to accept it. She drew away. "I'm Katie. I'm sorry—you might not have recognized me. Katie O'Hara."

"Of course, Katie, I remember you well, and thank you for the greeting," Kelsey said. By then, the men at the table were standing.

"Let's see who you remember, and who you don't," Liam said. "My cousin, David. You can't miss Sean O'Hara. And I don't know if you ever met Vanessa, though she's been down now and again over the years. And these are our friends Ted and Jaden. And Clarinda, and Jonas."

David and Sean greeted her like a long-lost kid sister, Vanessa was charming but reserved, and Jaden and Ted were as loving as any good flower children might be. Clarinda welcomed her, and Jonas quickly apologized. "Wow, I'm sorry. I mean, it is my opinion, but—" He broke off and grimaced. "You remember me, don't you? We had a house just across from you near the wharf. I still have it. It's called the Salvage Inn now. I run it as a bed-and-breakfast."

Kelsey grinned. "Yes, of course I remember you. You groaned anytime I was over at your house with either of my folks."

"Okay, well, I'm afraid I have a few years on you. You were a pest back then."

"Not that much of a pest," David Beckett said, "I remember really liking you. I can't believe that you're an adult now."

Kelsey seldom flushed, but she did so. David Beckett had an amazing sense of class and kindness.

Like Liam.

But her mother had always said that their grandfather, Craig Beckett, was one of the most honorable men she had ever known. He had taught his progeny well, she thought.

She needed to take a step back; this did feel like old-home week. And she wasn't staying. She had started life over again, and she was comfortable where she was. She loved her work, her neighborhood, and she wasn't sure why she had come, other than guilt and a sense of debt, and she was very afraid of falling back into…she didn't know what. Maybe the *oddity* of belonging to the house and being Cutter Merlin's granddaughter.

"Thank you, David. And Jonas, it's really okay—I wasn't so fond of you back then, either," she said, and the group laughed.

"Have a seat—I'll get you a Guinness," Liam said.

"Oh, wait! I'm supposedly working," Clarinda said.

"It's all right—I know the owner," Liam said laughing. He headed straight back behind the bar to pour the beer himself.

"We're right across from you," Clarinda told Kelsey. "I live with Jonas, and if you need anything at all, we're really close."

"Thank you."

"Yes, honest. Now I'll be glad if you stop by," Jonas said. He made a face. "And I've got rooms if you want out of the old place."

"Actually, I loved living there," she said.

"Oh, I don't know," Katie put in. "Liam said it's in pretty bad shape. Although I'll be happy to come over and help you put things in order, if you like."

"That would be great," Kelsey said. Could she really ask someone else to sweep up spiderwebs and dust with her?

"I would absolutely adore getting into that house!" Jaden said. "That's what Ted and I do. Well, not exactly. We own a place called Sunken Treasures. Most of what we do is restoration of things that divers bring up. Salvage restoration. But I worked at an auction house for a while before Ted and I opened our own place, so I'm pretty good at assessing the value of old treasures."

"That's great to know," Kelsey said.

Liam returned with two pints of Guinness, setting one in front of her. She thanked him, and Ted said, "Well, you do have an army here for help, if you want it. I must admit, I'm fascinated by the prospect of getting into the house, too."

"We could have a clean-the-house day," Liam said.

"Do you all have a conception of just how bad the house is?" Kelsey asked.

"Oh, hey, well, it doesn't take a lot of talent to get entangled in spiderwebs," Katie told her.

"There's still a barbecue out back, isn't there?" Jonas asked.

"Oh, Lord, if there is, God knows what's in it," Kelsey told him.

"We have an old portable barbecue somewhere," Sean said. "Why don't we dig it out? I mean—if you want an army trampling over on Saturday. I'm thinking Saturday would be the best day?" He looked at Katie and the others. "Katie, you don't start until nine or ten on Saturday night, Clarinda can come in late, and Ted and Jaden can close early. Liam, you take Saturday off, don't you?"

"Unless someone calls in with a real problem," Liam said.

The pretty blonde at Sean's side—Vanessa—cleared her throat. "Excuse me—we've all just invited ourselves over, you realize."

Kelsey laughed. "It sounds great. Sean, you can bring

the barbecue, but I'll supply the food. If you're cleaning the house for me, the least I can do is supply the barbecue."

"It's not that bad. The weather should hold," Liam said. "We can clean—then wash all the spiderwebs off by taking a dip. The water is a little cool right now, but not that bad."

"Hey…I've got to get started," Katie said. "We have a group of coeds looking at the suggestion books, and I'm not sure they'll like the choices."

Kelsey glanced over to the stage area. She smiled, as well—it looked as if the cast of a college comedy had just walked in. They were beautiful people; three girls who were blonde and slim and wearing tiny shorts and belly-baring ripped-up tees had come in with two young men who looked like linebackers—young ones. They still had baby faces.

Katie slid behind her computer, politely salvaging her songbooks and apparently telling the crew that she probably had what they wanted right on the computer; they just needed to name their songs. She made an announcement using the microphone.

"This is O'Hara's, and it's Katie-oke here, four nights a week. Sometimes, it's actually Clarinda-oke, but it's all the same fun. O'Hara's offers twenty-five beers from the cleanest taps you'll find from here to Canada, so enjoy—responsibly, please." Katie said the last with a hopeful but ironic twist in her tone. Key West and responsible drinking weren't really known for going hand in hand. Luckily, partygoers usually stayed within walking distance of the bars on Duval, while a lot of the major-chain hotels farther around the island sent shuttles to drop off and pick up their guests in the Old Town area.

Katie started the music. The college crew whooped and hollered and began dancing energetically to the music.

"It really wasn't that long ago, but I don't ever remember being quite so young," Liam said, his grin wry as he seemed to echo her thoughts.

"It's a good-looking group, and they seem friendly and ready to have fun," Kelsey told him.

Liam nodded. "Cheerleaders," he said solemnly. "You can tell."

"A bit too happy for me," Jaden said. She yawned. "Ted, feel like calling it a night?"

Ted nodded. "We're still working on a lot of treasure recently brought up from that film shoot." He shuddered. "Ugh. We'll tell you all about it at the barbecue, Kelsey." He stared at Vanessa. "It was bad. Very, very bad."

"Hey!" she protested. "We did capture a pair of truly deranged murderers."

"That's true," Jaden said happily.

"Oh! I did hear about that!" Kelsey said. She stared at Liam. She had been so caught up in her own situation, she had forgotten that she had seen their names online, and one night on the news. Sean O'Hara and the Becketts had gotten involved with a film crew, recreating the situation in which two people had been brutally murdered on an uninhabited island. A documentary would air sometime the following year.

"And it's over," Vanessa said with a shudder. "Next

week, I'm filming dolphins for a public-service feature. I'm much happier!"

"That sounds great," Kelsey said.

"Okay, we're really out of here," Jaden said. "It's wonderful to meet you," she told Kelsey. "And thanks for letting us get in the place on Saturday."

"My pleasure. If anyone is allergic to dust, they're in trouble," Kelsey warned as Ted and Jaden left.

It was a warm group, and she was apparently accepted.

Sean and Vanessa decided to brave the bouncing coeds and dance; Liam looked at Kelsey. "Want to try it?"

Dance. He was asking her to dance. Just dance. And yet...

"Do you remember grade school? Mrs. Miller insisted we have something like a cotillion!" she said, grinning.

"We can probably still manage."

Clarinda was busy taking drink orders at another table; Jonas and David were deep in conversation. She still hesitated.

It was a dance, just a dance. She wasn't being sucked back into this actually being her home.

"Sure," she said with a shrug.

By the time they reached the floor, however, Katie was singing at the request of the coeds—she was doing a Shakira number, and Liam told her, "Salsa!"

"Oh, Lord!" she said.

"You've been gone too long. We have a major-league

Cuban influence down here—everybody salsas. You'll be fine!"

Oddly enough, it all kicked in. *Maybe it was like riding a bike.*

Liam knew what he doing. She remembered in ballroom dance, her job was to follow. He led well. And it was fun, exhilarating. She didn't remember the last time she had been out like this.

By the end of the number, they had the floor. The bouncing coeds came over and hugged them enthusiastically, then decided to drip their inebriated adoration on Katie.

It was too easy to have too much fun. To feel his hands on hers, and his arms around her, and feel as if time had evaporated. They'd never taken a step past friendship, but then, they'd still been so young….

"This has been wonderful," she said. "I think, though, Liam, if you don't mind, I should get back home."

"Hey, I can take you," Jonas said. "I'm a stone's throw from you."

"Clarinda is still working," David pointed out.

"I'm fine taking Kelsey home," Liam said. "I want to walk around the place a bit, too."

"The new locks are on, right?" David asked.

"Yes. I just want to take a walk around the place," Liam repeated.

"Sure, but, Kelsey, don't forget—the Salvage Inn, right across from you. Clarinda and I are in room one—it's the left half of the house. Our breakfast chef and server are in at five-thirty in the morning, and we have a bartender at the tiki bar until two a.m., so if you're ever nervous at all, someone is there. And, of course, don't hesitate to wake us up!" He rose.

"Thanks," Kelsey said. "That's really nice. Especially since I was such a pain in the ass as a kid!"

He laughed. "Hey, David, tell Clarinda I'll be back. I'm just going to go home and check on the B and B for a few minutes. Make sure we don't have any calamities going on."

"Will do," David said.

When they walked out to Liam's car, the coeds decided that they were all best friends, too. Kelsey endured a round of hugs from the cheerful cheerleaders and their bruiser dates.

At the cars, they waved good-night to Jonas.

Liam turned down Simonton rather than Duval, knowing that Duval would be filled with jaywalkers. It was seldom an easy street to traverse—except maybe at five in the morning.

But the backstreets could be quiet and pretty. There were so many fine Victorian houses, since the great age for Key West—when the city had boasted one of the highest per-capita incomes in the country during the age of wreckers—had occurred when building had been seen as artistry. There were bungalows, shotgun houses and many a grand dame in Old Town.

"Have you missed the place?" Liam asked her. He had apparently been watching her as she surveyed their surroundings.

"Of course, I've missed it. I mean, I think—unless a place were absolutely terrible—you'd miss it if you'd basically grown up there," Kelsey told him.

"But you like where you live now," he said.

"Yes."

"And you're in Hollywood," he said.

"Yes, but it's not as… All right, well it *can* be plastic, but my neighborhood is great. My dad worked at UCLA, and so I went to UCLA, and they have a great school of art and animation."

"I've seen your column. But you do gaming, too?"

"I don't. My partner, Avery, does."

"Ah."

When they pulled in front of a house, he turned off the car's engine and sat staring up at it for several moments.

"My grandfather was not some kind of evil wizard who cursed the house and set a dozen demons loose in it," she said, surprised that she sounded so resentful.

He flashed her a smile. "I wasn't afraid of demons. I'm afraid of real people breaking in to steal things and not caring much if they take a human life in order to do so."

"Liam, honestly, if there was some kind of really terrible thief who knew about the strange treasures that might be found here, they could have easily broken in while my grandfather was alive. He was an old man living alone."

He was quiet, and that disturbed her.

"He died of a heart attack, right?"

"Yes."

"If you're trying to unnerve me, it isn't going to work. I grew up in that house," she reminded him. Kelsey wasn't sure why she was being so insistent. Maybe she felt that she had to stay there to honor her family in some way. No one in the world would ever understand Cutter Merlin the way that she had. If she didn't stay in the house, she would just perpetuate all the rumors about it being evil and Cutter being some kind of a devil worshiper.

He lifted his hands. "I'm not trying to make you angry. I'll come in and take a walk around the place, just because some kids and a couple of the barely employed were recently inside."

"But the locks are new—and the entry over the washer and dryer is sealed now, right?" Kelsey said.

He nodded while exiting the car. She wasn't sure if he meant to come around and open her door or not, but she hurriedly stepped out herself before he could do so. He was staring up at the house.

"Do you see something?" she asked.

He turned to look at her. "No."

"There you go, see?"

She started walking toward the house. He followed her. She opened both locks and pushed the door in.

The house was just as she had left it. A gazelle—obtained at an auction of objects from an 1890s safari—stared down at her from the far wall, its glass eyes baleful.

"See?" she asked Liam.

"Yeah."

He walked through to the dining room. She stood where she was in the parlor, halfway closing her eyes.

It had always been a beautiful house. Her mother had been a historian, a perfect daughter for Cutter Merlin, and her father had been an anthropologist. Her parents had met at a university function at Oxford, and her father, a California native, had been madly in love with her mother, and in awe of Cutter.

What had changed that? How had an accident on a stairway made her father so determined that he had to get her away? Or had it been, in truth, the insanity of grief?

Liam appeared again, coming through the family-room archway. "Okay, just the office—" He broke off, opening the door to Cutter's library. He walked in, and she heard him moving about, shuffling boxes around. He reappeared. "The upstairs," he said.

"Okay. Mind hauling my suitcase up while you're at it?" she asked, smiling. He had no right to stop her from staying, and he knew it. But it wasn't making him happy.

"My pleasure, Miss Donovan," he said, but there wasn't a lot of pleasure in his voice.

She'd brought only one bag, because it was Key West. One jacket was enough, a few pairs of jeans and shorts, two dresses and sandals. If she needed anything else for her time here, she could buy it in dozens of shops.

"This is all you brought?" he asked her.

"It does weigh a full fifty pounds," she assured him.

He grunted, hefting the bag. "Yes, I believe it does."

She followed him as he climbed the stairway without pausing. Of course, he knew the way to her room. The last time she had seen him before tonight had been in that room.

"You might have waited one night," he said, entering through the doorway of her room. It faced south, toward Jonas's Salvage Inn. There were two more rooms on that side of the hall, while the large master bedroom and another guest room were on the other side.

"Why?"

"Dust!" he said, and sneezed.

She laughed. "It's okay. I'm really tired. I'll fall asleep fast, and wake up and start with the cleaning. With any luck, the washer and dryer still work."

She flicked the switch by the side of the door. Light flooded the room.

He set her bag down and looked around. "I'll check the other rooms. One of the thieves who broke in said that the kids had used these rooms to smoke pot. I'll just check them out."

She laughed, and he turned back, frowning.

"I'm sorry. There's a real fear—kids smoking pot!"

He wasn't amused. He left her. As he did so, she walked to the closet. She was touched to see that Cutter had never gotten rid of her things. She would have to do so now. But she saw a set of clean sheets that had been sealed in a plastic zippered bag.

A little tremor touched her. Cutter had probably never stopped hoping that she and her father would return.

She had the bed halfway remade when Liam returned to the room. "Any evil weed smokers?" she asked him.

"No." He helped her finish pulling the clean sheets onto the bed. "Where did you find these?"

"In the closet—the miracle of sealed zipper bags," she told him.

When the bed was made, he stood looking across the room at her. "You have my number in your cell, if you need me—if you need anything."

She smiled. "Yes, thanks."

"All right, then. Hey, give me a call in the morning, all right?"

"Absolutely." They stared at one another for a minute. She wondered if he remembered the last time they'd been there together. She'd been in so much pain. He'd been so compassionate. She found herself wondering what might have happened if she had stayed in Key West.

They might have become a couple. They might have even married young, and then, like so many people she knew, grown apart, either apathetic or hating one another....

They could have been divorced already, she thought dryly.

But she didn't think so.

Something inside of her seemed to ache. All the could-have-beens.

"Come on and lock me out," he said.

She nodded, following him back down the stairs. When they came to the front door, they both hesitated a moment.

Such a hugging group. He was probably going to hug her good-night.

But he didn't. He seemed to need to keep a distance. That was good.

"All right, then. Good night, kid."

He brushed her cheek. She was suddenly tempted to step closer, to hug him. To cling to him for all the amazing strength he offered. But he offered a great deal more now. He was incredibly tall and well-built, and his eyes were hypnotic, blue like her own but different: more like silver-gray. She suddenly felt an odd jealousy, wondering what had transpired in his life over the years, what women he had known—and how it was possible that he was able to still be such a friend to her.

He walked out the door.

She made sure to lock it quickly behind him so he heard the clicks.

She heard him walk across the porch, and then she didn't hear his footsteps as he reached the overgrown lawn and driveway.

For a moment, she was tempted to throw open the door and beg him to come back in. She was tempted to actually ask him if he'd stay the night…ask if he wasn't the least tempted to sleep with her.

Her cheeks burned with the thought. And with the remembered brush of his fingertips upon them.

She turned to look around the house. The things that seemed so scary to others were not so to her. She loved the mummy—it had given her such great stories, both those told to her by Cutter and those she made up to scare her friends. She smiled at the thought of her dream, because, as Liam had once said, the mummy was dead and gone, locked in its elegant sarcophagus. That, she decided, must go to a museum. Cutter would have a particular museum listed, she was certain.

It was actually three hours earlier in California,

and she shouldn't have been so tired. But she was exhausted.

She was going to go to bed and sleep, and in the morning, she'd start dealing with it all.

She started up the stairs and paused. She silently cursed all the rumors about the place.

Once again, she had the odd sensation of being watched.

With a shake of her head, she went up the steps and into her room. She fell down on the clean sheets without bothering to undress.

Cutter, forgive me, she thought.

He emerged from his special place, that place that not even Cutter Merlin had known about.

And he watched as the car drove away from the house, a sense of elation filling him.

They didn't know; they just didn't know. They didn't see him, and they wouldn't find him.

They didn't understand. He was protected by the power within. They would never see him.

Old man Cutter had thought that he'd understood, but he never had, not until the very end.

Cutter's daughter... She'd known, and she'd seen. And the granddaughter had the same gift, so it seemed.

He was elated. What he had thought was lost might now be found.

She was back!

She was going to stay at the house. He thought of all the things that he could do, but he knew that he would wait. He had to wait. Kelsey Donovan was the only one who could find the source of the power that he needed, the true relic and the true wealth.

People looked at the house, and they shivered, and they thought of horror movies, Psycho, House on Haunted Hill...

And, yes, the house could seem to breathe in the moonlight, but... Ah, yes. Power. It lay in wealth. And in the ability to haunt and tease the mind. There was no weapon as great as the mind!

To Kelsey...he would do no evil.

He needed her, but then...

Great power did demand great sacrifice.

4

Kelsey woke with a hint of sunlight streaking through her windows; the curtains hadn't been fully closed. She lay for a minute, enjoying the dazzle of the light on the dust motes in the air. She smiled and stretched.

She'd slept beautifully. No dreams, no bumps in the night.

She rose slowly and searched the closet for towels. She found that a stack had been wrapped in plastic as well and thanked whoever had helped Cutter after she and her father had left.

The concept of a shower wasn't quite as appetizing. A patina of dust was on everything, and in the end, she decided that it was best to scrub down the bathroom, get all hot and sweaty and dirty first and then relish a shower. Luckily, cleaning fluids didn't seem to go bad.

Finally, refreshed and clad in shorts and tank top, she headed downstairs. The morning light pouring into the house gave her pause—the task ahead of her was daunting.

"Cutter, what were you doing?" she asked aloud.

She walked into the kitchen and winced. Before

anything else, the kitchen had to be cleaned. Then she'd be able to brew coffee and buy food. The thought that she really wanted coffee put everything in order. Kitchen first, then a trip into town for a new coffeemaker and some groceries. Then dusting and vacuuming her room. Then she would delve into Cutter's office and try to discover what was in some of the boxes. She wanted to go through Cutter's things carefully. She didn't want to discover that she'd thrown away what appeared to be junk and was really a precious relic belonging to an obscure religion.

The kitchen didn't appear to be quite as bad as the rest of the house. Cutter had used the kitchen, whereas he probably hadn't been in her room since she had left. Delving under the sink, she found sponges, scrubbers, dishwashing detergent and all kinds of cleaners. It took her about thirty minutes to do a thorough go-over, and then she was happy to find a coffeemaker, and some coffee in the refrigerator. She prepared a single cup in the little coffeemaker and enjoyed it without cream or sugar.

She started to make a list of things she would need for the next few weeks, then remembered that she was hosting a barbecue and added the items she assumed she'd need for her impromptu party. While she was mulling what the group would enjoy, her cell phone rang and she answered it.

"Kelsey?"

"Hey, Liam."

"You're all right?"

"Of course, I'm fine. I told you I'd be fine. You sound so distressed."

"You were supposed to call me and tell me that you were fine," he said.

She was disturbed by the flutter that teased inside. What was the matter with her? She hadn't seen him in years, and yet those years had melted away. She'd naturally been attracted to several men throughout the years, and she'd had friends who'd made her laugh, who intrigued her with their interests and hobbies, but she'd never known someone who seemed to have such a physical pull, and who haunted her soul and mind, as well. Liam still cared, after all this time. She didn't think that he'd spent his life waiting for her; he was an extremely attractive man physically, sensual, vital, honed, and she was sure he'd had his share of relationships. But he wasn't in one now, unless she was imagining things and he was about to tell her that he was bringing his wife or his girlfriend to the barbecue.

Maybe he'd been a lot like her—meeting people, enjoying them, their company, and spending time, even making love, but never finding whatever it was that was needed to make it a real and total commitment.

Or maybe she was reading far too much into a friend's concerned call.

"I'm sorry. But I slept great, and everything is fine," she said.

"So, what's on your agenda?"

"The grocery store, and a call to Joe Richter, and probably a drive over to his office. I was Cutter's only living relative, and the only one mentioned in the will.

But I knew even when I was a kid that he kept a log—he wanted a lot of his pieces in various museums. He trusted his family never to let greed get in the way of what he wanted, and he wasn't all that fond of paperwork and lawyers. So…it's good and it's bad. I have a lot to figure out, trying to fulfill all his wishes. Anyway…that's the agenda."

"If you need anything, don't hesitate to call."

"Thank you."

"I'll see you later, then."

"Great."

Kelsey hung up. She hesitated, and then dialed him back on his cell phone. *Later* was a little too vague.

"Is everything all right?" he answered.

She hesitated again. Maybe he was just concerned about her welfare. But they had been friends once—sparring, perhaps, but close.

"How do you feel about dinner?" she asked.

"It's a necessary meal," he said. "Just teasing. Was that an invitation?"

"Yes. I'm going to the store. What do you like?"

"I'll tell you what. We'll head out somewhere to-night. You can make use of all your culinary skills tomorrow."

"I don't remember saying that I had any," she said, smiling.

"Ah, well, that's to be seen, then, hmm?" he said. "I'll be around sometime after five. I'm day shift—unless something serious happens at night," he added.

She smiled, a little dismayed that the fact that he was coming over seemed so wonderful. She realized, too, that coming back was easy. The property was just as it had been. The house seemed like home. Even as cluttered and dusty as it had become. Her mother had died here, but before she had died, there had been many good times. She remembered the grand parlor when it had been all decked out for Christmas—her parents had always gone all the way. There had been ornaments on the antlers of the mounted animal heads on the walls, and the mantel had been strewn with decorations, from a Nativity to Christmas-clad Disney characters. Lights in a multitude of colors had blazed all around the property, making it a beacon in the night.

"I'll see you soon, then," she said softly.

They said goodbye and clicked off. Kelsey decided to put her call through to Joe Richter and then decide whether to shop first or drive out to see him.

Dialing, she left her list on the table, walked to the family room and then outside. Looking northward, she saw nothing but the endless horizon. The sky was a beautiful blue; the ocean was calm. The little snatch of sandy beach was inviting.

As she stood there, though, she thought that she smelled something unpleasant.

Death. It was the smell of death and decay, organic matter.

It was gone with a whisper of the breeze. She shook her head and winced. Cutter had died inside. She didn't smell it inside. Whoever had been there had cleared the house of the smell.

Liam had probably seen to it.

Her heart seemed to take a little lurch. She had to

stop; she was getting sucked back into the past far too quickly.

Determined, she turned around and headed back inside.

The phone call to Joe Richter put the day in order; she'd stop by to see him, and then she'd head out shopping.

But when she stepped out of the house to drive to the lawyer's office, she was struck again by a strange and haunting scent on the air.

Death.

It was in her mind, she thought. It had to be.

Franklin Valaski was in the middle of an autopsy when Liam arrived at the morgue. His receptionist, Lizzie Smith, had worked for the county almost as long as Franklin. Between them, the pair might have been an advertisement for clean living and longevity, except that Liam knew well that Franklin enjoyed an evening glass of single-malt Scotch—perhaps several—during the week, and also indulged in cigars.

So much for clean living.

Katie had always said that the old folks from the morgue had hung around their embalming fluids for so long that they were alive and well and preserved. Since everyone liked both Franklin and Lizzie, it was a good thing.

"Lieutenant, what can I do for you today?" Franklin asked, coming out to reception. He had stripped off his gloves, but he still wore his magnifying goggles, and his eyes appeared huge. He might have been the mad professor from a movie about aliens.

"Hey, Franklin," Liam said. "Who is on the table? Anyone I should know about?"

Franklin shook his head. "No, thank the good Lord above! No young traffic fatality or victim of foul play, though, of course, by law, since Mrs. Annie Merriweather died alone in her trailer by the sea, I am responsible for assuring the state that she indeed died a natural death. Alas, good Annie produced three children, outlived all of them, and actually has doting grandchildren and great-grandchildren who were not present when she expired in front of her television. Annie recently turned one hundred and one, and indeed the autopsy has proven that she expired when her dear old heart gave out probably while she was dozing through an episode of *Jeopardy*. What can I do for you?"

"I just thought I'd stop by. I know that you ruled Cutter Merlin's death as natural, but I was still curious. You commented about his expression. And you said that you'd seen it before on his daughter's face. You didn't find *anything* out of the ordinary during the autopsy, did you?" Liam asked.

"Like Mrs. Merriweather, Cutter Merlin expired when his heart gave out," Franklin said. "But I am having a strange anomaly with the man," he said.

"Oh?"

"Come, I'll show you."

Liam followed the M.E. down the hall, trying not to breathe too deeply. There was an excellent air-conditioning-and-exhaust system here, but even so, the smell of chemicals clung to the air: chemicals that spoke of death.

In the area Franklin referred to as "the fridge," the medical examiner went straight to a metal door that was second down from the top and pulled. Cutter Merlin, covered reverently in a sheet, lay on his cold metal bed.

Franklin pulled down the sheet that covered the face. To Liam's surprise, he saw that coins had been set on the eyes, something he had seen before only in historical pictures.

"His eyes keep opening," Franklin explained. "This is an old method of keeping them closed, but…well, I am an old man, nearing retirement, you know. Best I can do until his granddaughter tells me where she wants the body taken. I expect I'll hear shortly—talked to Joe Richter earlier, and he said that he was expecting her to make final arrangements today."

"She just got into town yesterday, after hours, so, yes, I'm sure she'll make her decisions today, though I'm assuming she'll have him interred in the family plot at the Key West cemetery. Her mother is there," Liam said.

"Yes, of course, I remember that interment. So very sad," Valaski said, shaking his head. "Such a young and beautiful woman. Such a tragedy."

"You performed her autopsy, right?" Liam asked.

Valaski nodded.

"And she died of a broken neck from a fall down the stairs—but her eyes were open, as well," Liam said.

Valaski shrugged. "When I first arrived at the Merlin house, she was in her husband's arms. But, yes, her eyes were open."

"And you're certain that Cutter Merlin died of heart failure, or cardiac arrest?" Liam asked.

"As certain as I am that night follows day," Valaski said.

"I'm still wondering how Chelsea Merlin Donovan managed to fall down a stairway she'd known since childhood. She was young, thin, coordinated, and she managed a terrible tumble. And yet you said that she had the same terrified expression that Cutter was wearing when we found him," Liam said.

"She saw that she was tumbling down a staircase," Valaski suggested. He waved a hand in the air. "Liam, I know you're busy, so I never should have spoken that day. I didn't mean to suggest anything. Naturally, they resembled one another. Chelsea was Cutter's daughter. And good God, man, Cutter was nearly as old as Mrs. Merriweather, since he didn't settle down to procreate until he was in his fifties!" He sighed. "Sadly, Cutter Merlin rather slipped through the cracks. He wanted to be a hermit. In Key West, we respect that. God knows, he might well have been suffering a form of age-related dementia. The human brain is the most miraculous computer out there, and we all know what happens when a computer gets a virus."

Valaski studied Liam, frowning.

"Liam, you can't be thinking that anything wasn't what it seemed in either death…can you?"

"Hey, Doctor, you're the one who mentioned that Cutter and his daughter had the same expression on their faces when they died," Liam told him.

"Yes, yes, I did," Valaski admitted, casting his head

to the side and staring at Liam with his still-enormous, magnified eyes. He shook his head. "But I'm good at what I do. Chelsea died of a broken neck. Cutter died of heart failure. Cutter was old. He had Lanoxin in his system."

"A heart medication?"

"Yes. And it can cause hallucinations."

"Can a person die of being frightened to death?" Liam asked.

"Sure—if fear causes the heart to give in," Valaski said.

"Or if it causes someone to misstep, and they go crashing down the stairs?" Liam asked.

"They died years apart," Valaski pointed out. "There were other people in the house—it was a normal house when Chelsea died. Well, an almost-normal house. It was still filled with all kinds of oddities. Hey, Ripley had nothing on old Cutter Merlin, really," he added, and grinned suddenly. "What? You think the mummy arises and scares folks to death? If there had been something there, wouldn't George Donovan have seen it, too? He was in the house. If I remember right, he heard his wife's scream, and the thudding as she fell. He would have run to her in a split second. If he had seen something, he'd have been after whoever or even *whatever* in a flash. That man loved his wife."

"I'm sure he did. What about Chelsea, though? She was young—she couldn't have been on any kind of medication."

Valaski was quiet for a minute, his brow furrowed. "Actually, if I remember correctly, Chelsea had been

taking a pain medication at the time. I'm…I'm thinking it might have been Darvocet-N. I'd asked about it,
naturally. She'd been seen by Dr. Nealy, who has passed
away now, too. He'd given her a prescription because
she'd twisted her back on a dive excursion."

"You're telling me that both of them might have been
scared to death by hallucinations they experienced in the
house because of medication?"

"I'm not telling you anything except for the medical findings. Autopsy is my job, Liam. Anything else is
your job. You want me to pull the records on Chelsea
Donovan and find out?"

"Actually, I would appreciate it," Liam said.

"Sure. I'll get back to you." He cleared his throat.
"And I'd appreciate it if you'd see to it that arrangements
are made for Cutter's body."

"Yeah, well, thanks, Franklin. I'm sure you'll hear
about funeral arrangements for Cutter today. If you don't
hear, I will see to it."

"Are you planning on seeing Miss Donovan soon?"
Valaski asked him.

"Yes, I'll see her."

Valaski lifted a hand. "I need you to wait one minute.
I'll have you sign out his effects. You can take them to
her."

Liam waited while Valaski disappeared into another
room, and then returned with a dull gray plastic bag.
"I've kept his clothing for the mortuary. If Kelsey wants
him buried in something else, she can let the mortuary
know."

"All right."

"Open the bag, Liam, so you can sign for the contents."

Liam did so. The bag contained Cutter's old seafarer's watch, his Masonic ring and the little casket he had held along with the book that had been in his lap, *In Defense from Dark Magick*.

Liam signed the log, stating that he had taken the items.

"What do you think the old coot was seeing in his mind's eye?" Valaski asked, shaking his head.

"He never called the police. As far as I know, he wasn't afraid of anyone," Liam said.

"The book is titled *In Defense from Dark Magick*," Valaski said. "I think he was having delusions, and *believed* that someone was out to hurt him, or take something from him. You wouldn't call the police against magic, would you?"

"No. Thanks, Franklin. I'll see you soon."

"Socially, I hope," Valaski said with a grimace.

"Yeah, socially."

Liam left, wondering why he had come, and yet still disturbed. After all, Valaski was the one who had made him think that there had to have been *something* that had frightened both Cutter Merlin and his daughter, Chelsea. One had died from a fall, and one from old age.

Both with eyes wide open in fear.

What possible connection could there be?

Both had been on medications that might have caused hallucinations.

He thought about the kids who had broken into the

house, and the way he had found them, cowering in the kitchen.

They hadn't been on pain medication. And he was pretty damned sure they hadn't been on any kind of drugs, at least not that night.

It was a scary house—unless you were accustomed to such a collection of oddities.

When he stepped outside, he found Bartholomew waiting for him.

"Why didn't you come in?" Liam asked him.

Bartholomew shuddered. "It's a morgue, Liam. Why would I go in?"

Liam lowered his head, smiling. *Not even ghosts liked morgues.*

"You tell me—why were *you* here?" Bartholomew returned.

"I don't know. Yes, I do. I don't like the house. And Kelsey is staying in it."

Bartholomew was silent for a minute. "I don't like the house, either."

"But you can't sense or feel anything that might be a clue as to *why?*" Liam asked him.

Bartholomew shook his head. "No. There's just… something. Maybe it's the house itself. It's creepy."

"Some people might say that talking to a ghost is creepy," Liam said. He tried to mentally shake off his feelings of impending doom as he walked to his car.

There was other work that needed his attention. And all he had here was a *feeling* that something wasn't right.

But he had to ask himself—if Kelsey hadn't come

down to stay in the house, would any thought of a wrongdoing, unseen, even be in his mind?

"What's in the bag?" Bartholomew asked.

"I picked up Cutter's property to return to Kelsey. His ring, his watch—the little casket he had clutched in his hands and the book."

"Let me see, please?" Bartholomew asked.

"Wait 'til we're in the car, please?" Liam suggested.

Bartholomew grinned. Once they were in the car, Liam opened the bag again. Bartholomew studied the casket with a frown.

"Do you know what it is? Anything about it?" Liam asked.

"No. Maybe Jaden and Ted can help."

"Maybe. I'll suggest Kelsey let them study it. What about the book?"

Liam opened the book to show to Bartholomew. Bartholomew could actually open a page, but it took a great deal of energy, effort and concentration.

"It's a first edition," Bartholomew noted. "Publication date 1838."

"Cutter had a number of first-edition books," Liam said.

"Perhaps I can find out more about the book," Bartholomew said. "I'll get on it, and I'll do what I can," he promised.

"You think a Key West ghost might know something about it?"

Bartholomew tapped the book. "It was published in England, so I don't know. And you know that I don't necessarily know every ghost in Key West, any more than you know all of the living. But I can prowl around the library, and…"

"And?"

Bartholomew smiled. If it was possible for a ghost to blush, he blushed. "Lucinda might know something about it," he said softly. Lucinda, the lady in white, the ghost who had finally talked to him recently and become the love of his life…or, rather, death.

"She was extremely well-educated," Bartholomew said softly.

Liam nodded. He studied the little casket. He found himself wondering if there were any powers in it, and then felt foolish.

It was just a box, with a gold ball. And he felt nothing, nothing at all, as he held it.

Why had it been clutched so tightly in Cutter Merlin's hand?

For the first ten minutes Kelsey sat in Joe Richter's office, all she heard were legal terms that might as well have been Greek. Or Latin—since she assumed that many of the terms in a will were Latin or derivatives thereof.

"Well, that's it, then," Joe Richter said at last, taking off his reading glasses and setting the folder he had been reading from back down on his desk. "Once you sign these papers for me, I can get everything into your name. It's all yours, and the disposal of all Cutter's 'earthly goods' is up to you. The second page dealt with the fact that he believed that you will 'abide by all my wishes, as set down in my ledger.' So, that was easy enough, right?"

"So far," Kelsey said. She smiled. "Have you been in the house?"

Joe laughed. "Not for a bit. But I liked Cutter, and admired him, Kelsey. He was a good man. I think he might have been a great man if—"

"If my mother hadn't died," Kelsey finished when he broke off, his face reddening.

"He loved the world. He didn't like the fact that artifacts were stolen from other countries, and he was instrumental in seeing that a great deal of material taken from Greece by the *allied* nations was returned in the decades following World War II. For his private collections, he never wanted anything that was pertinent to the history of another country."

"He kept a mummy."

"Ah, yes, but there are mummies all over. He didn't keep the remains of a great pharaoh! He told me that when the English and northern Europeans first started their excavations in Egypt, mummies were so plentiful that people used them as tinder for their fireplaces." Richter ran his fingers through his white hair and shrugged. "Countries would often exchange their treasures. Native American artifacts can be found in many museums on other continents. He didn't believe in stealing what *belonged* in the country of origin when it was precious to that country. Otherwise, he was a great collector of objects that might have been thrown away when an attic was cleaned out. He was brilliant with his knowledge at auction houses, and when he went around the world and made discoveries himself, he only kept objects with the blessing of the country's finest archaeologists and historians. But, yes, frankly—I imagine you will have your work cut out for you."

"I don't mind. I did love him," Kelsey said.

She wondered if the expression he gave her then suggested that she might have returned long ago if she had really meant her words.

Then, again, there were those who understood that her father would not return to the place of his wife's death, and that it might perhaps be painful for Kelsey to do so, as well.

"I'd like Cutter sent to the funeral home down the street from St. Paul's," she said. "I'd like to have a wake for him on Sunday evening, and have him interred in the Key West cemetery on Monday. He preferred St. Paul's, so if one of the Episcopal priests from St. Paul's will officiate, I'll be grateful. I'm afraid I don't know anyone, so—"

"I'll see to the arrangements," Richter assured her.

She thanked him and rose.

They shook hands, and he stood awkwardly as she exited.

His secretary, Lilly, smiled as Kelsey came out of the inner office. "Is everything all set, then? Do you need another appointment?"

"I don't think so," Kelsey told her. "If I have any problems, I'll call in."

"Are you planning on selling the property?" Lilly asked her. She was a sweet woman with bleached blond hair, slim features and, somehow, the look of an Afghan hound.

"I'm not sure yet."

"Well, if so, you just let Mr. Richter know. He says that the property is worth a mint. A mint! The house is protected—it's on the historic register—but the things that could be done around it are just amazing. You could honestly come out of this with quite a fortune," Lilly told her. "Why, just a few weeks ago—before poor Mr. Merlin's demise—Mr. Richter was saying that he'd studied the place, and he'd let Mr. Merlin know just what it was worth!"

"I really haven't thought about it at all," Kelsey said, "but if and when I do, I'll certainly let Mr. Richter know."

Kelsey thought about Lilly's words as she left the office. Property in Key West was prime, she knew, especially a property the size of her grandfather's house. It was doubly waterfront as well, being on the tiny spit of a peninsula, and it was in Old Town.

She'd never thought about the value of the property. She'd never thought about coming back.

Maybe she had just assumed that Cutter would live forever.

At the car, she hesitated, curious.

Joe Richter had told her that it had been months since he had seen Cutter.

Lilly had said that he'd been out there just a few weeks before Cutter's death.

She almost walked back in to ask Joe Richter, but

then she wondered just what it could matter. Richter was confused on dates, maybe.

He wasn't exactly a spring chicken, either!

It was a different world with Kelsey Donovan in the house. The place smelled like pine, and fresh, as if a great ocean breeze had come through.

She was gone for some time, of course. And he had spent so many hours in the house, insanely going through boxes and drawers. Insanely, and yet with an excellent organization, so that no one else would know. It was imperative that he find what he sought now.

But for once, he sat in the chair by the fireplace. He sat in the chair where old Cutter had died, almost a week ago now. All he had to do was wait.

Kelsey Donovan would find what he needed.

He stood and stretched and walked to the door, noting the new locks, the bolts. And back in the laundry room, the screens had been fixed, the windows had been fixed and locked down. Good Lieutenant Beckett had seen to that.

He smiled.

Ah, well. Beckett knew how the kids had always broken into the house. But the lieutenant would have no idea how he *was getting in.*

No idea just how often he stayed there, in the house. Hiding, listening.

Waiting.

Returning from the grocery store, Kelsey wished that she'd called someone for help. She seemed to have at least twenty bags, big ones, and, on top of that, cases of water and beer. Heavy stuff.

She was on her second trip into the house—wondering why they had always parked on the *wrong* side of the house and why there had never been a carriage drive that would place the car park somewhere near the kitchen, at least—when Jonas came walking into the yard.

"Hey!" she said.

"Hey, I saw you from my place. Looked like you needed a hand," Jonas told her.

"I can't say that I won't be extremely grateful," she told him.

"Well, especially since I plan on partaking of the feast, I think the very least I can do is help!" Jonas said.

He was tall and lanky, with a thatch of brown hair that fell across his forehead, but, like the others, Jonas had matured. He had a good smile. And despite his lankiness, he was good with grocery bags.

They both grabbed up two and headed for the house. Kelsey had left the door open. On the porch, though, she found herself pausing.

"What?" Jonas asked her.

"I don't know. It's bizarre. I know that someone aired this house out—I'm sure Liam had it done—but every once in a while…it's just strange. It may be my guilt complex. Every once in a while, I feel like I'm being overpowered by…"

"By?"

"The smell of death. Do you smell anything?"

Jonas stepped into the house and inhaled deeply. He

turned to her and shook his head. "Kelsey, I don't smell anything. But…" He paused, wincing. "Cutter was dead awhile before he was found."

Kelsey nodded.

Jonas smiled at her. "The house smells like pine to me! Clean and fresh. Hey, want me to open windows?"

"Maybe I should open everything up today," Kelsey said.

"We'll get everything in, and then run around and open everything," Jonas suggested.

On their third trip out, Kelsey saw Katie come walking down the dirt-and-gravel drive from the mainland.

"Hey, Katie!" she called.

"Hey—thought I'd take a walk over. Sean is at the house, and he and David are editing something, and so… I see you did the shopping. Want some help?" she asked.

"Help is always great. But you have to work tonight…."

"I have four hours," Katie told her.

"I think you should dive right in," Jonas said. He looked at Kelsey. "Ask Katie what she smells," he suggested.

"What I smell?" she asked.

"Yes, do you smell anything?" Kelsey asked.

Katie arched a brow, her hands on her hips.

"Um…maybe the water is a little stagnant somewhere?" she suggested.

"Do you think that's what it is?" Kelsey asked, relieved.

Katie laughed. "Hey, when they work on broadening

the highway from Florida City to Key Largo, and they're reclaiming land, the smell of rot can be horrific!"

"I suggested that we open all the windows in the house—there's a decent breeze today," Jonas said.

"But if it's the smell of the water, we'd be letting it in rather than out," Katie said.

"Hmm. Good point," Jonas agreed. "But—"

"Let's do it anyway. With all the cleaners I've been using already, it's probably a good idea," Kelsey said.

"Hey, I'll run back over and get my iPod and speakers," Jonas said. "Might as well do this to some music."

"Great," Kelsey said.

"So, you'll be staying here a while?" Katie asked her.

"There's a lot to be done," Kelsey told her.

"I think it's great," Jonas said enthusiastically.

"So do I," Katie agreed. "Jonas, go get us music to heft and haul by!"

Grinning, he took off at a trot back toward the mainland. Katie snatched up a couple of the bags and headed into the house. "I think it smells great in here!" she said. "Okay, you're right. It smells heavily of cleaner, and I think that will get worse as we go."

"I'm sure," Kelsey said.

In another trip, they had the last of the bags, and Kelsey was delighted that Katie had come, because she helped clean out the shelves in the kitchen as they put groceries away. "It's amazing, what you've done already," Katie said. "You know, I was a little girl the last time I was here, but this is an amazing house. I thought it was the coolest place on the whole island. I mean, it was as if you *lived* in a museum. That was incredibly neat."

"I did love living here," Kelsey said. "I loved all the stories. One night my parents were going to a major fundraiser at the Casa Marina. I remember how gorgeous my mother was coming down the stairs. Then, of course, I remember the day she died."

"Of course. I understand. That must have been so painful." She hesitated. "So, what do you think you want to do with the place?"

"I don't know. How strange—I don't think that I want to let it go, but I'm not sure I could actually ever live here again."

"Rental property?" Katie suggested.

"I don't know yet. I just don't know," Kelsey said.

Jonas returned while they were in the kitchen, shouting to them from the porch and then as he entered, pausing to stare at them. "Girls! Or young women, if that's somehow politically incorrect! You left the door open. That's not a good thing. Opening windows is fine—inviting in all the possible drunken riffraff in the city is not!"

"We stand corrected," Katie said cheerfully. "All right, windows! I'll head upstairs."

"We'll handle it all down here," Jonas said. He turned toward the laundry room.

Kelsey headed in the opposite direction, to the family room, and then on into Cutter's study.

She paused, coming into the room. As a child, she had loved this room so much. It was where she came to sit on her grandfather's lap to have him read to her from one of the books in the endless rows of shelves, and where he weaved his great tales of adventure. It could be a dark room, though, with only the one window that led out to the porch.

She turned on the light switch, and the room came to light, revealing Cutter's large mahogany desk, his ledger open on the old blotter as if he had been reading just before he had gone to sit down and die. Egyptian statuettes sat on one edge; a family picture taken twenty years ago sat on the other. The lamp on the desk was a beautiful Tiffany piece, and the hardwood floor was almost completely covered with a Persian carpet showing some signs of age but still beautiful. The fireplace was shared with the parlor, where the mantel was marble; in this room, it was hardwood. Elegantly designed fire utensils sat on the limestone apron around the fire, and a firebreak from the early eighteenth century hid the fact that the hearth area itself was shared.

It really was a beautiful old house. She hadn't talked to Joe Richter yet about the actual value, but it occurred to her then that the house really was probably worth a small fortune.

And yet, oddly enough, she couldn't imagine selling it.

She walked across the carpet and pulled back the dark crimson drapes and opened the window. Natural light flooded in softly.

The entire house had been screened in the seventies, she knew, so she wasn't going to have to deal with an onslaught of bugs or other creepy-crawlies. When her parents had lived here, when it had been a family home, it had been wonderful.

She looked around the office. Except for the archway from the family room and the living room, and the large expanse of the fireplace, the room was shelved. Cutter's library of books took precedence here, but there was also a stack of crates and boxes between his desk and the window, and on some of the shelves she could see his collection of bookholders and curios. Porcelain cats guarded one shelf, old seafaring nautical instruments were on another, and replicas of Mayan gods adorned another. The bookcase behind his desk had one relatively empty shelf just about six feet from the ground holding one of Cutter's favorite pieces, a replica of King Tut's gold mask purchased from the Egyptian Museum in Cairo.

Memories here were good.

She turned to walk out of the room and then paused, certain that she'd heard something. A rustling sound.

She turned back and waited. Nothing. She smiled at herself. She'd opened a window. The breeze was coming in. And right now, it smelled clean and just a bit salty.

She headed for the door again, but once there, paused once more. She'd had the oddest feeling that...

She was being watched.

She turned back.

She gave herself a mental shake.

There was no one there.

"It's my house now, you know," she said softly aloud. "And I will love it as Cutter did, and allow no evil!"

What a ridiculous assertion. And how bizarre to feel

that someone was staring at her. It had to be the gold death-mask replica of King Tut.

But the death mask was a beautiful piece. Nothing evil about it.

She shook her head and determinedly left the room, closing the door firmly behind her.

5

Liam arrived at the Merlin house at five-thirty, just in time to see the house against the first pastel colors of the dying day.

It rose large and mysterious on the landscape, gray peeling paint and darker dormers giving it the look of something that lived and breathed.

He parked and, as he walked up to the house, he noted the open windows.

He knocked on the door and waited, then tried the knob.

It was open.

He entered and heard voices from the kitchen. He walked through the living room, noting that the floor had been swept, some of the clutter of boxes rearranged, and that it was already beginning to feel lived-in once again. He was still disturbed by the carelessness of the open door and windows.

Jonas, Katie and Kelsey were in the kitchen. They each had a bottle of beer and appeared to be happily chatting in a casual way.

Kelsey saw him enter the kitchen. He thought that

her blue eyes were immediately guarded. She had been leaning on the butcher-block counter but straightened.

"The door was open," he said. "I knocked, but no one heard me."

"Liam!" Katie said, pleased to see him. She came to give him a kiss on the cheek. "It must be getting late, then. I'm out of here."

"We're going to dinner. Wouldn't you like to come?" Kelsey asked.

"It's a work night for me. I've been asking Uncle Jamie to bring someone else onto the floor so that Clarinda can take over for me more often, but Jamie isn't a trusting soul. He keeps putting it off. He actually needs to bring in a few more people, but… Anyway, I'm going to go home and spend some quality time with David! See you all tomorrow, or later, if anyone is bored and wants to come by. Jonas, I know I'll see you soon. 'Bye all," Katie said and stepped around Liam.

"I'll follow you out. And lock the door," Liam said.

"I'm out of here, too," Jonas said. "I'm going to go home and wake Clarinda up! She's looking forward to a lighter schedule, too."

"Thanks, both of you, for all the help," Kelsey said.

"No problem. When I see you struggling, I'm your man," Jonas said lightly.

Liam wasn't sure why, but it didn't make him particularly happy just then to think that Jonas lived so close to the house, he could literally see Kelsey anytime she came out the door. He should have been glad; friends should be close. Jonas was a friend.

He winced inwardly, wondering if he was seeing the

man as a rival. Jonas and Clarinda had been together for years, so that was pretty foolish. Jealousy was not an attractive emotion. But he wasn't certain he was jealous. He was uneasy. And he wasn't sure why. He seemed to be making things up in his head.

But he had been the one to find Cutter Merlin dead, in the chair, his eyes wide open in fear.

"I'll walk you both out," he said lightly.

Kelsey followed him through the dining room and then parlor to lock the two out. She smiled at him, but he thought she still had a guarded look in her eyes.

"What?" she asked, when he had locked the door after the other two.

"Kelsey, you know what. Twice, I came here and people had broken in."

She waved a hand in the air. "Liam, people knew that Cutter was dead, that the house was empty. An easy mark."

"People know this place is a treasure trove," Liam said.

She frowned, looking at him. "This house is my home, and I'm not going to set myself up to be paranoid to live here, Liam." She lifted her hair, letting it fall on her neck again in an offhand manner. "Where did you have in mind to go?" she asked him.

"Nowhere—until we've gotten the windows closed again," he said firmly.

She frowned, ready to protest.

"Please, Kelsey. Don't be paranoid—do be responsible. I've had a lot of officers busy around here, you know, clearing out teenagers and opportunists," he said.

"Sure. I'll run upstairs, if you want to run around downstairs," she conceded.

He nodded. He watched her head for the stairway, then decided to do a circle of the house himself.

Odd. When they had been kids, they had never thought about any kind of danger when Kelsey had forgotten her key and they'd crawled in through the broken screen in back, over the washer and dryer. Now the thought that the house was vulnerable in any way made him extremely unhappy.

He quickly secured the windows in the dining room, kitchen, laundry room and family room, and then went into Cutter's office. He walked over and closed the one big window, securing the bolts on it. He paused, looking around the office. Even with the crates and boxes aligned between the desk and the window, there was something different about the room.

He thought about it a moment and realized that it looked lived-in. Naturally. It was where Cutter had spent most of his time.

He didn't know why, because he knew what he had just done, but he went back to secure the window once again. He liked the room, but for some reason it gave him an uneasy feeling.

When he came out, he met Kelsey in the living room.

"All locked up," she said cheerfully.

He tried to shake his feelings of tremendous unease, remembering that his life had not been particularly normal in the last year. His own grandfather's death had brought David home, to answer an unsolved murder.

Vanessa Loren had come to them specifically because of the brutal killing of her coworkers, and none of the mysteries had afforded easy answers, not to mention the fact that they had all been cast into extreme danger. Perhaps he had become so jaded and suspicious that he couldn't even look at his friends with trust.

And if he kept behaving like a law-enforcement tyrant, there would be no reason for Kelsey to pay attention to anything that he had to say.

"Turtle Kraals?" he suggested. "It's just across the bight."

The Merlin house was on a tiny spit of land that was actually just a geographical feature of the bight. The bight was about a twenty-acre span in the bay—although the word itself came from the Old English *byht,* which meant bend, or a bay created by a bend. By the bight was a bigger bay, which confused many people.

The marina was close. Tourists boarded old schooners and other craft to sail in the bight.

The Merlin house still seemed remote.

"Turtle Kraals it is," Kelsey agreed. "Shall we swim," she asked with a grin, "or drive on over to the marina? Or walk?"

"We'll play it lazy and drive," he said.

In less than twenty minutes, they were seated in the restaurant.

Liam brought the gray plastic bag in with him, but didn't mention it at first.

They both apparently knew the conversation was going to grow more serious, but they began with casual suggestions about food. "Conch chowder! I haven't had any in ages," Kelsey said.

"It's good here, very good," Liam said.

"Ah, fresh snapper. That sounds good," Kelsey said.

"What are we having tomorrow?" Liam asked.

"Oh, everything I could think of!" she said. "They had fresh mahimahi, so I bought some fish. Ribs, chicken, hot dogs, hamburgers…corn, salad, potato salad, baked beans, all kinds of stuff. A pack of desserts—you name it!"

"Well, then, snapper might be a nice choice tonight," he said.

She nodded. Their waitress arrived, and they ordered. When the woman had gone, Kelsey stared at him. "All right. What's in the bag?"

"Cutter's belongings. Valaski, the medical examiner, gave them to me," Liam said.

She didn't reach for the bag. "Valaski," she said softly. "He came when my mother died. I thought he was ancient then. But I was young."

"He's closing in on retirement. But he's good at what he does," Liam said. "He kept Cutter's clothing for the mortuary," he said.

She nodded. "He'll have a viewing on Sunday night, and I'm having him buried in the family plot on Monday morning."

"That's good," Liam said. He handed her the bag. She didn't open it.

"Kelsey, when I found him, he was clutching the little casket in the bag, and a book titled *In Defense from Dark Magick* was on his lap," Liam said.

"Oh?"

"Don't you want to see them?" he asked. "Oh, and his watch and Masonic ring are in the bag, as well. I'm sure they will mean something to you."

She nodded. "Thank you."

Their drinks and salads arrived. She took a long sip of iced tea, as if it were something alcoholic and might give her warmth and false strength.

He leaned toward her. "Kelsey, I didn't want to tell you on the phone, but now I think you need to know. The reason I'm worried about you out there is because I think that Cutter... Well, I think that he was scared to death."

"Liam, I'm not leaving the house."

"Do you know anything about the book or the casket?" he asked her.

At last, she set her fork down and looked in the bag. She frowned. "I...think he had both for a very long time," she said. "I remember that he used to keep the casket on his desk, and I know that the book was on one of the bookshelves."

He nodded. "Would you mind if I took the casket back and asked Ted and Jaden to take a look at it and see if they can find out anything about it in their reference materials?"

"No. I don't mind at all," she said.

He sat back. She smiled at him. "Liam, the more I'm in it, the more I love the house."

He nodded uneasily. "It's a great house," he said flatly.

She seemed more at ease. "So, why don't we talk

about you for a while? It's not a surprise that you're a cop, you know. You always wanted to solve every riddle. So…what have you been doing all these years? Did you graduate, go right into the police force?"

He shook his head, wishing that his tension would ease. "I went to the U of M. I went into criminal studies, spent some time in Miami, took special classes that were offered up in Quantico, thought about the FBI and came back to Key West. I loved Washington, D.C. It was a great place to live, but I missed the water. Yes, it's on the Potomac. I miss the kind of water you can go in every day."

She laughed. "That was an easy roundup of a lot of years!" she told him.

Their main courses arrived. She talked about her drawing, and about her partner, Avery. He was a whiz with animation, and they worked well together. She loved being her own boss. "Which, of course, is why I'm able to spend time down here now," she said. "But you're kind of the boss now, aren't you? I heard about the shake-up in the police department—and about David coming home to vindicate himself from any suspicion," she said.

"The chief is a great guy. I'm under him," Liam said. "But since I'm known to work all hours and all days, I can take time when I need it, which I did recently, when I went off with David, Katie, Sean, Vanessa and others on the film shoot, trailing the recent massacre on Haunt Island."

She set a hand on his. "That's the problem, Liam. You've been so busy with really horrific events. Please—you're worrying about me too much. I'm fine."

When she touched him, he felt as if time and place whirled around them. Her fingertips created an instant tension in his muscles, ignited a fire in his blood and caused dangerous things to happen to his state of arousal.

He drew his hand back. "I just want you to be careful, Kelsey, that's all."

She seemed troubled that he had drawn away. He didn't want to explain.

Soon after, they finished and walked out on the docks. They could almost see the Merlin house from the pier; some of the high-growing pines obscured it, but she had left on lights in the front and back of the house, so a glow could be seen.

"It's pretty, huh?" Kelsey asked.

"Um…"

"Let's go back and sit on the beach?" she suggested.

They drove back to the house. When she unlocked the front door, he was tense again. He didn't know what he expected. That something might have changed?

But nothing appeared to be any different.

Kelsey seemed happy. She suggested they bring drinks and cookies out to the sand, since they had passed on dessert. He agreed. They went out through the family room and down to the small beach area. The wash of the waves against the shore was a pleasant sound. Light glowed from the house and from an almost full moon above. Light clouds could be seen drifting over the water.

"It is really beautiful, isn't it?" Kelsey asked.

"Just like Eden," he said dryly.

She smacked his shoulder. "Liam."

It was arousing to just touch his shoulder!

"Hey! It's beautiful," he agreed. He was quiet a minute. "You own an amazing piece of property, with the best view around. It still worries me. I still wish you'd stay with me. Or Katie and David, or Sean and Vanessa, or—"

"I'm not staying with any set of lovers, thank you very much."

"Jonas runs a B and B," Liam reminded her.

"That would be silly."

"He wouldn't charge you."

"Then I wouldn't stay there. And it actually isn't money. Cutter was solvent, and I'm already on his banking accounts, and, thank you, but my career is actually lucrative!"

"I assumed it was. You said that it would be silly."

"It would be silly."

"What about staying with me?"

She was looking out on the water. A slow smile touched her lips, and after a moment she answered softly, "I can't stay with you."

"Why not?"

"I'd wind up sleeping with you."

"How crazy," he said.

"Oh! Well, I—" Her words faltered; she seemed to think she had received a rejection.

"It's crazy," he interrupted quickly, "because I believe we're going to sleep together anyway, and I believe we would have slept together years ago had you stayed, and not staying with me is not going to prevent what surely seems to me to be just a little bit desperately inevitable."

The breeze from the ocean whispered by, lifting a strand of her hair, an ebony that seemed to burn with a blue depth in the moonlight. Her lips curled slowly back into a smile. They still weren't touching; they were just inches apart, seated on the sand, legs stretched out before them while the surf came near enough to brush their toes.

She stared at the night.

"I'll never understand," she said quietly.

"What?"

"Time, places, life, the world, people," she said, and she turned to him at last. "And it is crazy. I've been gone so long, I haven't seen you in forever, and many a day went by when I didn't even think about you or Key West, or even the water and the way it feels to sit outside and see the endless dark undulation of the water at night...."

"And?"

"And when I came back, the moment I saw you... You'd changed so much, and you hadn't changed at all, and I felt like I did that last night, that I could still crawl into your arms, and you would be there to comfort me."

"I wasn't exactly thinking about comforting you," he admitted.

She looked at him, and he knew how hard he was trying to play it all cool and rational, and yet...he was melting. Everything in him was melting, burning, and he felt the tension of desire rip through his limbs and his core, and he prayed that the longing to pull her into his arms, rip off her clothes and hold her wasn't glaringly apparent. There was a glow in her eyes and a breathlessness about her; he thought that he could feel the pounding of her heart.

"I think I've been in love with you forever," she said, and it was barely a whisper, hardly sounding above the breeze. "Oh, no! I'm so sorry, don't take that as... I mean, I suppose I've always been drawn to you. If I hadn't been quite such a good kid... I think a few of our schoolmates and friends might have been involved, but... I'm babbling, aren't I?"

"Babble—it's quite all right," he managed huskily.

She burst out laughing, and so did he, and he would never be sure if he did reach out and grab her with force or if she actually turned to him, pouncing upon him. He went back flat in the sand, and she was on top of him. She stared at him a moment longer, and then her lips fell down upon his and her body stretched out atop his. For a moment they were locked in a wickedly hot, wet, passionate kiss with their tongues violent in the quest for the most intimate kiss in the world, and then they rolled so that they were side by side in the sand, still in one another's arms, still melded together in the kiss, and yet freeing themselves to touch and pull closer and closer.

At last, somehow, she was beneath him, and his hands wandered freely over her length. She reached up to touch his face, then pulled him back, her fingertips pressing down the length of his spine. His lips touched hers again, and he felt the tremor of her heart, the rapid rise and fall of her breath, the vibrant movement she made beneath him, arching closer, touching....

He gasped, breaking away from her.

He leaped to his feet and reached down to her. She caught his hand, allowing him to draw her up from the sand. He pulled her against him again, laughing as he whispered, "It's private, it's remote. It's not that private or remote."

She grinned, turned and kicked up sand as she ran for the house. He bolted after her, following her into the family room. She had already sped through it, on her way to the stairs.

Panting, he forced himself to pause to lock and secure the door.

She had raced up the stairs to her room, and he followed. She had jumped upon the bed in the shadows; the room was lit only by the light escaping from the bathroom. Everything in him seemed to be pulsing to a painful degree as he started toward her.

To his astonishment, she stopped him.

"The door!"

"I locked the door."

"The bedroom door!"

He had to admit: the biology of his male mind had gone beyond thought. He stood still as she leaped back up, ran to the bedroom door and locked it. But when he would have questioned her, he never got the chance. She made a running leap to him, arms and legs locked around him, knocking him back down to the bed.

And there, breathless, they began a disorganized and frantic removal of clothing, she tearing at his buttons, he lifting the hem of her knit pullover, both of them using their feet to try to remove their shoes. When clothing was cast away at last, they stared at one another, breathing heavily again, and then his hands were on the firmness of her breasts and she was locked around him again, fingers upon his chest, kissing against his throat, his collarbone, his chest. In a tangle they kissed and petted and explored, and at length he found himself straddling her, feverish, his longing to be a good lover waging war with his desperation to be inside her.

She dragged his mouth down to hers and wrapped her legs around his hips. He forced himself to a certain finesse as he slid slowly into her. At first he was aware of nothing at all but the incredible scent of her body, of the amazing movement, of being with her at last, forceful, his urgency matched by her own, the eager vitality and need of their lovemaking akin in an undulating motion like the ocean in a tempest. She writhed against him, increasing his arousal to a maddened frenzy, as if he were an adolescent, as if life and the state of the world rested in her touching him in return, coming to the same state of wild, frenetic ecstasy.

As if he had been waiting all of his life.

He didn't know how many minutes went by; time was meaningless. He didn't know where they were anymore, nor did he care. He moved and moved, and felt as if he moved deeper into her with each touch, and it seemed that his heart and limbs would explode in a savage burst of fire that would consume the world. He refused these feelings in his mind, refused in his soul to let go, until he felt the eruption in the softness of her body, the sweet feminine cry in his ear…and then climax wracked through him with a vengeance.

Ripples, afterquakes, seemed to rip through them both as they lay panting, no words coming to their mouths, and still, he knew, if he tried to speak, he would be too breathless to do so. He didn't want to speak, to think of time gone by, of the distance that lay between their real worlds. It was best just to take these moments, the darkness and shadows around them, and pretend that the feeling could last forever.

In time, she stirred. "Liam, I didn't mean…"

"That was pretty good if you didn't mean it," he teased.

She laughed, lying against him, her fingers then playing down his chest. "I didn't mean that…that I expected anything from you, you know."

"Oh?" he said, heart thundering.

She laughed. "I didn't mean it that way! I meant… things like that are so easy to say. I've always cared about you, and I think we *would* have, and…"

"I think so, too. And it was really a long, long time for all that tension to build up!" he told her.

She was so relaxed. It was homecoming as it should have been.

Homecoming to him.

No sadness, no fear.

Just the easy laughter and honesty that been theirs once when they'd been so young.

"Liam—"

He pressed his fingers against her lips. "Let's take tonight, hmm?" he queried softly. Tenderly now, and with time and care, he pressed his lips to her forehead, to her throat and to her lips. "It was a lot of tension, you know. Tons of tension, and…"

She didn't seem to mind. She was slow and lazy then, just as he pressed his point in an achingly slow and thorough manner. She did the same. He explored the length of her body, luxuriating in the perfection of each limb, the incredible sleekness of her skin, the wonder of her breasts, belly, calves, thighs and everything in between. And she in turn teased with an erotic touch that was equally slow and taunting, with whispered words against his flesh, until neither could bear it any longer and they became entangled in one another's arms again, her legs locked around him, his heart thundering to a roar and his breath as frantic as a man deprived…for years.

He never stirred from the bed. He wasn't about to suggest that he go home.

She never seemed to think about him leaving, either.

The moon was full out; it was what they called the wee small hours of the morning.

And still, of course, it was Key West. Some places were just closing. There were still those stumbling around on Duval Street. Workers—servers, managers, musicians—many cold sober, would be annoyed at those who drank themselves silly and had to be carried home by others.

Soon the sun would begin to rise.

In another hour or so, the early crew would be out. There wasn't much of it. The docks would get busy quickly for the morning fishing charters, dive boats, snorkel boats and sightseeing trips. Restaurant person-nel who worked breakfast venues would be struggling up, and the earliest coffee places would start to prepare for the day. Those on the night shift at the desks, bell men, bouncers, security workers and others would be bored, idling away their time in this strange in-between hour that came to Key West.

Time meant nothing to him, and everything. He em-braced the darkness.

And yet, he enjoyed functioning, totally hidden within himself, in all the brilliance that the sun could possibly bring.

He stood for a moment, simply enjoying the time of the day. Enjoying where he stood, the sight, the memory, the scent.

He looked over at the house. His enjoyment faded, and he felt bitterness well inside him.

So now that prying bastard, Liam Beckett, was stay-ing there, with her, in her room, sleeping with her.

It didn't matter. He was protected, and they were all blind, and it was euphoria to watch them all, having no idea of all that went on that they didn't see.

It was no matter, truly. The house was still his, and he needed Kelsey Donovan. There was no way that Beckett could be there all the time. Beckett was a cop. He had to go to work. He had to do things.

He smiled. He liked being in the house, and he would be in the house again. And it would be amusing because Beckett would be sleeping with her, and he'd changed the locks, and he was so self-confident, and he would never know.

Maybe something could happen to the cop.

He calmed himself. He inhaled.

And he inhaled the scent of death.

Ah, yes, different, but the expression was still there.... Of course, they were idiots. He'd thought they would have found the last victim by now.

He was too good at what he did.

It was more time to enjoy the expression on his victim's face, more time to savor the kill....

More time to relish the scent of death that was like a teasing whisper on the air, mingling with the salt sea breeze. There and not there...

He inhaled deeply, and looked toward the house.

He would have his time with Kelsey Donovan.

6

"Kelsey, what do you want us doing about the packing crates and boxes?" Katie asked. "Some of them have been opened, but there's packing stuff all over the place."

"You should go through them all carefully," Liam warned, making a face as he noted a pile of strawlike packing material sitting on top of a box. "Cutter might have had tiny things packed in with big things."

"That's true," Kelsey said. She looked across the room at Liam. The Merlin house was alive as it hadn't been in years. The cleaning party had arrived, and they were a dedicated crew. Heads had been dusted on the wall, floors had been swept and swabbed, carpets had been vacuumed and surfaces cleaned, shined, scrubbed and polished.

"Maybe we could just organize them all better," she said, not sure what to do herself. She hadn't had a chance yet to go through Cutter's office and his desk, something that had been first on her agenda. But she'd felt obliged to join in with the cleaning crew. Katie was a whirlwind, while David and Sean followed her directives for moving heavy furniture. Ted and Jaden had taken it on themselves to work with the more delicate collectibles and art pieces in the house, dusting gently. Jonas and Clarinda had appointed themselves cleaners of the floors, and Liam had worked with Vanessa and Kelsey, trying to manage the organizational part of the work.

All of them were aware that Kelsey and Liam were acting like a couple, but no one said anything about it. They just all smiled to each other.

"How about if we move them all upstairs to the guest room?" Katie suggested. "There's nothing up there but a bed and a dresser, and we can stack them around the walls. They'll be out of the way, and then I can go through them one by one."

Sean groaned softly and then laughed. "Up the stairs."

"Oh!" Katie said. "That's a bad idea."

"No," Liam told her firmly. "It's a fine idea. Everyone will be very careful on the stairway. And it's perfect. Most of them have a number or some kind of title on them. We can leave the identification sticking out, and you'll know what's in everything."

"Yeah. I'll dust up the packing down here," David teased.

"Wait—the broom is in my hands at the moment, and I'll be keeping it!" Vanessa said.

"I will follow around behind you to make sure nothing is dropped," Jaden said.

"Works for me!" Ted told her.

"You'll head right on over there and pick up those boxes, sir!" Jaden told him.

"Which box?" Ted asked Liam with a sigh.

"Let's get started with the boxes and crates here, closest to the stairs. Then we can move on to the office," Liam said.

He and Ted picked up one of the large boxes, Sean and David went for the next and Jonas determined he could take one of the smaller ones on his own. Kelsey stood by the stairway, her heart in her throat for several minutes, until she felt Katie's arm around her shoulder. "They're going to be very careful, Kelsey. It's fine. Let's put some of the snacks out—we can all run down to the beach for a few minutes to cool off and dust off and do some munching before firing up the barbecue. Come on."

Kelsey nodded and turned away. They were all young, strong, and in good health. They could handle the boxes. And, once the boxes were organized, the task of going through them would not seem so daunting.

In the kitchen, she scrubbed her hands for the umpteenth time that day and delved into the refrigerator for dips and chips, cheese cubes, veggies and the other appetizers she had purchased. Katie started carrying things out the back door, setting up on the long picnic tables she had found in the family-room closet. By the time the boxes were moved and the last of the packing swept up, the backyard was set up. Kelsey was about to walk into the house when David and Katie came running out, screaming something about the last one in being a truly rotten and tough old conch.

They'd all worn bathing suits beneath the jeans, shorts

and T-shirts they'd donned for cleaning, so clothing went flying as they raced for the water.

The beach itself wasn't more than fifty feet, but there was a good sand bottom for a stretch, before the entangling mangroves and foliage began to take hold to the west, and the little peninsula curved back toward the mainland on the east. There was plenty of room for a group of ten to run in, splash, swim and torment one another.

"Am I dust-free yet?" Jaden asked, rising in four feet of water.

They all laughed. She still had a splash of black on her nose. "Grease!" Ted announced, walking over to rub his thumb over the top of her nose. "I got it, I got it, I got it—nope, nope, it's on your cheek now!"

"Hey!" she protested.

Kelsey leaned back in Liam's arms as they idled in the water, laughed and realized she hadn't had this kind of fun in ages, and she didn't really know why.

It was Liam, of course.

Her life in California was good. She was going back to it. This kind of…day couldn't last forever. Real life overtook you wherever you lived. She couldn't really just pack up and come back here to live.

They remained in the water awhile longer, then one by one trailed out, grabbing the towels from the picnic tables, munching on the snacks and setting up for the barbecue. Apparently, Jonas was the head chef at the portable barbecue pit, and he liked pretending the others were all his sous chefs, making announcements on how the different meat should be cooked and snapping his fingers for plates and other dining paraphernalia.

Finally, the food was cooked, and they all sat around the tables. Kelsey thanked everyone for all the work they had done. Soon after, however, Katie, David, Clarinda and Jonas left, saying that they had to get to O'Hara's for the night.

The others remained around the picnic tables, watching the sun begin its descent into the horizon.

Sean, straddling the left side of the picnic bench, said, "You know, we were all lucky. We have great places down here, and the property our parents purchased might well be out of reach for us—even now, with property values struggling around the country." He grimaced. "Katie bought our house from our parents, and now I'm buying it from her, but obviously, we're keeping it reasonable! Still, not even the Beckett house could possibly be worth as much as this place, Kelsey. What a view! You can't see a sunset like this even down on Mallory Square, or anywhere else, for that matter. I hope you intend to keep it."

"With all that Cutter left behind, you should be able to keep it, even if you choose not to live here," Jaden said.

"I do love the house," Kelsey said. "Creepy as the world chooses to see it!"

"I think it's an absolutely beautiful house," Vanessa said. She grimaced and glanced at Sean. "Actually, right now, it would make an amazing place to film a movie."

Sean groaned.

"No, no, no," Liam protested.

"Nothing bloody!" Vanessa protested. "Something psychological."

"Shades of *The Haunting* or *House on Haunted Hill!*" Ted suggested.

"That would be a way for the place to keep itself afloat," Vanessa said. "Renting out to commercial and movie companies."

"I really don't know what I want to do yet," Kelsey told them. She rose suddenly. "The box, the casket—whatever it is. We need to show it to Jaden and Ted," she told Liam.

He nodded. "I'll get it," he said.

"What—casket?" Jaden asked.

"It's a box, like a jewelry box, with a gold filigree ball inside it. It's just big enough to hold the ball. I *think* it's some kind of a reliquary, but I'm not sure. I have to go through all of my grandfather's papers, and I may or may not find out what it is when I've gone through them. But he was holding it when he died," Kelsey explained.

"Cool!" Jaden said. Her eyes were bright. "I love that kind of mystery!"

"I have to admit, I'd love a shower and a nap," Vanessa said, yawning. "Kelsey, thank you, it was a great day."

"Thank you—the house is livable."

"I know," Vanessa said, grinning. "We should have gotten a lot of footage before we cleaned it!"

"Vanessa," Sean said.

"Hey, opportunities like that don't come along so frequently," Vanessa protested.

Vanessa told Sean that he didn't need to leave because she was leaving, and he admitted he needed a nap, as well. "Work is easy—this house-cleaning thing is a real chore."

Sean and Vanessa said goodbye to Liam as he came back out of the house carrying the bag with Cutter's personal belongings. He waved to them and headed to the table, taking a seat again.

He produced the little casket and handed it to Jaden. Her eyes were instantly alight.

"It *is* a reliquary," she said. "Fascinating! It's really delicate workmanship. I'm going to guesstimate Italian, early Renaissance."

"Beautiful workmanship, absolutely beautiful," Ted commented.

"Do you know of any special significance it might have?" Kelsey asked.

"Well, the obvious. The Catholic Church always honored saints, and to have a bit of a saint in a reliquary was kind of like…well, you know, nowadays like wearing a cross or a Star of David. Any religious symbol. A reliquary would be an extremely precious belonging to a devout believer," Jaden said. "Was Cutter very religious?"

Kelsey thought about the question. "Actually, I think my family was originally Catholic. Cutter liked the Episcopal Church here, though. And I don't think he particularly believed in *organized* religion. He was a spiritual man. He held the concept that man saw God in different ways, and if you looked at even old pagan religions, things somehow corresponded."

"Ah," Jaden said.

Kelsey laughed softly. "What does 'ah' mean?" she

asked. She noticed that Liam wasn't laughing. His forehead was knit in a frown, and he seemed to take the concept of the reliquary very seriously.

"Well…I don't know exactly," Jaden said. "I'll start going through books and see if I can find this particular piece. It would be interesting to find out how it came to be in Cutter's possession."

"Take it. Let me know what you can about it," Kelsey said.

"Great. Well, thank you. I guess Ted and I will get going now, too," Jaden said. They both rose, Jaden carefully putting the little casket in her bag.

"We'll walk you out," Liam offered.

They went through the house. In the drive, as they waved goodbye, Kelsey frowned. For a moment—just a moment—she thought she smelled the scent of death again. But it was quickly gone.

"What's wrong?" Liam asked her sharply.

She had the feeling that he was going to go into his speech on how she shouldn't be staying at the house— *especially* if she thought she smelled death.

"Nothing! Nothing." She slipped her arms around him. "Nothing at all. It was an amazing day." It *had* been an amazing day.

She pulled him close to her. She closed her eyes and enjoyed the simple feel of her body against his, the natural way it was to be with him. They were both still salt-sticky from the sea; he was shirtless, and she had a throwover on, and his warmth and ever-vibrant energy seemed to spill into her. She was happy just to be with him, happier to be close to him. It was exciting to tease, to touch, and making love was, of course, electrifying. The acuteness of that kind of feeling couldn't last forever, she knew, and yet she also knew Liam so well, even if it had been years since they'd seen one another. Ecstasy could lead to comfort, but comfort could remain exciting.... The whole thing was actually terrifying. It could be easy to find others attractive, but the excitement of sex could fade so quickly unless there was that incredible something there that made a lover totally unique, his body warm and wonderful in the morning, and his face something that you longed to see. That was Liam. But it was happening too quickly, and she wondered if he also felt they were being swept away like leaves in a whirlwind, that they needed to stop, slow down....

But his arms wound around her. "The day isn't over," he said softly.

She looked up at him and smiled. Laughing, he swept her off the ground and headed for the door. He started when they both heard a clanging sound from the back of the house.

Kelsey shimmied to her feet. He grabbed her hand and didn't rush around but hurried back into the house. His service revolver was in its holster, hidden beneath his jacket, which hung on one of the pegs just inside the door.

"Liam!" she protested.

He shook his head. Still gripping her hand and keeping her behind him, he walked through the house to exit through the back.

Jonas was there, scraping utensils from the barbecue.

He looked at Liam and the gun.

"Jesus, Liam!"

"Sorry," Liam said, clicking the safety and slipping the gun into his waistband.

"My heart nearly stopped!" Jonas told him.

"How the hell did you get back here?" Liam asked.

Jonas arched a brow. "Walked?" he said.

"We just came through…oh!" Kelsey said, and laughed. "We were walking Ted and Jaden out through the house while you were walking around it."

"I guess," Jonas said. "Man, Liam, you are jumpy."

"People broke in here twice," Liam said.

Kelsey placed a hand on his arm. "Kids, and the idiots," she said softly.

"And I'm well-trained," Liam said, his tone edgy. "I wouldn't have shot anyone, but this house is set by a nest of pines and mangroves and overgrowth. It doesn't hurt to be safe now."

"Yeah, yeah, it's all right," Jonas said. "I didn't mean to startle anyone. Just thought that I'd help pick up."

"And we didn't expect you, because you left with Clarinda," Liam said.

"Well, since the poor girl has to go to work and I don't, I like to get her there and walk her home, at least," he said. "But I didn't want to leave this place a mess, either. Hey, you want to go down to O'Hara's for a while later?" he asked brightly.

Liam had eased at last, Kelsey knew. She could feel him relax. He smiled. "Maybe," he said. "But not for a while."

Jonas laughed. "I hear ya. Okay, I'm really leaving!"

He hefted his bag of utensils over his shoulder and started to roll the barbecue over the lawn. "Give me a call if you're interested. I may walk on down early anyway."

"Okay," Liam said.

"'Bye. Thanks again," Kelsey told him.

They watched him go. Kelsey was very afraid that the mood was broken, but Liam's arms came around her waist. "Where were we, now? Oh, yeah!" Again, he swept her off her feet. They entered through the family room, and he balanced her weight to lock the door.

"Ah, hell, the front!" he said.

She laughed as he whirled her around, pretending to whack her head into the wall as he hurried through the house to lock the front door.

He started toward the stairs, and to her surprise turned back. Still balancing her weight, he headed to Cutter's office. He opened the door, turned on the light and looked around. He turned off the light and headed for the stairway again.

He must have felt her tense.

"I'm all right on this, really," he said softly.

She didn't protest. He carried her up the stairs, and once in her room, he dropped her on the bed and gasped dramatically.

"Oh, you jerk!" she laughed.

He fell down on the bed, reaching for her.

She eluded him, jumping up to run to the bedroom door.

She locked it.

He stared at her, frowning, but she ran for the bed and pounded down on it, crawling on top of him and slipping her arms around his waist as she leaned down to kiss him.

Neither of them asked any more questions.

The funeral home had served the residents of Key West for years. It would be on the ghost tour tonight, but hopefully, the visitation for Cutter Merlin would be a quiet and decent affair.

Liam and Kelsey met with the funeral director at ten o'clock, Sunday morning, to finalize the details.

They were both stunned to see the many arrangements of flowers that had arrived, especially since the event hadn't been well-publicized.

"Wow," Kelsey whispered to him. "And sadly, Cutter would be horrified. He would have told people that they had much better use for their money these days. I should have written somewhere that he would have preferred donations to charity."

"I'm sure some of these are from the old-timers here and around," Liam told her. "And they would feel that a funeral needed flowers, no matter what you had said."

She nodded. They spoke to the director for several minutes, and when all the final arrangements had been made, the director asked Kelsey, "Do you want an open or closed casket?"

She opened her mouth without speaking, apparently taken aback by the question.

"Closed," Liam said firmly.

The director scratched his answer on his notepad.

"And what about the family? Do you want a private viewing first?"

"No," he said, answering for Kelsey again.

"As you wish. Then, we're all set. The hours for visitation have been set from seven to nine. If you arrive about six-thirty, that will be fine."

They walked out into the bright sunlight.

Then Kelsey asked him, "Why were you so determined that I not see Cutter's body? Was there something about his death that you haven't told me?"

He hesitated, wanting to tell her the truth and not really wanting to do so.

"Liam, I want to know," she said stubbornly.

He looked down the street. It was just after ten. Music was beginning to pour from a number of the bars over on Duval.

"Kelsey," he said, looking at her at last, "I told you—he wasn't found immediately."

"I know that," she said quietly. "But the funeral director didn't make it sound as if it were so terrible that I shouldn't have seen him. Sadly, I'm not a stranger to seeing the bodies of those I love when they're in their coffins."

"I don't think you should see him, Kelsey. That's all."

"No, it's not."

He sighed. "I gave you his belongings. His ring, his watch—and the book and casket he was holding when he died."

"You're still not telling me everything," Kelsey said, confused.

"All right, Kelsey. It appeared that he'd been scared to death."

"Scared to death? You mentioned that before, but I thought you were just trying to get me to be more cautious," she said incredulously.

"I'm trying not to make you nervous," he said.

She laughed. "You don't want me to be nervous, but you don't really want me staying in my own house. I guess it's better if you're staying there?"

"Of course." He paused, looking down at her. "And what's with you? We lock the house—but you want the bedroom door locked, too."

She shrugged, looking away. "I don't know. If those kids did break in again, I wouldn't want to be taken by surprise, that's all."

"That's not why," he said.

She stared at him. "Yes, yes, it is."

She was stubborn, and she wasn't going to say anything else. That was that.

"Breakfast?" he asked her.

"What?"

"Breakfast?"

She smiled and nodded. "That sounds good. Blue Heaven still here?"

"It is."

They walked down Duval. On a Sunday morning, despite the fact that some of the musical acts were already starting up, the street was fairly quiet. Kelsey commented on the slogans on the T-shirts in the windows they passed, Liam pointed out that the models in the windows now had gigantic breasts.

They were halfway down the street when Liam's phone rang. It was David, asking him if he wanted to meet him and Katie for breakfast. Liam told them to head over to Blue Heaven.

The building had been there for over a hundred years. Once, the structure with its great patio beneath an array of trees had served spirits to thirsty guests. Then it had been a venue for cockfights, and, at one time, there had been boxing matches that took place there, with none other than Key West's famous one-time-resident Ernest Hemingway presiding. In the early nineties it had become a restaurant, and since then, its popularity had grown.

The food was good. There was usually a bit of entertainment going on. The place had a Ping-Pong table for idle guests as they waited for their tables, and, of course, a shop.

Kelsey and Liam opted for Ping-Pong, which was fun, with both of them spending most of the time chasing after the ball rather than hitting it back across the table. David and Katie arrived, and they tried doubles, which worked somewhat better, with all of them arguing over who got a ball in bounds, and who didn't.

It was during the game that Liam saw Bartholomew. He was standing beneath the old almond tree, his arms crossed over his chest as he watched. Liam, distracted by the ghost, missed a ball as it went flying by him. Kelsey batted him on the shoulder, laughing.

Bartholomew nodded to him, as if he had something to tell him.

Katie O'Hara was the one in their group who tended to see and befriend ghosts. David could see Bartholomew now, as could Sean, though the others didn't have the same talent as Katie to sense, feel or see other spirits that might be around.

If it had been just the three of them, they could have spoken to Bartholomew as they ate without anyone noticing.

Frankly, Liam hadn't believed that spirits could roam the earth after death in any way—until, of course, he'd found out about Bartholomew. Katie insisted that she wasn't psychic—she simply saw ghosts. She couldn't tell the future, and she didn't read palms. She had always seen ghosts. Sean had kept her from admitting it until Bartholomew had come so strongly into all their lives.

Liam found himself wishing that he could introduce Kelsey to Bartholomew. But things between them were on the edgy side. He knew she wasn't telling him everything.

But he could ruin whatever tenuous relationship he had with her now if he sat down and tried to explain that his friend, the dead privateer ghost Bartholomew, had something to tell them. Bartholomew, meet Kelsey; Kelsey, meet Bartholomew. It was difficult enough as it was. He was a high-ranking officer in the police department. Best for people not to think that he was a total lunatic.

"Game!" Kelsey said, lifting her arms.

"What?" David protested. "No, it's game point now."

"I say we call it a draw," Katie said.

"Yeah, 'cause wait, I might have miscounted!" Kelsey agreed.

She looked happy, laughing with Katie. Her cheeks were flushed, her eyes appeared exceptionally blue and, in the sunlight, her hair was still as glossy as a raven's wing. She'd started to acquire a tan, and he realized that, in his mind, she was the perfect woman. Not too tall, not too short, lean and athletic, beautifully shaped, not enormous in the chest but perfectly formed and firm and… if she weren't, he'd still be crazy about her, her honesty, her laughter…

"Hey, let's look around in the shop for a minute, Kelsey," Katie said. "My side is hurting."

Katie, of course, knew that Bartholomew was there, and that he apparently wanted to talk to Liam, and for once Bartholomew wasn't going to try to get him in trouble or make him look like a fool.

There were a few tables near the bar. David and Liam took a seat and Bartholomew came over to join them. "So, what's up?" Liam asked. People walked around them, not noticing anything. Every once in a while, he saw someone pause. They didn't see Bartholomew, but they had a touch of the sixth sense that let them know something was in the air. Usually, they would stop whatever they were doing for a heartbeat, frown and move on, forgetting the sensation.

"I described the book to Lucinda," he said. "And she remembered it. We were chatting in the cemetery, and another fellow came by. Pete Edwards. His real name wasn't Edwards, of course, but that's what he was called after his death. He owned the book at one time, and I believe that Cutter Merlin bought the book from his estate. Pete died and his estate went into probate for ten years. Then his belongings went up for auction."

"And?" David prompted.

"And someone should read the book and find out more about its history," Bartholomew said. "Cutter Merlin probably paid a very high price for it because of all that happened after the book was salvaged, and what happened during the Civil War."

"What happened during the Civil War?" Liam asked.

"Something with the fight in Key West between the Northern and Southern states," Bartholomew said.

"It was a strange time. Florida was the third state to secede from the Union, but the forts stayed in Union hands, both Fort Zachary Taylor and Fort Jefferson," Liam said.

"Look," Bartholomew said, "I was dead during the war. I've gone this far. You're a cop, Liam. Investigate. My new spectral friend, old Pete Edwards, says that there was a book written about himself, a fellow named Abel Crowley and all sorts of stuff going on in Key West. We should find that, too."

"Thanks," Liam said. "What's the name of the book?"

"He didn't say."

"Great. Does it even exist still?"

"I don't know. Hey. What do you want out of a ghost?"

Bartholomew asked. "It's not as if I can walk into the library and ask to get on one of the computers."

"You're getting very good with computer keys," Liam told him.

"Excuse me—do you want my help or not?" Bartholomew demanded.

Liam smiled. "Yes, of course, and thank you."

"Your Miss Donovan is returning, Liam," Bartholomew noted.

Liam turned. Katie was announcing their return as they walked toward the table from the shop. "I don't know—you have so many *things* already! I perfectly understand you wanting to sort through what you have before buying so much as a magnet!" she added with a laugh. Katie looked at Bartholomew. He grinned. He wasn't leaving. He was going to torment the three of them through breakfast.

And he did. He might pretend he couldn't push the keys of a computer yet, but he did well at knocking over the salt, making Liam's cup rattle and shaking the table now and then. If Kelsey noticed, she didn't comment.

David and Katie helped Liam trying to rescue various items on the table. Maybe it didn't matter; Kelsey seemed distracted throughout the meal. When they had idled over a second cup of coffee, she said, "I think I'm going to head home. I have no idea what will happen at the viewing tonight, whether there will be a dozen people there or a hundred."

"It might be a huge turnout," Katie commented. "People were fascinated by Cutter Merlin."

Until we all forgot him at the end of his life, Liam thought ruefully.

"Anyway, I'm going to head home and get ready," Kelsey said.

Liam started to rise, too.

She placed a hand on his chest and smiled. "I'm all right. Honestly. I think I need a little time. I'll see you there. Early." She smiled. She did want him with her at the funeral home.

She also needed time alone.

He nodded, wishing he didn't feel as if his stomach knotted each time she was going to head to the house alone.

She left them, and he sat back down.

"I think you should do some studying on the occult," Bartholomew told him.

"Because of the book Cutter Merlin was holding when he died?" Katie asked.

"A ghost is telling me to go study the occult," Liam said dryly.

"Has Jaden found a description of the reliquary yet?" David asked.

Liam shook his head. "I have to give Jaden time." He stood himself. "She just took the reliquary last night. I'm going to head out to do some research into the occult— as our friendly neighborhood ghost suggests."

Bartholomew rolled his eyes. "And I try to help you people."

"Deeply appreciated," Liam said. "I'll see you at the funeral home this evening."

They both nodded, and Liam left them. Bartholomew followed behind him.

Kelsey enjoyed the walk back to her house. It was about a mile through the heart of Old Town, and she gazed into windows as she walked along, noting new businesses that had sprung up and those that had been there as long as she could remember.

She walked by the beautiful Episcopal church that had burned and been rebuilt, added to, changed through its many decades. She smiled, thinking about the ghost story that involved the sea captain who was still buried in back—and who didn't enjoy backpackers sneaking in to sleep on his tomb.

She passed the funeral home, and felt a little shiver of sadness sweep through her—Cutter's body would be there by now.

Eventually she reached Front Street, passed by the Pirate Soul Museum and walked down around the wharf.

Jonas's house was clean and whitewashed, welcoming as a bed-and-breakfast inn now. She saw couples out on the side patio enjoying afternoon drinks from the little tiki bar.

Finally she started out at the stretch to the Merlin house. She wondered how long she would think of it in that fashion. It was actually her house now.

She smiled.

It would always remain the Merlin house.

She walked up to the porch. At first, she smelled

nothing but the sea breeze. She slipped her key into the lock and hesitated.

An odd moment of fear swept over her. And once again, she thought that she smelled death.

She gave herself a shake. She was letting Liam's fears get to her. She had grown up in this house. She had loved its oddities and curiosities.

She walked in determinedly and closed and locked the door. She leaned against it and inhaled deeply. It was gone. She wasn't smelling death. She inhaled pine cleaners and every other substance they had used for their scrub down of the house.

She started into the kitchen, but again felt a creeping sensation along her spine.

Something had moved.

Someone had been in the house.

Someone was in the house, watching her.

She looked around. Nothing was out of place. They had carefully locked up when they had left. She walked through the house and assured herself that the back door was still locked, that the windows were closed and the locks were secured on the windows, as well.

That took some time.

But it was good to feel that the house was entirely safe and all bolted down.

She started up the stairs, then paused again, thinking that she had heard a sound from Cutter's office.

She walked back down the stairs and into his office. She turned on the light and looked around. No one was there.

She walked to his desk and saw that a little figurine

had fallen to the floor. Laughing at herself, she picked it up and put it on his desk.

The house was safe and sound.

She hurried up the stairs, wanting to shower, wash her hair and dress for the evening.

When she reached her own door, she was surprised to note that she still had goose bumps on the flesh of her arms.

Giving herself a mental shake, she stepped into her room.

Wondering what she was locking herself in against, she firmly slid the bolt on her bedroom door.

She felt safe. Alone.

None of it made any sense.

And yet, when she walked into her bath and turned on the shower spray, she knew that she still trying to wash away a certain scent.

That awful scent of death.

7

As they headed for the library, Bartholomew said to Liam, "It's all quite strange. I mean, Key West is famous for the unusual person here and there, for some great ghost stories and history. Anything that hints of devil worship and the like, though—that's unusual. But then again, I think it might all have had to do with the fact that Key West went into the spiritualism craze along with the rest of the world when the Fox sisters started their whole craze."

"The Fox sisters?" Liam asked. He frowned. He seemed to remember something about a movie that had featured the Fox sisters. They had begun an entire movement into spiritualism—but then they'd been proven to be faking their "manifestations."

"I wasn't alive when it all came about, so once again, I say you might want to do some research," Bartholomew advised.

"But you were here. You were just dead."

"Yes. But I wasn't running around tapping three times for yes and twice for no or participating in any such ridiculousness!" Bartholomew said.

The library was quiet. Liam might have gone on the computer at home, but if the book that Bartholomew was referring to did still exist, he might be able to get it at the library. And with no one there, it seemed a comfortable place for his strange investigation.

It was extremely slow that afternoon. He had his pick of computers.

Bartholomew sat by him, talking as they went from site to site, starting with the Fox sisters and spiritualism.

The ghost pointed to an old picture on a page of three children—quite innocent and grim in appearance. Liam read, "'When the Fox girls were children, they lived in a house with a reputation for being haunted. They soon found the attention they wanted when they spoke about the situation, and convinced the world that the house was indeed haunted, that there were taps and lights and all manner of manifestations within their home. The girls became mediums, and had the world fooled. When they were older, one of them recanted and proved how she could make a tapping sound with her toes. The girls' words meant nothing—spiritualism had taken hold across the known world, and with it, man's belief in the occult and paranormal in all varieties.'" Liam looked at Bartholomew, frowning. "All right. This all became a 'movement.' All kinds of people began to believe that mediums could allow them to talk to dead relatives. The Fox sisters *were* more or less proven to have invented the entire thing. But it didn't stop people from believing—or pushing it all further?"

Bartholomew looked at Liam and shrugged. "The point is, the whole spiritualism thing went wild. And with that, 'witchcraft' came to the fore again—and Satanism."

"I can't believe that Cutter Merlin was a Satanist," he murmured. "Or even that he was afraid of Satanists." But he thought about the afternoon when he had found Cutter Merlin. Cutter had been holding the book, a reliquary—and a sawed-off shotgun. Cutter had wanted to be prepared.

And he had died anyway.

Liam keyed in a different series of words that included Key West, Satanism and books.

He scanned another site quickly. "A ship called the *Queen Caroline* wrecked off Key West in the 1840s, and a large majority of her cargo was salvaged by a local character, Peter Edwards, a man known for his love of magic and his reputation for using occult practices. As a young man, he was feared for his abilities to 'curse' his fellow Southerners, thus helping the South's defeat in the Civil War. Edwards was a staunch Unionist. While many in the area were suspected of abetting Southern ships during the blockade, Pete was known to report any possible activity of Southern ships to the Union military. It was an uneasy time in Key West, since Key West was part of the state of Florida, which had seceded from the Union, but with the Union firmly holding both forts in Key West. The activity at the forts is believed to have been effective in preventing numerous blockade runners from bringing needed supplies to the South, and Peter Edwards was credited with supplying the officers at the forts with valuable information. Historians suspect that his alliance with the Federals caused a great deal of hatred among his fellow citizens, and so his reputation for the practice of 'black magic.'"

"There. That's him. The Pete Edwards prowling the Key West cemetery," Bartholomew said.

"Makes no sense," Liam murmured.

"Here," Liam noted, pointing to another reference. He moved onward. "The end of the 'War of Northern Aggression' was as strange in Key West as all else. Old hatreds died quickly. Northern soldiers went home, and little of what was suffered in areas of the Deep South was felt in Key West. Peter Edwards soon began a practice of magic again for the purpose of entertainment. It's during this time when he told friends that he had turned to his book—the book he had salvaged from the *Queen Caroline*—to make amends for whatever deaths he might have brought about during the war. He was living for a long time in peace and harmony and the eccentricity known to exist in many a *conch* when another visitor headed down to Key West, Abel Crowley, a man who claimed to be related to the notorious Aleister Crowley."

"Aleister Crowley," Liam murmured. Sadly, he remembered his days of studying rock bands who had been obsessed with Aleister Crowley better than some of Crowley's history. But he knew that Crowley had practiced black magic, supposedly worshipped Satan and, according to some, offered up human sacrifices in his pursuit of dark arts. During his time, he had been known as "the wickedest man alive."

In retrospect, he might have been nothing more than an extreme exhibitionist, rebelling against the Victorian society into which he had been born, Liam thought. Give a man enough money, enough time, boredom and curiosity, and he might delve into anything.

Not to mention the fact that he was fond of hallucinogenic drugs.

Liam noted a link on the page to a book—possibly the book that Bartholomew had learned about from Pete Edwards. Liam hit the key to the link and found that a book had been published titled *Key West, Satanism, Peter Edwards, and the Abel and Aleister Crowley Connection.*

Liam hit the connection and began scanning the publisher's and reviewers' information on the book.

"An intriguing look into little-known historical figures who brought the dark arts to the bright sunshine of Key West!" read one review.

Another touted the book as "A little-known treatise on some most unusual men."

It went on:

Aleister Crowley is a well-known figure in the chronology of the supposed "Anti-Christ" movement. He began to live with a tenet of "Do What Thou Wilt," believing his wife was a mystic and that an Egyptian exhibit—numbered 666—specified the year of the beast. Whether his claims to possession of power and magic were in any way real has never been proven or disproven. His exploits in Great Britain and elsewhere were legendary. History cannot even prove or disprove whether Abel Crowley was or wasn't a bastard cousin of Aleister. Some people believed Abel

Crowley was an eccentric, an accepted personality in Key West, a man like Aleister also rebelling against the Victorian principles of his day, and others suggest that he, too, was a human-sacrificing devil worshiper.

Bartholomew poked Liam and whispered, "I think you need to check *this* book out of the library. I'm thinking Key West may be one of the only places to have this book now." He sighed. "Maybe I can get you to see the fellow I met. Pete Edwards. Pete Edwards believes that he remains walking the streets of Key West because he tried to practice some of Aleister Crowley's rites—taught to him by Abel Crowley—in his house on Margaret Street that was bulldozed years ago—at the end of his life. He tried to use the book, *In Defense from Dark Magic*—which had been salvaged off the *Queen Caroline*—in order to atone for his actions during the war, and for the evil he had done during his time with Abel Crowley. Pete Edwards believes he began his way back to goodness and grace through the use of *In Defense from Dark Magick*—but he died before he could fulfill his task of freeing others."

Liam looked at Bartholomew, grateful and yet not sure of what the information might give them that they didn't already have. He knew, whether Kelsey ever wanted to admit it or not, that Cutter Merlin had suffered his fatal heart failure because he had been afraid.

Liam had returned the book and the reliquary to Kelsey, but Ted and Jaden now had the reliquary and would hopefully find out what they could about it. He needed to get *In Defense from Dark Magick* back from Kelsey, read it and hope that the library had the other book, about Pete Edwards and his friend Abel Crowley, as well.

The librarian was a friend—Key West was a small community. Jeanie Fry was tall and slim and tanned and loved books. She was surprised when he asked about the book and told him that they didn't usually lend it out. "It's in the room with our special editions. It's very old, and we only have one copy."

"Oh," he said, looking at her with disappointment.

She smiled and shrugged. "But you are an upstanding citizen, and I suppose we could trust you with it. After all, we trust you with our lives, right?"

He smiled appropriately in return. "Thank you. I really appreciate it, Jeanie."

"Follow me," she said, heading for the reserved and special-editions section of the library. "This isn't your usual reading, Liam," she said as they walked. "In fact, it's not the usual reading for anyone I know. Is this all about Cutter Merlin?"

"Yes, he was a strange old fellow, and once, he was my friend."

"I heard his granddaughter has come back. And I saw the announcement that there's a viewing tonight, and he's going to be buried tomorrow."

"True."

"So—was he practicing some kind of dark magic?"

"I don't believe so."

"Then why the interest?"

"I'm not sure."

"He died of a heart attack, right?"

"Yes. There were a couple of break-ins over there, though. I'm just trying to hunt down what someone might have been looking for," Liam said.

Jeanie rolled her eyes. "That house must be like a mystery treasure trove, delving into an attic of lore!"

She used her passkey to allow them entrance, and then signed in at the stand that held a ledger keeping track of all who entered the section holding the library's rare editions.

"Hmm. Looks like we've been busy in here lately."

"Oh?"

"Cutter himself was here about a month ago," she said. "There—see where he signed in?"

"Yes, and there are a half a dozen entries after—or seven," Liam noted, frowning as he read the names. He was surprised to see several that he knew.

"Barney Thibault. He's a professor who comes down from the University of Miami. And Mary Egans—she teaches high school down here. Actually, Liam—"

"Yes, I know Mary. She was my high-school English teacher."

Jeanie nodded and then shook her head. "Ah! Old Joe Richter was in here. The attorney. I don't know George Penner. I do know Jonas Weston—oh, so do you, I'm sure! Here—your friends Ted and Jaden were in, but that's not in the least surprising—Jaden uses the library frequently. And I don't know this last fellow or woman, maybe? This Bel Arcowley."

She shrugged and moved over to the shelves, searching along them until she came to an empty position.

"Oh my," she said.

"What's wrong?"

"It's gone."

"The book is gone? I thought you said that you didn't lend it out," Liam said.

She turned to look at him, shaking her head. "We don't. I'll talk to my fellow librarians, Liam. I'll get right on it."

"Maybe it's just out of place," Liam suggested.

Jeanie nodded. "Well, you can help me search," she told him.

Bartholomew was in the room with them, of course. He searched along with Jeanie and Liam. But the book wasn't on any of the shelves. They looked thoroughly for at least thirty minutes.

"I suppose it might have gotten put back outside the room," Jeanie said, sounding weary. "We'll start a general search for it."

"Thanks. Tell me, is someone always with visitors in this section of the library?"

"Sadly, no. We don't have the funding."

"It would be too much to hope for a security tape, right?" he asked, looking around. He didn't see any cameras.

"No. We don't have the—"

"Funding, right."

They looked at each other for a minute. Liam grimaced. "All right, let me take that list of names. I'll give all the visitors a call after you check with your coworkers."

"Thanks, Liam. Do I need to fill out a report or

something? I mean, once I find out one of my coworkers didn't suddenly decide to read up on Satanism in Key West?"

"Yes, we'll fill out a report," he told her. "I'll go ahead and get an officer out here for you to do that. I don't think you'll find that any of your coworkers took the book."

She thanked him, flustered, and they went out. Liam headed to his house to change for the viewing at the funeral home. He was determined to be there when Kelsey arrived.

Kelsey left the house, locking it carefully as she did so, ridiculously pleased that she was leaving while it was still daylight.

She thought she smelled the scent of death and decay again, but she was impatient with herself; she had it set in her mind that she could still smell the horrible lonely end that had met her grandfather, and she wasn't going to change what was set in her mind. She felt oddly irritated with Liam, though at the same time, she wished that he was with her. She wasn't a scaredy-cat. He was turning her into one.

She walked slowly to the funeral home, knowing she was a little bit early. But that didn't matter. Liam was there when she arrived. He was extremely handsome in a dark pin-striped suit, clean shaven, his hair still damp. He met her at the entrance.

"You're early," he told her.

"You're earlier," she noted.

He smiled. "I didn't want you to be alone."

"Thanks."

They walked on in. As Liam had predicted, the hallway was alive with flowers. The funeral director came out to greet them, telling Kelsey that her grandfather's was the only viewing that night, and so they had been liberal with the layout of the arrangements, which he hoped was fine with her. She assured him it was.

"Where is…Cutter?" she asked.

"Right here, first door to the left," the director told her.

They walked into the room with its rows of chairs, multitude of wreaths and flower arrangements, and, at the far end, the podium, stand and coffin.

The coffin was open.

Liam walked in ahead of her, moving quickly. She heard him make a strange sound, and then he turned back to her.

"Kelsey, please. Let me have them close the coffin. I thought they were going to leave it closed," he said, irritated.

The funeral director, correctly solemn in his dark suit, said in quick explanation, "In such cases, we wait for the family to arrive."

Liam was aggravated, she knew. Yet why he didn't want her seeing her grandfather perplexed her, and made her want to see him more.

She pushed past Liam and came to the coffin.

She'd seen what ravages disease could cause the human body, and in that sense, he didn't look *horrible*.

He was pasty and slightly plastic-looking, as she'd expected. Pale. Sunken. She could see that his eyes had been delicately sewn shut.

But his eyes were open.

Tiny trails of spiderweb-thin thread clung to his eyelashes.

He stared out at the world in horror, as if, even in death, he was still seeing something eternally malignant and evil.

"Kelsey."

Liam was behind her; his hands rested on her shoulders.

"It's all right," she said. "I've seen death before."

"Please, let's close the coffin," he said softly.

She nodded.

She had brought a tiny cross Cutter had given her when she had been a little girl. She pulled it from her purse and set it around his icy-cold fingers.

The director had called for one of his assistants. As they closed the coffin, the first visitor for the evening arrived, the Episcopalian priest from Cutter's favorite church on the island. He greeted Kelsey with familiarity, and she remembered him from her childhood. She felt oddly detached and cold, still stunned by the look in her grandfather's eyes, open and dusted with the remnants of the stitches that had held them closed.

But she felt that people were what they were—creatures of social habit. She greeted Father Tom warmly, thanking him for coming. He told her that her grandfather had been a beautifully spiritual man—loving God no matter what his thoughts or disagreements with any organized religion might have been.

She tried to make sure that she gave all the proper responses. Father Tom was speaking with sincerity. She

had known that her grandfather had always respected
and cared about him and that her parents had enjoyed
him as well. It was wonderful that he was here.

She refrained from shouting out, *What made my
grandfather die with that horrible terror in his eyes?
Tell me, tell me, please, that he was never into devil worship, that he never delved into the black arts, that...*

"...and so wonderfully intelligent, Kelsey. He was a
brilliant man. He knew the world, and what was so wonderful was that he understood all God's creatures—and
humanity with its different cultures and beliefs. Well,
you knew him. Rest assured, he is in God's hands now,"
Father Tom said.

She thanked him. He told her to let him know anytime
she wanted him to start the prayer service she'd planned
for the evening.

By then, the next visitor had arrived.

Cutter Merlin's attorney, Joe Richter, had arrived.
He awkwardly told her how sorry he was and patted her
hands over and over again. Once more, she wanted to
scream. They had been fine in Richter's office, but now
he didn't know what to say and she didn't, either.

"Ah, well, at least he left you in a very nice position.
That can't be said in many such a situation," Richter told
her.

"Mr. Richter, my parents left me in a fine position.
They taught me to get an education, and I have my own
work and my own income," she reminded him.

He blushed to the roots of his white hair. "I didn't
mean...forgive me. But, you know, Cutter seriously left
everything in your hands. He left you instructions, but

he also left a sizable fortune and incredible riches, you know."

"I haven't begun to go through his collections yet, Mr. Richter. And I plan to honor all of my grandfather's wishes."

Maybe she looked uncomfortable. Liam was speaking with the priest and the funeral director, but Jonas had arrived and came over to rescue her. "Kelsey," he said, excusing himself as he came between them. He gave her a warm hug, steering her away from the attorney. "You all right?" he asked her, studying her eyes. "You seem a bit shell-shocked."

She shook her head. "I'm fine. Honestly. Where's Clarinda?"

"She'll be along in a minute. She had to finish getting ready for work—it's Sunday night, and she and Katie are both on the schedule, but they're coming by."

Just then, Katie, David, Sean, Vanessa and Clarinda came in, all giving Kelsey hugs and saying appropriate things. She assured them she was fine.

People she didn't remember began to arrive. Then there were those she did recognize. Several of her old teachers were there, and others from her grandfather's and her parents' generations. If she'd been afraid that it would be a lonely viewing, that fear was quickly set to rest. The room was overflowing by the time Father Tom gave his little eulogy and prayer. The priest was already speaking when Jaden and Ted slipped in, nodding to her across the room and giving her the kind of "we're here for you" smiles that friends gave at such a time.

It was nice; it was good. Cutter would have been

happy. He would have wanted all the money that had gone into flowers used in a more productive way, but other than that, he would have been proud. Old cronies spoke of better, brighter times. Days gone by when they'd argued over beers, dressed up for Hemingway Days just to outdo one another, and various other events. One of her old teachers spoke about how wonderful Cutter had been about coming in to talk to different classes about different cultures or one of his many escapades.

It was eleven by the time everyone trailed out. Kelsey felt drained.

Clarinda, Jonas, Katie and David had slipped out early, heading off to a Sunday night's work. But Jaden and Ted lingered.

Kelsey yawned broadly, certain Liam would notice.

He didn't.

"Jaden, how are you doing on the reliquary?" Liam asked.

"I think I might have it pinned down to the time and place," she said. "There are some markings on the bottom. I went in a few wrong directions, but I think it's French," she said excitedly. "And, if I'm right, it might hold a fragment of the remnants of Joan of Arc."

"What?" Kelsey gasped.

"Don't go getting excited. There are a few more tests to perform, and for a real assessment, you're going to need at least one other expert. But it's fascinating," Jaden said.

"We know people who are experts, of course," Ted said. "But you might want to bring in an independent, as well. Someone from one of the world's major universities, someone specializing in Roman Catholic history, relics and symbolism."

"Joan of Arc was burned at the stake. To ash," Liam said.

"Even burning at the stake allows for bone fragments," Jaden said.

"So, Cutter was holding a reliquary that might have contained the bones of a highly regarded saint?" Kelsey asked.

"Thought by many to be exceptionally holy, to place the possessor in a position to combat evil," Jaden said.

"I think that the Church has gone beyond that kind of thought process," Kelsey said, puzzled. "I mean, such relics might be honored, as we honor our dead…or bow to a cross, but to actually believe that a reliquary could ward off evil? I don't know about that."

"I didn't say that the Catholic Church had such a belief or doctrine," Jaden said. "I believe that there are people out there who might believe it."

"Everything is in belief, isn't it?" Ted asked, and shrugged.

"If it is what I think it is, it's worth a small fortune," Jaden said.

"If it is what you think it is, I'll find a way to give it to the Catholic Church," Kelsey said.

Jaden laughed. "I honestly don't believe that God will smite you for selling it."

Kelsey shook her head. "You don't understand. I don't need the money. I don't need to be incredibly wealthy. I like working. I will have a nest egg to fall back on, certainly, even if I send everything that Cutter wanted in specific places exactly where he wanted it all to go. He didn't collect for the wealth of it—he collected because he loved history and the objects that taught history. He was like one of the last great adventurers."

She felt Liam watching her then, and felt the warmth of the small smile that had crept onto his features.

And then, at last, he noted that she was tired.

"We'd better get going. Big day tomorrow," he said softly.

She nodded. They rose, and she hugged Jaden and Ted, thanking them. "Wow. I appreciate all that you've done on this."

Jaden laughed. "Are you kidding? I love this! Can't wait to just see more and more of what is in that house!"

Ted said the same.

They parted ways.

Kelsey thought that she might fall asleep as they walked through the darkness toward the house.

She held Liam's hand, and leaned against him.

They hit the little spit of land leading out to the house.

She felt a sense of cold and fear sweeping over her as they did so, and she wondered why.

Then she realized that the odd and wretched odor was coming to her again.

The scent of death.

She was imagining it. She had it set in her mind. She had to stop, get control of her thoughts and her emotions.

But it wasn't in her mind.

"Lord, that is strong! There has to be a big animal dead on this property somewhere," Liam said, pausing.

"You smell it, too?" she asked.

"Big-time. The closer we get to the house, the stronger the smell is," he said.

He caught her hand, and they walked faster. He paused, breathing in and grimacing.

"It's not—it's not *in* the house, is it?" she asked.

"I don't think so, but let's see what's going on."

He kept her hand in his as they walked up the steps to the porch. She opened the door, and they stepped in.

He stood in the entry and shook his head.

"It's outside," he said.

"What is it?" she asked.

"I'll go out and look," he told her.

She didn't know why, but she didn't want him out in the night. She had to admit to feeling squeamish. She didn't want to find the dead thing.

And she didn't want to be left alone.

"No," she said, her fingers tightening around his. "No, please, let's find out what it is in the morning. Please."

"Kelsey, I can get a flashlight and find out what it is," he said.

"I know you can. I don't want you to. Please. It's not in the house. It's not in the house at all. Please wait until the morning."

She looked at him earnestly. He touched her face and smiled after a moment. "All right, we can wait until the morning. It might be a dolphin, I'm afraid. It's something fairly large, I think. A large mammal."

"Or small and pathetically bloated," she suggested.

"But, whichever, please, let's let it wait until the morning."

"All right."

He turned and checked the door.

He paused again, looking around the house. For once, she didn't feel uneasy, or as if someone had been there, or as if she were being watched.

She felt safe. He was there.

But he told her, "I'll be right up. I'm just going to take a look around and make sure that everything is locked up."

She laughed. "You won't be right up. It's a big house."

"I can move quickly," he promised.

She smiled and headed for the stairs. When she was up in her room, she wondered if she might actually carry a bit of the scent on her, having walked through it.

She cast her clothes into the wicker hamper in the bathroom and turned on the shower.

A few minutes later, Liam joined her. For a moment he was silent as he slipped in behind her, caught the soap and rubbed it erotically down the length of her back. "I must say, we are extremely clean people," he whispered against the back of her ear.

She laughed and turned into him. "I just…I just wanted to make sure we smelled like soap."

And not death.

She didn't say the words; neither did he. While the water cascaded down around them, he cradled her head with his hand and kissed her lips slowly. The steam created a breathtaking mist, and the soap was slick against their bodies. They touched their lengths together, and their hands began to roam, and in the wickedly delicious heat that rose between them she forgot about fear and unease and gave way to the pure decadent pleasure of arousal.

They played, stroked and teased in the shower, until at last they turned off the water, groped for towels and headed halfway dry and still steaming into the bedroom. She fell upon him on the clean white sheets, her heart and mind and desire filled with him…

And then she pulled away, rising quickly and racing to the door.

She heard him groan softly as she turned the lock.

"Kelsey, we're alone, I checked the house!" he whispered to her.

She didn't answer. She slid back down him, unable to explain.

And then it didn't matter. Her lips were locked with his, his tongue was thrusting into her mouth, hot and fast, and their hands were all over one another, and then their lips, hot wet kisses that covered and seared against flesh, and he was within her, and the world was gone.

They made love until sheer exhaustion took over. She slept, curled against him, their limbs entangled.

When she awoke, he was gone.

She glanced quickly at the clock, hoping that she hadn't overslept. Cutter's funeral was that morning. But, of course, he wouldn't have let her oversleep.

It was just seven-thirty. The funeral wasn't until ten.

She groaned, still tired, and dragged herself out of

bed, washed her face, brushed her teeth and had one thought.

Coffee.

He would have set it to brew by now, she was certain. He was probably downstairs, maybe just about ready to come wake her up.

Kelsey walked downstairs and into the kitchen. She poured herself a cup of coffee, but still didn't see Liam.

She looked out front, but didn't see him, and so she came around back.

He was there. He was standing stiff as a poker, staring into the mangrove brush near the beach. Frowning, she opened the back door and started out.

The scent hit her like a massive wave.

She couldn't seem to stop herself; she started walking toward him.

"Kelsey, get back to the house," he said.

But she couldn't do so.

She was almost to him.

But then she saw what he saw.

She dropped her coffee cup.

She choked back a scream.

Yes, it was definitely a large mammal that was dead.

After all...

Human beings were mammals.

8

Liam had believed that he could find whatever had died on the property, call animal control and have the poor deceased creature gone long before Kelsey had to see it.

He hadn't expected the corpse of a man.

It had lain in the marshy ground by a knot of mangroves, their roots stretching out and into the water, soil accruing by those roots and creating marsh. It appeared that crabs had done quite a bit of damage to the fingers; white bone stuck out from darkened hands. The face was likewise unrecognizable, eaten, darkened, showing bits of cheekbone. The nose appeared to be gone.

The birds had taken the eyes.

The man's clothing was so darkened by the dark sand, soil and marsh water that they appeared to be just black at first sight.

There was no obvious sign of death. The corpse was at an angle, caught in the gnarly arms of the mangrove roots, water washing over it at high tide, receding at low. The corpse was in a severe stage of decomposition, but due to the water, the ground and the creatures that had fed upon it, he knew he wouldn't be able to tell himself in any way just how long it had been here.

A week? Five days, seven days?

When had they first noticed the smell?

That, too, was hard to determine, because the scent of death had lingered about the house itself after Cutter had died.

"Kelsey, I've called for the medical examiner. He'll be here—soon."

Before he said the last word, he heard the sound of the police sirens. The medical examiner would be there in minutes, along with a crime-scene unit to gather whatever clues they might.

He wasn't sure if there was anything at all a crime-scene unit might gather. He tried to remember how much rain there had been in the last few days. It wasn't summer, so the rain hadn't been constant, but they'd had a shower here and there. Footprints? Had the corpse been here during the barbecue? Yes, probably. It had been fresh then, though, hidden by the mangroves, roots and brush; he had found it this morning because he had been looking for a dead animal.

"Kelsey, please, go back inside. Maybe you could make a really big pot of coffee. I'm sure that it will be greatly appreciated. I think there are still a lot of paper coffee cups left over from the other day." He was accustomed to crime scenes. He knew that he was speaking calmly.

He winced at the way she was staring at the corpse.

"Kelsey!" He snapped her name.

She looked at him at last, her blue eyes wide with empathy and horror.

She cleared her throat. "Oh, God, Liam, who is it?"

He shook his head. "Kelsey, I have no idea. I believe that the medical examiner is going to have to give us an ID."

"But it's not—"

"I don't think it can be anyone we know well, Kelsey. We saw everyone last night, remember?"

She nodded, still frozen in place.

The first of the cars he had called were coming down the drive in front of the house.

"Kelsey, coffee? Please. And then go on, get ready. We have Cutter's funeral today."

She turned at last and went walking stiffly toward the house. He could see a few of the officers from the crime-scene unit moving toward him along with a few of the uniformed officers, armed with their crime-scene tape.

Behind them came Franklin Valaski, followed by two of his assistants bearing the body bag and stretcher that would shortly be needed.

"That's my path," Liam said, pointing to the direct line he had taken from the lawn and the rear of the house through the marsh.

Valaski snorted. "Like there are going to be footprints!"

Beth Ingram and Lee Houston from the crime-scene unit shrugged. "This is…this isn't promising," Beth told him.

"I know. See if you can find anything. Valaski, come on through."

He stepped back as Valaski moved in to see the body. He swore softly. "Jeez, Liam, think you could find 'em for me when they're a little fresher?"

"Think you can tell me time of death?"

Valaski stared at him, and then hunkered down by the corpse. He muttered beneath his breath again, shook his head, reached almost blindly for his bag and got a mask and gloves.

"Any clue as to how he died?" Liam asked.

"You mean you didn't check for a pulse?" Valaski asked dryly.

"I left him in situ for you."

"I could check for petechial hemorrhaging—oh, wait, no, I can't. I'm sorry, there are no eyes."

"Good Lord, Franklin—"

"Sorry! I'm sorry. But this poor boy... I'm not seeing a gunshot wound. It might have been strangulation. I need to get him back to the morgue, that's all there is to it. I can't tell you much of anything until we get him out of here and cleaned up. I'm sorry, Liam," Valaski said.

His hands were gloved; he wore high galoshes, having known he was headed into the marsh. He had on his huge magnifying glasses, the mask over his nose and mouth. He did a cursory inspection of the body, and then seemed to freeze.

He looked at Liam.

"What?" Liam asked.

"I can't give you much info on how and when he died yet, but..."

"But?"

"I can tell you who he is."

Liam was startled. "Who?"

Valaski waved a hand toward him to come around and hunker down as well. Mercifully, he offered him a mask.

Valaski pointed at markings on the blackened T-shirt the man was wearing.

Liam had definitely seen the shirt before. Even as he stared at it through the stains of marsh water and body fluids, he saw the emblem on it more clearly defined. There was a bird with flapping wings, a large bird, and *White* in cursive over the emblem.

It was Gary White, Key West's own part-time musician.

The man who had been trying to break into the place with Chris Vargas just a week ago.

Now dead and decaying at the Merlin house.

Kelsey paced in the kitchen, drinking a third cup of coffee and glancing at her watch. She had to be at Cutter's funeral soon. It wouldn't be right for the deceased's granddaughter to be late.

But she felt as if she'd been wired and charged.

Someone had been dead on the property for days now, and they had just discovered the body. What had happened to him? She felt it highly unlikely that anyone could have decided just to walk down to the Merlin property to die of natural causes.

At last, Liam came back into the house.

Involuntarily, she took a step back from him. He reeked.

He winced. "I'm heading up to the shower."

"Who was it? How did they die?" she demanded. "Did you know him?"

He nodded. "Not real well, but he was a Key West character. Gary White. He was a part-time musician. I don't know how he died." He hesitated. "The body is in very bad shape."

"Yes, but—I watch TV," she said. "They have ways—"

"Yes, they do. Franklin Valaski, the medical examiner—"

"I know him," she interrupted curtly. "You mentioned he checked out Cutter, and he came when my mother died."

Liam nodded. "He's taking him back to his morgue. He'll conduct the necessary autopsy and tests. We'll know what we can soon enough. I don't believe he's been dead more than a week—I saw him then—but when he was killed after that, I don't know. Because of the situation with the water and the marshy ground, mangrove roots, birds…crabs…it may be difficult to pinpoint the time of death very clearly."

She jerked a nod at him. "I noticed the smell when I got here," she said. "I kept thinking that it was something…left behind by Cutter."

"That would be natural," he said softly. "I'm running up." He moved toward her as if he would touch her, comfort her, but then stepped back. "Sorry. I'll be fast. Is there time? Maybe you should go ahead."

As he spoke, they heard the heavy brass knocker bang at the front door.

Kelsey jumped.

"I'll get it," Liam said. He shook his head. "No, you get it. Hey, look out the peephole first."

"Right," she said.

Liam went by her, flying up the stairs. She walked to the front door and looked out. She opened the door quickly.

David Beckett, Katie, Jonas and Clarinda were there, all dressed nicely for the services, the two men in jackets and Katie and Clarinda in dresses and low heels.

"We thought we should bring some support," Katie said.

"And find out why the yard was filled with cop cars and an ambulance," David said flatly.

"Liam found a man named Gary White dead on the property," she said, opening the door farther to let them all in.

"Gary White!" Katie said with surprise.

"Oh, that's so sad," Clarinda said.

"Sad, but he was a bum," Jonas said.

"He could play his guitar. He just found drugs instead of ambition," Katie said.

"What happened to him?" David asked, frowning.

"The medical examiner is going to have to figure that out," Kelsey told them.

Katie looked at her gravely and nodded. "We were at Jonas's place and saw that you two were still here. And, of course, all the stuff going on. And we knew nothing had happened to either of you, since we saw Liam out there with the officers and you out there earlier. But I knew you'd want to get to the church for the services, so…"

"So here we are," David said. "Why don't you four go on, and I'll wait and come with Liam."

"That's the best plan," Clarinda said. She looked tired, weary and, Kelsey thought, oddly worried.

It was probably just exhaustion. She worked an awful lot, and Sundays could be busy with the tourists who thought they'd be clever and stay the Sunday night while others were headed back for work on Monday morning.

"Let me just run up and tell Liam," she said. "And thank you."

"We're happy to be here with you," Katie told her.

"Yes, that we are," Jonas said.

Kelsey nodded, ran up the stairs, tapped on the bathroom door and stuck her head in to tell Liam what she was doing. He called back that he'd be another two minutes, but, yes, she should get going with the others.

David had brought his car, an SUV, and they all fit comfortably. The church, like almost everything in Old Town, was easily reachable, but under the circumstances it did seem prudent to drive. She hadn't asked for a car or a limo of any kind, knowing that she'd rather be with friends.

When they arrived, the reverend was there, quick to take her hand and sympathize, and bring her to a front pew. Cutter's coffin was there, draped in purple. She was afraid the bucket of tears she could shed for the years gone and the lives lost would come to her when she saw the coffin; she felt numb. Thoughts of Cutter raced through her head, but they were dislodged by the thought of a dead man rotting for days on the property.

Katie, Jonas and Clarinda took seats near her, and within minutes Sean O'Hara and Vanessa arrived, and then Ted and Jaden. They sat in the row behind her.

A few minutes later the church began to fill in. She wondered how many people had been Cutter's friends, and how many were there because they were curious. Cutter had been legend.

He had real friends there, as well. Kelsey smiled, touched as she saw Liam's and David's elderly aunts, Alice and Esther Beckett, come in and find seats in a pew in the back. She was saddened to see how they had aged, but then, they were actually great-aunts, and Esther had to be almost ninety, with Alice the baby of the two at eighty-eight. They both had beautiful heads of silver-blue hair, wore neat little boucle suits, hats, and carried hand-embroidered handkerchiefs.

Liam arrived with his cousin moments later, stopping to kiss his aunts before coming up to join her, and the service began. It was an Episcopalian mass, and many on the island participated. Then the eulogy was given, the reverend doing the speaking and doing it beautifully. He talked about a fine man who had suffered much, and had always been kind to his fellow beings and to lost and frightened critters, as well. He spoke about Cutter's brilliance, and his talent, and his adventurous soul.

Kelsey was invited up. For a moment, she stood at the lectern and looked out. She did feel a hot flash of tears at her eyes. So many people were there. She saw Joe

Richter out in the crowd. She saw strangers. She saw the
medical examiner, Franklin Valaski, looking as if he'd
taken a two-minute shower, crawling into a back pew.
It seemed that every old conch in Key West had turned
out.

She said goodbye to her grandfather, to the world's
finest storyteller and the man who had taught her to draw
and had given her the world. The service ended, and it
was time to move on to the cemetery.

She tried not to focus on her mother's name, beautifully etched in brass on the stone wall of the small family
mausoleum. The Key West cemetery was eclectic, with
many graves above ground as they were in New Orleans,
and for the same reason. All kids who grew up there
knew that a vicious hurricane in the mid-eighteen hundreds had sent bodies floating down Duval from other
sites. This ground had been chosen because it was in
the center of the island at the time, and on high ground.
There were little mausoleums here and there, in-ground
interments and even a grave that looked as if it were a
small brick smokehouse. There were sections and monu-
ments. The cemetery was in the true spirit of Key West,
with one grave that made the profound statement, "I told
you I was sick."

Kelsey stood outside the family mausoleum she hadn't
seen since her mother's funeral.

It was while they were there, with Liam not far from
her, that she felt a strange touch.

It was a comforting touch, as if someone had reached
out to stroke her cheek gently. She heard a voice speak
softly.

"He rests in peace. He was a good man, and he has now entered into the final great adventure, where he will do well."

She turned around, looking for the speaker who had given her the kind words. Liam was to her left, having just spoken softly to Katie. Sean O'Hara, Katie and Vanessa were just behind her, a respectful step back.

Katie, however, was frowning.

At someone who wasn't there.

She found herself closing her eyes and trying to feel the air around her. Silly. There was nothing there, and she had imagined the words, or a friend had come close....

The service finished. She went to throw a rose on the grave, and others followed suit. Cutter Merlin's coffin was carried into the mausoleum by representatives from the funeral home, Liam, David, Ted and Jonas.

The grave would be sealed later. People she knew, and people she didn't know, came by to squeeze her hand and remark that Cutter had been an extraordinary human being. Jamie O'Hara was there, assuring his nephew and niece to take their time; he had others working, as they'd arranged for a good Irish sendoff for Cutter at O'Hara's, a celebration of the life he had lived.

Alice and Esther Beckett came to her, supported by David and Liam.

"Oh, child! It was a wonderful service," Alice said.

"Nonsense, my dear," Esther told her. "Cutter was a blessed man, living all those years, and really living while he could. Too many old geezers—ah, well, hmm, like Alice and myself!—have given up on adventure. You be proud of Cutter, and all that he did!"

"I am very proud," Kelsey assured them.

"And you come see us, dear, promise?" Esther asked.

Alice took her hands. "Oh, Kelsey, dear! You are just beautiful, even more beautiful than your sainted mother, may she rest in peace. Thank God you've come home to us. Liam, didn't I tell you once? I knew that Kelsey would come home to us. Remember, dear, we must never live for the past. Only for the present, and a bit for the future."

Esther grinned wickedly. "Right now, I'm believing in the present. At my age, dear, one doesn't count on a future."

"Oh, Esther, we all pray you'll be with us much, much longer!" Liam said.

She smacked him sharply on the arm. "A few good years, my boy. Then you'll gracefully let me go. Now, you two young people come to see us, you hear? Where is my dear Betsy? She'll see us home."

Betsy was the woman working for them. She was young, kind, had glossy dark skin and spoke with a beautiful and melodic Bahamian accent. She gave Kelsey condolences and led her charges away, Liam assisting them over the ground of the cemetery.

More people came to offer their sympathy and welcome, Joe Richter among them. He frowned, taking her hands. "Kelsey, I've heard about that guitarist fellow being found dead on the property. You might want to stay somewhere else while… Well, I just don't know how safe that house is, young lady!"

"Why?" she asked him.

"Well—the fellow was dead, Kelsey!"

"I don't know if I ever knew him, Mr. Richter. I doubt if it had anything to do with the house or me, really."

He shook his head, unhappy. "It's a strange place, Kelsey."

She found herself remembering that he had said he hadn't seen her grandfather in months while his secretary had said that he'd been out recently. She made a mental note to mention the fact to Liam.

It was right after Jamie O'Hara stopped by to give his condolences and kiss her cheek that she noticed Katie, David, Sean, Liam and Vanessa standing over by the Beckett mausoleum. They all seemed to be in the midst of a strange conversation, talking and yet not seeming to be looking at one another. It was bizarre, and she wanted to walk over, but others kept coming by, and she couldn't be rude enough to ignore what seemed to be sincere sympathy.

Liam looked up, as if he knew she was watching him. He smiled and waved.

But they all looked so odd. As if they were talking to air.

It was a cemetery. Maybe they were talking to ghosts.

She thanked a stranger for his kind words and made her escape. But before she got across the cemetery to see them, she heard her name being called.

"Kelsey, Kelsey, my poor, dear girl!"

She turned around, stunned to see her partner, Avery Slater, tall, handsome, muscled and as well-dressed as ever, racing across the cemetery to her.

"Avery!" she managed.

He reached her, wrapped his arms around her and pulled her close. He drew back, studying her face. "My poor, poor, Kelsey. I'm sorry I'm late. But I'm here now. And I'll stand by you. Everything is going to be all right, my love. He passed in the right time. He had a long life."

"Avery. You're here," she said.

"Well, of course, I'm here. You're my partner," he said.

Kelsey noticed the group over by the Beckett mausoleum. They were all staring at her, and it looked as if they had received a group Botox injection, they appeared so surprised.

"Come on, you need to meet some of my old friends," she told him. She remembered to hug him, then reached up and planted a kiss on his cheek. "Thank you. What you did was so sweet, so kind. But I'm really all right. Really, I'm all right. I do have friends here, Avery. Really good friends."

"No!" he said, his dark eyes flashing. "I was by the Merlin house…your house. I saw all the crime tape. You may have friends, but now I'm here. The police wouldn't let me near the property. They said a man was found dead on your beach today."

"Yes, but…we don't know what happened."

"That house may be cursed!" he said.

"Avery, I don't believe in houses being cursed."

Liam reached them. He didn't appear as stunned; he was still frowning, and obviously confused. He was followed by their entire contingent.

"You have a posse?" Avery whispered.

She began introductions. The group were wonderfully accepting and friendly—and obviously beyond curious and in awe. Well, Avery was beautiful. Simply beautiful, and because he was so perfectly sculpted, he looked rough and tough and rugged. There was no way she was going to make the announcement that she wasn't sleeping with him to everyone close to her, that Avery was a dear friend and just that, and gay. Announcing his sexual preference was something she left to him, and he told those he chose to tell.

"So you came down to be with Kelsey now. That's wonderful of you," Katie said.

"She's the best. She's like a wife but with her own house, so I can go home if she gets in the mood to nag. And I watch out for her, of course. When we go out. You know, to bars and the like. Oh, not that she's a boozer," Avery said. He looked around the crowd and smiled at Liam. "So, you're the cop. What's going on with the body?"

"Too soon to know much. The crime-scene folk are still scouring the property, looking for any kind of murder weapon. There were a couple of break-ins at the house before Kelsey got here, but we've secured the house itself now. We'll find out what happened," Liam assured him. "Now, I believe, we should get over to O'Hara's."

"O'Hara's?" Avery asked.

"My uncle's friendly neighborhood pub," Katie told Avery. "The reception."

"Of course," Avery said. He paused for a minute. "I have a car. Am I taking it?"

It was agreed that Avery could leave his car at the funeral home for the time being. Liam made the call, and then, in a group—since the other cars were parked legally around the cemetery—they began the four-block walk to O'Hara's.

When they got there, another good family friend, Marty, had a group of his "pirate" friends playing together as a small band. They played quietly, and they mixed laments with sonnets and soft songs that seemed to fit the bill just right; they weren't making the room fall apart, and yet, both the fact that it was a celebration of a good life and the mourning of a passing seemed to have been met perfectly.

Kelsey was sitting at the bar, Avery at her side, Sean telling her a story about Cutter giving drifters dollar bills and hamburgers, when Katie sidled into the chair next to her.

When the story was finished and Jamie had moved on, Katie whispered, "That is surely one of the most gorgeous men I have ever seen. This is really none of my business, but…well, yes, it is—Liam is a dear friend. Wait, he will be my cousin-in-law. Were you and Avery involved?"

Kelsey looked at her and smiled. "No. Never. I'm not his type."

"And he's not your type?" Katie asked.

Kelsey laughed. "No."

Katie frowned and said softly, "He's really—just the most stunning man I've ever seen."

David had come up behind her and slipped his arms around her. "The most stunning?" he teased.

Katie winced. "Almost the most stunning," she amended.

Kelsey decided to be merciful. "I'm not his orientation," she said.

"Well, that is a relief!" David said.

Avery turned then, grinning. "Wish the guys I fell for thought I was the most gorgeous thing in the world," he said.

"Hey, it's none of our business," David said.

"Oh, hell, yes, it is—we're very nosy," Katie said.

"Watch out—she's already plotting," David warned him. "Thinking of friends who would love to meet you."

She wasn't sure if Liam heard the remark or not, but he came up behind her then. "I have to go, but I'll be back as soon as possible."

"Can I go back to the house?" she asked him.

"She won't be alone," Avery assured him.

He glanced at Avery and tried to smile. It was a weak effort. "That's great," he said. "I know David and Katie and Sean and Vanessa and maybe some of the others can hang in for a while, too. My cousin and his group are editing a documentary on strange incidents around here, so they're on their own schedules. Well, except for Katie, but she's off tonight, anyway."

"Whatever," Avery said staunchly. "I won't be leaving her."

"I'll call you as soon as I can leave today," Liam said. He grimaced, meeting her eyes. "I do have to deal with Gary White. He was a drifter, but not an evil man, and every human being deserves justice. I will find out what happened to him."

He looked awkward, as if he wanted to kiss her cheek or give her a hug but wasn't sure if it was appropriate. She stood up and put her arms around him. He held her close for a long minute. He lifted her chin and whispered softly, "Is it cool if I still hang around the house, too?"

"I wouldn't have it any other way," she assured him.

She watched Liam go. And she knew that to her mind, he was the most stunning and beautiful man she had ever known.

Liam was barely out of the bar before his phone rang. It was Katie.

She wasted no time.

"He's gay," she said.

He almost laughed out loud. He'd realized, when he'd seen the man and it had seemed that his entire body knotted with jealousy, that the way he felt about Kelsey had to include trust. If she'd been that close with someone in California, Kelsey would have told him. He hadn't understood completely, but he was going to go on trust.

"Did you hear me? It's all right, Liam. Oh, my God, though, I can think of so many friends for him!"

"Katie, whoa, calm down. He may be in a relationship in California already."

"I didn't want you to be worried."

"I wasn't worried."

"Like hell!" She laughed.

"Okay, I was a little worried. The guy could win in Olympic wrestling. But I'm glad he's here, because he'll hang tightly with her while everything is sorted out," Liam said.

"Yeah? You think that finding Gary White's body could have anything to do with Cutter Merlin, Kelsey or the Merlin house?" Katie asked.

"Let's just say I believe…I don't know what I believe. But I won't stop until I find the truth. I've got to work, Katie. Hang in there for me, huh?"

"We're all here," she assured him.

He thanked her and hung up. He headed first to his office, sinking into his chair. The desk sergeant gave him slips with all the calls they had received from the local media, so he quickly wrote up a statement for what they knew thus far and set the desk sergeant to returning the calls with the information. It was a mistake to tell media "no comment."

They would make up their own comments. And Key West was certainly small enough for everyone out there to know that the body of a local had been found on the Merlin property.

Liam's first order of business was to find Chris Vargas. He and Gary White had been caught together seeking some small item to steal from the Merlin estate.

A walk down Duval Street and a few questions to old conchs and fresh water conchs might help him find out where Vargas had last been seen. Bartholomew, who had been pacing quietly beside him, said, "You know, she saw me today. Or she heard me… Felt me, at least."

"What are you talking about?" Liam asked.

"Kelsey Donovan. She was rather breaking my heart at the cemetery. I touched her cheek. I whispered to her. She heard me," Bartholomew said. "You should tell her that I exist."

"Just like that. Hey…you sensed something at the cemetery. Don't worry. It's Bartholomew, the ghost of a pirate—"

"Good Lord, when will you stop saying that? I was a privateer," Bartholomew interrupted, deeply aggravated. "Over and over again, I must explain this fact!"

"I'm sorry. Truly sorry," Liam said, almost as aggravated. "You *look* like a pirate."

"Then every man of my decade looked like a pirate, as well," Bartholomew said.

"All right, so we associate the fashion of the era with pirates," Liam said, distracted. "Bartholomew, I have a dead body on my hands. I think the fellow was murdered, because I don't think he headed out to the Merlin property to die of natural causes or to commit suicide. We need to concentrate on the *murder*."

"You don't know that it was a murder. You don't know that Cutter Merlin was murdered," Bartholomew protested.

Liam stopped in the street and stared at him.

"All right, so…there is something going on at the house, and it certainly looks as if the fellow, Gary White, was murdered," Bartholomew said. "But I think you're overlooking someone who can really help you solve everything that's going on."

"Oh? Who?"

Bartholomew looked at him seriously. "Kelsey Donovan," he said.

Liam paused, hands on his hips. "Okay, Bartholomew, when you think that she has actually seen you, we'll bring her on the paranormal side. Otherwise, I can't just ask her to go into a trance or something and connect with the ghosts of her dead grandfather, her mother—or Gary White!"

"She'll see me soon enough," Bartholomew assured him. "It would be easier if you just told her about me first, but…"

Liam groaned and kept walking. He realized a moment later that the *privateer* was no longer following him.

He stopped by a coffee shop and questioned a man who hired Vargas now and then for cleanup work. The man shrugged and told him that when Vargas wasn't working, he usually spent his days on U.S. 1 with an inventive sign so that he could beg cash from visitors.

Liam drove around the island and found that Vargas was doing exactly that—he had a sign that proclaimed him a Desert Storm vet, a family man with kids to feed, who was just out of luck.

Vargas saw him, and paled.

Liam parked his car and walked over to the sidewalk by the light where Vargas had been begging.

"You gonna arrest me?" Vargas asked.

"I should."

"I'll quit right now," Vargas said earnestly. "It's just been bad lately, you know? I mean, stockbrokers are out of work, you know?"

"Yes, it's been a bad time," Liam agreed.

"So…you gonna give me a break?" Vargas asked.

"I need to know about the last time you were with Gary White," Liam told him.

Vargas looked puzzled and scratched his head. "Gary? Well, we went to the Merlin place together—but you know that. You saw us together. Why? Oh, Lord, what did Gary do?"

"Gary is dead," Liam told him.

"Dead?" Vargas said, horrified.

"Dead."

"Dead—as in deceased?" Vargas said.

"Very. He's been dead for days—I don't know how many," Liam said.

"Oh, God!" Vargas said. He put his hands on the sides of his head and sank down to the sidewalk. "Dead… how? Where?"

"I found him on the Merlin estate. I don't know how he died yet. The medical examiner is going to have to answer that question," Liam said. "I need to know the last time you saw him."

"Oh, man…the last time I saw him was when you caught us in the house, Liam. He must have gone back. I told him not to. I told him that you were watching the place…that the cops would be keeping an eye on it. But…oh, man! You don't know what happened?" Vargas asked. He sounded scared.

"That's the last time you saw him?" Liam pressed.

Vargas squinted hard, thinking. "Yeah, that was the last time I saw him. Oh, man. He was young. He might have… Well, he could play a guitar. He might have had a chance."

"Yeah, he was young," Liam agreed.

"Lord, oh, Lord," Vargas said.

"Look, did you see or hear anything unusual? There were kids who had broken in as well, and they were terrified. They thought that someone—or something—was in the house with them," Liam said.

Vargas sniffed loudly, about to burst into tears. He shook his head. "No. But you know what? I think that Gary was scared that day. He wanted to get out. He seemed uncomfortable in the house, you know?"

"Uncomfortable—that's it?" Liam asked.

Vargas thought and lifted his hands. "Yeah. Well, you know, old man Merlin was a weirdo. There were all kinds of things in that house. I mean, there's a god-damned mummy in the place. Gargoyles. Coffins. He was weird. And those animal heads! It's a flipping horror house, really, you know?"

"There's absolutely nothing else you can tell me?" Liam asked.

Vargas thought. "Yeah, yeah, there is," he said.

"What?" Liam asked.

"There's the guy across the water."

"What guy across the water?" Liam asked.

"Jonas. Jonas Weston. The guy who owns the bed-and-breakfast. Hell, I remember him when he was a little kid. Always watching the place. You know what? I think, even when he was a kid, he was jealous. I think he loved the house—weird as it was. You know what else? I think he had a thing for Kelsey Donovan. Yeah.

Really. I think he wanted Kelsey Donovan, and I think he wanted Cutter Merlin's house. I mean, he has a place, yeah. But it's nothing like the Merlin house."

"Vargas, Jonas Weston has always lived across the water. You can see the Merlin house from his place. There would be no way that he wouldn't look at it," Liam said.

Vargas sniffed. "He's a fuckin' Peepin' Tom, that's what he is. I've seen it. I've seen him watching the place."

"You've seen him watching it?"

Vargas gave a brittle laugh. "Hell, yeah. Of course, I watched it before I went in. I watched him watching it. I had to wait until I knew he wasn't watching it before I went in with Gary!"

"You're telling me that you think that Jonas Weston did in Gary White—over the Merlin house?" Liam demanded.

Vargas shrugged. "What? You think Gary walked there to drop dead? No, I've seen that guy staring at the place, like he coveted it or something. And not just him. Oh, man. There's the lawyer."

"Richter? Joe Richter?" Liam asked.

Vargas nodded grimly. "He's always hanging around. Driving out… I mean, before old man Merlin died, that guy was always driving out to kind of case the place, too, you know?"

"No, I don't know. Not really."

"Ask him. Ask Richter if he's seen Gary White," Vargas said. Tears welled into his eyes. "Gary. Gary's dead. Maybe there is a curse on that house."

"You believe in curses, Vargas? You don't seem the type," Liam told him.

"There's one more person you should find out about," Vargas said.

"Oh? And who is that?" Liam asked.

"That fellow—*your* friend. Your friend Ted, the guy who is such a genius and such an expert on old stuff. Yeah, you ought to be talking to him," Vargas said.

"But shouldn't I be talking to you?" Liam asked. "You were with Gary—the two of you broke into the house together."

Vargas shook his head. "That's the ticket, sir. That's the ticket. Gary and I were in that house together. You need to check out all these people that you didn't catch in it. I'm giving you three men *I've seen* staring at that place, dying to get their hands on the things that are in it. Mr. Joseph Richter, fine attorney, Mr. Jonas Weston— and Ted and his girl, Jaden. They're the ones you ought to be grilling, Officer! Oh, yeah. Those folks." He paused, shaking his head. Tears welled in his eyes again. "Gary. Oh, Lord, poor, poor Gary."

He shivered ferociously.

"That house! That wretched Merlin house. There's something that goes on there. Something in the brick, the concrete, the wood." He looked up at Liam. "Don't you understand? There's something about it. It's the house. The house is evil. Merlin was up to something. Devil worship, had to be. And because of what he did…something is there. Something that has lived there. Something malignant. Something that is… I'm telling you, something that is pure *evil*."

9

It was five o'clock when they finally left O'Hara's. Kelsey felt exceptionally brave due to Avery's presence and several pints of Guinness. When Katie expressed concern and said that she and David and their immediate group would happily return to the house with her, she told Katie that she was going to be fine.

"There's crime-scene tape all over your property," Katie reminded her.

"Ah, but I don't plan to go home and play in the mangrove swamp," Kelsey assured her. She kissed her friend, who looked exhausted as well, and assured them all she was just going to take a nap, and she'd see everyone the following day. Clarinda needed to get to work, Jonas had to act as host at his B and B, and Jaden admitted she was eager to get back to the little box and the research she was doing. David, Sean and Vanessa had their own work to return to as well. Kelsey really was fine—and tired. Tomorrow, with Cutter now restfully buried, she would start reading the book he had been holding, *In Defense from Dark Magick*.

It was still daylight when Kelsey and Avery returned to her house.

They walked back to the funeral-home parking lot where Avery had left his rental car and drove the few blocks down Front Street to the little road that led out to the house.

The driveway and the house were free of crime scene tape. It still stretched from the far left of the house to the end of the land, encompassing all but the immediate front and back yards of the house and the house itself.

"Creepy," Avery announced.

"It's not creepy—it's a house. Cutter was a collector, that's all," Kelsey said.

"Creepy. I'm sorry, Kelsey, unless you're a born-again vampire or something, the place is damned creepy," Avery told her. "Seriously! Look at it. Peeling gray paint. Those windows that look like eyes." He shuddered. "And a dead body to boot!"

She turned to him. "Avery, are you afraid of staying here? Jonas Weston owns the place right across the water. He turned his family home into a bed-and-breakfast. I can get you a room over there if you'd prefer."

"Don't be ridiculous. I'm not a coward," Avery said. "I was just pointing out that the house is—creepy."

"Okay. Fine. It's creepy," she said.

She exited the passenger side of the car. She was feeling a little tipsy. The "celebration of life," or reception, or whatever they had hosted at O'Hara's, had lasted all day. It had included a few too many beers. Luckily, Avery had been determined not to have more than one or two drinks, and then switched to diet soda and coffee. She was feeling a little unbalanced—and a little defensive and belligerent, as well.

"I suppose that 'creepy' is good for the artist's soul," Avery said.

"Yes, and it's really a beautiful house, and Cutter was a fascinating man. He wanted to preserve artifacts and cultures. He always said that it was both good and bad that the world was homogenizing, and that it was incredibly important that we recognize cultures and beliefs." She headed for the house, dug in her purse and finally found her keys. By then, Avery had taken his suitcase from the car and joined her on the porch.

"Need help?" he asked.

"Funny, funny," she said.

"No, I'm being serious. Think you can get that key in the door?"

She twisted the key in the lock, staring at him.

"Hey, I think you should be a little inebriated. You found a body on your property this morning, and you buried your grandfather. Drink yourself into oblivion, if that will help."

"I don't want to be oblivious."

"Then we should make some coffee," Avery said.

Kelsey didn't want coffee; it seemed like a nap would be in order. She slipped her arms around Avery and hugged him tightly. "Luckily, you got here after the cleaning. I have to dig some sheets out of a closet to get you a bedroom going, and then I'd like to lie down for an hour or so? Will you forgive me?"

"Only because we were ahead enough on work so that I'm not going to go down because of you," Avery said, his voice gruff. He smiled. "You know, you're the stickler, always wanting to be a month up on everything."

"It works, huh?" she asked.

He shrugged. "I'm still on California time. Flew into Miami yesterday and took a puddle jumper down this morning. Body clock is still adjusting. Take your nap. I'll find a room, and sheets. I prefer taking care of myself, which I will do, and then grab a bit of a snooze myself."

"I would never be so rude—"

"Hey, you know me. I remake beds in hotel rooms. I'll be fine," he told her.

She kissed his cheek. "Explore my childhood, then. Enjoy," she told him, waving an arm to encompass the house. "It is truly entertaining. Mummy is by the fireplace. What else? Coffin is over there, gargoyles… Well, knock yourself out. Sheets are actually in bedroom closets."

"I'm already taking in the animal heads," Avery assured her. "And I'll find my way around just fine. Maybe I'll go out and see the sunset."

"No!" Kelsey cried. "No, no, no. Promise me you'll stay right in this house. I don't want you out on the property alone. Please, Avery—a body was discovered this morning."

"Hush, my darling, fine. I'm not going anywhere for a while. I'll see the famous Key West sunset on another night, all right?"

"Promise?"

"I promise."

Upstairs, in her room, she crashed down on her bed. She just needed an hour or so of sleep.

She had almost drifted off when she found herself jerking up again. She had to lock the door to her room.

Avery was in the house, she told herself.

But it didn't matter.

Even when Liam was actually sleeping with her, she had to lock the door to her room. It was paranoia, she told herself. Dangerous.

No. She wanted to be in the house.

She just wanted her door locked at all times. She wasn't sure why, but she feared sleeping to wake up and find that someone *was* there.

Someone staring down at her as she slept.

It was getting late in the day, but when he left Chris Vargas on the street, Liam called Franklin Valaski to see if he was still at the morgue.

He was.

Valaski, like many a Key West old timer, had taken the morning hours to attend the funeral of Cutter Merlin.

"Come on in, Liam. Come on in. I have Mr. Gary White on steel right now, and I can give you my initial findings," Valaski told him.

As he drove toward the medical examiner's office, Liam reflected on the events of the last several hours—finding Gary White's corpse, and Cutter Merlin's funeral. As long as he lived, he would never forget the look in the man's eyes.

Had Gary had that same look? They'd never know. Gary had no eyes left in his skull.

The corpse didn't look much better when he saw it stretched out on the gurney. Some of the skin had dried out from the sun, and was now stretched out taut, ripped in places over bleached white bone. Some of it looked like…soupy goo.

Gary White had been given the customary autopsy cuts and sewn back together.

The face was best described as gruesome. The mouth was open, contorted, as if it had frozen in a scream. A great deal of soft tissue had been eaten away by the sun, sea, salt and creatures of the mangroves.

"Not a pleasant sight, our old friend Gary," Valaski said.

"I don't know of any relatives. They're working on that at the station," Liam said.

"Well, let's hope they don't find any," Valaski said.

Liam nodded. The scent in the room was a horrendous mixture of chemicals and decomposition. Valaski handed him a white mask to filter the air. Liam accepted it without comment.

"Hell of a day, huh?" Valaski asked.

"Agreed. So?"

"Well, our friend Gary died of something like a pinpoint prick to his heart. Actually, the death appeared to have been a heart attack, or heart failure, but!" Valaski announced. "I'm an old buzzard, and I don't fall for many tricks. Even if a man is someone on the fringe of society. In this morgue, no matter how rich and powerful or poor and sad in life, we find the truth."

"Franklin, there is no one more grateful for your

honor and your expertise," Liam told him, "but, come on. Please. Explain."

"Well, here you go. Come here…look at the scans. It might have appeared that the heart was ripped up soon after death, the body was in such a sad state. There are bits and pieces of sharp coral in the area of the peninsula spit where he was found—probably dredged up years ago when harbors were fashioned for the ships…or, who knows? I'm no geologist or geographer. God knows how we have more of a key now than we did before, though I suppose I could—"

"Franklin. All right. We're looking at an area where mangroves are growing, and thus it's enlarging constantly, and away from the beach that was also dredged out long ago, we have roots, we have crabs…and there's an occasional toss up of long-dead coral. I got that. So?"

"Well, where he was found, it just might have appeared that he'd fallen on rock, and thus causing this area—" Franklin pointed to a mass in Gary White's chest "—where the heart itself bled out. Aha! But before the chewing and decomposition, I don't believe there was a tear of any kind in the man's chest, or in his heart. This looks like it was caused by a needle of some kind. I don't think it was done by something so many centimeters in circumference as an ice pick, but…there is that possibility."

"He was murdered, and murdered by a slim stiletto-like object, possibly a needle, and, less likely but possibly, an ice pick," Liam said.

"Precisely!" Franklin Valaski said, looking pleased. "Well?"

"Well, a man was murdered and left to rot," Liam said.

"Yes, yes, but at least he didn't die like Cutter. He was cleanly murdered. No mystery—no strange look, no books or guns or talismans in his hands," Valaski said.

"Franklin, he was murdered," Liam said. "When?"

"I don't know exactly. It might have been three or four days, or maybe a week."

"What? You can't pin it down more than that?" Liam asked, dismayed.

Valaski shook his head. "There was water in the lungs, so if he hadn't died from the piercing of his heart, he would have drowned. I believe he was caught under a root or something, beneath the water, but for how long, I don't know."

"I thought you people studied larvae, flies?"

Valaski rolled his eyes. "We *people* do. But he was underwater. No flies. No maggots. No larvae, not at first. It's impossible for me to tell you what day he was killed. Please, Liam! He was half-eaten. It's amazing I have what I do."

"I'm sorry. I'm just frustrated."

"Ah, yes. Man's inhumanity to man, but nothing as eerie as Cutter's death!"

Liam shook his head. "Please, Franklin. It's more of a mystery," Liam said.

"Oh?"

"Why on earth murder a poor, down-and-out man specifically on the Merlin property? There was nothing to steal from him. He wasn't high-powered. He didn't have a wife or a mistress. There was no reason in hell for anyone to kill him," Liam said.

"Well, you're quite right, Liam," Valaski agreed.

"Unless he saw something. Unless he knew something," Liam said.

"And so it does have to do with Cutter and the Merlin house," Valaski said.

Liam nodded. "He saw something, or he knew something, or..."

"Or?"

"Or he was simply the right victim, lured out to the Cutter estate because he was an easy mark. No family, a drifter, no friends who would immediately worry about his whereabouts."

"Why would anyone kill for that reason? Unless you have a serial killer on your hands who just seeks out victims," Valaski said.

"Not this time, Doc," Liam said.

"Then?"

"He may have been lured out to the Merlin house and murdered there precisely because the property had belonged to Cutter Merlin. And someone wants everyone to be afraid of the house, to think that it's hexed or cursed."

Valaski stared at him, frowning. Then he shrugged. "I solve the mystery of the body, my friend. The mystery of murder is up to you."

Darkness had fallen when Kelsey awoke.

She felt puzzled for a moment, not sure where she

was. Then she knew, of course. She remembered the compulsion that she had to keep her door locked or she would awaken to find someone staring at her.

She felt a moment's pure terror; there was someone there. Someone just staring at her, watching her sleep.

She jerked up in panic, desperate for light. She felt encompassed by the night, certain someone was there and horribly afraid that she would discover that she was right.

She wasn't alone; there was someone with her, watching her in silence.

She jumped out of the bed and stumbled to the light switch by the wall. Her room was instantly bathed in a glow, and she flung around in terror, searching out every corner of the room.

The edge of her fear began to fade away. She gave herself a shake. She was alone. It had been her imagination, the paranoia that was growing within her—even while she insisted she wasn't afraid of the house.

The bathroom!

She strode to it with long, angry footsteps. She had to *see* if someone was there. Better to face whomever or whatever it was!

But the bathroom was empty.

She shuddered and then laughed aloud at herself.

She wasn't even alone in the house. Avery was somewhere napping, poking through the oddities or reading and sipping a cup of tea.

She walked back and checked her door; it was still locked.

She shook her head, smiling at her own foolishness,

and opened the door to the hallway. The entire house was dark.

With the glow from her room guiding her, she walked along the hallway and turned on the overhead light.

"Avery?" she said her friend's name softly and decided he had to be in one of the rooms upstairs, sleeping. She backtracked. He would have chosen the guest room just a few doors down from her own. She opened the door quietly and saw that Avery was indeed there, snoring softly.

"Ah, yes, gorgeous, but you do snore!" she whispered affectionately. She closed the door again, letting him sleep. It couldn't be very late; Liam would have been back. She glanced at her watch. It was just seven.

A two-hour nap had been good. She had slept off the effects of the Guinness and felt alert and decent. When Liam returned, she'd find out if they would just cook in or take Avery out to a good Key West seafood restaurant. Avery ate just about everything, but he loved fish.

She headed toward the stairway.

Then she froze.

The upstairs hall light wasn't enough to clearly illuminate the grand parlor below.

The parlor with its mounted heads, gargoyle, mummy, coffin and more.

Between two neat stacks of boxes and crates, near the authentic voodoo altar and fireplace, there was a shadow, dark against gray, swirling and moving in the night.

She stared in pure open-mouthed terror as the thing rose and waved, wafted, disappeared and returned.

It seemed like a massive black swatch of evil, taunting and teasing her.

It was malignant; it was the darkness that lived in the house, that came out and killed.

She wanted to scream; the sound choked in her throat. She wanted to turn and flee down the hallway and waken Avery, but she couldn't.

Rising, falling, rising, falling...

And there was a sound. Like a growl on the air, a whir, a laugh. Oh, God, yes, a soft laughing sound that mocked her.

She blinked.

It didn't go away.

She worked her throat.

And then, somehow, she found the light switch for the stairway, and the switch that brought the parlor alive with a brilliant glow.

And it was still there, sleek and black, and moving...!

Turn! Scream!

She did neither. She was so frozen, she stared at it. And then, as she did so, she realized that it was doing the same thing, over and over again. And she wasn't hearing a growl, a laugh, a whisper or any such thing. It was a *whir,* like the sound of a motor.

"What the hell?" she demanded, speaking aloud.

Angrily she walked down the stairs, straight toward the boxes. The closer she came, the more evident it was that she was seeing some kind of a magician's trick.

When she reached the ground level and the boxes,

crates and voodoo altar, she almost laughed aloud at herself.

One of the large crates was open. The evil, black, malignant shadow was nothing but a silky cloth, and it was springing up from a motorized board that sat in the open crate.

"Cutter!" she said, shaking her head. "Great trick! You almost gave your granddaughter a heart attack, you dear old geezer!"

She caught the flying material and twisted it around enough to see that it was controlled by wires, and the wires were controlled by a motor within the box and a simple switch turned it off. Something must have triggered it to start.

She heard her cell phone ringing from a distance, and she tried to remember where it was. In her purse, up the stairs, in her room. She hurried back up the stairs.

"Hello?" She caught it when it rang again for the second time.

"Kelsey!" It was Liam.

"Yes!"

"Oh, my God, you had me so worried. Are you all right?"

"I'm fine, thanks, Liam. I'd fallen asleep. Avery is napping, too."

"Why are you so breathless?"

"I was downstairs, and I left the phone upstairs."

"Oh." He sounded relieved. However, she must have sounded strange.

"Then what's wrong?"

"Oh, I just gave myself a scare," she said.

"How? You weren't outside, in the secured area, were you?"

"No, no, of course not."

"What happened?"

She laughed. "I really have to go through Cutter's boxes. He's got some magic tricks in them. He has something like a magician's gig—black sheets that shoot up out of a crate."

"What?"

"It's all right, it's all right, really. It's a mechanized magician's trick, that's all. Where are you?" She tried to be casual. "I was just wondering if you wanted to stay and hang here and get started on something, or if you'd like dinner out."

She thought that he hesitated a minute. "I'll be right there," he said. "Then we'll decide, if that's all right. But don't do anything until I get there, okay? It's locked up tight, right?"

She laughed. "Yes, sir, it's locked up tight. Honestly. We came home, took naps and haven't been out. I swear."

"I'll be right there."

He hung up.

The house seemed too silent. Kelsey wanted to start reading the book her grandfather had been holding when he died, so she took it from the bedside table where she'd decided to keep it. She found her iPod and went downstairs. She turned on every light, brewed herself a cup of tea and walked past the crates with the magic trick toward Cutter's office.

She felt uneasy. She had spent so much time working

in the house. She didn't remember seeing the open crate, or the magic trick. She set the tea and the book down, went back and opened the crate again.

She was perplexed. Magic tricks weren't Cutter's interest. The voodoo altar had been a piece of history—it had been taken from an old home just outside the French Quarter in New Orleans, and Cutter had purchased it from the new owner, who intended a redo of the entire place. He had been a businessman, uninterested in voodoo.

The mummy…Egyptian history. The coffin, a beautiful piece of Victorian funerary art. He had never, in her memory, purchased a cheap magician's trick. Then again, she hadn't really begun to go through his ledgers yet.

For some reason, the book seemed more important.

She went into Cutter's library and took a seat behind his desk. Even with every light in the house on, she was surprised to still feel uncomfortable. Looking around, she found herself believing that something was just slightly out of place.

As if someone had been there.

But no one had been in the house.

Or had they?

Had someone gotten in somehow, set up the magic trick to scare her and moved things around in Cutter's study?

She stood up uneasily. She heard the brass knocker at the door, and she jumped. She laughed nervously when she realized that Liam had arrived. She checked that it was him through the peephole and let him in.

He clutched her shoulders and looked into her eyes. "You're all right—really all right?" he asked her.

She smiled. "Yes, of course. Liam, I have an odd request."

"Oh?"

"Is it possible to dust that magic box for finger-prints?"

He arched his brows. "Yes. Why? You don't think that someone was in here, do you?"

"I don't see how anyone could have been in here. The place was rekeyed. We've bolted all the windows, and the doors have been locked," she said. "I don't know, I guess it's bizarre, but…"

He didn't act as if she was getting paranoid or losing her grip on reality. She wasn't sure that made her feel better.

"Avery is with you, right?" he asked.

She smiled. "Yes. He's napping upstairs. I guess we should wake him, or he'll never sleep tonight."

"Maybe he wants to do the town tonight," Liam suggested.

"Maybe," she said with a shrug. "I was about to start reading the book. *In Defense from Dark Magick.* I thought it might give me an insight into Cutter's state of mind."

"It might." He frowned. "By the way, where's the shot-gun he was holding? It was left by the fireplace when his body was taken."

She frowned. "I believe someone must have moved it the other day, when we were cleaning. I don't actually remember seeing it."

"Hmm. I'm thinking we should find it. You read—I'll start looking for it," he said.

"Read? Doesn't anyone ever think about eating around here?" Avery asked suddenly. They looked to the top of the stairs. He was standing there, grinning down at them. She felt a moment's discomfort, seeing him there and remembering her mother's fall.

"Come down here, now," she said.

He frowned at her tone, but obliged.

"Of course we eat," Liam assured him. "We'll head out to Duval Street. There's a nice little place that isn't too touristy right off of Front Street."

"Lovely," Avery agreed.

Liam looked at Kelsey. "We're meeting Jaden and Ted," he told her.

"Oh, how nice," she replied.

"Ten minutes? I'm going to hop in the shower," he said.

"Very clean," she teased.

He hesitated. "I've been back at the morgue," he said.

"Oh, of course," she said. "Oh, Liam, I feel horrible. What did you find out?"

"Gary White was murdered. Someone pricked him in the heart, and he bled out internally."

Kelsey gasped. "How horrible!"

"When?" Avery asked.

Liam shook his head. "Days ago, maybe a week. Valaski can't really tell. The body was too compromised."

"But…shouldn't bugs tell him…or…larvae or…"

"No. He was probably underwater at first. But he

was murdered, and he was murdered here, on this property."

"Kelsey, you've got to leave now. Come back to California!" Avery insisted.

She felt numb, uncertain. There were so many possibilities. She'd been scared. Very scared. But Avery was here now, and when Liam was working, she wouldn't be alone.

It was possible that this man's death had to do with drugs or a heist gone wrong; he had broken into her house. He had lived in a world where bad things happened.

Or...

There was also the possibility that someone was trying to scare her out of her grandfather's house. That someone might have done something to hurt Cutter.

She didn't want to be scared away.

"Avery, you're here now, and Liam is here every night," she said.

"Oh," Avery said, looking at the two of them.

She looked at Liam. "I don't want to be scared out of here. I want to know what happened. I want to have answers. I need to be here—I haven't begun working on his collection. Let's go to dinner. Is there a reason we're meeting Jaden and Ted?" she asked.

"Yes," Liam said. "Jaden thinks she's found out something about the little gold reliquary box that Cutter was holding when he died."

One of the nicest things about the people in Key West was that they were quickly accepting of friends of friends.

Ted and Jaden greeted Kelsey as if she'd never gone away, and greeted Avery warmly, even though they had only met him that day.

Once they were all seated, before they ordered drinks, Liam asked, "All right, come on. Give. What have you discovered?"

Jaden reached into her bag for a book. For a moment, Liam thought that she was going to produce the book that was missing from the library, but she did not. She brought out a large hardcover book on reliquaries of the fourteen hundreds.

"Wow. It's that old?" Kelsey asked.

"Yes and no," Jaden said.

"What do you mean?" Liam asked her.

"Well!" Jaden said, leaning closer. "I found the exact reliquary. I'll show you!" She opened the book. There was a painting done by an obscure artist from the time period. It showed a man in a monk's robe holding what looked to be the same reliquary.

"So it is that old?" Kelsey said, puzzled.

"The reliquary first held a fragment of a charred piece of bone obtained after Joan of Arc's death. The little gold ball that held the saint's relic inside the box was designed by the monk in the picture, Brother Antoine. He also designed the little casket, or box, that holds the gold ball."

"So, it was considered an especially holy item," Kelsey said. "If my grandfather had such an object, I honestly believe he would have wanted to return it to the Catholic Church."

"Maybe. There's more to the story, which perhaps Cutter Merlin knew—and then again, maybe he didn't," Ted said, nodding sagely.

"Was such a relic supposed to ward off evil?" Liam asked.

"Joan of Arc became an incredibly honored saint, so of course," Jaden said. "She was a victim of betrayal after serving king and country, and it was said that the fires for her burning were set before sentence was pronounced on her. She recanted her pleas, but in the end was true to herself, her God and her voices. In the fire, she was heard to call out to Jesus many times, and those in the crowd were brought to pity. It was in the marketplace in Rouen, and when she was dead it was recorded that her ashes were spread in the Seine. Naturally, there were holy men and women who sought a piece of such a famous or infamous woman—there were many such beliefs. The severed fingers of dead men were believed to hold different magical properties depending on whether the deceased had been a murderer, a thief—or a saint. Any relic with an historical claim to holding so much as an ash from Joan of Arc would be highly esteemed."

"That's why Cutter was holding it, surely," Avery told Kelsey. He patted her hand.

Kelsey was staring at Jaden, and Jaden looked as if she were about to burst. But she held silent as a waitress came to take their drink order and ask about appetizers.

Kelsey looked at them all and then at the waitress, asking if they could give her the entire order. It was obvious Kelsey was trying to be polite but was far too anxious for many interruptions.

Their puzzled waitress agreed and discreetly moved on.

"Jaden, spit it out!" Kelsey begged. "What else are you trying to say? Cutter was using it in some kind of a spell against evil? That's why he held the book, too, *In Defense from Dark Magic*?"

"We need the next book," Jaden said. She reached into her bag and pulled out another. It was titled *Nazi Treasures Secreted from Germany*.

"Okay, so the Nazis stole the relic from the monks?" Kelsey asked.

Jaden nodded. "The relic was at a church in Rouen, in the center of the altar. It was taken—not for holy purposes, but for the gold. The relic was secondary—the gold was what they valued."

Kelsey sat back, puzzled. "I'm lost. Cutter was sitting in the house, the book, the relic and a shotgun on his lap. We're assuming he was frightened by something or someone. But if the person who had frightened him so badly was there, wouldn't he have taken the relic?"

"If there was someone there, he might have tried to take the relic," Jaden said.

Liam spoke up. "All right, wait. He was dead quite a while before I found him. If someone had been there to steal the relic, that person had plenty of time to take it."

"Yes. But you haven't heard the rest." She flipped open the second book. "Herr Hubert Eichorn. She pointed to the picture of a man in a distinguished pose before a fireplace. "He was never in the German military. He was a 'consultant.' He was a consultant on how to most quickly and efficiently kill people—he was a chemist. He had left the bunker long before Hitler's last days, and he knew he had to get out of Germany. He left the country disguised as a priest—carrying the reliquary."

"All right, so that's how it left Germany," Kelsey said. "I'm still—"

"Ahem!" Jaden said. "Here!" She flipped a page in the book. They saw a picture of a brilliant-cut but unset diamond. It was an old picture, and the caption beneath it announced that it had been taken in 1942. "The reliquary is worth ten to twenty thousand dollars. This diamond—called the Koln diamond, a gift from a prince to his princess at the time of Joan's death, is worth a million or more."

"They make diamonds worth that much?" Avery said.

"Perfect clarity, perfect hue…nearly ten carats. A size that fit perfectly into the reliquary," Jaden said.

Kelsey sat back, staring at her. "Jaden, you're telling me that this diamond was in the casket?"

Jaden shook her head. "That's the point. The diamond isn't in this reliquary."

"So it was taken?" Liam asked.

"No, I don't think so," Jaden said.

"And why not?" Kelsey asked.

"Because this reliquary is a fake!" Jaden announced, sitting back, flushed and triumphant.

"What?" Liam, Kelsey and Avery asked simultaneously.

Jaden reached into her bag again, producing a little gold ball. "This is your gold ball, Kelsey, or the gold ball from the reliquary. It's really perfect. The workmanship is incredible. It's worth ten to twenty thousand, so it seems that a thief should have taken it. But it's nothing next to the diamond. I don't know who made this, or why, but our tests have dated it back to the early twentieth century. So, the thief must have figured out that Cutter didn't have the real reliquary, and so he left it."

Kelsey stared at her blankly. "That doesn't make sense. If you were a thief—why not at least take something that was worth twenty thousand dollars or so?"

"I don't know that," Jaden said. She fell silent as their drinks were delivered. "I can only tell you what I discovered. There was no sign of bone or ash in the little gold ball."

"So what was in it?" Liam asked.

Jaden grimaced and produced her last object from her bag. It was a little swastika on a gold pin. "Worth something, I imagine, even if distasteful," she said.

"None of it makes any sense," Kelsey said.

"Actually, it does. It makes perfect sense," Liam said.

They all looked at him. He didn't explain right away. "Hey, Jaden, I saw that you and Ted visited the rare-book room at the library recently," he said, sipping his iced tea.

They both looked at him blankly, and then at each other. "Recently, and always," Ted said. "How do you think we do research? Online, yes, but we have to look at rare books for the pieces we're asked to restore. Why?"

"Just think back for a minute, did you ever take out a book called *Key West, Satanism, Peter Edwards and the Abel and Aleister Crowley Connection*?" Liam asked.

It seemed as if the entire table was looking at him as if he had lost his mind.

"I've never even heard of such a book," Jaden said.

"Someone has. It's missing from the library," he said.

"And you're accusing us—of stealing a book?" Ted asked, sitting back.

"No, I was asking if you happened to have it," Liam said. He noted that Bartholomew was sitting at an empty table near them, studying the reactions everyone had to his questions and comments.

"I have never taken a rare book from the library, and I don't even know why I would want the one you're talking about," Jaden said. "Nor would I know why you would want it, Liam!"

He didn't rise to the bait. He leaned back casually himself. "I'm interested in the book because it supposedly has a reference to Cutter's book, *In Defense from Dark Magick*," he said.

"Where did you even hear about it?" Ted asked.

"Oh, some old-timers mentioned it. Apparently, there was a connection to Crowley and his interest in dark arts."

"Aleister Crowley was in Key West?" Jaden asked, still confused.

"No. A supposed relative. I was just asking because

your names were on the list of people who had been in the rare-book room. It wasn't an accusation," Liam said.

They both still appeared to be confused. "Well, you had best ask the rest of the people on the list," Jaden said. "I didn't take it. And if Ted has slipped it out for any reason—which he wouldn't have!—he'd tell you straight away."

"Hey! I didn't take the book," Ted protested.

"Of course not, dear," Jaden said, squeezing his hand.

"Who else was on the list?" Kelsey asked him.

"Mary Egans—" Liam began.

"A high-school teacher," Jaden said, dismissing the possibility.

Liam shrugged. "Barney Thibault."

"He'd die before he'd steal a piece of gum!" Ted said.

"I agree," Liam told him. "Someone named George Penner—I don't know the name, and neither did the librarian. Jonas—"

"Our Jonas?" Jaden demanded.

"Let him talk, please," Ted said.

Liam nodded. "Yes, our Jonas. Oh, and Joe Richter."

"Richter!" Kelsey said.

Liam studied her. "What?"

"I—I'm not sure." She shook her head and hiked her shoulders. "Richter can't be guilty of anything. He had free access to Cutter's place. He was the attorney. He had the only access, really, for a while. I mean, once you reported Cutter dead."

There was something more there, Liam thought, but he'd ask her later.

"Then there was someone named Bel Arcowley. Do you know him—or her?" he asked.

Ted and Jaden looked at him solemnly, shaking their heads.

"Why is the book so important?" Kelsey asked.

"I don't know," Liam said. "I'd just like to find it."

"You know, I can do a rare-book search for you tomorrow. There has to be a copy somewhere else," Jaden said.

"I can do a search," Liam said.

Jaden sniffed. "Bet I can do a better search than you!"

He smiled. "All right, then. Thanks. Do a search for me, will you?"

She nodded.

Their food arrived. The tension that had gone around the table eased somewhat. He worried that he might be ruining a long running and close friendship.

He had no choice.

Kelsey toyed with the blackened grouper on her plate. She stared at him and asked, "So what do you think is going on?"

He wasn't sure. Maybe it was best to just state his suspicions.

He shrugged.

He realized that they were all silent, staring at him, including Avery, who was wide-eyed.

"Oh," he said, and set down his fork. "I have a theory. The thief—or murderer, as he might be—wanted the reliquary. Cutter knew that it was a fake, and that was why he had the shotgun, though, of course, he never used it. When Cutter was dead, the thief did try to take the reliquary, but discovered it was a fake."

"Still worth money!" Kelsey reminded him.

"But not compared to the real prize," Liam said. "I'm not sure who did know about it, but I think that Cutter had the fake—and the original. The thief didn't take the fake because he was determined to find the original. While Cutter sat there, dead but undiscovered, he had a chance to search the house. But then I came when Cutter didn't pick up the mail. The thief was probably there when the kids broke into the house—and scared them half to death. He was probably there when Gary White and Chris Vargas broke in as well, and went back to work once I had shooed them out. Looking for anything in that house is like looking for a needle in a haystack. He was neat as he searched about, knowing that he was after the real prize. If he gave himself away, how could he get back in to search? Now, however, we have every window bolted and new locks on the doors. And, of course, Kelsey has a cop sleeping with her, as well."

Avery cleared his throat. "I might not exactly be sleeping with her, but I'm not chopped liver," he said.

Kelsey stared at Liam in silence. So did Ted and Jaden.

Jaden cleared her throat and spoke at last. "So—you think that this will make whoever it was give up the quest?"

"No, I don't. I think that Gary died because of something he knew or saw."

Jaden gasped and shook her head. "No, no…Cutter was old. He might have had a heart attack no matter what. But…you're saying Gary White was *murdered?* We still have the death penalty in this state for murder!"

"True," Liam said. "But people have committed murder for a lot less than a million dollars."

"But…" Ted spoke and broke off, confused. "Cutter Merlin died of a heart attack. He was holding a book, this little reliquary and a shotgun." He looked at them both. "You have the book, right?"

Kelsey nodded. "In safekeeping?" He lifted his hand, staring at Liam. "*Don't tell anyone where.* Liam will start accusing of us of stealing another book."

"I was asking, not accusing," Liam said. "For all I knew, you might have slipped it out just to borrow it because you needed it for more research, and meant to put it back."

"Oh, yeah. Jaden and I sit up nights and think about new ways to worship Satan," Ted said, an edge to his voice.

"It's on my mind every morning when I wake up, too," Jaden said.

"Hey," Liam said. "A man has been murdered. Cutter might have been frightened to death. Give me some slack. I have to ask questions."

"You're all old friends. Stop it. Let's think about it. Where do the books fit in?" Kelsey asked.

"I don't know. But that's what we have to find out," Liam said. "Would you pass the salt, please?"

***

He sat comfortably in the handsome chair at Cutter Merlin's desk. Three of them in the house now, and he was still invisible.

What a lovely time.

Last night, he had stood at the door to her room. He had imagined them together, and he had imagined the time when the cop would be there.

He had to be patient. Well, he'd been patient a very long time. Maybe he had never imagined it would really be this long, but in the end, the prize would make up for it all. Watching them…watching the idiots when they had found the body at last…well, that had been a thrill. Watching them—from the house!—while they had been so certain that their new locks, bolts and wary care could keep him out, was worth his effort.

He heard them coming home, and he quickly rose. It would be no good being found at the desk. That could ruin everything.

He turned away, feeling more powerful than Cutter Merlin, Pete Edwards, Satan himself—or the bastard, Liam Beckett.

He was invisible.

He had committed murder, and he was invisible.

He watched, he waited, he stalked.

And he was invisible.

For a moment, he felt a flash of anger so deep it shook him to the core.

He was invisible, yes.

But he hadn't found the real reliquary.

He gave himself a shake. He could hear their voices.

Kelsey knew where the real reliquary was, she had to, or she would. He would wait. Patience. So long, and just a little longer, then. And stalking Kelsey... Well, it was fascinating to consider what the end might finally be.

10

Despite the discovery of the decomposing body of Gary White, her grandfather's funeral and Liam's theory of the events surrounding her, Kelsey woke feeling rested, strong and ready to face anything that came her way. She stretched a hand out over the sheets, found that Liam's side of the bed was empty and sat up and stretched. She forgot sometimes that he was a cop, high in the city pecking order, with a great deal of responsibility.

She rose and headed to the bathroom to shower, then paused. If he wasn't in the room, the door was unlocked. She couldn't get over the need to lock her bedroom door. It was as if a sixth sense kept telling her that she needed to do so.

She obliged.

Last night, Liam had teased her.

"Okay...Avery doesn't have nightmares and decide to come crawling in, does he?"

They'd both been able to laugh, and she shook her head, and he humored her, as he had all along, and she had locked the door, fallen back into his arms, felt the breathless, heart-pounding emotion of being with him, and then the glorious, starkly carnal, wild and raw wonder of letting the world go away in his arms, lost in sensation, knowing nothing but the earthly force of their bodies. Surely she slept so well, so beautifully, so peacefully, because she was so replete, and because she was in his arms still, flesh damp and touching his, limbs entangled.

Showered, she unlocked her door and went downstairs. Liam was in the kitchen, dressed and ready for work, coffee cup in his hand as he read the paper.

"No way out, I guess. I tried to control the media, but there's always going to be sensationalism. Don't take it to heart," he told her.

She poured her own coffee and came to stand beside him, reading the headline.

Death Strikes Again at Cursed Merlin Estate.

"Hey," she said, sighing softly. "At least it's an estate. I'm so sorry for that poor fellow. Is he going to need help…being buried?"

"Probably."

"I'd like to take care of it—or Cutter would, more exactly," she said.

He set his coffee down and pulled her to him. His chin rested against the top of her head, and there was something wonderfully intimate and tender in the gesture. "That's nice," he whispered softly. Then he looked at her. "Hey, I just thought about something. Last night, when I was talking about the book that was missing from the rare-book room at the library and mentioned Richter, it seemed there was something you were going to say, but didn't."

"Oh, he'd said something about not having seen Cutter for a while, but his secretary told me he'd been out recently. But I still can't see how Joe Richter could be responsible for anything…or that he would *kill* over anything in Cutter's house. He did have free rein here."

"After Cutter was dead," Liam said.

Kelsey studied him for a minute. "How do you know that the people who registered in the rare-book room might have anything to do with this?"

"I don't. I have to start somewhere."

"But you don't even know all the people."

"I know the names—I'm going to run traces on the people I don't know. I don't have evidence, but I have a really good hunch, and I believe I'm right. Jaden really cast a light on things. A million-dollar diamond can create obsession, and an obsession can create a complicated case."

"Satanism—and diamonds," Kelsey said.

"Connected somehow," he assured her.

He was whispering, and they were close together. Touching. Kelsey started at the sound of Avery's voice.

"All right, all right, enough already," Avery said, entering the kitchen. He walked past the two of them, heading for the coffeepot. "So, you know, I have to admit, this is an amazing place. I'm a West Coast boy, but this is pretty cool. You've got a dolphin that hangs around by your dock, did you know that? Cool creature. I walked out, and it followed me, watching me. I was talking to it, and it's as if it listens to me."

Kelsey turned and leaned back against Liam. His

arms were around her waist, and she set her arms and hands on his, basking in the comfort of the moment.

Liam said, "Dolphins are incredible creatures. I have a friend at one of the facilities just a few islands up, over the Seven-Mile Bridge. They've done amazing research with them. They can count, they know colors and they definitely have personalities. This one may have escaped captivity. I'll make a few calls."

"And lock him back up?" Avery asked.

"If he was born in a facility, his life will best be spent in his—or her—home. You didn't check out the sex, did you?" Liam asked.

"I wouldn't know how to check out the sex," Avery said.

"When a male decides to show himself, you know," Liam said, chuckling. He let go of Kelsey. "I have to go in—I need to do a lot of interviews and try to trace Gary White's movements. I have officers working on it, but…I need to be out there. Your assignments until I return are to find the shotgun, read the book and search for a little golden reliquary worth a million bucks. Got it?"

Kelsey nodded, smiling at him. "And lock the doors, be careful if we go outside—"

"The crime-scene people were just wrapping up when I walked down to the little beach and dock area," Avery said.

"I'll check with them before I leave," Liam said. "Careful with going out the back entry, too. Keep an eye on any open door."

"I'll be watching out for Kelsey," Avery told him, his tone fierce. He heard the sound of his own voice and tried to lighten the tone. "Hey, what do I animate if she doesn't draw? And she's so damned good for my ego. Our superhero is based on my extraordinary good looks."

"Has his ego, too," Kelsey said lightly.

Liam smiled at her, kissed her lips and said softly, "Stay safe, watch yourself, watch the doors, stay with Avery."

"You trust Avery?" she teased.

Liam looked across the kitchen at Avery. "I do." He grimaced. "I ran a background check. Avery has no ties to Key West. He was at Hollywood High years ago, has two unpaid parking tickets and is otherwise an upstanding citizen."

"You did a background on me?" Avery said incredulously. He laughed. "Good man!"

Kelsey was surprised to see that Liam gave pause. "I need someone to trust completely," he said.

He headed toward the living room. "Come on—lock me out."

Kelsey followed him. He was a few steps ahead of her. Morning's light was pouring in, and the house did look like a fascinating museum-home, with dusted antiques and curiosities here and there. It felt like the home she had always known and loved, unique but warm.

And then...

She thought she saw someone standing by the front door. Waiting. But...

He was just an outline in the air, and he wasn't real, he was certainly part of her imagination.

He was leaning against the wall there, thumbs hooked

into the low pockets of the period coat he was wearing. He had on a hat. A tricornered pirate hat.

He was dark and strikingly handsome, and not really there….

She blinked. The apparition faded. But then she heard Liam whisper, "Yes, stay, thank you."

"What?" she asked.

He turned back, looking at her. "Hmm?"

"You just spoke. You said, 'Yes, stay, thank you.'"

"Must be muttering to myself. Sorry." He walked back to her, taking her shoulders. "Be careful, do you hear me? Please be careful. If my theory is right…"

"Someone has a great deal at stake. I promise I'll be careful."

"Kelsey, I almost forgot. Where's the box with that magic trick? You wanted it dusted for prints. I'll take it into the station, let them look into it there. I can't promise you much—there may be a number of prints on it. Or just yours."

She hurried to the crate and produced the box with the motor and the jumping black shadow cloths. He kissed her lips lightly and headed to the door again. She followed him and locked him out. When she had done so, she leaned against the door for a minute. Oddly, she felt as if she weren't alone. She moved her hands through the air as if she could feel an unknown entity, but she couldn't.

She didn't feel the fear that she sometimes did, the fear that made her lock the door to her room at night.

But she still didn't feel as if she was alone. She had

seen something. Or she had almost seen it. She couldn't quite touch it.

She had things to do. She gave herself a mental shake.

But then she paused again.

When her mother had died, she had wanted so badly to believe in ghosts. She had wanted to be able to see her, feel her, just tell her one last time how much she had loved her, what a good mother she had been, what a brilliant and kind woman. At least, with her father, she had been there at the end. He had known her heart, known how much he was loved.

Of course, her mother had known, as well. But her life had been cut so short.

"Mom?" she whispered aloud. "Cutter?"

The empty room gave her no answer. She walked back into the kitchen to find Avery. She had a lot to do, and, eventually, she was going to have to get back to work.

Outside, Liam cursed himself. Bartholomew wasn't next to him, since he was going to stay at the house to watch over Kelsey, so he couldn't curse the ghost for making him look like a fool again. No choice but to curse himself.

He saw Yolanda Egert, a pretty young civilian in the crime-scene unit, packing up her box.

"How did it go?" he asked her.

She stood, shaking her head with disgust. "Nothing. And we searched, and we're good. I know some folks figure we have to be yokels down here in the islands, but we're good at our jobs, and better than any outsider because we know how to search beaches, the water, swamps, marshes, hammocks, you name it. We had divers out. We did a grid out there. There was no sign of anything. No one even left a damned foam cup out there!"

"I didn't think there would be anything to find," Liam said. "The killer took his weapon, there's been rain, so no footprints, and I'm sure whoever did this was extremely clever."

"You don't think it was just a fight of some kind?" Egert asked.

"No. Who the hell has a stiletto-type weapon on them when it's just a fight gone bad?" Liam said. "Someone is trying to get into this house. They want something in it. Gary White saw them and knew who they were, maybe even what they were doing. Or he was killed on purpose just to scare people away. That's my theory. Anyway, I know you and your group are the best. I'll see you later, Yolanda."

"Well, you're good at what you do, too, Liam. Wish we could give you more."

"Not your fault. It's just that a murder weapon is such a good thing to find."

"I hear you. But the killer was smart. Took it with him."

He said goodbye to her and headed to his car. The crime-scene tape was all coming down. Liam waved to a few of the other workers, calling in to the station as he did so. He wasn't going in right away; he had a few stops to make, and he wanted to make sure that his officers were following up on questioning just about everyone everywhere to find out when Gary White had last been seen.

He headed to Truman and around U.S. 1 on Roosevelt to reach the "new" part of the island and the shopping center where Joe Richter had his offices. Richter's secretary asked him politely if he had an appointment; Liam offered her his badge.

"Oh. Oh!" the secretary said. "Uh, sure." Nervously, she pressed a button to announce Liam's arrival.

Joe Richter came straight out of his office to greet him. "Liam Beckett. How are you? Sad business, yesterday. Poor Kelsey. She comes home to bury her grandfather, and a corpse shows up on her property. Sorry—did you know Gary White? Folks say he's been around, that I must have seen him, but I don't think that I knew the man." He pumped Liam's hand and indicated his office. "Come on in and let me see how I can help you."

"Thanks," Liam told him.

Seated across from Richter's desk, Liam said, "You know, Joe, Gary White was one of the people I caught breaking into the Merlin house after Cutter died."

"Bad business," Joe said. "Cutter was such an old coot. Amazing man, but I guess that house has so much in it, it's just a major temptation."

"A lot in it, but it's not always easy to recognize what's valuable."

Joe shrugged. "I knew the man's legal dealings. I don't know much about his collections. He left all that for his granddaughter to handle."

"Do you think that Gary White might have been searching for something specific?" Liam asked. "Did you know of any piece that Cutter had that might be extremely valuable—and easy to slip out without anyone knowing any better?"

Richter lifted his hands. "I know there's a lot valuable in there. Believe it or not, the damned mummy is extremely valuable. There was a time, when the English first delved heavily into Egyptian archeology, that mummies were a dime a dozen, in many places. I don't think that Cutter's mummy was someone incredibly important historically, but I know that the coffin and sarcophagus are considered fine examples of Egyptian art during the reign of Ramses II."

"A sarcophagus is rather big to slip out," Liam commented. He sat back comfortably in the chair and tapped his fingers lightly together. He had alienated Ted and Jaden last night, and he'd hoped he'd made it up and explained. Ted and Jaden were longtime friends. He didn't want to alienate Richter, because he didn't want the man on the defensive. If he was clean, he might be able to help. If he was dirty, it would be good to have him think that he was getting away with everything.

Which the perpetrator was, at the moment, he reminded himself dryly.

"Well, that's true." Richter shook his head. "The damned property is worth a mint. But I guess you can't walk away with property."

"That takes a different kind of thief," Liam said lightly.

Joe Richter drummed his fingers on his desk. "I always think of that big beautiful living room. The heads on the wall, the voodoo altar right there…the mummy…

the Victorian coffin. I guess I've always been struck by the larger artifacts. I know he has gargoyles from medieval churches, stained glass, lamps, some kind of Chinese good-luck cats…you name it, Cutter Merlin had it. Crosses, ankhs, relics of all kinds." He frowned, sitting back. "The ledgers and notes and instructions were all in the house. It was left to Kelsey Donovan as it was when he died. Disposal of the estate is up to her. He might not have seen her in years, but he had no doubt she'd follow all his wishes."

"That's true, of course," Liam said. "I had just hoped you might be able to help. The place is so vast, and I've got a murder on my hands."

"You have my sympathy, that's for sure," Richter told him.

"Then—well, you know, I found Cutter holding one of his relics, a shotgun and a book. A friend told me about another book, and I looked for it at the library. It's gone. I noted that you'd been in the rare-book room."

Something passed over Richter's face.

Was he wary now?

The man made a pretense of shrugging casually. "I go there a lot. What was the book you were looking for?"

"Key West, Satanism, Peter Edwards and the Abel and Aleister Crowley Connection," Liam said.

Richter blinked. Was it because of the title, or because he'd been nailed?

"There is such a book?" he asked.

Liam nodded.

"Why would you want a book like that, Liam?"

"Friend of a friend said that it talked about the book

that Cutter was holding, *In Defense from Dark Magick,*" Liam explained.

Richter frowned, shaking his head. "Cutter Merlin was eccentric—he wasn't crazy."

"You don't think he might have suffered some dementia at the end?" Liam asked.

"I...I...I'd say the man was sane. How do you judge eccentric from dementia at all levels?" Richter asked. "I was at the library. I enjoy the rare-book room. But I've never seen the book you're talking about, and I certainly don't have it. Why would you think it was me?"

"I didn't say I thought it was you. I was just asking. I'd like to find the book. Read it. Apparently, there was a man who lived in Key West during the Civil War who did believe in magic and wanted to use it to keep the enemy forces at bay. Then he wanted to atone for his sins, or felt demons were chasing him or some such thing. I'd like to find out what was going on in Cutter's mind. It might just have something to do with the murder of Gary White." Liam shook his head. "Were you around a lot? Were you friends with Cutter? Is there anything you can think of to tell me?"

For a moment, he didn't think that Richter would answer truthfully. Then the man shrugged and folded his hands on the desk. "We had a good working relationship. I can't say we were really good friends. I found him fascinating. I tried to get him to be more specific about his will—he wouldn't have it. And, in all honesty, I wanted the property."

"The property?" Liam said.

"Yes. That little spit of land is a gold mine. Get some

zoning, build it up as an exclusive resort, or even a bed-and-breakfast. It's perfect land. There's a dock, a little beachfront and a pack of mangroves bordering it all that could be filled in to add acres to the place. I went out a few times, just to walk around the property. I was trying to figure out if I could swing buying it, if I could convince Kelsey Donovan to sell. I mean, the kid spent the last decade in California. She may want to hightail it back there fast as she can when the dust settles."

Liam nodded. "You didn't want that property badly enough to try to scare her out of it, did you?" he asked.

Richter stared at him angrily. "I'm a respectable businessman. And I'm an attorney. You better have evidence if you want to cast any accusations against me," he said.

Liam stood. "Trust me, Mr. Richter, if I had evidence against you, attorney or no, you'd be down at the station." He set his card on the desk. "If you think of anything, call me."

He watched as Joe Richter stared at him and picked up his card. "Sure."

He knew that the minute he left, Joe Richter threw the card in his trash basket.

The possibilities ran through his mind. Jonas had been at the library, he lived across the water from the Merlin property and he seemed to be around when he shouldn't be at times. Jaden and Ted knew the truth about the reliquary—and were always at the library. Joe Richter had been the one to have access to the house, and he'd just admitted that he'd wanted to buy it. Chris Vargas, petty criminal, had been in the house. None of it meant anything; as evidence, it would all be laughed out of a court of law. The reliquary had to be the key; the real one was far more than a talisman against evil.

It had been the receptacle in which a million-dollar diamond had been smuggled.

Who·did he really trust?

His cousin, David, and Katie. Sean and Vanessa. They'd been through enough together. But Ted and Jaden and Clarinda and Jonas had been around for a hell of a lot of bad stuff, too. They'd proven their mettle. They couldn't be guilty of any—evil.

Getting into his car, he swore softly into the air.

He had nothing. There could be someone out there he hadn't begun to suspect.

As he got in the car, he got a call from the station. It was Ricky Long, who was working computers and re-search for the week.

"Hey, boss," Ricky said.

"What did you get?" Liam asked him.

"George Penner is a tourist from Virginia City, Nevada. He went home three days ago. I spoke to him, and he told me that yes, he'd been in the library, in the rare-book room. He'd been researching shipwrecks, and he said he didn't know anything about the book that was missing. I checked with local police, as well. He was born and bred in Virginia City—it was his first trip to Key West," Ricky told him.

"All right. Well, that takes care of George Penner," Liam said. "What about the other name? Bel Arcowley?"

"Well, boss, I can keep going, but I haven't found a reference to him—or her. I swear, I called most places in town, I still have a few to go—you know how many inns, bed-and-breakfast places, private homes, hotels, condos and time-shares there are in Key West?" Ricky asked him.

"Yes, I do, but keep checking, all right?" Liam asked.

"Sure. You're the boss. This is about the Merlin place, isn't it?" Ricky asked.

"Yep."

"That's one screwy place. But I don't understand what the book has to do with anything."

"I don't know, either. That's what I need to find out."

"You know, it's probably a fake name," Ricky said.

"That's possible. You just have to sign in—they don't ask for ID. A librarian has to open the door to let folks in, and they try to keep an eye on letting folks out," Liam said. "I think I should get over to the library. See if I can find out which librarian let the man—or woman—in."

"Should I give up on the calling?" Ricky asked.

"No, keep trying."

"Will do," Ricky said. "Anything—just so long as I don't have to go back in that house!"

Liam twisted his key in the ignition and headed back north toward Old Town.

If someone had come into the library with the express purpose of stealing a book, that person would have used a fake name.

He pulled off on the side of the road and took a

notepad from his glove compartment. He wrote the name. Bel Arcowley.

He started to move letters around. It didn't take long. The words were an anagram.

Abel Crowley. Someone out there was really playing games.

Deadly games.

Sitting in Cutter's study, Kelsey read from *In Defense from Dark Magick.*

She had started first delving into more boxes and crates, looking for more magic tricks, but she didn't come across any. She found some ancient Chinese funerary forms and a collection of communion chalices, but at that point decided that reading would be better than delving.

"Too bad it's not an audiobook!" Avery told her. "We could listen together and get all kinds of things done!"

"I don't think they were doing audio when this came out," Kelsey told him.

"I'm going to take care of shelving these chalices in the glass cases out there—two shelves have room, if I move some of the Chinese lucky cats," he said.

"That's great. Thanks, Avery," Kelsey told him.

It was comfortable; he shelved and she read.

The first part of the book was a series of prayers against different forms of evil. "Lord, protect me from the miasma in the air, in the disease of the Devil's making, that travels in the air we breathe. We lift the cross to thee, we beseech thee in the forms of Father, Son and Holy Ghost. Cast out thy evil that we take into our lips and lungs, and guard us from that form of his torment," Kelsey read aloud.

"And if it had been the right time in history, they could have taken vitamins!" Avery said.

"The whole first part of the book is just incantations like this, nothing that strange," Kelsey said. "The concept was that the devil was in everything, in people, in the air, in illness…in the weather! Listen to this one. 'Dear Father, in the name of the Holy Mother and all the Saints, cast the demon Devil from the seas, from the wind that blows, and rocks our ships, devouring them to a watery grave.'" She looked over at Avery. "I can't believe that Cutter believed any of this!"

"I'm sure he didn't. He might just have been holding the book…for something to set the little gold casket on," Avery suggested.

"No…I don't think so. I think that maybe… Okay, he knew or suspected that someone out there knew he had two of the reliquaries—the real one, which he had discovered held the diamond, and the fake one, the one he was holding. Or, he hoped that the thief *didn't* know that he had two of them, and he planned on handing over the one. The fake one, the one that he was holding. He had the shotgun, but…oh, I don't know, I give up! If he was being threatened, why didn't he call the police?"

"Because," Avery said thoughtfully, "whoever it was came and slipped in through a window and was using… trickery to scare him. And he couldn't call the police and tell them that he had shadows in the house. He was getting older. Maybe he was afraid he was getting dementia. Maybe he didn't trust the police."

"I wish I'd been here," Kelsey said softly.

She carefully turned a page and was startled to see that there was a note folded into the book. She pulled out the note, opened it and saw Cutter's large, perfect cursive handwriting.

She read aloud.

"Note: Read from description of Pete Edwards that he practiced black magic at night on the beach. A black candle carried, and an incantation to Satan to show him the Southern ships in the darkness so he could sound the blockade alarm. Many of his neighbors despised him, but they feared him, as well. Most probably, he found the ships by seeing the dimmed lights in the darkness of the beach. Those around him might well have believed that he was in league with the devil and that his hatred of the Southern cause was so great, he was willing to make any sacrifice. Some say that on the night the ship Southern Comfort *was captured by Union ships, Pete reported the ship, having discovered it on the horizon by Satanic rite and then sacrificed a goat. The ship's captain, Ethan Rutger, suffered a heart attack during the capture, and it was said that Pete's rite brought about the heart attack, the man's death and, consequently, the capture of the ship."*

"Ugh. Cree—eepy!" Avery announced.

"Cutter was just making a note on what he had read," Kelsey said. "He must have been at the library. He must have read from that book Liam was talking about."

"Certainly sounds like it," Avery agreed.

She began searching through the book for more notes. Two chapters in, she found another one.

Avery was gently wiping dust from a little porcelain cat, and she frowned and found herself reading in silence.

Morning, June 10. I asked Marabella if she had moved anything in my office. She had not. I believe her, and trust her; she is the kindest woman, and the only housekeeper for me. She understands that I must have a clean kitchen, clean sheets… bathroom, and the rest does not matter. I know she did not move the book. I do not believe in demonic forces, though I believe there is a devil, Satan, if you will, and he lives in the hearts of many a man. There is not a ritual that awakens evil; there is a man's belief that he can harness it, and in his own belief is his power. I can't ask Marabella to stay any longer. Someone comes here, and I have not fathomed the method. There is only one thing he might be thinking. The reliquary. I should have gotten rid of it the moment it came into my possession; the money might have gone to so many causes. I waited just seconds too long, and the fact of what I had was known. Too quickly, my precious daughter was gone, and I will live the rest of my life seeking her killer.

Dumbstruck, Kelsey stared at the page.

She started turning pages again, one by one, seeking more notes. Finally, she came across another.

Kelsey will find the truth. I dare not write it anywhere. I wait, because I believe the thief is out there. I wait forever.

He killed my daughter.

It was extremely quiet when Liam arrived at the library. A different librarian, Matilda Osbury, was working, but he knew her as well.

Matilda was in her late fifties. She was slim and nervous and always reminded Liam of a saluki dog. She was a retired schoolteacher, and he'd been her student in first grade.

"Liam, hello, young man," she told him, looking up when he came to her at the desk. "I hear we're seeing a lot of you these days. Oh, such bad business going on lately. But it's lovely to have so many of our dear friends back. Your cousin, David, living here again! And all that horrible tragedy regarding his old girlfriend cleared up. And Sean O'Hara back as well, and now Kelsey Donovan." She spoke quickly, as if it were important she say everything without taking up too much of anyone's time. "Oh, but now a murder—that guitarist fellow—out at the Merlin place. Such a shame. Who would murder the poor dear man? He wasn't brilliant, but he hurt no one. He was a pleasant enough young fellow, indeed, that he was. He loved his guitar."

"That's what I'm investigating, Mrs. Osbury," Liam said.

"Liam, you have been out of school a very long time. Please call me Matilda. Now, how may I help you?"

"You knew Gary White?" Liam asked her.

"Of course," she said.

"I'm sorry, Matilda, help me out here. How did you know him?"

"Why, he loved the library."

"He did?"

"Oh, yes, he came frequently."

"Did he have a library card? Did he take out a lot of books?"

She frowned, pursing her lips. "No. I told him he could get one. He didn't want one. He just came and read all the time."

"Did he ever go into the rare-book room?"

"Yes, I believe he did."

"His name isn't on the list of those who entered," Liam said.

"Oh, it must be!" Matilda protested. "I brought him back there myself."

"Matilda, I need you to show me the list."

She nodded, rose and started off straight for the rare-book room. He followed behind her. She keyed open the door and showed him the book on the pedestal.

She frowned after a moment. "Well, I'm sure he signed in. I might have been a bit distracted, but I saw him at the book."

"Matilda, I need to take this book. Can you bring out a new register for people to sign in?" Liam asked.

"Well, of course. Do you think it can help solve the mystery of his murder?" she asked. "Oh, Liam, this is so frightening!"

"Matilda, I don't think you need to be afraid."

She shivered. "But I heard the missing book is all about Satanism."

"I haven't read the book, but it's not really about Satanism, Matilda. It's about people who thought they could use it, and how they connected with Key West. I'm sure you're safe. Carry on with the usual, Matilda. Lock your doors, don't walk around in the dark…. You know all about being smart and safe." He offered her a reassuring smile. "You taught us all about it. Now, if you don't mind, will you help me again? Did Gary talk about any of his friends, or his work, or anything else he might have been doing or anywhere he was attempting to go or anything at all that might help me?"

She frowned again, pursing her lips. It seemed to be her mode for thinking.

She shook her head. "We didn't have long conversations. We talked about books, and his guitar. Oh!"

"Oh?"

"Yes, yes, the last time I saw him—a week or so ago—he was in a bit of a hurry. He was about to go and do a few odd jobs for Jonas Weston at the bed-and-breakfast. Maybe Jonas could help you?" she suggested hopefully.

He smiled. "Thank you. I'll check into that."

He took the book and left.

"Avery, he knew," Kelsey whispered.

"Hmm?" Avery looked up, and then came over to her. "Who knew what, honey?"

"Look at this, read this."

Avery bent over her and read the notes. "Oh, Lord.

This is frightening, Kelsey, really frightening. Your grandfather thought that—despite the fact that she fell down a staircase—your mom was murdered. But you were there, weren't you? Wasn't your father right in the living room?"

Kelsey closed her eyes and thought for a moment, then shook her head. "No. When I came running out of my room, my mom was already in my father's arms, and rescue was on the way. But I'm pretty sure that my dad and Cutter had been right where you and I are now." She shook her head, trying to conjure up a clear picture of the day she had long ago tried so very hard to forget. "My dad ran out to California. He was trying to get as far as he could from the site of my mom's death without leaving the States, I'm certain."

"I'm glad he picked California!" Avery said.

"And that explains so much!" Kelsey said excitedly. "My dad never hated my grandfather, but he wanted me away from him. He thought that Cutter might risk too much in order to find the person he was convinced had killed my mother. I know that my father believed that it was a tragic accident, and he spent the rest of his life brokenhearted. He didn't want to risk keeping me in Cutter's house."

"So sad," Avery said.

"So sad, yes. But here it is. Cutter owned a reliquary that was worth a million dollars. He also came into ownership of the copy. I don't know which he owned first. But someone else out there knew that he had it. Cutter believed that people were breaking in. He believed one of those people managed to kill my mom, though I still don't understand how or why. My father took me away, knowing that Cutter would spend the rest of his days obsessed with finding a murderer. Cutter died of a heart attack, with a shotgun, the fake reliquary and a book in his arms."

"Then, within a week, Gary White is murdered on the property," Avery said. He pulled a piece of Cutter's monogrammed paper from beneath the heavy jade paperweight that held it down. "List it all out. God knows, it might help."

She did so. When she was done, he took her by the hand, making her get up. "Come on, we'll get back to this, but let's take a break. Come on out—we'll see if the dolphin is still hanging out by your docks."

Her back was cramped. Her muscles were tense. She smiled. "Okay." They walked through the house and out the back together.

He waited. He waited until he was certain that they were gone.

He reminded himself that he was powerful and invisible.

He came to the desk, and he read the sheet that lay there, not touching it. He was tempted to rip it to pieces. He didn't. He didn't need anyone suspecting that he was invisible, and that he could come and go at will.

He felt a tic in his cheek. He was angry with what he was feeling. She was close, so close.

Oh, yes, close...close to everything but giving him the real reliquary.

Patience. He had to have patience.

He turned away. He'd had his chance to take the damned book, but he hadn't. How the hell could he have known that Cutter kept notes in it? He knew that Cutter would find a way to tell Kelsey about the reliquary.

He slipped away, tamping down his fear. He had a real face when he wasn't invisible. Maybe he could do more with his real face.

In this house, though, he had to take care. He had to remain invisible.

Until it was time. Until Kelsey Donovan had the reliquary.

And he had Kelsey Donovan.

11

"Jonas, hey," Liam said. It was easy enough to park at the bed-and-breakfast—on a Tuesday, few places in town were full, and the bed-and-breakfast inns tended to fill up last simply because hotel chains were more readily visible on travel sites.

Jonas was sitting on his front porch, reading the paper, eating his lunch. When Jonas had been growing up, the place had been a single-family dwelling. It was a nice house, with its own little spit of beach, six bedrooms in the main house and, now, two in the old carriage house. He and Clarinda lived in the master on the ground floor of the first house. He was a good innkeeper, with many guests being people who were from the state and returned often during the year. His tiki bar was well-run; his breakfasts were known to be both inventive and very good.

It was impossible to think of him as a thief or a killer.

But, of course, Liam had learned the hard way that you seldom ever really knew another person.

"Liam, hey," Jonas said. He started to stand. Liam

waved him back down. "Join me. Want some lunch? Clarinda is inside making herself a sandwich. At least have some iced tea or something,"

"I'm fine, really. I've got to get back to the station. I just wanted to ask you a few questions."

Jonas's brows shot up. "Officially?"

"Casually. I'm hoping you can help me."

"How?" Jonas looked baffled.

"Two things. I'm looking for a book," Liam said.

"Um—have you tried the library or a bookstore?" Jonas asked.

Liam grinned. "No, I was at the library. I'm trying to find a book about Satanism in Key West."

Jonas laughed. "Watch it! People will talk. You're supposed to be one of the good guys."

"No, I'm not planning on taking up the black arts," Liam said. "I was trying to find this particular book. It's missing from the rare-book room, and you were there. I don't know, but it's like I told Jaden and Ted—honest people have been known to slip rare books out of rare-book rooms and slip them back when they're done with them. Saves a lot of trips to the library."

"I was there, and I was in the rare-book room," Jonas said. "But I wasn't looking for a book on Satanism. I'm still Catholic. Well, my own form of Catholic." He paused. "You're not here to talk about religion. What's the deal with the book?"

"I think it has something to do with Gary White's murder," Liam said.

"A book on Satanism?" Jonas asked.

"And the Key West connection," Liam said.

"Apparently, there was a fellow here during the Civil War. He supposedly caught Southern blockade runners by practicing black magic. Later in life, he knew a fellow named Abel Crowley, who was related to or an admirer of the Aleister Crowley, who was known to be the 'wickedest man alive.' Gary, using the name Bel Arcowley, might have taken the book."

Jonas nodded, and then shook his head. "So why did you think I had taken the book?"

"Gary might have taken the book, and he might not have done so. When he was in the library last, he told the librarian he was headed out here to do some work at the B and B. I don't know—I thought you two might have talked about it."

"I hired Gary to do some painting. Upstairs in the old carriage house," Jonas said. "He wasn't a bad guy."

"You didn't mention it," Liam said.

"I didn't think to mention it. We all knew him. Sort of—at least."

Liam turned; the door to the house was open. Clarinda had come out, a plate with a sandwich in her hands.

"Liam, I don't believe this! Are you accusing Jonas of something?" she demanded.

Liam sighed. "I'm not accusing. I'm hoping someone will be able to say something that will help me."

"Well, I was the one who was here most when Gary was working. He came over a few mornings—he worked the streets at night, when he couldn't get himself some kind of a gig. He'd play on a street corner or down at Mallory Square and hope to make his rent on tips. We seldom got into any heavy conversations, though," she said.

She set her plate down at the table and glared at Liam. "I don't believe this! How long have we all known each other?"

"I'm looking for help, Clarinda," he said. She was truly outraged. He was fairly certain that if Jonas was up to anything foul at all, Clarinda didn't know.

"Right. What do you want? We'll help you. Sure. It was me. I just decided that I didn't like the guy and it would be fun to kill him and trap him in the tree roots at Kelsey's place," Clarinda said.

"Clarinda," Jonas said.

"Well, a friend we've known forever is accusing us of God knows what!" she said angrily.

"I don't think he was accusing you," Jonas said.

"Why not? We all know that women are capable of anger. Let's see, Gary White was always so clean and fresh. I seduced him. And I shot him. Or stabbed him. Sorry, the papers and the news haven't said just how he was killed," Clarinda said.

"And he's not going to tell us, Clarinda. This is his job," Jonas told her.

"This is outrageous, is what it is," Clarinda said.

"Clarinda, honestly, I'm hoping you two can help me. You can see the Merlin place from here. I need all the help I can get. I'm asking you both if you'll keep an eye out, write down anything that you see. I'd greatly appreciate it," Liam said.

Clarinda stared at him, looked away and sighed softly. "It's just infuriating, Liam. How long have you known us? Good God, I serve you dinner half the nights of every week. And Jonas is from here. He's lived in the same house all his life!"

"Clarinda, I'm looking for answers. I need help."

"Sure." She was quiet a minute. "Do you want some iced tea? A sandwich?"

He stood. "No, but thank you. I'm going to head to the station, drop a few things off and start looking into some leads." He almost said *other* leads. Luckily, the word didn't slip out. He didn't need to make her any more antagonistic toward him.

"You have to eat," Clarinda said.

"I'll grab something in an hour or so," he assured her. "Thanks."

He waved and left them on the porch. As he got back into his car, he noted that there was a telescope on the upstairs wraparound porch.

It was aimed at the Merlin estate.

"See?" Avery said. "It's friendly. It wants to play."

"It's friendly, all right," Kelsey agreed.

The dolphin, swimming up and down along her dock, watched them. It seemed pleased to entertain them and didn't make any effort to disappear. Nor did it grow bored, but rather seemed to be listening to their conversation. It swam up and down and hovered, and then disappeared for a minute, only to reappear doing a majestic leap out in the deeper water.

"I wonder if Liam was right, and he's lost from one of the dolphin facilities—there are several in the Keys," Kelsey said.

"Do they ever act like this when they're just wild?" Avery asked.

"Hmm. Honestly, I don't know," Kelsey said. "I mean, I've seen them swim alongside boats when we've gone out, and they leap as a natural behavior. He does seem to like human interaction. I'll mention it to Liam again. Maybe he's heard of a dolphin that was lost somehow. I get the feeling that they're pretty good at knowing where they're going, though. I don't know. But he is fascinating."

"He's a nice diversion," Avery said. "I think I'll call him Jimmy. Is it a he?"

"I can't tell you," Kelsey said. "He's looking at us and leaping around pretty quickly."

"Ah, well, if it's a girl, Jimmy can be short for Jimima. How's that?"

"Sounds fine to me. I'm going to head back in."

"I'm going to talk to Jimmy for a while longer," Avery said.

"Okay."

"But I'm here for the long run, Kelsey. I'll be helping you from here on out."

"It's okay, spend some time with Jimmy."

"Maybe I'll get in the water later."

"They can be aggressive," Kelsey warned.

"I'll watch myself."

"The water is probably pretty cool. It wasn't bad the other day, but it can be cool in winter."

"Hey, I dive in the Pacific, Kelsey. I'll be fine."

"Why don't you wait a bit? I want to keep looking through that book, find more of my grandfather's notes,"

Kelsey said. "Later on, I'll break for the day and we can go for a bit of a swim together."

"All right. We'll talk a bit—Jimmy and me—and then I'll be in."

Kelsey turned around and walked back into the house. When she entered the office, she held still, a scream caught in her throat.

She wasn't alone.

Liam drove back up to the new side of the island, looking to see if Chris Vargas was out pounding the pavement again with a sign and a cup.

He didn't see him.

He went to the station and dropped off the magic trick that had so badly scared Kelsey, and the rare-book room registration ledger, asking Ricky Long to get it to a hand-writing expert. He wanted to know if Gary White had been the person who had signed in as Bel Arcowley.

Art Saunders had been with the officers who had gone through Gary White's tiny efficiency studio on Petronia Street. Liam stopped to talk to him, and Art assured him that he hadn't found a rare book.

In fact, he hadn't found a book at all.

"I looked at his bills, found his checkbook, searched his drawers, his shelves—I didn't find anything at all. He didn't have a cell phone or a landline. There was nothing."

"Thanks. I'll probably do a double check," Liam said.

Art nodded. He wasn't offended. Another pair of eyes was never discounted.

Liam left instructions for Art to question a number of the bars where Gary had done his one-man song-and-guitar routine, and left. He drove up and down Duval looking for Chris Vargas again, and at last saw him with his rickshaw on Front Street.

Vargas saw him and flinched, but he didn't try to move away from the corner where he'd been standing, calling out his services to passing tourists.

"What?" he groaned when Liam pulled his car over and came out to talk to him.

"What do you mean what?" Liam demanded. "A man is dead. A man who was supposedly your friend."

"My friend, that's the point, Lieutenant Beckett. Please…"

Vargas winced, looking down at the ground.

"I need to know what Gary White was doing before his death," Liam said.

"Doing? The usual. He was playing his guitar. Trying to make ends meet. He bussed tables and washed dishes sometimes. When he was lucky, he played his guitar and sang. You know, neither one of us needs all that much, and so, even at what it was, his life was good the way he saw it. We're not druggies. We know the cheap bars and the cheap eats. If anything is cheap down here. But we did well enough."

"If you were so happy with the status quo, why were you in the Merlin house?" Liam asked.

Vargas groaned. "Can't you figure that by now? Kids had broken in. It seemed like something easy to do. We weren't going to steal anything big. We were just looking for an easy object to pawn and make enough to get ahead a bit, that's all."

"And that was the last time you saw him?"

"Yeah, that was the last time I saw him."

"Do you know why he was going to the library, entering the rare-book room with an assumed name?" Liam asked.

"What?"

"Never mind. Let's start over. Whose idea was it to break into the Merlin house?"

Vargas flushed, looking away. "Mine," he admitted.

"Have you been visiting the library?" Liam asked him.

Vargas's face twisted in a frown. "The library? No. I'm not much of a reader. Neither was Gary. I don't know what you're getting at."

"There's a book missing from the rare-book room."

"I didn't steal any book," Vargas said. "Look, I've been telling you the truth. I knew about the kids breaking into the house. I thought we could slip in, find some little thing and slip back out. I admitted it that night. I did not steal a book. I'm not a library kind of guy."

"Who else was Gary hanging around with?" Liam asked.

Vargas shrugged. "I don't know. Gary just hangs around. Look, can I go back to work now?"

"It didn't really look like you were working," Liam commented.

"I was trying to work. And a cop hanging around me doesn't help bring in the inebriated tourist who may need a little help getting back to his hotel room."

"Yeah, yeah, go ahead," Liam said, frustrated.

Vargas stared at him.

"Go on."

"I need you to leave. This is my corner," Vargas told him.

One of Key West's innumerable roosters crowed off-hour and went walking by them. "Watch yourself, Vargas," he warned.

"I will. Swear it," Vargas said.

Liam returned to his car. He sat there a minute, wishing that he wasn't grasping at straws.

"You see me," the apparition said quietly.

It was the pirate. The outline she had seen walking behind Liam. She was either falling under too much pressure, or she was staring at the ghost of a long-gone swain, a handsome man, perhaps thirty, decked out in the fashion of his day.

He might have been flesh and blood as he stood there. He had been staring broodingly out the study window, until she had opened the door.

And seen him.

"I see…" she whispered, "something."

She blinked. He didn't disappear.

It was still broad daylight. She was wide awake, not dreaming.

"Well, you're not screaming or running," he said, moving away from the window to come to the center of the room.

He still looked real. So damned real. And his voice.

She could see him speaking just as if he were Liam or Avery or any other living man.

"May I introduce myself?" he asked, sweeping off his hat in a broad and elegant gesture, bending low in a bow. "Captain Bartholomew, privateer, unjustly led to the gallows, though that travesty has since been righted. And still I remain. The Becketts and I are connected, you see."

She was silent, staring at him, trying to determine if she could possibly be seeing—and hearing—a ghost.

Ghosts. Apparitions. Spirits. They were supposed to be nothing but mist. They roamed the fields of Gettysburg and such places as the Vatican or Westminster Abbey, Notre Dame, the Lizzie Borden house. They went about their spectral existences without stopping to talk to people, for God's sake, and a man such as Liam, a cop, for God's sake, did not walk around with a ghost for a friend.

Definitely, it had to be the pressure.

"I am having some kind of a mental breakdown, brought on by the events surrounding my grandfather's death, and the fact that a man was murdered on my property," Kelsey said.

He smiled. It was a charming, handsome smile.

"I knew you sensed me before," he said. "Many people do. Well, they sense me, and others, of course."

Kelsey made her way to the desk, skirting around the ghost, keeping her eyes on him all the time. She tried to sit calmly and rationally in Cutter's desk chair.

"If ghosts haunt this house, they should be the ghosts of my mother or grandfather," she said. "Ghosts are supposed to haunt the places where traumatic things happened."

He reflected on that. "I'm ever so sorry," he said.

She swallowed. "Liam—sees you?"

"Yes."

"We're sharing a mental breakdown?" she asked.

He walked around and sat at the chair in front of the desk, crossing one stockinged leg over the other. She noted the heels on his shoes and the buckles, the brocade of his coat and the elegance of his waistcoat.

They were so real.

He sighed. "No, I'm quite real. Or surreal, I suppose. For quite a while, I couldn't begin to imagine why I was still here, but first there was the issue with David Beckett, although I had been attached to Katie O'Hara. She's quite amazing, with a sight that rivals any I've come across. Oh, there are others out there, of course. Liam? He doesn't have great sight. But he is a Beckett, and he's been forced to see me, poor boy. It's just been the way that things have come about."

"Just how many people are sharing this breakdown?" she asked.

He smiled again, setting his hat on his lap. "Now? Hmm. Well, Katie and Sean and Vanessa and David, Liam—and now you."

"Are we crazy?"

"Aren't we all, just a bit?"

Kelsey closed her eyes, keeping them closed. She opened them. He was still there.

She hadn't even been drinking.

"I'm glad that you see me," he said. "It does make trying to protect you so much easier."

"You're trying to protect me?" she asked.

"Of course. Ghosts aren't evil. Well, wait, I retract that statement. Most ghosts aren't evil. But people are in death as they were in life, and sometimes…well, I don't know what hell is, myself, and I'm hoping I never do. I don't believe I'm headed in that direction, wherever it may actually be. I have seen the darkness of evil come up to claim its own, but never mind, that's neither here nor there. As it stands, I believe that I've remained though the remnants of the past that directly involved me have been solved in order to see that justice befalls all Becketts."

"I'm not a Beckett," Kelsey said.

"No matter. A Beckett has involved himself with you. Oh, please, don't take that wrong! You're a lovely young woman. I'm delighted to help in any way that I can."

"You're a ghost."

"Yes, I believe we've established that fact."

Was there such thing as dreaming while one was wide awake? Had she blacked out, blanked out—without knowing it? Maybe she would wake up on the floor, having been hit on the head with a candlestick or a gargoyle or Chinese good luck cat.

"My dear young woman, you're gaping. Not that you're unattractive even while staring at me openmouthed, but you are lovelier still with a more customary and benign expression," he said.

"I still don't understand." She suddenly felt tears pricking her eyes. Figment of her imagination, creation of stress or real remnant of the past, she couldn't understand why she would see an unknown privateer and not her mother or her grandfather.

"I don't think any of us actually understands," he said.

"Can *you* talk to my mother or my grandfather?" she asked.

"I'm sorry. Truly sorry. If they've remained behind, I've yet to come across them," he told her. "And I've been in this house quite frequently lately. Nor have I met either in the cemetery."

This was crazy.

A crazy that she wanted.

"But if you're here, isn't it possible that they are here, too? Somewhere?" she asked.

"Yes, it's possible. But I've told you—I have not had the pleasure of the acquaintance of your mother or grandfather."

"They could still be here," she said stubbornly.

He appeared to inhale and exhale, sighing, but, of course, he was a ghost.

He wasn't breathing.

"I'm sorry, Kelsey. Key West sometimes seems to crawl with spirits, and yet they are but two or three percent of those from this area who have passed on to whatever it is the next life brings to us," he said. "Some walk down Duval, seeking what they lost or never had, lovers come and gone, wives, husbands, children. And there are those who see one, and those who see many, like Katie O'Hara. Still, I don't suggest you share your sighting of me with those who don't already know of my presence. People do tend to think that you've lost your mind."

"I think that I've lost my mind," Kelsey said.

"I rest my case."

She frowned suddenly and gasped. "It was you—you staring down at me in my sleep. Or, you are what I fear, what I feel."

He sat very straight, staring at her indignantly. "Never!" he said.

"Was that fear, my imagination, then? My paranoia? Or was it as real as seeing a ghost?" she asked.

Once again, he seemed to sigh. "My dear, dear Miss Donovan. I don't have all the answers. I don't even have all the questions. This lack of life is much like life itself in several ways. I can only be one place at one time. I can only travel with the speed of my legs or that of any conveyance in which I might be seated. One day, before I pass over, I'd like to take an airplane ride. How wonderful! Soaring above the earth. Ah, but that is not for now. Now I am trying to discover what I can that will help you. I don't have the power to push large pieces of furniture, but I am quite proud of my prowess with a modern coffee brewer. I can push buttons. I can think. I can see. And what I see, I can tell those who see me. Am I making sense?"

Kelsey smiled. She was seated at her grandfather's desk. A ghost was sitting across the desk from her, speaking as if they were at a casual meeting.

Did the ghost make sense?

"You see me," he said quietly. "I'm trying to tell you in what ways I can help—and in what ways I cannot."

"Did you know my grandfather when he was alive?" she asked.

"I'm afraid I did not. I saw him a few times about town. But I did not know him. I spent years being nothing more than a shiver or, perhaps, upon occasion, a source of comfort, before Katie O'Hara finally spoke to me."

"Did you know my mother?"

"No, I am afraid I did not."

"Then how do you know that neither she nor my grandfather are about, haunting Key West?"

"This house is filled with pictures, Miss Donovan. I would recognize both."

"Oh," she murmured, disappointed. "What about Gary White?" she asked excitedly. "He was murdered. Surely his spirit must be wandering around seeking justice!"

"I've tried to explain—not everyone remains behind. Some pass through life to death and what comes after without this time in the midst of the veil."

"Is that what it is, really?" Kelsey asked. "A veil between life and death?"

"I don't know. That's just what I've heard it called," he said.

"I keep closing my eyes. You're not disappearing," Kelsey said.

"I won't disappear. I've been coming clearer and clearer to you since we were first together," he said. "Now…well, I'm sorry if it distresses you. You will continue to see me."

Kelsey shook her head. "It doesn't distress me. It

makes me believe that I might see those I loved once again."

"Kelsey, please don't count on that," he said.

"You were in the cemetery," she said. "You spoke softly to me. You comforted me."

He smiled. "I thought that you had felt me there."

"My grandfather believed that my mother was murdered. My grandfather might have been murdered, and Gary White was murdered," she said.

"Yes," Bartholomew said. "I've heard. And, of course, forgive me, I've been reading over your shoulder."

"But you don't know who killed Gary White?"

"I wasn't here," he explained.

"And you haven't seen Gary White? His ghost, I mean?"

"Miss Donovan, if I had the answers, I certainly would have given them to Liam by now! All I can do is help him trace what we know and…tell him what information I can get from others, like myself, I have had the pleasure of meeting. Well, usually, it's a pleasure. Now and then, one does come across someone quite unpleasant who has stayed behind. I'll tell you what I know, and what I believe. There was a man named Peter Edwards. Whether all the stories about him are true or not, I don't know. But, supposedly, he used black magic to curse or hex or kill Southern blockade runners during the war, and, later on, got mixed up with a very evil man named Abel Crowley. At some point in his life, he truly began to regret what he may or may not have done. Tattling on a man during wartime is much like killing him. Pete rued his transgressions, and he tried to use the book your grandfather had—the book in this very room—to atone for his sins. Pete is still walking around the cemetery. Perhaps he can help us again, and perhaps knowing about the books and what they are supposedly capable of doing, or enabling, is the key to what is going on now. I don't believe that men can bring about hexes and curses. I believe they are capable of greed, envy, viciousness and violence."

"All right. What do you think of Liam's theory? After reading my grandfather's notes, I think he's right that someone knew about the real reliquary, and the fake reliquary, years ago. I believe that person somehow killed my mother—though exactly how her fall was caused, I don't know. After my mother's death…" Kelsey paused, perplexed.

"What?" Bartholomew asked.

"Nothing happened. My mother died, my father and I moved away, and nothing happened. Not until Cutter died."

"A million-dollar diamond is a prize well worth waiting for," Bartholomew commented.

She nodded, and then frowned again. Out the window, she saw someone moving.

The someone was running, running around from the front to the rear of the house.

"What in the world…?" she began, jumping to her feet.

Leaving Bartholomew to follow in her wake if he chose….

If he was real….

She raced around to the back.

She saw a man at the end of the dock.

And then she saw Avery.

He was facedown in the water, twenty feet from shore.

12

Ah, but it was invigorating, fascinating, exciting beyond imagination to watch!

Ah, they didn't know....

He had been the one to do the screaming. Ha-ha, ha-ha, ha-ha, and it had worked so well.

He was invisible.

He paused for a moment. Today, he had shaved it very close. He had barely disappeared into himself before the others had come, before the frantic quest for life had begun. But then again, cutting it so close led to the brilliant wonder that he was feeling now.

Victorious. Amazed, amused, so vastly entertained.

He watched, and he felt himself so incredibly clever, so jubilant.

He backed away....

Soon, the fun would really begin.

After questioning Chris Vargas, Liam returned to the station. He realized he never had bothered to have lunch, and he managed to eat a rock-hard bagel as he looked over the reports from the day.

Gary White had played at a small coffeehouse on Margaret Street in the days before he had disappeared and died. The owner hadn't had much conversation with him. Gary wasn't a brilliant performer, but he'd been fine, playing soft tones that fit the bill for people who didn't want loud music. Getting away from loud music in Key West wasn't always easy.

He had fixed a leaky pipe for a Mrs. Vinnie Wilfred over on Simonton Street the following afternoon.

He hadn't been seen since.

He hadn't spoken to anyone about the Merlin house, nor had he mentioned visiting the library, and he had certainly not spoken to any of them about reading any books.

Liam's head was pounding. He was getting nowhere. He might be running down chimeras. No. Gary White was dead. Murdered. Someone had murdered him. The clues had to be out there.

He had died on the Merlin property.

That had to mean something, too.

It meant a killer was laughing at him as he chased his own tail.

He left the office at precisely five, thinking that Kelsey might have discovered something else helpful in her grandfather's book.

He was just pulling into Kelsey's drive when he heard the sound of her scream.

It was coming from the back of the house.

He jerked the car to a halt and went tearing around the house.

There were people in the water. Clothed people in the water.

Kelsey.

Avery.

And Jonas.

Liam rushed to the shore and saw that Kelsey and Jonas were pulling Avery from the water. Kelsey was speaking to her friend, words tumbling from her lips.

Avery was pale and bloated-looking; his lips were blue.

Jonas and Kelsey had just dragged him ashore when Liam met them there. He had his phone out, and he dialed in for emergency assistance.

His phone slipped from his hands as he reached the three upon the beach. "Kelsey, I've got the training!" he told her, pulling her from Avery's prone body so that he could begin CPR. He could hear her sobbing softly behind him, and he knew that Jonas had his arms around her, trying to reassure her. He tried to block out the sounds of life around him and give his total attention to the man before him, counting out, breathing in, pressing down, breathing out.

Nothing.

Then, after he did his best to breathe life into the man, Avery suddenly coughed and spit out a stream of water. He inhaled.

He was breathing.

He twisted Avery, trying to make sure he didn't choke on the water, and by then, the emergency technicians had arrived.

He stood up. He felt Kelsey move against him, trying to get to Avery, sobs shaking her body.

"Good work, Lieutenant," one of the EMTs said. "He's alive."

"Why isn't he moving?" Kelsey asked.

"He…might have suffered a concussion, if he fell off the dock," the EMT said. "We'll get him airlifted to the hospital."

"I'm coming with him," Kelsey said.

"Of course."

She was dripping wet.

"Go, Kelsey, they'll airlift you. I'll get there in the car," Liam said.

The emergency medical technicians had a stretcher and two of them were positioning it to lift Avery's muscle-bound and heavy body upon it. While they were doing so, Liam knew he had to get some answers.

"What happened?" he asked.

"I don't know," Kelsey said. "I saw Jonas running—"

"I was watering the plants in front. I heard a scream. I came tearing over," Jonas supplied.

Liam looked at Jonas, hoping that the raw anger and suspicion he was feeling wasn't written all over his face. "And what did you see?"

"Nothing. He was in the water."

"Kelsey?"

"I saw Jonas racing out to the water. I followed him. I saw Avery."

"He was facedown," Jonas said.

"You didn't see how he got that way?" Liam asked.

Both Kelsey and Jonas shook their heads.

"But you arrived first?" Liam asked Jonas.

"I saw Jonas race past a window, and I came after him," Kelsey said. "I was a split second behind him."

"I told you, I heard a scream," Jonas said.

"But you didn't hear the scream?" he asked Kelsey.

"I was inside—all the windows are closed and bolted," she said.

"We're ready," one of the med techs said.

"Go," Liam told Kelsey. "Stay with him. I'll be on the phone with you, and I'll be there as fast as I can drive up. They have to get to the airport, and get him in emergency transportation. I won't be that far behind you."

Kelsey nodded jerkily. "Oh, my God, if Avery isn't all right," she whispered.

"He'll be fine," Liam assured her. Of course, he didn't know that at all.

Kelsey started to follow the med techs around the side of the house.

"Kelsey, grab your purse and a sweater," he said. "Your phone, you'll need your phone," he told her.

She nodded again and went through the house. He followed her; Jonas Weston followed him.

He lowered his head and bit his lip.

Kelsey said that she saw Jonas go by the window. She'd reached the water area just a split second behind him.

Jonas couldn't have caused this.

"You want to hear something odd?" Jonas asked him.

"What?" Just inside the back door, Liam spun to face him.

Jonas backed away, his jaw tight. "I came over and helped save that man," he said.

"Sorry. I'm sorry. What?" Liam asked.

"It looked like there was something in the water. Something big. It was right beneath him," Jonas said.

"Like what?" Liam asked.

"I don't know. It's nearly dusk. The water is dark. It—it just looked like a dark shadow." He tried to offer a weak smile. "Well, you got the man breathing. I'm sure when he comes to, he'll be able to tell us exactly what happened."

What the hell had happened? Avery Slater was a well-built, coordinated man who didn't seem the type to slip off a dock.

"Thanks, Jonas. Thank you. I'm sure Avery is going to be very grateful as well. I'm glad you were here for Kelsey," he said.

He tried to keep sincerity in his voice.

He wanted the man to leave.

He had to get a few things together for Kelsey and get up to the hospital. No matter how quickly he moved, it was going to take some time to get there.

Screw it.

He would call the station and say that he'd need his own helicopter.

"Thank you, Jonas," he said again pointedly.

"Right. Right," Jonas said, backing out the door. "Call me. Call me, please, and let me know how he's doing."

"Of course," Liam promised as Jonas finally left.

Liam called the station and ordered his helicopter. He asked for a crime-scene unit to be sent out to the Merlin estate again.

He was asked what they were supposed to be looking for.

"A large black shadow," he said. "I don't know. Hopefully, the victim will be able to tell us what happened."

Ricky Long had answered at the desk. He didn't seem to think that the request was odd, but before he hung up, he asked, "Lieutenant, are we sure we have a victim?"

"What do you mean?"

"The man might have just fallen off the dock. I mean…never mind. *I* don't have any problem telling people they're supposed to be looking for a large dark shadow. After all, they're going out to the Merlin house."

Naturally, they had to save a life first. Ah, yes, running around like chickens with no heads. Desperate to get a man out of the water, desperate to make him breathe.

It had all worked very well, especially considering that it had been a spur-of-the-moment plan. He'd heard Kelsey speaking. The book! That damned book! He could have taken it; it had been right in front of him. But he'd never imagined that old Cutter had stuck notes into the thing. He'd needed Kelsey there, needed her to point the way.

But now he needed the book. God knew what else the notes said, what Cutter Merlin might have suspected or figured out by that time. Merlin had been a fool. He should have gotten rid of the real reliquary years ago. But he had held it, determined to catch his daughter's murderer....

The excitement began to ease as the med techs left with the body, with Kelsey.

He slipped back in, ready to go for the book.

Kelsey wasn't sure who gave her the blanket she was wearing. It helped, though. Winter in Florida was doing the right thing, being mild at the moment, but still, being wet, and drying slowly and stiffly, was not comfortable. And yet, other than the fact that she'd been shivering, she hadn't thought much about it. She simply realized she had acquired a blanket somewhere along the line, and she was grateful for it. She hoped she remembered to thank all the right people.

Avery didn't come to while they were in the helicopter.

He didn't come to at the hospital.

She was terrified that any minute, a doctor would walk out of the double-swing doors with a sad expression and shake his head sadly while her heart and mind rebelled at the horror of such an impossible tragedy.

Not Avery, too. Please, God, not Avery, too. Please don't let him be touched by whatever monstrosity of greed or fate plagues my family.

The day had been absurd. She should pinch herself and discover that the entire thing had been a nightmare or a daymare, or a hideous creation of her mind.

But it wasn't.

She'd never felt the wet and the cold so thoroughly in a dream. It was real. At least, this part of it was real. Before…before she had seen Avery floating facedown in the water, she'd been talking to a ghost. A ghost named Bartholomew. And everyone knew him, of course. At least, Liam knew him. Liam, the dead-steady, capable, solidly sane cop. Or so said the ghost. But the ghost knew Katie, David, Sean and Vanessa, too. Naturally. The ghost was a conch. Conchs were friendly.

She couldn't bear sitting there, waiting….

When she thought that she would lose her mind, she saw Liam walking down the hallway. How he had gotten there so quickly, she couldn't imagine. She jumped up and went running to him.

"How is he?" Liam asked huskily.

"I don't know. He wasn't conscious, but they keep telling me that I shouldn't be horribly worried about that. But they won't tell me that he's okay, either. How in God's name did you get here so fast?" she demanded.

"I decided to abuse a little power and order a copter for myself," he told her dryly. "It is police business. I believe he was attacked."

Kelsey shook her head. "Liam, Jonas didn't attack him."

"I didn't say it was Jonas."

"It's obvious that you've been suspicious of Jonas."

"Really? It's that bad?"

"Why?"

"The bone-thin leads I have point to him," Liam said.

"He didn't hurt Avery. I saw him run by the window.

I ran through the house. I was one step behind him when we plunged into the water to get Avery. Oh, God, he wasn't breathing. You resuscitated him. I don't know how long he wasn't breathing. He hasn't come to. In movies, when someone spits the water out of their lungs, they wake up!"

"Let's believe that he's going to be all right, Kelsey."

"Liam, I don't know how long he was in the water!"

"But Jonas heard him scream. That means he couldn't have been without oxygen that long. The human body is remarkably resilient, Kelsey. He'll be all right," Liam said.

She wasn't sure she dared believe him. But she was glad that he was there. She was more than glad, she realized. He was a steadying influence. He was the love and support she needed.

How strange that she realized it so clearly now. She'd been away so long. They'd been out of one another's lives. And she knew now that she had always loved him, and it had been so easy to be with him because she should have been with him long ago.

Ah, but could he feel the same? How could anyone be certain about her, when it seemed that her family and even the house itself were cursed?

Not cursed. There was someone out there killing people. A real live human being. She didn't know what forces were driving that person, but a person was trying to steal the reliquary, and that person was committing murder because of greed.

And, after all, Liam was friends with a ghost. They were all a bit different, so it seemed.

"I'm going to see what I can do," Liam told her. "I'll be right back."

When he stood and left, she saw Bartholomew. He had apparently accompanied Liam.

"You said that you wanted to fly," she told him, smiling weakly.

"Not this way," he said.

"It's all right. How was the ride?"

"Tense," Bartholomew said.

"But did you enjoy it?" she asked.

"I think I'd like to fly first class in an airplane, someplace with first-class hotel accommodations," he said. He shrugged. "I've roamed the Caribbean, I've set sail on majestic waters, I've walked streets of mud and seen a great deal of time pass. I'd like something contemporary and modern, and, of course, I can't really feel it, but I'd love a hot tub and a cushion-top bed."

He made her smile. She wished she could really touch him, squeeze his hand.

"So, does Liam know that I see you, that we converse?" she asked him.

Bartholomew grinned wickedly. "Not yet. We'll let him know at an appropriate time."

Liam came back down the hallway. He wasn't smiling, but he didn't look as if he were going to have to give her awful news, either.

"Avery's brain was not deprived of oxygen too long," he assured her quickly. "He really should make a full recovery."

"Should?"

"He's still unconscious. He took a tremendous wallop on the head," Liam said.

"So someone struck him?" she asked.

"I asked the doctors about that—they can't say for certain. They don't know how he fell into the water. The injury could have been caused by the dock if he fell a certain way. We won't know until Avery wakes up and tells us," Liam explained.

"When can I see him?" she asked.

"I brought you dry clothing. Why don't you go change, and then you can go in and see him," Liam suggested.

Kelsey nodded and thanked him for the duffel bag of belongings he had brought for her. He pointed down the hall to a restroom.

Kelsey changed from her damp clothing and immediately felt better. Oddly enough, simply being dry and warm seemed to give her more strength.

When she came out, Bartholomew was seated in one of the hallway chairs, listening. The doctor was talking to Liam.

She hurried up to the two of them, anxious to hear what was being said.

"Kelsey Donovan, Dr. Lee," Liam told her. "Kelsey is Avery's business partner and best friend. He was staying with her."

"He's going to be all right? Has he come to yet?" Kelsey asked.

"We've done scans, and we're not seeing anything worrisome. His brain activity is functioning well by all our standards, so we don't believe that he was deprived of oxygen long enough to cause damage. We're concerned that he hasn't come to yet, but such an injury to the head can, naturally, cause a coma. We're still hoping that in a few hours, he'll be doing much better."

"Thank you. May I go in and sit with him?"

"Yes, and go ahead and talk to him. Don't upset him, but talk to him. Maybe your presence will help."

He pointed to a room. She hurried through the door.

Avery looked much better than he had when she and Jonas had first fished him from the water. His color was back. There was an IV needle in his arm, and he was attached to a monitor with waving lines. Kelsey had spent enough time with her dad in the hospital to know which monitored his respiratory function and his heart, and both seemed to be functioning at an even keel.

She sat by his side and took his hand in hers. "Avery, I'm here. I'm so sorry! I wish I knew what happened. I shouldn't have left you out there alone. I'm so sorry. I love you. You're my best friend."

She thought that his hand twitched. She could swear that there was movement behind his closed eyelids.

But he remained silent.

Liam felt as if a hand were constricting around his heart; it was horrible to watch Kelsey sit next to Avery and be powerless to lessen her worry and her pain. He thought about her life, her mother gone when she was so young, her father passing when she was young as well, and then the news about Cutter Merlin.

And a friend, who had nearly died, in her house, as her guest.

But he couldn't do anything except watch her sit there.

He called down to the station and was glad that Ricky Long didn't seem to mind working overtime at all. Apparently Ricky's experience at the house had made him determined to stay out of it himself while doggedly pursuing every task Liam handed to him.

"The crime-scene unit combed the property. They looked for prints on the beach, but by the time everyone had come and worked on the victim and headed out, the beach was a mess. They couldn't get anything. They tried the dock, but there wasn't really anything to dust." He was quiet for a minute. "Lieutenant, I have to tell you, some of the crew were grumbling. They're not sure that there was a crime. They think that Kelsey's friend just fell off the dock and bumped his head." Ricky cleared his throat. "And they didn't find a large black shadow in the water."

"Thanks, Ricky. I didn't think that they'd find anything."

"No?"

"There was no trace, no clues, no leads, after a man was murdered. We know that he was murdered. Franklin Valaski verified that fact. Something is going on at the Merlin place, and I will find out what it is."

"I believe you, Lieutenant," Ricky said. He was quiet again for a minute. "Do you believe in ghosts?" he asked.

"Pardon?"

"I still swear that armor moved the night I was there with you."

Liam paused for a minute. Did he believe in ghosts? It wasn't a matter of belief. He knew that they existed. But he didn't believe that the Merlin house was cursed. He believed in a very live culprit, influenced by a belief that words on a page and incantations could help him achieve what he desired. Killing people who got in the way was simply a way to get what he wanted.

"There's a human being out there who murdered Gary White," he said at last. "I believe the same person might have tried to murder Avery Slater. We're going to get him, Ricky. That's that."

"He's good," Ricky said. "He has to be really good. The Merlin house is on a little peninsula. One way on, one way off."

He walked the street, aware of the people around him. Always, there were people. It was quiet, though. Late Tuesday night.

He walked, and he closed into himself, and he thought of all the years gone by, all that he had done, how he had waited, waited and watched, believing that if he was patient, the reward would be his in the end.

He felt sorry for himself.

He'd looked, and he'd looked, and he'd looked, but he hadn't found it. He'd been careful, then careless. Then he'd tried to return everything as it had been.

He'd had the house to himself again. All to himself. For hours. He had searched, but he was back to where he had begun.

The book was gone.

The bastard cop must have taken it.

And he couldn't find the reliquary.

He still needed Kelsey Donovan for that.

He tried to tell himself that it was fine; Kelsey might need the book to find the reliquary. She didn't know where it was. If she did, he would know it. But Cutter Merlin had left her the clues. She would find it. He had to make sure that he was ready when she did.

He looked up at the moon. He had the book that would explain what had been done. He had the book that had the Crowley rites in it.

The moon was full. Tonight, there would be another rite.

Liam went in to sit quietly next to Kelsey for a few minutes. She looked at him, and she appeared to be angry. "You know, I've known Avery a long time. We met in college. We've worked together ever since."

"Kelsey, I'm so sorry."

"You have nothing to be sorry for—you've tried to talk me out of staying at the house."

"The house isn't cursed, Kelsey."

"Oh, I know that. My family was a loving family, and the house itself was always filled with warmth and caring. It was a bit crazy, completely eclectic and fun. And I'm more determined than ever now. I am going to find out what's going on."

"Maybe you shouldn't stay there—"

"Oh, when I'm there from now on, I'll make absolutely sure that I'm locked in safely until there are a number of others around." She smiled, and her smile was anguished but still tender. "I have you with me. When you're with me…the world is right," she said softly.

The world is right, he thought. And he wondered if, when it was all over, she would still feel the same way. He wondered if she remembered that she wanted to go back to California, that she had built a life there.

"Kelsey, I'll never stop. I will find out what's going on."

She nodded.

He had his briefcase with him, and he reached into it. He produced the book, and she was surprised, and then she smiled deeply.

"You brought it with you! I'm so glad."

He nodded. "I knew you'd stay here with Avery, and I'm going to fly back tonight. I'm going back to work tomorrow morning, so I thought you should have this."

"I forgot!" Kelsey said excitedly. "Liam, I forgot all about the notes I found in the book."

"The notes?"

"Yes! Thank you so much for thinking about it. Cutter left little notes to himself in the book, or maybe he intended for me to find them. Cutter definitely knew that there were two reliquaries, and he knew that someone was after the one with the diamond."

"I wonder why, after your mother died, he didn't produce the real reliquary and sell the diamond or give it to someone," Liam said.

"Because he believed that my mother was murdered. That something caused her to fall down the stairway. He intended to spend the rest of his life waiting patiently to force whoever had killed his daughter to show his hand. It finally happened. That's why he had the fake—he was probably going to try to convince whoever broke in that the reliquary in his hands was the only one—the book, because he thought the person *believed* in Satanic power and might believe that Cutter was protected by it—and the shotgun, so he could shoot the son of a bitch."

"Well, it makes sense," Liam said softly.

"He has a note about Peter Edwards and the Abel Crowley connection. Edwards must have believed in the end, especially after he met the Crowley fellow, that he had practiced evil and would go to hell."

"I agree with that," Liam told her. "But Aleister Crowley wasn't even born until 1875. Pete Edwards must have had another source that gave him whatever Satanic rites he was practicing during the Civil War."

She nodded. "I'll bet there's reference to it in the book that disappeared from the library."

"Maybe. Jaden is doing a book search for me. It's out there somewhere. We'll get a copy."

She was sitting back, her attention all on him. He took her hand and idly stroked her fingers. "I think that we have a murderer and a thief who began it all with one obsession—stealing the diamond. He did what he felt he had to do in order to find the diamond. But he also knew Cutter, and he seemed to know some island history. He had to have a life in the Keys as well, because he spent so many years believing that he would get the diamond from Cutter. I have to ask you one question. I believe that your mother may have had a hallucinogen in her system. Did she use any drugs?"

"I told you she was on pills for pain," Kelsey said.

He nodded.

"There was an autopsy when my mother died, you know," she said.

"But they didn't test for everything so we can't be sure," he told her.

"Right."

He looked into her eyes. "Kelsey, I have to ask you this. Are you absolutely certain that Jonas was just ahead of you?"

"I saw him, Liam. I saw him racing by the window toward the back. That's why I went out."

He nodded. "All right. Thanks. I'm going to get going. Keep in touch with me by the cell phone, please. Let me know the minute that Avery wakes."

She nodded. "Of course," she whispered.

He wanted so badly to take her into his arms. He wanted to punch the world, beat it to a pulp, do something that could make the nightmare end.

He stood instead. "Kelsey, may I take the notes your grandfather left that you've already read?"

"Of course."

In a businesslike manner, she quickly went through the book, extracting finely folded papers, opening them and checking them, and handing them to Liam.

"I'll take good care of them, I promise."

"I know you will."

He kissed her gently on the forehead and left her.

Reading Cutter's notes, Liam felt a sharp pain in his heart…or perhaps it was his conscience. All those years,

Cutter Merlin had lived just waiting for the murderer to return.

He hadn't tried to get police help—it would have been in the records, or even in the memory of an older officer who would have talked about the "kook" out on the peninsula.

"Cutter, we owe you," he told himself softly.

He went back to another of the earlier notes.

"Lieutenant!" the copter pilot called to him. "Landing any minute."

"Thanks!" he shouted in return.

Back at the airport, Liam glanced at his watch while he walked to his car. It was nearly 5:00 a.m. He was going to have to try to get a few hours of sleep.

He started to head for his own home, and then changed his mind. He drove to the Merlin house.

He came slowly onto the peninsula, searching the brush and bracken along the way through the glow of his headlights.

Nothing.

At the house, he entered with the key he'd kept when the place had been rekeyed. He stepped in quietly and waited, but he heard nothing. He sheepishly admitted to himself that he wished Bartholomew was with him, but Bartholomew had chosen to stay behind and watch over Kelsey.

Bartholomew might sense if something was awry.

But after a moment of standing there, he believed that he was alone in the house.

Still, with his police-issue revolver in his hand, he

walked around. It seemed as if things were different. Just subtly different.

He went from room to room, and checked every window. Nothing had been opened. It had to be his imagination. A statue of the Virgin Mary on the voodoo altar seemed just a bit out of whack. The suit of armor that had so terrified Ricky Long seemed to be a step forward. The mummy in his open sarcophagus seemed to have shifted.

But there was no one in the house, and it was locked tight.

As he walked, Liam decided that he'd have an alarm company out the next day. He didn't know why the place hadn't gotten an alarm system years ago. Maybe Cutter had wanted the perp who he believed had killed his daughter to come back. He had spent the remaining years of his life waiting.

At last, he went upstairs. He opted for a hot shower.

He missed Kelsey. He could smell the scents of her soap and shampoo. He'd taken what he had thought that she might want for an overnight stay in a chair at the hospital, but she was still there, everywhere, in his senses and in his mind.

When he came out, skin still hot and damp from the shower, he started to hit the bed.

But Kelsey seemed to be with him. He grinned and locked the bedroom door.

He went to bed, thinking he was so exhausted that he would sleep quickly. But he didn't. Her sweet, clean, erotic scent was in the bed, and he stretched his arm out where she should have lain, and he missed her. It hurt. Deeply.

What the hell would he do with himself if she left him for another life?

He couldn't dwell on it; he needed sleep. He tried to will himself to rest.

He finally drifted off.

He woke, eyes flying open, and not knowing why.

He had heard something downstairs.

He got up quietly and slipped into his chinos and pulled a polo shirt over his head. He didn't put shoes on, but quietly opened the door and started down the hall.

He tiptoed down the stairs.

Morning's light was pouring in; it was later than he thought. A glance at his watch told him that it was almost ten o'clock.

There was nothing.

He looked across the living room. He went from room to room, swearing when he stubbed his toe on the giant gargoyle.

He went back upstairs, and through every room, and still there was nothing.

He stood still, listening. There were just the usual sounds of a winter's day in Key West. Birds. A distant sound of laughter and music. A ship's horn.

Shaking his head, he went back to Kelsey's bedroom and finished dressing.

As he did so, his cell phone rang.

"Boss?" It was Art Saunders.

"Yes, what is it?" he asked tensely. He groaned inwardly. "Another murder? What's happened?"

"Well, it's murder in a way."

"Art, spit it out, what the hell has happened?"

"Um, it was the murder of a goat. The poor thing sure as hell didn't die of natural causes. We have a dead goat on Smathers Beach. Looks like its throat was slit and its entrails were arranged across the sand. You'd better come quickly."

13

The little notes her grandfather left were on thin, delicate paper, folded discreetly in the pages. She couldn't just shake the book to find them; she had to go page by page.

As she did so, she read aloud when a particular passage seemed relevant.

"Here's an interesting one, Avery," Kelsey said. Avery hadn't opened his eyes yet, but she was speaking to him, just as the doctor had said that she should. "It's a prayer for a house! 'Oh, Lord, let your presence protect this time and space, may you bless those who dwell within, and may you blacken and burn the hearts of those who do work against thee. Cast Satan and all his minions from here, and let all that is done here, and all that abide here, rest in your arms, the arms of Goodness, and Mercy, and Peace. Let us reflect your Divine Spirit, and no other.'"

"Very wordy," Bartholomew said. He was leaning back in a chair at the far side of the room. He'd been there with her, and she was touched to realize that he had watched over her when she had drifted off through the night. Sleep hadn't been easy. The chair extended, the hospital staff had given her a pillow and blankets, but she was cramped and tired.

When she had gone for coffee earlier, Bartholomew had been torn. He didn't want her alone; he didn't want Avery alone.

In the end, he had decided that whoever was attempting murder at every turn was still in Key West—obsessed with the reliquary and the Merlin house. She had gone for coffee and an egg sandwich, and he had stayed and watched over Avery.

"Nice."

It wasn't Bartholomew who spoke; it was Avery.

Kelsey gasped, nearly throwing the book from her hands. She looked at the bed. Avery was offering her a weak smile.

His eyes were open.

Bartholomew jumped to his feet, looked at Avery and sank back into his chair, arms crossing over his chest as he smiled at them both like the Cheshire cat.

"Oh, my God! Oh, thank God! Avery, you're all right!" Kelsey said.

She managed to set the book on the hospital bed before she bent over him, kissing his cheek, his forehead and his lips.

"Wait, wait!" he told her.

She jumped back. "Did I hurt you? Oh, I'm so sorry."

"No, no, I'm fine, you didn't hurt me, only my head is spinning just a bit. Where am I? No, no, dumb question. We're in a hospital."

Kelsey furrowed her brow, worried. "Avery, don't you know what happened?"

He was thoughtful for a second, touched his head and winced. "Yes, I do. I was talking to the dolphin."

"Yes, you were out at the docks. You were fascinated by the dolphin. I went in, and you were going to talk to the dolphin awhile longer. When I came out, you were in the water."

He nodded.

"Avery, what happened?"

He looked at her as if something was dawning in his mind. He smiled. "She saved me. He saved me. I'm certain. I felt myself falling, falling…and the creature lifted me up!"

"Avery, Jonas and I pulled you from the water. Liam administered CPR."

"I don't remember that, but thank you. No, bless you. I'm assuming you all saved my life. But, Kelsey, honestly, I do remember the creature, the dolphin, being there. I think I would have gone straight down if it hadn't been for the dolphin."

He was obsessed with the dolphin. He was marveling about the animal, and, of course, she was amazed and gratified, as well. She'd heard such stories before, about dolphins rescuing swimmers, divers, surfers and shipwreck survivors. She didn't think it at all impossible that a dolphin had kept him from drowning initially, and she was deeply grateful.

But she needed information from him.

She pulled out her cell phone and dialed Liam. He

sounded a little tense when he answered, but she told him quickly, "Avery is awake."

"Thank God," he told her. "Does he know what happened? Can he talk to me on the phone?"

"He thinks that the dolphin saved him at first—the dolphin that hangs out by the docks next to the beach."

"Okay," Liam said. "And before? Can he talk to me?"

She held the phone up to Avery's ear. She didn't hear Liam's question to him, but Avery's response was clearly audible.

"Hell of a headache, and hell of a thing. I don't know what happened. I was leaning over the dock. Then my head was killing me, the world was going black and I was in the water."

Kelsey was certain that Liam asked him to think, to try to remember every second leading up to what had happened.

"I was…was talking to the dolphin. Do you know they make noise? It was kind of making a little noise and moving back in the water…and…"

Avery stopped speaking. "I think I did hear something. Like a pounding. Yes! I felt a vibration on the wood, too. I thought that Kelsey had come back out. But before I could really register the sound or turn…I was in the water, my head killing me, the world going black and spinning."

Liam spoke again.

"I didn't scream!" Avery protested. He waited, listening. "I'm telling you, I didn't scream. I would remember screaming. In surprise, in pain, in…whatever! I didn't scream. There was no time. It was bang, and then the rush of the water and the pain in my head."

Avery listened again to Liam, closing his eyes for a minute. "Of course. Of course, I will do my best to remember more, but…it was sudden. So sudden. Seriously, I went into the water. How the hell do you scream in the water? I mean, I suppose you could try, but…no one would hear it, certainly. Oh, my God. I was attacked on that property by some bastard!"

Kelsey, watching him, shook her head. "You don't ever have to go back there!" she whispered.

"Like hell! I want to know who did this!" Avery told her.

He spoke to Kelsey's cell phone again. "Sorry, Liam. Kelsey was telling me that I didn't have to go back there. I told her no slinking ass was driving me away from staying with her. Whoever this is wants to separate her from the rest of us. I'm not letting that happen! What? Oh, I haven't seen the doctor yet. I woke up with Kelsey reading to me, and then she called you right away. All right, yes, of course." He closed the phone and handed it back to her.

"You hung up on him?" she asked.

"He wants a doctor to come in and see me, and see how I'm doing, and decide how long I have to stay here," Avery explained. "He was in the middle of something. Blood and guts on the beach."

"What?" Kelsey demanded.

Bartholomew was back on his feet, anxiously frowning.

"There was a dead animal on the beach, that's what

it sounded like. Not a human being," Avery explained. "Are you going to go and get the doctor for me?"

"Yes, of course!"

Kelsey ran out to the nurses' station, excitedly told the woman on duty that Avery had come to and ran back to the room. There was a different physician on that morning, but he came in just seconds after Kelsey had returned to the room.

He spoke to Avery, listened to his words, asked him to point his fingers in different positions, alike and opposing, and stared into his eyes carefully with a light.

Afterward, he supported Avery as he stood for the first time, and they took a few steps together.

Finally, the doctor said, "You're looking very well, Mr. Slater. Very well indeed. That was a nasty bump you got on your head. We'd like you to stay one more night for observation, then take it easy for a week or so."

"Oh, I can't stay," Avery said.

"Avery, they said that you needed to stay in the hospital another night," Kelsey said.

"Well, I can't. I need to be with you. And you know that you can't stay here. You need to be working on your grandfather's estate," Avery said firmly.

"I don't want you here alone," Kelsey said.

"Here's the deal, Kelsey, and that's that. I'll stay, if you'll go home. And if you'll have another friend come over during the day while Liam is working. That's it, that's my final offer!"

The doctor looked from one of them to the other.

"This *is* a hospital, miss. Your friend will be safe here."

"I take it he never saw *Friday the 13th,*" Avery said, grinning. "Parts one or two!"

"I beg your pardon?" the doctor said.

"I'm sorry, nothing," Avery said. He looked at Kelsey. "I will catch up on *People* and *US*. I will be fine. You'll call someone to come and get you—someone who will stay with you. And I'll think about what happened, and try to remember."

Kelsey felt as if she were being ripped in two. She knew now that her grandfather had counted on her finding the reliquary, on doing the right thing with it.

She needed to go through his ledgers, to find out how he had labeled the various pieces and where he wanted them to go.

But she didn't want Avery to be alone.

"Avery, you're staying. I'll get on the phone with Liam and work things out."

She looked across the room. Bartholomew had proven he was a willing if spectral guardian.

Bartholomew was staring back at her.

"Oh, no!" he said firmly. "Where you are going, I'm going. I am not staying here and leaving you and Liam alone down there. No. No, absolutely not! *No*—and I mean it!"

No goat had ever deserved to end its days so heinously.

Franklin Valaski stared at Liam, shaking his head. "Liam, not to judge, but why me? Shouldn't animal control have been called on this one?"

"We have laws against animal abuse, and this is abuse

if I've ever seen it," Liam said. "Hell, I don't even know where anyone got a goat on this island!"

"Up on Stock Island, sir!" Ricky Long told him. Along with members of the crime-scene unit, he and Art Saunders were working the bizarre crime.

Liam looked over at him and shrugged. "There's a fellow up there with goats. I mean, there may be some down here, but…roosters. We have roosters and chickens everywhere. You'd have thought this nut might have gone for a rooster. It wouldn't be all that easy getting a goat!" Ricky Long continued.

Liam hoped that was true. That would help him a great deal.

He looked around. The men and women of the unit were all working diligently, searching the beach for any evidence—gum wrappers, cigarette butts, footprints, trash in containers, anything and everything—but he was afraid they were also thinking that he was losing his mind. They were all still working a murder; there were drug busts daily, prostitution rings, grand larceny, gang violence, smuggling and any number of other serious events happening, and they were looking for clues to a goat-murderer.

"Hey!" he snapped loudly, drawing everyone's attention. "I have good reason to believe that whoever butchered this goat killed Gary White. We're looking for an organized man who functions well day by day but has a seriously delusional personality. He's taking after Peter Edwards, an historical character who supposedly sacrificed goats on the beach in a like manner to curse Southern blockade runners. And if I hear one more snicker, someone is going to be on trash duty for the next month!"

Everyone went back to work.

Liam turned to Franklin Valaski. "Cause of death?" he asked flatly.

Valaski stared at him. "Liam—"

"Cause of death!"

"All right, thankfully, I think the throat was slit first. This is an isolated area, near the fort, busy by day, dark by night. Perfect for someone to get a goat out here, and even if anyone had been around to hear, the animal would have died so quickly it wouldn't have had much time to let out a noise. Get the windpipe, and, well...."

"What kind of a weapon?" Liam asked.

Valaski sighed, his gloved hands on the wound.

"Something incredibly sharp. Like a sacrificial knife."

"It's not a problem at all, really, I don't mind!" Vanessa assured Kelsey. "I have work with me. Copies of a lot of the film we took, my computer...right now, I'm weeding through, looking for the best footage and clearest explanations of different events we chronicled, along with the main event, the massacre on Haunt Island... so I'll be fine. And Sean will be fine without me for a night," she said, grinning. "It's good to miss each other now and then—it makes you know how wonderful it is when you're together!"

Kelsey smiled. "Thank you."

"And I will be with you. I don't work at all today. I can help you at the house," Katie assured her.

They were in Avery's hospital room, and Avery wasn't pleased.

"I'd be fine alone," he insisted.

"You'll be fine giving me your opinions of what we've got," Vanessa said firmly.

He threw up his hands. "I feel useless. I feel worse. I'm taking up time that people need."

"Avery, please, deal with it!" Kelsey said firmly.

Avery looked at Katie. "You won't leave her for a minute? I can't believe that Liam approved this, but…" He lifted his hands in aggravation once again. "I am overrun by women!" he moaned.

"But we all have cute friends," Katie teased.

"Don't add insult to injury," he moaned. "I do not need to be fixed up!"

Kelsey laughed and kissed him on the cheek. "Behave. Promise?"

"I'll keep him in line," Vanessa said.

Katie and Kelsey waved, leaving the hospital room at last. Katie O'Hara had driven up, and she and Kelsey would drive back. In the morning, when Avery was released, someone would make the trip back up to bring him down to Key West and the Merlin house. He was stubborn; he was not going to stay anywhere else as long as Kelsey was staying there.

As she drove, Katie said, "So we've determined that Avery was attacked. It's a pity that he didn't see anything. Or hear anything. Whoever is doing all this is incredibly good, I'll give him that much."

"He did see something. He saw a dolphin. Well, we

both saw the dolphin. It is a fascinating creature—it observes people as we observe it," Kelsey said.

"I should have been outside, watching over him," Bartholomew said from the backseat.

Kelsey saw Katie frown at the ghost in the rearview mirror.

"It's all right—I see him," Kelsey said wearily, closing her eyes as she leaned back in the passenger's seat.

"What?" Katie asked. The car swerved slightly.

"Sorry, sorry!" Kelsey said, opening her eyes and sitting up straight. "I shouldn't have spoken while you were driving. I can see and hear Bartholomew just fine, thank you very much."

Katie's jaw dropped.

"Katie, it's fine. I'm glad that Bartholomew is such a wonderful ghost, that he's so watchful. I'm thrilled to know that ghosts exist. I have to believe in a concept of heaven—it's the only way I can live with everything that has happened in my life. I'm sure many people feel that way, and some scholars say that's why we invented religions. But Bartholomew is great, he gives me faith and hope and all kinds of good thoughts," Kelsey said.

"Bravo," Bartholomew murmured.

Katie still couldn't find her voice.

"It would be lovely if he had come across my mom, though," Kelsey said.

"I'm so sorry," Bartholomew said.

Katie gazed over at Kelsey. She started to speak, then stopped. "Wait! Tell me again—there was a dolphin at your docks. One that watched you. One that seemed intelligent and interested in people?"

"Yes," Kelsey said slowly.

"Kelsey...oh, never mind! Wait! We're almost there. You'll remember when we get there. Never mind," she repeated excitedly. "Kelsey, your mom was always watching out for injured sea creatures. She helped save all kinds of animals, and instigate legislation, but...I think that dolphin does know you."

Kelsey frowned. She and her mom had been in a group that had gone out and saved a beached dolphin off of Smathers Beach years ago, and they'd gone north in the state once to help rescue a stranded manatee, too.

Katie turned on her blinker, and they turned off into the parking lot of one of the Keys's dolphin research establishments, a nonprofit organization that did swims and interaction with the creatures and worked with them on intelligence levels. They also took in old animals that were no longer working at various theme parks across the country.

"You remember this place, don't you?" Katie asked.

"Yes, of course. We came several times." She gasped. "Oh, they took in the dolphin we rescued that time! And it somehow made it back to our docks...and came back here on its own. Yes, yes, I do remember! Its name was Morgan. The guys were all drinking Captain Morgan rum after the rescue, and he became known as Captain Morgan!"

"Morgan, for short. They like to work with quick, short names," Katie said.

She set the car into Park and headed across the stone parking area to the front door. A woman at the counter told them that Betty Garcia, director of animal management, was in, and she would call and see if she was available.

While they waited, Kelsey bought Avery several T-shirts with dolphin emblems and sayings. She smiled as she did so.

Bartholomew groaned softly at a few of her choices, but she ignored him.

Betty Garcia appeared to be about sixty; she had a sprightly step, a beautiful smile and sparkling blue eyes. Kelsey didn't remember her.

She remembered Kelsey.

"How lovely to see you, Kelsey! You've grown up just beautifully. Your mother would be so very proud of you!" She held Kelsey's hands for a moment, and then turned to Katie, giving her a hug and a kiss on the cheek. "I'm so glad you drove up. Of course, I heard about Cutter, dear. Were you able to see him at all before he died?"

Kelsey swallowed and shook her head.

"Well, well, he led a good life. So, how can I help you?"

"Betty, I think that Captain Morgan might be down by Kelsey's place again," Katie said.

Betty smiled. "I think you might be right. He is out. But we don't worry about him. He's one of the dolphins we let swim when a storm is approaching, and he always comes back. And once every two or three years, he takes an outing." Her beautiful smile faded. "He's all right?"

"Oh, yes," Kelsey said quickly. "My friend is convinced that a dolphin saved his life."

"He fell into the water with a conk on his head," Katie explained briefly.

"Well, look who you're giving this information!" Betty said. "Are you asking me if I think it's possible? Yes. Dolphins have been known to go so far as to push drowning victims to shore. They've been trained for the military, which, of course, doesn't thrill me. I always try to weigh human life against animal life, but...well! There are those who think we're wrong to keep dolphins in captivity, but we have all manner of animals in captivity, don't we? Many of ours wouldn't survive in the wild, but to some, that's not the point. In my mind, God gave the world to all creatures. Man rose above the rest. He eats cows, makes glue from horses' hooves and does many a deed far more evil than rescuing and learning about wonderful mammals like dolphins." She laughed softly. "Did you two want a tour? I'll send someone down in a few days if Morgan doesn't come back up. I'm not surprised that he's at your place, though, Kelsey. That animal loved your mother. He was in your little lagoon there right after he was rescued. Don't you remember?"

"Vaguely," Kelsey said. "I—I've been away a long time. A really long time. I forget."

"Well, your mother loved that dolphin, and that dolphin loved your mother. If you go in the water, he'll swim alongside you. He's very friendly. I just worry about him because he is so friendly. We'll take a drive down soon."

"That's great. Thank you, Betty," Kelsey said.

"Now, really, how about a tour? It's been so long since you've been here," Betty said.

"We'll come back," Katie promised. "I just wanted...I just wanted Kelsey to have a chance to see you and ask about Captain Morgan."

"Anytime, girls. And we'd love to have you back as volunteers."

"I actually live in California now," Kelsey said.

"Ah, well, this will always be home though, won't it?" Betty asked. She gave them a wave. "I've got to get back to work! Therapy session with some of my best girls and some autistic children this afternoon. Now, that's something so enjoyable! If everyone just saw those children with the dolphins... Ah, well, it takes all kinds to make a world, right?"

Back in the car, Katie smiled at Kelsey. "Okay, so I couldn't give you the ghost of your mom, but...I don't know. Maybe Captain Morgan came back as her representative?"

Kelsey felt Bartholomew's hand on the back of her head, a gentle stroke.

"Love never dies, Kelsey. Maybe that is her way."

"And that from a ghost," Kelsey said. "I'll take it. Thank you. Thank you both."

Liam took the short drive to Stock Island by himself.

The last key before Key West, it had been so named because, for years, it was where all the stock had been kept.

Now, of course, it still had much more land for animal

facilities, but it also had its own share of bars and restaurants and hotels, a theater and much more.

He was at the third farm that sold goats when he met with success.

"Yes, we sold a goat just yesterday," the clerk in the farm's office told them. "Henry. He was a three-year-old, sold to a man with a preserve up in the middle Keys."

"How do you know that?" Liam asked.

"Because the man told me!" she said.

"Please tell me that it was a credit-card sale," Liam said.

"Oh, no. The man paid cash!"

Liam winced. "You wouldn't still have any of those bills in the register, would you?"

"No, I'm afraid we deposit every night."

"You have a bill of sale?" he asked.

"Of course!" she said.

"May I see it?"

"Of course," she said again, eager to be helpful.

"What did this man look like?" Liam asked.

"Oh, um, regular height. He had a beard, a mustache…and he was regular build. You know, not skinny, not heavy."

"What was he wearing?"

"A sweatshirt with a hood. It has been cool a few of the days lately."

She was describing anyone, he thought.

She handed him the bill of sale.

He wasn't surprised to see the name of the purchaser.

Bel Arcowley.

* * *

"Go to the cemetery," Bartholomew said.

Kelsey turned back to look at him. "You think that... we might find my mom?" she asked. "Or Cutter?"

"I haven't seen them yet," Bartholomew said patiently. "But I thought you might like to meet Pete Edwards."

"Will I be able to see him?" Kelsey asked.

"I don't know," Bartholomew said. "But Katie will."

That seemed good enough.

Katie drove to the Key West cemetery, parking as close as she could to the open gate.

They had been there just a few days ago, Kelsey thought.

Burying Cutter.

They walked down Passover Lane, moving slowly.

"Where does he usually hang out?" Katie asked.

"By the Confederate Navy section," Bartholomew told her.

Kelsey glanced over at Katie, wondering what she was seeing.

"Anyone?" she whispered.

Katie glanced at her. "Several people," she said softly. "I don't know how to tell people to see ghosts. Just... I guess just knowing that they may exist is the best way."

"Open yourself up," Bartholomew told her.

She wasn't sure how one "opened" themselves up, but she tried to concentrate on the cemetery. It was peaceful, eclectic and beautiful in an odd way. A glorious angel rose above one tomb, and she appreciated the beauty of the funerary art.

"I believe I see one of the Curry women," Katie said. "She's mourning the death of her husband. She might not know that she has joined him."

Kelsey looked. The air seemed to ripple.

"She's a lovely woman in a draping dress, short bobbed hair," Katie said. In the same tone, she continued, "Do you think I've had too many island drinks?" she asked Kelsey.

Kelsey smiled. "I know that we're walking with a handsome man in a hat and elegant brocade coat who is manly in tights," she said lightly.

"Hose, my dear girl. Hose. I do not wear tights," Bartholomew said.

The woman to whom Katie had been referring suddenly began to become a form before Kelsey's eyes. First there just seemed to be an outline of a figure, and then Kelsey saw her.

Katie gripped her by the arm. "Don't stop and gape."

"Very rude, I'm afraid," Bartholomew said.

"I'm so sorry!" Kelsey said.

"Leave her to her thoughts," Bartholomew said.

The Beckett family vault was ahead to their left, while the O'Haras had their small mausoleum farther on, toward the monument to the sailors of the *Maine*. Kelsey's family members were in a vault in the back section. The cemetery also had avenues, but she wasn't sure where everything was, so Kelsey simply followed Bartholomew and Katie.

As she did so, shapes and figures slowly began to form here and there before her. She saw at least ten spirits walking in the graveyard.

She couldn't help scanning the specters or spirits before her, hoping against hope.

"There," Bartholomew said.

She saw the man. He was old, perhaps eighty or ninety. His clothing had something of an Edwardian appearance to it, and he knelt down in prayer.

"Slowly," Bartholomew said.

They walked behind him.

"Peter," Bartholomew said.

The man looked up. He saw Katie and Kelsey. He stared at them both. He seemed to want to struggle to his feet. Bartholomew reached down to help him up.

"You see me," he said. Kelsey was surprised that he addressed her, rather than Katie.

"Yes," she said softly.

"Why? Why are you here?"

"People are dying, Peter," Bartholomew said. "Someone is copying your rituals."

The ghost shook his head slowly. "I tried to atone. I knew that the hatred in my heart was so deep that it was the evil itself. I did not make things happen. I made people believe that they could happen. I had the book, the book of goodness against evil."

"*In Defense from Dark Magick,*" Kelsey said softly.

He nodded. "I prayed with it. I prayed for those I hated, and those who were betrayed. And I prayed for forgiveness, for the war took so many souls, and I added to the misery."

Kelsey moved closer to him. "What about a man named Abel Crowley, Mr. Edwards?"

He waved a hand impatiently in the air. "A fake, a fraud! A man who had heard of me and my supposed powers during the war. He came wanting to know about my rites and my sacrifices. He wanted to be known as a wicked man, a Satanist. He came to me as a friend, and I told him of many of my sins."

"What did you sacrifice?" Katie asked.

"Goats, roosters, on the beach. But they became dead goats and roosters, and no more," Peter told them. "Crowley was a fool—I doubt he had any relationship with Aleister Crowley. He wanted to be revered and feared. He opened his house to the desperate, and he told them he could help them through secret arts. Only fools believed him. He worked as many a voodoo priest or priestess or fortune hunter has worked. He would gather information and pretend to *see* it, and then he would sell that information in his work. He gathered together the very rich for a coven, and he took their money and caused them to do the evil deeds he wanted done." He stared at Kelsey again. "I'm sorry. I'm very sorry for whatever is happening. But I have nothing to do with it now. I learned. Evil people will use fear and awe to make others do their bidding. Know that, and don't be afraid, and you will find the truth." He waved a hand in the air. "There's nothing else I can tell you," he said. He turned.

Bartholomew helped him back to his knees. "Thank you, Peter," he said.

They walked slowly out of the cemetery.

Kelsey kept looking.

She didn't see her mother.

And she didn't see Cutter.

She couldn't sense or feel them, either.

She did feel a sense of overwhelming sadness.

It was time to get back to the Merlin house.

And time to find the reliquary.

14

"I've got it, I've got the book!" Jaden said, the excitement in her voice radiant through Liam's cell phone.

"Already?" he asked.

"FedEx—and you owe me," she assured him. "I put a rush order out, and it was a rare-book shop in upstate New York. Oh, and you owe me for the book, too. It isn't a first edition—but it wasn't a megaseller by any means, so each new print run was fairly small. It's a fourth edition, and it was still two hundred dollars, so you can head over and pay me and pick it up anytime you like."

"Thanks, Jaden. I'm on Stock Island. I just brought a sketch artist out here, so I'll be about another half an hour."

"Why don't you meet us at O'Hara's?"

"All right—be careful with the book, huh?"

"I need to be worried about an old book most people would pay me not to take?" she asked.

"Hey, who knew a goat needed to be worried on Smathers Beach last night?"

"I heard about that. What the hell happened?" she asked.

"That's what I'm investigating now."

"The murder of a goat?"

"The *sacrifice* of a goat," he said.

He rang off from Jaden and watched as the clerk gave one of the station's forensic artists a description of the man who had purchased the goat, watching as the face took on life. There was something about the eyes that seemed familiar, but in the end, Liam was disappointed.

The sketch looked like a drawing of the Unabomber.

But it might help.

He was still waiting for the artist to finish with the last details when his phone rang.

"Liam?" It was Kelsey.

"Hey, how is Avery?"

"Doing really well. We had to force him to stay in the hospital," she said.

"We?" he asked.

"Katie, Vanessa and I. Vanessa is staying with him tonight. I'm back at the house. Don't worry, I'm not alone—Katie is with me."

He frowned. He'd had an alarm company over there during the day; she hadn't known about it.

"Kelsey, how—"

"Katie knew the two men setting up the system. We all met, chatted and had tea before they left. I came home, Liam, because I had to. I have to figure out where that reliquary is. And, thank you. The alarm system should have been a given. Anyway, Katie and I are here, we're reading and sorting, and looking through everything we can find."

He wasn't sure why he felt so worried.

"They finished setting the alarm system?" he asked.

"Yes, and I have the secret codes down pat and all that. I'll show you when you come home."

When you come home. The words were sweet.

"I have a better idea. I'm just finishing up on Stock Island, and Jaden got the copy of the book that was taken from the library. The book about Abel Crowley and Pete Edwards. I'm going to meet her at O'Hara's. Come on up with Katie, and we'll head back to the house together."

She agreed, and they hung up.

He looked at the sketch again. He wondered if the goat purchaser and ritual sacrifice slayer had worn fake eyebrows to match his beard and mustache.

When she hung up from Liam, Kelsey thought that he had called her right back. Her phone rang, and she answered it.

"Hello?"

At first, she heard nothing.

Then, she heard breathing.

"Liam?"

There was no answer.

She hung up and looked at the number on her caller ID. It was listed as Private.

Thinking little of it, she shoved her phone back into her pocket.

"Ah, another one!" Bartholomew said. He was sitting behind the desk in Cutter's office, reading from *In Defense from Dark Magick*. He seemed to have the art of turning pages down quite well, but he looked at her. "Sorry, I'm not talented enough to unfold the paper. It's parchment thin."

"Thanks, I've got it," she said.

Katie had been going through the bookshelves one by one, picking up, dusting off and returning books and objects, and making sure that nothing was hidden behind any of the books. She walked over as Kelsey took the little parchment from Bartholomew and carefully opened it. She read aloud.

"Kelsey was always my little wonder child. She was fascinated with history. Her friends' parents sometimes thought I must be very odd, even scary, because of the objects I collected. But Kelsey knew and understood peoples and cultures, and as we often discussed, there are so many paths to God. Kelsey knew that the true path to God only came through great sacrifice. She knew this even as a child."

"What a fascinating fellow. I'm so sorry that I did not know him," Bartholomew said.

"But what does it mean?" Katie asked.

"It means that he was the rare fellow who respected all beliefs, no matter his own. Glorious, really. What a fine man," Bartholomew said.

Kelsey shook her head. "Keep looking for more notes. If that's the last, he was trying to tell me something— I just have to figure out what it is. Oh! I forgot. Liam wants us to meet him at O'Hara's," she said. "Jaden got a copy of the book that was missing from the library."

"Intriguing. Let's go," Katie said.

Kelsey picked up the book in front of Bartholomew. "I'm not leaving this anywhere," she said.

"Good idea," Katie said, nodding sagely. "Give me a minute just to finish this shelf—then I'll know where I am when we start up again."

"Okay. I want to run upstairs and just wash my face quickly, too, if that's all right," Kelsey said. "Dust in my eyes. I'll be right back down."

She headed out of the study and across the living room, but paused there. She took a good look around. There were still boxes and crates to be gone through, but she had the strange feeling that whoever had gotten into the house when Cutter died had already gone through them. After his death, Liam had caught kids in the house, and then Gary White and Chris Vargas.

But who else might have gotten in before the locks were changed?

And why was she too afraid to leave her own door unlocked at night?

She did a circle as she stood there, noting the mummy. The large outer sarcophagus stood with the head end against the wall to the right of the fireplace; the open inner coffin was braced against it, and the mummy, still completely wrapped, lay within the inner coffin. To the other side of the fireplace was the voodoo altar. She kept turning. The giant gargoyle looked at her benignly. Gargoyles kept away evil spirits, she reminded herself.

She liked the gargoyle. She'd called it Harry when she'd been a kid.

The animal heads looked down mournfully from the wall. The medieval suit of armor, standing near the staircase, stared blankly at her.

As she stood there, her cell phone started ringing again. Absently, she pulled it out and answered it, thinking it must be Liam to tell her something he had forgotten.

"Hello?"

Once again, she heard the breathing.

Impatiently, she hung up and started for the stairs.

In her room, she washed her face, felt a lot fresher and started back down again. As she did so, the phone started to ring.

She glanced at it. The caller ID once again said Private Number.

Irritated, she answered it. "What?"

She expected the breathing.

She didn't get breathing.

A man's voice, a whisper, spoke to her.

"I'm watching you. I'm watching your every move," the voice said.

She felt as if the hair rose on her flesh, as if she were frozen in place. The voice sounded detached, and it sounded close. It was rough and husky, and menacing. It seemed to creep right into her body.

She fought the fear.

"Good for you, buddy," she said and hung up.

She met Katie and Bartholomew in the living room.

"What's wrong?" Katie asked her.

"Nothing—obscene phone call," Kelsey said.

"Probably a prank, but let Liam know," Katie advised her. "I hate that!"

She nodded, and they headed out. She carefully punched in the code for the alarm. As they walked down the porch steps, she suddenly paused.

"What?" Katie asked.

"I want to run around back to the docks for a minute. See if Captain Morgan is there. He may not understand, but I want to thank him. For Avery! Avery is convinced that the dolphin saved him," Kelsey said.

"Sure," Katie agreed.

Dusk was coming, and it was beautiful out. The colors of the sky were pastels, except where the sun sank in the west in a fiery ball that shot out streamers of gold.

When they came around the house, the docks, the trees—even the mangrove area where Gary White's body had been found seemed mysterious and beautiful.

Katie and Kelsey walked down the dock. Bartholomew remained on shore, arms crossed, as if he guarded the dock.

"I don't see Captain Morgan," Kelsey said.

"I don't, either," Katie agreed.

Just as they spoke, water and air spurted from the surface just below them at the right edge of the dock. Kelsey went down on her knees.

The dolphin was there. He looked at her with dark eyes that gave away nothing.

"Captain Morgan, my friend. You are a marvelous creature. My friend thinks that you saved his life, and I hear it's quite possible. Thank you," Kelsey said.

"Hi, there, big fellow," Katie said, hunkering down by her.

The dolphin let out shrill squeaking noises, and backed away, flapping its flippers.

"I think he's answering us," Katie said.

"Maybe. He does work with humans," Kelsey said.

"It's getting dark soon," Bartholomew snapped from the beach end of the dock. "Let's go."

"Good night, Captain Morgan!" Kelsey called, and she and Katie turned and walked toward Bartholomew.

As they started around the house to the road off the peninsula, Kelsey's phone started to ring. She saw that it said Private Number, and she ignored it.

They had reached Front Street when her phone rang again. She was certain it was going to say Private Number.

It didn't. It had a local phone exchange, 305.

She answered.

She heard breathing, laughter and the throaty whisper.

"Don't get wet, Kelsey. Remember, I'm watching you."

She didn't have a chance to reply.

The line went dead.

Liam headed from Stock Island back to the station. The sketch artist was going to scan his drawing into his computer that night, and tomorrow they could play with the image, taking away hair, trying to remove anything that might have been costume or artificial.

Checking on the fingerprints, he found out that there

was only one set on the magic box with the floating silk forms Kelsey had given him.

The prints were hers. They were in the system because her parents had believed in fingerprinting children, should they tragically be kidnapped or find themselves lost.

"It was wiped clean," the tech told Liam. "There are smudges, so I know that it was wiped down, and wiped well. If someone is pulling apart that house when no one knows it, that someone is wearing gloves."

Liam wasn't surprised.

He left the station, eager then to meet Jaden, Ted, Katie and Kelsey. He was anxious to see the book.

When he walked in, O'Hara's was quiet. He didn't see the others at first; Jamie was behind the bar, and he directed Liam out to the back patio.

Clarinda was there, working her evening shift as a server. She was seated with the others, taking a break, so it seemed.

Jonas wasn't with her, he noted.

"Hey, all," he said.

"Hey!" Kelsey said, rising to greet him.

He wanted to reach for her, enclose her in his arms and just hold on to her. He hated being away from her, and it hadn't even been a full night.

He kissed her lightly on the lips, longing to linger and bask in the scent of her skin and her hair but aware of their audience. He crawled onto the bench by her side.

Bartholomew was there, seated at the far end of the table. Through some of the foliage, he had a view of Duval Street. He seemed to be brooding.

And watching.

"Voilà!" Jaden said, producing a copy of the book. *"Key West, Satanism, Peter Edwards, and the Abel and Aleister Crowley Connection!"*

He took it from her. "Thank you, Jaden. Have you looked at it?" he asked her.

She nodded. "Well, yes, sorry, of course. Page two hundred twenty. You'll love it."

"Read it aloud," Kelsey told him. "We just got here. We haven't had a chance to get into it yet."

He did so.

"In his golden years, Pete Edwards rued his sins, and made public much of what he had done. He said that he'd never committed murder, but that he had relied on rites learned from a Santeria priest on an excursion in the islands, and from a voodoo priestess in New Orleans. While neither religion worshiped Satan, voodoo practitioners were known for communication with unhappy spirits, and Santeria also recognized malignant beings in the underworld. He concocted his own formula, partially drawn from his affection for Dante's Inferno *as well—drawing a pentagram on the beach and placing lanterns at each point. Animal sacrifice was carried out in the center of the pentagram. Though he sought the help of Satan, it was for a godly reason, Pete Edwards believed. The South claimed the war was fought over state's rights, but in Pete's eyes, the Confederacy stood for slavery and nothing else. He was doing God's work through the devil to end the war. In the end, he turned back to God, the Christian God, and did penance. The man calling himself Abel Crowley came to Key West at a*

time when Pete was trying to atone. Crowley had heard about Pete's exploits during the war, but was of the belief that Pete had downplayed his role. He was convinced that Pete's mumbo jumbo of Satanism, voodoo and Santeria demanded blood, and that there was an incredible power in worshipping dark forces. From eyewitness accounts, it's suspected that Abel Crowley was a magician and a hypnotist; he could use mind control to force what he desired."

"Sick people," Clarinda noted.

"Very, but it's interesting to realize that people don't really change, don't you think?" Ted asked.

"Yes, but…," Kelsey began.

"But what?" Liam asked her.

"I don't know. I believe in the power of the human will, and in goodness, and in evil—in men's hearts. But it's night. Me not believing it is night will not make it day," she said.

"Yes, but," Katie argued, "isn't every reality a perception?"

"Only if we let it be," Kelsey said. "Think of *The Emperor's New Clothes!* Someone out there knows that what isn't real, isn't real."

"You all are giving me a headache," Ted said.

Clarinda stood. "Let me get your orders. Jamie said I could take an hour and hang with you all, but let me get the ball rolling here. Fish sandwiches are fresh and delicious," she suggested.

"All the way around? We'll make it easy?" Liam suggested.

It was agreed.

While Clarinda went in to get drinks and put in the food order, Jaden told Liam, "You might want to move on to page three hundred."

He did so.

"Aloud, please!" Kelsey asked him.

He read, *"At the turn of the century, with Spiritualism still a rage across the western world, the concept of owning holy relics became popular. Throughout Europe through many ages, and in other societies as well, holy relics were said to be godly. Lockets with hair from dead saints, reliquaries with bone fragments, even pieces of the deceased kept in small caskets, were said to ward off evil. In contrast, the fingers and toes of hanged criminals were also said to keep away evil. Abel Crowley became obsessed with the collection of these reliquaries, but on his deathbed, Peter Edwards swore that he had never owned such a relic, and that Abel Crowley had been a hypocrite—he had only ever sought out such reliquaries for their monetary value in gold, silver and gems."*

"Well, there you go," Katie said softly.

Kelsey sighed. "It's still so hard to fathom. Mind control, good spirits, evil spirits, my mom gone a very long time, Gary White just murdered, Cutter…and Avery."

"And," Ted pointed out, looking at Liam, "the slaughter of a goat on Smathers Beach."

Liam shrugged. "The mind can go awry. Perhaps it all began innocuously enough—a man wanted to steal a diamond. The diamond was in a reliquary. We're back to the whole point of perception. If the thief *believed* he could practice black magic—maybe in context with the fact that he knew people were on certain medications that could cause hallucinations—he could project fear and terror and make it happen. I don't know. I'm hoping we have a real lead. The clerk who sold the goat gave an artist a description of the culprit. Tomorrow, we'll put it through the computer and see what we can come up with."

Coming out of the back door of O'Hara's, Clarinda suddenly dropped her tray. The drinks exploded in a shower of liquid and glass.

"Oh!" Clarinda gasped. "What a klutz! I don't re-member the last time I did something like that," she said.

"Let me help you," Katie said, leaping up.

"It's all right," Clarinda said.

"Nonsense. My uncle owns this place, and I've picked up many a spill, mostly my own."

Kelsey was quickly over by the pair. "Your uncle owns the place, Katie. You go get more drinks, and I'll help pick up."

"I know where to find the broom," Liam said, rising and walking past Clarinda. She stared at him, wide-eyed, and he suddenly found himself wondering if she was suspicious of Jonas herself.

Was she afraid that the picture, when cleaned up via computer image, would show them a clear shot of Jonas?

He swept, the girls collected large glass frag-ments and Katie came out with more drinks and their sandwiches.

Liam was determined not to betray his suspicions in

any way, and while they sat around and ate, he asked Kelsey how she liked the alarm system.

"I'll get used to it," she said. "Believe it or not, I've never had one before. But it's good. It's a very good idea."

"You had an alarm system put on the house today?" Ted asked.

"Yes. Well, Liam took care of it," Kelsey said.

"And your friend Avery is all right?" Jaden asked. "Vanessa is staying up with him?"

"Yes, and I'm sure they're getting along fine. He's an animator, and she's a scriptwriter, editor—they'll be fine," Katie said, waving a hand in the air. "Oh, Kelsey, we don't have to go up and get them tomorrow—Sean is going to go." She laughed softly. "I guess my brother wants to make sure he gets the love of his life back."

"That's great," Kelsey said.

"You're busy, huh?" Clarinda asked.

Kelsey nodded. "I'm going through my grandfather's logs. I'm going to find out everything he has, and exactly what he wants done with it all."

Liam noted that she didn't mention the reliquary.

That night, when they finished eating, they were ready to head out. Clarinda was still working, so they bid her good-night and went in to say good-night to Jamie O'Hara.

Bartholomew was standing on Duval when they emerged from the pub. He was waiting for an elegant woman. She was his lady in white, Lucinda, not the woman he had died for, but the love he had found in the afterlife.

He bowed low as she came to him; he straightened, and she accepted his arm.

He looked back, aware that Liam was watching him. He smiled. "Good evening, friend. I'll see you tomorrow."

He nodded. Katie saw Bartholomew, but Ted and Jaden, anyone on the street, *and* Kelsey would surely consider him mad.

He turned away from Bartholomew, glad of the glow of warmth and love that seemed like an aura around the two.

Ted and Jaden went their way—after he'd paid Jaden—and he and Kelsey drove Katie back to the Beckett house.

"Oh," Katie said, getting out of the car. "Kelsey, tell Liam about the phone calls."

"Pranks," Kelsey said, waving a hand in the air.

"Tell me," Liam said.

"Some idiot is calling me. First he called and breathed. Then he called and told me he was watching me. Then he called and said something about me not getting wet."

"Not getting wet?" Liam asked.

"We had just walked out on the dock," Katie said.

"Let me see your phone," Liam told her.

Kelsey dug in her pocket and handed it to him. He saw the calls listed from Private Number and then the exchange and number on the other.

"The call with the actual number came after you'd gone out on the dock?" he asked.

Kelsey nodded.

"I'm calling this in tonight. Maybe the graveyard shift can help," he said.

He called in; none of the day crew was working over-time, but he knew Tony Santini, working the research desk. He gave Santini the number and handed Kelsey back her phone.

"Good," Katie said, satisfied. She bid them all good-night.

Liam waited until she got to the door; David opened it before she knocked, and waved to them as Katie went in.

They drove on to the Merlin house.

Lights burned from the parlor and the porch. The house seemed welcoming.

Amazing what a good alarm could do. Peace of mind.

Perception, Liam thought. Maybe life was all in the mind, all perception.

No, he'd been a cop too long to believe that.

"I was trying not to be obvious with the code," Kelsey told him as they exited the car. So I chose Av-ery's birth date, 1130, to get in, and backward to close up at night."

"We just have to remember to set it; an alarm is only good when it's set," he told her.

She twisted the key, stepped in and punched in the numbers on the alarm pad. Liam came in behind her, and Kelsey grinned and reset the alarm.

She turned into him. "Liam, I found another note today. I have a feeling that it might be the last I'll find in the book, but I think that I can find out what he's saying to me if I keep studying it. It's as if the answer is there—I just have to really put my finger on it."

He was suddenly, overwhelmingly tired. "Tomorrow," he said softly.

She nodded. She had set her bag down when she'd keyed in the alarm. She started toward the stairs without it, and then came back, looking at him sheepishly. "I can't help it. I need it in the room, and I need the door to the room locked."

He put his arms around her and drew her close. "Guess what?" he asked huskily. "I locked the door to the room last night."

She smiled. "You slept here?"

"I did. I couldn't be close to you, but I could sense you near me, and dream and imagine having you beside me," he told her.

He loved her eyes. They were great pools of brilliant blue, ever-changing in their depths, like the colors of the ocean when the sun was out, when a storm was coming, when night fell. Now they were tender, and soft, and sparkling, as well.

She pulled from his arms and headed for the stairs, turning back when she was halfway up.

"Well?" she demanded.

"Well!"

He raced after her. By the time they reached the bedroom door he caught her. He kissed her long and hard and deeply against the door, drawing her hands over her head and pressing against her. His heart thundered; he felt as if he were on fire, and still, he had to kiss her there, breathe her in and wonder how he had lived all the years she had been gone.

At last, his mouth still firm upon hers, tongues thrusting in a wantonly hot and probing kiss, he turned the doorknob, and they staggered into the room, laughing around the kiss. She drew her shirt over her head and let it fly and pressed against him again, her fingers looping beneath his waistband.

"The door," she whispered against his mouth.

"The door," he whispered back.

Still entangled, he backed his way to it and slid the bolt. Then he pushed her forward, and in a second they were on the bed. He released her bra, and her breasts tumbled into his hands and a spasm went through him, hardening him instantaneously. He covered her bare breasts with the curve of his hand, the molten caress of his tongue, and worked his way down. They were still half-clad, and entangled in their clothing, and they disentangled themselves while they made love, touching, stroking with fevered lips and tongues. Finally they were both fully naked and he rose above her and thrust within her, and for a moment he caught her eyes, and the honesty within them, and then she wrapped herself around him and they began to move, undulating slowly, then frantically, and when he came, he knew that sex had never been better, and that there would never be anyone in his life like Kelsey Donovan again. She'd been the ghost in his heart since she had left, and it seemed that all his life, he had been waiting for her return.

Exhausted, sated, they fell against one another. Entangled in one another's arms, they slept.

* * *

He sat in Cutter Merlin's chair at Cutter Merlin's desk, and he felt elated. An alarm system!

They were such fools.

So clever, and they knew nothing. The invisible could see so much while unseen. Even alarm codes.

Nothing. They knew nothing.

He was brilliant, and the last episode on the beach was going to give him everything that he needed.

Everything.

Because it was time. Kelsey knew. Even if she didn't know that she knew, the whereabouts of the reliquary were in her mind.

The time had come.

A spasm of anger ripped through him. She was up there now, in her room, with Beckett. They were probably naked. Sweating and copulating. He could imagine the feel of her skin. The feel of her breasts. And that bastard Beckett was with her. He was tempted to get the shotgun that they still hadn't found, and go in, guns blazing. He'd see the look on Beckett's face when he fired straight between his eyes. And then Kelsey would be there, naked on her knees in the spill of the cop's blood, and she would be begging him; she'd do anything for her life….

He couldn't do that. He still didn't have the reliquary.

He had to stop thinking about her.

In her room.

Locked in. It irritated him beyond all reason that she locked that door. Why? Why the hell would she lock the door in her house, when she was alone, and when she was with the cop?

And why...why in hell sleep with the book?

Kelsey, in the room, naked, sweaty, making love to the cop.

He winced.

The reliquary was the prize.

But he had waited long and patiently.

The prize would come now as he chose it.

Well, the cop had to go to work. Investigating him! Ha ha, that was a laugh.

The cop would go to work.

And he would be alone.

With her.

It was time.

He smiled suddenly. He rose and moved in silence through the house. He knew the house so very well.

There were things he could do this night that would ensure all would come to him tomorrow.

15

That morning, Kelsey beat Liam downstairs. When he dressed and came down for work, she was reading the newspaper. The sacrificial murder of the goat was the lead story.

"Poor goat," Kelsey said softly. She turned, leaning against the counter, and told him, "Yesterday, Katie took me by the dolphin center, and we spoke with Betty, the director there. I think the dolphin in back did save Avery. I'm pretty sure it's a dolphin we called Captain Morgan, and my mom was instrumental in saving him years ago. Isn't that amazing?"

He reached for a coffee cup. "Amazing, and amazingly good—for a change," he said.

She looked down at the paper again, a small smile on her face. "Well, the coffee is good, too. Bartholomew brewed it."

He nearly dropped his cup. He forgot all about the coffee. He set the cup down and turned to Kelsey. "What?"

"She sees me, old fellow. I told you she would," Bartholomew said. Liam frowned, not seeing him. He walked to the entrance to the dining room. The ghost was comfortably seated at the table, his feet up on the next chair as he read from Cutter Merlin's book.

He carefully looked back at Kelsey. "You—see a ghost?"

"Yes, I do."

"Describe him," Liam said skeptically.

"He's very handsome, actually. And quite charming," Kelsey said.

"Thank you!" Bartholomew called.

Kelsey walked to stand in the doorway with Liam. "Great hat, white hose, buckled shoes…brocade coat, waistcoat, fantastic poet's shirt. Really, Liam, you should have introduced us at the very beginning."

"I was supposed to tell you that we have a friendly neighborhood ghost?" he asked.

Kelsey smiled and walked back into the kitchen. "He's an amazing ghost."

Liam caught her by the shoulders and turned her around to face him. "You really see him? And hear him…and talk with him?"

She smiled. "Yes."

"And you weren't…afraid?"

Her smile deepened. "Well, I did have a bit of a start, but I began to see him slowly…but no, I'm not afraid. I'm thrilled to know him. It means that there really is more," she said softly.

He pressed his lips to her forehead. "Well, good, then."

"I really wish I could see my mom, that's all."

"None of us, including Bartholomew, really understand how it works, who stays, and why," he said to her.

She nodded. "I understand. I'm still—glad."

He leaned to kiss her lightly. She moved against him.

He eased back, knowing he had to go to work. "You've heard from Avery?"

"Yes, he's doing well. David is going to drive up with Sean and pick him up—and Vanessa, of course. They'll be back by early this evening."

"Good," Liam told her. "All right, I'm out of here. I'm going to go over and tear Gary White's place apart, give the guys in Forensics some time to work the computer picture and to track down that number that was calling you. Keep in touch."

He started out, then came back. "Kelsey?"

"Yes?

"Do me a huge favor. Stay locked in. Don't go visit the dolphin, don't get your mail—stay locked in, please?"

"Liam, it's broad daylight—"

"Just today, please, Kelsey. Bartholomew is with you. Handsome and charming, right?"

She laughed. "Are you jealous of a ghost?"

"He should be!" Bartholomew called.

"Handsome and charming is in love, did he tell you? Her name is Lucinda, and they like to haunt the streets together," Liam told her.

"Lovely. Go to work. I'll stay in. I'll be fine. I have a lot of reading and a whole lot of looking to do."

"A needle in a haystack," Liam said.

Kelsey smiled. "I have a few ideas," she assured him. "The religious angle. All paths to God. Hey, I haven't found it yet. I'm thinking about a few things. I think that it all fits in together. I'll call you as soon as I have found it."

"Bartholomew," he called.

"I'll be here, I'll be here!" Bartholomew assured him.

He left the house at last. His first stop: Gary White's apartment.

Kelsey sat at the dining-room table with Bartholomew, going over everything with him and wondering if truth and lies and perception weren't the same thing. Was she really talking to a ghost? Was it a mass hallucination? Had they all hypnotized one another?

She preferred the concept that she was carrying on a conversation with a charming ghost named Bartholomew.

"Well, was it worth it? He almost dropped his cup when I mentioned that you had brewed the coffee," Kelsey said.

Bartholomew laughed. "Ah, yes, the look on his face. Well, he deserved it. He was the worst skeptic in that group. Poor boy, though. He never had a cup of coffee."

"And it really is excellent," Kelsey said.

"Thank you."

"Well, down to it! The truth, the answers, are in this note, I know it. Listen, I'm going to read it again," Kelsey said.

"Kelsey was always my little wonder child. She was fascinated with history. Her friends' parents sometimes thought I must be very odd, even scary, because of the objects I collected. But Kelsey knew and understood peoples and cultures, and as we often discussed, there are so many paths to God. Kelsey knew that the true path to God only came through great sacrifice. She knew this even as a child."

Bartholomew shook his head. "I don't understand. If he's giving you clues, I'm not getting them. Why not just say where he left the reliquary."

"He couldn't do that. Someone else might have found the book and the notes," Kelsey explained.

"So, what you're getting out of it is—religion?"

"Yes, and he's using it for two reasons—he found a great hiding place, and because he was a believer in a higher power—God." She smiled. "He was also a believer that love—love for each other or love for God—sometimes involved making sacrifices. He didn't believe in the book he was holding. But he held that book because the perpetrator believed in the power of that book. Oh, I'm not sure, nothing is a direct clue. But, anyway, time to get started."

"Where?" Bartholomew asked.

"Corner table, the runes and the masks of the Norse gods. The cabinet with the chalices, the mummy and the voodoo altar," she said.

"I'm not much help," he said ruefully.

"Being with me helps me," she assured him.

"Start with Odin," he suggested.

* * *

Gary White's room was a cluttered mess.

Liam knew that officers and a crime-scene unit had gone through it and found nothing, but he wasn't satisfied.

He was certain that Gary White had been in on some part of what was going on. He had been too young to have been guilty of subtly finding a way to kill Kelsey's mother. He went through the clutter of magazines—most of them old, taken from coffeeshops or tables on the streets—paper bags, fast-food containers and junk. He wasn't sure if he was sorry for the man or angry when he saw the musician's guitar sitting next to the one over-stuffed chair.

The drawers were full of worn clothing; the hamper was overfull. He was about to leave the apartment in frustration when he looked at the chair again.

He strode to it and pulled up the cushion. It was heavy, with a zippered upholstery cover over it.

He unzipped it and stuck his gloved hand into the cushion. He felt around.

And he found something. A book.

He pulled it out.

It was *the* book.

Had he been killed because he had held out on someone?

Or had the murderer never thought that Gary White could hide something so completely?

"Not in Odin, eh?" Bartholomew asked, leaning against the wall as he watched her.

"Not in Odin. Not in the chalices, not in any of the rune cases," Kelsey said.

"The mummy?" Bartholomew suggested, wrinkling his nose.

She walked over to the mummy. Though the coffin was open, there was a sheet of glass over it, keeping the mummy from deteriorating. She lifted the glass. This mummy had been dug up long, long ago. Long before they had known about preservation techniques. Though the sarcophagus was nice, handsomely painted, she knew that it was common for the upper-class working masses. The mummy hadn't been buried with jewels or anything of value.

"I'll probably break it to dust," Kelsey muttered. She had on a pair of gloves, not the best, but the kind that came with certain hair products. She'd found them under the sink. Cutter's last housekeeper must have used them.

"Dust to dust," Bartholomew reminded her.

She tried to feel around the mummy. The old wrappings made her sneeze.

"Finding anything?"

"No."

"How about the sarcophagus?"

"I'm going to have to crawl in it."

"You don't have to do anything," Bartholomew reminded her.

She crawled in and searched every corner, patting the sides. To her astonishment, a secret panel sprang up from the floor of the sarcophagus.

"Bartholomew!"

"You found it?"

"No! But…"

She sneezed and crawled out. Perplexed, she looked at Bartholomew. "But it… I'm not sure. It's just made me think."

She walked to the door of Cutter's office and turned on the lights. The room looked as it always did. She started walking around, pushing at books, stomping on the floor.

"Oh, dear," Bartholomew said.

She shook her head. "I'm not going crazy. I keep thinking that someone is in here, even when it's locked up. Even now, with an alarm. I lock my bedroom at night. Even Liam locked the door when I wasn't here."

"I can pat walls," he said.

"Perfect, help me!" she said.

He started around the room. As he did so, Kelsey's phone rang. Distracted, she answered it without looking at the caller ID.

"Kelsey."

It was Liam.

"Hey," she said.

"You're all right?"

"I'm fine. How's it going with you?"

"I just found the book taken from the library. It was in Gary White's apartment," he said.

"So…Gary White signed himself in as Bel Arcowley?"

"So it seems."

"But he's dead," Kelsey said.

"He had to have been acting for someone," Liam said.

"Who?"

"I don't know. But I know where he was going when he left the library. To work for Jonas. Kelsey, don't let anyone in. If anyone comes over, don't answer the door. Not until I'm with you."

"Liam—"

"I may be paranoid, but I'm a cop, and better safe, right?"

"Okay," she said softly.

"What are you doing?"

"Well, I was going through all the religious artifacts. I found a secret drawer in the sarcophagus. It made me think. I'm tapping around in his office, trying to see if I can find another hiding place."

"Keep in touch, all right?"

"Of course," she said.

"Call me if—anything," he said.

"I promise."

"Kelsey?"

"Yes?"

"Never mind, we'll talk later," he said.

They hung up.

She began looking around Cutter's desk. Her phone rang again, and she answered it, almost dropping it as she did so, she was so certain she would find something.

"Hello, Kelsey."

She recognized the voice instantly. She started to close the phone, but she heard laughter.

"Don't hang up on me so quickly, Kelsey. I just want

you to know… No, you don't have to do anything. You don't ever have to do anything you don't want to do. Except die."

Liam walked into the station and straight over to Ricky Long, who was working with the telephone number that the caller had used to threaten Kelsey.

"Sorry, Lieutenant. It's a prepaid phone, no contract necessary, sold all over, and the purchaser probably paid cash."

"Pretty much what I expected."

"But we're trying to trace it down to the most likely area through the satellites," Ricky told him hopefully.

"How close can they narrow it?"

"Down to a block, possibly, and if it lets out a signal again, it can be pinpointed more accurately," Ricky assured him.

"Great. Keep me posted."

He headed over to the desk where Dave Aspen, the sketch artist, was working with his sketch scanned into the computer.

"Well?

"Lieutenant," Dave said, looking up. "What timing. I've gone ahead and done a slide show with various different scenarios of facial hair and even nose putty."

"That sounds great. Let me see."

He pulled up one of the rolling chairs to sit next to Dave while he hit a computer key. "Okay, here's a cleaned-up version of what I drew yesterday from the clerk's description. Next, without the beard and the mustache. Now, the nose seemed a little too long and pointed, so I played with it. Oh, wait, this is the one with the eyebrows thinned. Now here's the one with the thinned brows, facial hair gone, best representation of the lips and mouth I can manage, and—"

He broke off; Liam was standing.

He should have known!

Just as he did so, Ricky came rushing over to him.

"Lieutenant!"

"What, Ricky, what?"

"He called her again. The phone is on the Merlin estate. He might be calling from within the house."

She'd had it. Completely had it. She was on to something, and this idiot was calling her, trying to scare her out of the house.

"Back off, ass," she said and snapped the phone closed.

"What was that?"

"A jerk!" she said angrily. "I'll fool around in here in a minute again. I don't know what I'm looking for. And I'm feeling… I don't know. Like I need to sit down, like I'm going to pass out."

"Then you need to sit," Bartholomew said. "Take a break."

"No, no, I can't. I think I have to keep going. Okay, I tried the mummy. The chalices, the runes…Odin! Time for the voodoo altar."

She walked back out to the living room and stared at the altar. There were numerous saints, little statues, big statues. There were offerings to the saints on the black velvet altar cover. There were Mardi Gras beads spread over it in a series of colors. A child had offered up a princess doll that was almost life-size. It had been given to the Virgin Mary, who looked down at her benignly, her hands spread in an offer of tenderness and peace.

There was a pounding on the front door. She walked to it and looked through the peephole.

Jonas was out there. Liam had told her not to let anyone in. And she was starting to feel like hell, so weak and disoriented.

He was waving at her wildly, saying something, but she couldn't hear him.

She shouted at him. "I'm sick, Jonas! Go away."

"Watch yourself, Kelsey," Bartholomew said. "What's wrong with you?"

"I don't know. I'm fine. I must have eaten something… bad."

She stumbled back to the voodoo altar.

Her eyes returned to the large princess doll. A great sacrifice for a small child who had surely loved the doll.

She stared at the smiling princess doll, and at its crown. The crown was large and covered in cheap gold paint. Perhaps the doll was supposed to depict Mardi Gras royalty.

The altar seemed to spin before her. She blinked, positive she was seeing something.

Her phone started ringing. It was difficult to reach for it. She managed to get her hands around it. She flipped it open.

"Hello?"

She sensed movement and heard the fall of a

surreptitious footstep. She looked up. The sound was coming from Cutter Merlin's office.

She saw him.

Just as she heard Liam's voice.

"Kelsey, get out of the house. Get out of the house quickly. I'm on my way," Liam said.

She wanted to answer him.

Then the phone was slapped from her hand.

She didn't have the power to resist.

He shouted his orders as he left the station. "No sirens. And no cars on the peninsula. No one into the house but me, and start surrounding it. He has Kelsey. If he sees us, if he has any idea that we're on to him, she's dead. I repeat, no sirens, and stay back! Move it, move it!"

He rushed out of the station house and to the car. He tried not to shake, knowing that if he did so, he'd wreck the car. He thanked God that it was a small island.

He parked at the wharf, got out of the car and started running.

He passed Jonas's bed-and-breakfast and burst out onto the road that led to the Merlin estate. As he came to the end, he saw Bartholomew standing there, his hands in the air.

"Not the door—he'll see you. Don't use the door," Bartholomew said.

"Then what? He's got her—get the hell out of my way!" Liam cried.

"No! Follow me. Get down, follow me."

He began a quiet, quick jog behind Bartholomew.

On the front lawn, he nearly tripped over the body of Jonas.

He kneeled down. Jonas groaned. He was alive.

"I...saw someone. In the attic. It wasn't Kelsey," he said. "I thought it was you, but I wanted to be sure. I was on the porch...and then..."

"Help is coming," Liam told him. "Hang on."

Jonas nodded.

"And stay down. Stay down, please."

Liam moved on, following Bartholomew.

To his amazement, the ghost ducked into the crawl space beneath the house. He followed the ghost.

He didn't see it at first. And then he did.

It was a trapdoor. It had been used frequently, and gave without a single squeak.

It led to Cutter Merlin's office.

"Give it to me, Kelsey," he said.

She blinked, trying to focus. She wanted to lash out, strike him. She couldn't. He had his hands on her shoulders, and she couldn't move.

"I know you."

"You know me well. I was your handyman around here when you were a kid. I took all kinds of bull from your sainted family. Now, I want the reliquary. Where is it?"

He shook her. She felt her head rattle.

"I haven't found it."

"You're a liar."

"You killed your friend," she said. "Why? You're Chris Vargas. You killed Gary White, and you had him doing all kinds of dirty work for you. Why did you kill him?"

"I had to kill him. He wouldn't give me the book. I knew that I couldn't beat Cutter without Abel Crowley's original book of spells. Cutter's book *In Defense from Dark Magick* was too powerful for the spells that I knew. I finally learned that Abel's spell book was talked about in *Key West, Satanism, Peter Edwards, and the Abel and Aleister Crowley Connection,* but Gary lied and said he couldn't find the book. When I found out he lied and that he was keeping the book for himself—I had to kill him. I wasn't ready for Cutter to die on the night he did. I was just continuing to scare him—leaving him clues about what I wanted—and hoping that he would finally just give up the reliquary. Things went too far that night, and he died of a heart attack. I knew, though, that he would leave you a clue."

She was scared, definitely scared. Terrified. But it didn't really seem to register. She was going to fall down, and there would be nothing he could do.

She started to slip. He dragged her up, shaking her again. "How much coffee did you drink?"

Her heart sank. Whatever he had drugged her with had been in her coffee. And it had been so good. She'd had several cups.

She smiled at him. "A lot."

Suddenly she saw that he had a huge blade out, next to her face. He forced her down to the floor, the point of his knife near her eye. "Kelsey, I'll cut you to ribbons before I do worse things to you and then kill you," he said. "Or, I'll tell you what. Your friend Jonas is lying on the ground outside. I haven't killed him. Yet. I'll drag him in here and cut out his eyes and tongue in front of you. How's that?"

"You want the reliquary?" she asked him. "Take it."

He slapped her. Hard. For a moment, her teeth rattled and the room spun.

"Where is it?" His voice was shrill.

"Tell me how you killed my mother, and I'll give you the reliquary," she said.

He started to laugh. "Your whole family loves coffee, Kelsey. That, combined with her painkillers and a phone call I made to her. She was rushing—rushing down the stairs because she believed a madman was killing you in the living room. That's how she fell. That was my first. I didn't know that it had worked. Stupid, huh? But I slaughtered a bunch of beautiful Key West roosters for that one. And it worked. So, you know how your mother died. Now give me the reliquary. Her death was supposed to force Cutter to give up the reliquary—I would have killed you, and your father next, if you hadn't left so quickly."

He pressed the blade of the knife close to her right eye.

"The crown," she said. "Take it. You won't get far with it. Liam will come after you."

"Liam is passed out cold somewhere. Maybe he had a traffic accident. Maybe he's dead. The world will know that the house is cursed. What do you mean, the crown?"

"The doll's crown," she managed.

She didn't see him reach for it. He'd had to drop her to do so. She heard his exclamation of pleasure.

And she knew then that he would kill her.

Liam took great care, crawling through the trapdoor as carefully and silently as he could. It took some effort; the Persian rug covered the trapdoor.

He made it into Cutter Merlin's study and carefully stood, drawing his gun.

The door was ajar. He could hear Vargas talking to Kelsey. She was still talking.

He started out. "Vargas!"

Vargas spun and dropped, dragging Kelsey up in front of him. Liam saw that he was holding a large bowie knife, and that the blade was now against Kelsey's throat.

"You've got the reliquary. Leave her," Liam said.

Vargas shook his head. "I need her. She has to come with me."

"Come with you where? There's no way out."

"There is," Vargas assured him. "Stay back."

With his eyes on Liam and his arm tightly around Kelsey, Vargas started to back up. Liam followed him.

He looked into Kelsey's eyes. They were glazed. She was trying to move, trying not to be dragged like such a limp rag doll.

"Shoot him," she mouthed.

"Stay back!" Vargas demanded.

He was going all the way through the house. Liam knew that his men were out back, but they'd also been told to stand down until given an order. They wouldn't risk Kelsey's life.

Where the hell did he think he was going?

Vargas must have read his mind. He started laughing. "I have a boat back there, Beckett, under the dock. When I'm some distance away, I'll let Kelsey go. You rush me now, and I'll slit her throat," he said. "I've been the smart one, you stupid cop. All these years."

"So smart I caught you killing a goat," Liam said.

That gave him pause. He hesitated. But then he started moving again, backing slowly away. The knife was chafing at Kelsey's throat. Liam saw a thin trickle of blood.

He lifted his hands. "I just want Kelsey."

"Drop the gun, then."

Liam dropped the gun. He lifted his hands again. "I just want Kelsey."

Vargas kept going backward.

Step by step.

They came to the back door. He keyed in the alarm and opened the door; the reliquary tucked under his one arm, his grip around Kelsey treacherous as he held her and the knife, and worked the alarm and the door.

A trapdoor. How often had the man been in there with him? He'd done work for the Merlin house. He'd found the door. And that had begun it all.

"Stay back!"

"I'm keeping my distance," Liam said.

He silently cursed himself, wondering when the man had gotten the boat to the docks.

He kept his eyes on Kelsey for a moment, willing her to live.

She stared back at him gravely.

The door was open; Vargas dragged her down the steps and slowly, slowly backward toward the dock and the beach. Liam followed at a distance, now keeping eye contact with Vargas. At the foot of the docks, Vargas tightened the knife. "Stay there, stay there…. No, come out. Do what I say or she dies, do you understand?"

"What do you want?"

"The boat. Get into the water. Drag it out."

Liam jumped down into the chest-deep water. His heart sank. The boat was a Donzi, a speedboat.

But as Vargas asked, he drew it from beneath the dock and loosened the ties.

"Now get back!" Vargas shouted. He was getting nervous, it seemed. Liam realized that he should have been drugged like Kelsey, and Vargas had imagined that he'd take the reliquary and dump her in the water before anyone was any the wiser.

He backed up slowly. Vargas had a bad time getting into the boat, trying to get his balance, drag Kelsey in and keep the knife at her throat all the while. It took him some time. Bartholomew was on the dock, trying to steady Kelsey, trying to trip up Vargas.

Liam prayed for the moment when he could move, take his chance to rush the man.

Vargas would never let her live. He'd throw her over in deep water. And she was drugged; she wouldn't be able to stay afloat.

Vargas was almost in the boat. Liam was ready to leap when the boat suddenly tilted out of the water.

Kelsey crashed overboard. Vargas tried to hold on to her, and he went in, too.

Liam made a dive into the water, desperate to find Kelsey. Something swirled around his feet.

It was the dolphin. A good twelve feet long, powerful. The animal had caused the boat to tilt. And, though he couldn't really believe it, the dolphin was leading him to Kelsey.

He dived, and dived again, following the large, sleek sea creature.

And his arms came around Kelsey. He pulled her from the water, screaming her name as they surfaced. She gasped, choked, coughed, and opened her eyes and stared into his.

"Liam," she said.

He half swam and half dragged her to the shore. As he did so, something like an iron fist landed on his back.

Vargas. Vargas, rolling him over, straddling him, lifting the knife high over him in a frenzy. He bucked with all his strength and threw the man from him. Vargas lifted his arm to throw the knife.

His aim went askew as Kelsey staggered to her feet and threw herself against him. The knife went flying to the ground, and Vargas shoved Kelsey aside, desperate now. He turned and ran for the house.

Liam jumped to his feet, racing after him. Kelsey came behind him. As they tore into the living room, Vargas suddenly stopped.

Just stopped, dead still.

"No." Vargas was staring at nothing. Staring toward the fireplace.

"No!" he repeated.

Liam started forward. Vargas rushed to the fireplace and reached into it, drawing out the shotgun that Cutter had held on his lap, the shotgun that had disappeared on cleaning day.

"Kelsey, down!" Liam said and made a dive himself for the police-issue Smith & Wesson he had dropped earlier.

Vargas shot wildly, at nothing.

But it wasn't nothing.

There was a woman in the room, slowly materializing. She was wearing a blue dress, and she had long dark hair and had beautiful blue eyes.

Kelsey's mother.

The shots went straight through her.

She walked to Vargas and said softly, "There is a hell, and you will rot in it. You will never touch my child!"

"Witch! You're not real. I'll show you your precious daughter!"

Vargas let out a long gale of hysterical laughter and spun around, aiming the gun at Kelsey. She rolled swiftly to the side, and Vargas tried to follow her. His finger twitched on the trigger.

Liam took fleeting aim with the Smith & Wesson.

And he shot the man.

Vargas fell.

Liam could hear his men out in the yard, running now toward the house. He hurried to Kelsey, trying to help her up. She was still staggering, but when she'd gotten to her feet, she whispered, "Liam, I'm…I'm fine."

He eased his hold on her. He watched as she walked to the apparition of her mother.

"I loved you so," Kelsey whispered.

A spectral hand touched her cheek with infinite tenderness, and then disappeared in a soft glow of light.

"Love is forever, my darling child," Chelsea Merlin Donovan said. "I will always love you."

Epilogue

"I must admit, I was afraid that you'd want to do one of those *Titanic* deals. You know, how the woman threw the gem back into the sea!" Jaden said.

Kelsey laughed. "Hell, no! That's too much money. I've divided it between a lot of Cutter's favorite charities. AIDS, cancer, heart, diabetes and the animal shelter! The reliquary itself is being returned to the Church and France, and I'm actually well on my way to getting a great deal of Cutter's collectibles to the museums where he wanted them to be. Oh—the fake reliquary? We're giving that to you and Ted, Jaden," Kelsey added.

Jaden gasped. "Oh, you can't. It's far too valuable."

"But you don't intend to sell it. And anything is only as valuable as what one pays for it. You two should have it. You will appreciate it, as Cutter did."

Jaden looked at Ted.

"We couldn't!" Ted said.

Jaden pinched him. "Maybe we could!"

Liam laughed softly. "Kelsey wants you to have it. Take it."

"Can you imagine, that monster lurking in that house,

on and off, all those years? I guess he found the way in when he worked for the Merlins all those years ago," Katie said. "Ugh! Too creepy."

"I think," Kelsey said, "that he got himself attached to Cutter, and he saw the book, and he found out more about the things that had gone on in Key West and decided bit by bit to put together everything that had been used over the years. He *was* invisible, because he could come and go so easily. He was a thief—and he was a psychopath! At least, that's how I see it."

"You don't hate the house now, do you, Kelsey?" David asked her, frowning.

They were all at O'Hara's. In the weeks since Vargas had attacked Kelsey, they had made a point of meeting each other every Sunday at four, if not during the week. They were at the back-patio table: Ted and Jaden, Clarinda and Jonas, Katie and David, Sean and Vanessa, and Kelsey and himself.

Good friends were hard to come by.

And all of his friends—including Jonas—had forgiven him for being a cop.

They still tried to figure out what could have caused such a madness, one that allowed a man to function in the world by day—and live in his own world of black rites and pure greed and obsession.

"No. I love the house," Kelsey said.

Vanessa asked her softly, "When are you going back to California?"

Liam couldn't help but answer for her. He leaned closer to the table, pulling Kelsey to him.

"She's not," he said, and he produced her hand,

displaying the ring they had chosen. It wasn't a diamond.

Kelsey had opted for an emerald.

"An engagement ring?" Clarinda asked, grinning.

"Absolutely, short engagement," Kelsey said. She turned and smiled at Liam, that dazzling smile that made his heart melt. "We lost a lot of years somewhere. We're hoping to make them up."

"Oh, oh! Oh, how sweet!" Jaden said.

"Saccharine, actually!" Ted said with a laugh. She elbowed him, and he grunted.

"But what about your partner and best friend, Avery?" Jonas asked.

"Oh, I can answer that!" Vanessa said, actually waving a hand in the air. "If I may! Well, Avery Slater met a nurse in the hospital. They hit it off right away. Avery is looking at property down here. There's a little Victorian on Whitehead, near the Hemingway House, that he wants to buy."

"Really!" Clarinda said, laughing. "Well, soon he'll be a freshwater conch."

"True."

Sean O'Hara lifted his beer bottle. "To engagements!"

They all toasted.

Jaden and Ted had to get back to work on a cache of silverware that had just been brought up by salvage divers, and Clarinda was about to go to work. They all hugged and parted, with Liam setting his bottle down and saying, "Well. It's time."

David nodded at him. "It's time."

Liam took Kelsey's hand, and they started off walking.

The cemetery wasn't far.

Naturally, on the way, Katie started crying softly. It was contagious. Liam squeezed Kelsey's hand, looking at her with tender assurance.

There, by the large sculpted angel, were Bartholomew and Lucinda, his beautiful lady in white. She was shy, but she smiled, and when Bartholomew came to them all, one by one, giving them his spectral handshake first, and then just hugging everyone with a breeze of tenderness, she did the same.

They each had a private word for him.

"Thank you for being here, my dear, dear friends," Bartholomew said.

"Thank you," Liam said huskily. "Thank you for our lives, and what's most precious. Those we love within our lives."

Trying to be jaunty, Bartholomew doffed his hat and bowed deeply.

Then he took Lucinda's hands. "We're ready, my love," he said. "Let it come."

And it came. A golden swatch of light. It settled over the pair, and it glimmered, and then they were gone.

It was a glorious moment. That shimmering light. The sun just beginning to fall. The palette of colors that was so beautiful on a winter's day that was gentle and balmy.

Then Katie let out a loud sniffle, and they all laughed and comforted one another, and it was time for them to leave.

But Kelsey hovered just a moment, and Liam waited patiently, watching her.

There were tears shimmering in her eyes, but she didn't shed them.

She walked over to him and placed her hands on his chest. She stood on her toes and tenderly pressed her lips to his.

"Love is forever," she told him.

When he kissed her far more firmly in return, she knew that he agreed.

*   *   *   *   *

Water, water, everywhere! And, naturally, lots of fish.

Grouper, snapper and dolphin are popular in Key West, the "dolphin" being a colorful fish and not the warm and cuddly mammal some people think the natives are consuming. With fresh fish in abundance, it's naturally a popular meal, from preparations that are hot and spicy to mild and flavorful.

Fish can be tricky. It needs to be cooked, and not overcooked. But fish is its own reward—lots of healthful aspects, low in calories and low in fat.

Here are just a few ways fish are prepared in Key West, South Florida and the Caribbean!

Sweet Key Lime Baked Grouper
(serves 4)

INGREDIENTS

4 four-ounce grouper fillets
2 key limes
Salt and pepper
1 diced tomato
1 diced sweet onion
1 teaspoon minced garlic
1 diced sweet red or yellow pepper
½ cup shredded coconut
1 cup sliced pineapple (fresh or canned)

Overnight, or for several hours, soak fillets with fresh-squeezed lime. Salt and pepper to taste; for a spicy dish, add a dash of hot sauce of choice. Cover while marinating.

Preheat oven to 350 degrees. Arrange fillets on lightly greased baking sheet. (Olive oil works well and adds a bit of flavor! A low-cal spray is fine, as well.) Arrange diced tomato, onion and sweet peppers on top of the fillets, cover with tin foil. Bake approximately one hour.

Fish fillets should be light and flaky.

Arrange coconut and pineapple around finished fish on the plate.

Broccoli spears and rice make nice side dishes.

Key West Red Snapper à la Caribbean
(serves 4)

INGREDIENTS

Splash of dark rum
2 tablespoons olive oil
1 medium onion, chopped
½ cup chopped red pepper
½ cup carrots, cut in strips
1 clove garlic, minced
½ cup dry white wine
¾ lb. red snapper fillet
1 large tomato, chopped
2 tablespoons crumbled feta cheese

In a large skillet, heat olive oil over medium heat. Add onion, red pepper, carrot and garlic; sauté 10 minutes. Add wine and the splash of dark rum and bring to boil. Push vegetables to edges or one side of the pan.

Arrange fillets in a single layer in center of skillet. Cover; cook for 5 minutes.

Add tomato. Top with cheese. Cover; cook 3 minutes, or until fish is firm but moist.
Serve with slices of fresh mango or peaches.
A nice side dish is vermicelli with just a touch of olive oil and a dusting of Parmesan.

Key West Dolphin (Mahimahi) on the Grill

INGREDIENTS

4 (six-oz.) Mahimahi fillets
3 tbs. olive oil
¼ cup shallots, chopped
¹/₃ cup yellow bell pepper, chopped
¹/₃ cup red bell pepper, chopped
¾ cup chunky salsa
¼ cup apricot preserves
1½ tbs. chopped cilantro
¾ tsp. garlic salt
Seasoning salt
Dash of Worcestershire sauce

In a large skillet, heat 1 tbs. of the olive oil over a medium heat until hot.

Add shallots and bell pepper and sauté 5 minutes.

Add salsa, apricot preserves, cilantro and garlic salt. Blend well and cook 2 minutes.

Brush fish steaks with the remaining olive oil and sprinkle with seasoning salt. Grill or broil 5 minutes on each side or until fish starts to flake.

Spoon bell pepper mixture over grilled fish before serving.

Great with a fresh salad and couscous!

REQUEST YOUR FREE BOOKS!

2 FREE NOVELS
FROM THE SUSPENSE COLLECTION
PLUS 2 FREE GIFTS!

YES! Please send me 2 FREE novels from the Suspense Collection and my 2 FREE gifts (gifts are worth about $10). After receiving them, if I don't wish to receive any more books, I can return the shipping statement marked "cancel." If I don't cancel, I will receive 3 brand-new novels every month and be billed just $5.74 per book in the U.S. or $6.24 per book in Canada. That's a saving of at least 28% off the cover price. It's quite a bargain! Shipping and handling is just 50¢ per book in the U.S. and 75¢ per book in Canada.* I understand that accepting the 2 free books and gifts places me under no obligation to buy anything. I can always return a shipment and cancel at any time. Even if I never buy another book, the two free books and gifts are mine to keep forever.

192 MDN E4MN   392 MDN E4MY

Name	(PLEASE PRINT)	
Address		Apt. #
City	State/Prov.	Zip/Postal Code

Signature (if under 18, a parent or guardian must sign)

Mail to **The Reader Service:**
IN U.S.A.: P.O. Box 1867, Buffalo, NY 14240-1867
IN CANADA: P.O. Box 609, Fort Erie, Ontario L2A 5X3

Not valid for current subscribers to the Suspense Collection
or the Romance/Suspense Collection.

Want to try two free books from another line?
Call 1-800-873-8635 or visit www.morefreebooks.com.

* Terms and prices subject to change without notice. Prices do not include applicable taxes. N.Y. residents add applicable sales tax. Canadian residents will be charged applicable provincial taxes and GST. Offer not valid in Quebec. This offer is limited to one order per household. All orders subject to approval. Credit or debit balances in a customer's account(s) may be offset by any other outstanding balance owed by or to the customer. Please allow 4 to 6 weeks for delivery. Offer available while quantities last.

Your Privacy: Harlequin Books is committed to protecting your privacy. Our Privacy Policy is available online at www.eHarlequin.com or upon request from the Reader Service. From time to time we make our lists of customers available to reputable third parties who may have a product or service of interest to you. If you would prefer we not share your name and address, please check here. ☐

Help us get it right—We strive for accurate, respectful and relevant communications. To clarify or modify your communication preferences, visit us at www.ReaderService.com/consumerchoice.

MSUS10

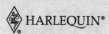
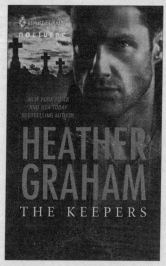

NOV   2010   2/11 -3

HEATHER GRAHAM

32801	HAUNTED	___ $7.99 U.S.	___ $9.99 CAN.
32816	THE PRESENCE	___ $7.99 U.S.	___ $9.99 CAN.
32915	THE VISION	___ $7.99 U.S.	___ $9.99 CAN.
32758	NIGHTWALKER	___ $7.99 U.S.	___ $9.99 CAN.
32676	UNHALLOWED GROUND	___ $7.99 U.S.	___ $8.99 CAN.
32654	DUST TO DUST	___ $7.99 U.S.	___ $8.99 CAN.
32625	THE DEATH DEALER	___ $7.99 U.S.	___ $7.99 CAN.
32527	DEADLY GIFT	___ $7.99 U.S.	___ $7.99 CAN.
32560	DEADLY HARVEST	___ $7.99 U.S.	___ $7.99 CAN.
32585	DEADLY NIGHT	___ $7.99 U.S.	___ $7.99 CAN.
32520	THE DEAD ROOM	___ $7.99 U.S.	___ $9.50 CAN.
32486	BLOOD RED	___ $7.99 U.S.	___ $9.50 CAN.
32916	THE SÉANCE	___ $7.99 U.S.	___ $9.99 CAN.
32424	THE ISLAND	___ $7.99 U.S.	___ $9.50 CAN.
32343	KISS OF DARKNESS	___ $7.99 U.S.	___ $9.50 CAN.
32277	KILLING KELLY	___ $7.99 U.S.	___ $9.50 CAN.
32900	GHOST WALK	___ $7.99 U.S.	___ $9.99 CAN.

(limited quantities available)

TOTAL AMOUNT	$ _____
POSTAGE & HANDLING	$ _____
($1.00 for 1 book, 50¢ for each additional)	
APPLICABLE TAXES*	$ _____
TOTAL PAYABLE	$ _____

(check or money order—please do not send cash)

To order, complete this form and send it, along with a check or money order for the total above, payable to MIRA Books, to: **In the U.S.:** 3010 Walden Avenue, P.O. Box 9077, Buffalo, NY 14269-9077; **In Canada:** P.O. Box 636, Fort Erie, Ontario, L2A 5X3.

Name: _____
Address: _____ City: _____
State/Prov.: _____ Zip/Postal Code: _____
Account Number (if applicable): _____

075 CSAS

MIRA®

*New York residents remit applicable sales taxes.
*Canadian residents remit applicable GST and provincial taxes.

www.MIRABooks.com

MHG0710BL